Above the brig...

Above the Bright Blue Sky

MARGARET THORNTON

Allison & Busby Limited
13 Charlotte Mews
London W1T 4EJ
www.allisonandbusby.com

Hardcover published in Great Britain in 2005.
This paperback edition published in 2006.

A CIP catalogue record for this book is available from
the British Library.

10 9 8 7 6 5 4 3 2

ISBN 978-0-7490-8294-9

The paper used for this Allison & Busby publication
has been produced from trees that have been legally sourced
from well-managed and credibly certified forests.

PEFC
PEFC/16-33-111
CATG-PEFC-052
www.pefc.org

Printed and bound in the UK by
CPI Bookmarque, Croydon, CR0 4TD

MARGARET THORNTON was born in Blackpool and has lived there all her life. She is a qualified teacher but has retired in order to concentrate on her writing. She began by writing articles and short stories for magazines and has since gone on to have fifteen novels published, most of which are set in Blackpool. Her family sagas range from the late Victorian period, through to the Twenties, the Second World War, and the Fifties and Sixties. She has two children and five grandchildren.

**Available from
ALLISON & BUSBY**

*Down an English Lane
A True Love of Mine
Remember Me*

Dedication

To my husband, John, with love, thanking him once again for his support, encouragement and understanding.

A special mention for Christopher, the youngest of my five grandchildren, who was puzzled as to why he was not included in some of the earlier dedications.

And to my agent, Dorothy Lumley, and Lara Dafert, my new editor at Allison and Busby; my thanks to you both for having faith in me.

Chapter One

M aisie crouched halfway down the stairs, her ear pressed hard against the bannister railings, listening to the conversation that was going on between her mother and her step-father. It was developing into more of a row though, now, than a conversation, but that was nothing fresh. Sidney Bragg spent a good deal of his time shouting, either at her mother or, sometimes, at his son, Percy, or – most of all – at her, Maisie. Not so much, however, at his two younger children, Joanie and Jimmy, aged three and two, the ones who had arrived on the scene since he had married her mother four years ago. The little kids were learning to keep out of his way as much as possible, just as Maisie herself had soon learned to do when he came to live with them.

She knew she would get a clout across the ear, or, even worse, what he called a 'bloody good hiding' with his leather belt if he were to find her eavesdropping. She knew that that was the proper grown-up word for it – Maisie loved words and what they meant – but it was usually thought of as 'nosy-parkering'. But she had a right to know what was going to happen to her. Her mum would tell her nothing any more; she was too scared of him, no doubt. Although Maisie knew that once, a long time ago – so long ago it seemed that she could scarcely remember it – her mother had used to tell her all sorts of things; and she knew her mother had used to love her very much... But that was before Daddy had died.

Maisie hated Sidney Bragg with an intensity that frightened her at times. She knew it was wrong to hate people. The vicar from the big church down the road who came into school sometimes to talk to the children had told them so. He had even said they should try to love their enemies. But Maisie shut her mind to that. In fact, she was not sure whom she hated the most, Sidney Bragg or his son, Percy.

It was Sidney who was speaking now. 'The kid's got to go, Lily. I keep telling yer. I've told yer till I'm blue in the face. It's for her own good.'

'It's because you want to get rid of her, you mean.'

'Don't talk so bloody stupid! Get rid of 'er? Why should I want to do that, eh? She's got her uses, when she can be bothered to take her nose out of her bloody books. She fetches me ciggies and me paper, an' I know you rely on her to mind the two nippers. Oh aye; that's why you want to keep her here, i'n't it? I gerrit. You're scared you're gonna lose yer little nursemaid. You won't have so much time to sit around on yer fat backside...'

'Give over, Sid,' came her mother's plaintive voice. Maisie knew she was well accustomed to her husband's insults and clouts across the head, so much so that she scarcely bothered to retaliate any more. 'I look after our Joanie and Jimmy as best I can; you know I do. And why shouldn't the lass help me out now and again? I've got me hands full, what with me job and you on shift work, and your Percy an' all.'

'Oh, stop yer bloody whining, woman! And leave Percy out of it. He's a good lad, our Percy, an' he pays his way. Anyroad, it'll be one less mouth to feed with your Nellie out of the way.'

Nellie! The little girl detested the name she had been called by ever since he had moved in with them. Her full name was Eleanor May Jackson, and her mother, and her daddy, too, had used to call her by her proper first name, Eleanor. But Maisie had been Daddy's pet name for her. 'My little mayflower,' he had called her, often shortening it to Maisie. Daddy had been a country lad, so he had used to tell her, from a village in the Yorkshire Dales. He had loved the coming of the spring every year, and the sight of the frothy white may blossom in the hedgerows, he said, had been a sure sign that spring had really arrived. Eleanor May had been so christened because both her parents had liked the name Eleanor, and because she had been born on the first day of May. That had been in 1930, and she was now nine years old.

But Sid Bragg had laughed and poked fun at her. Eleanor was far too pretentious – or swanky, as he had termed it – for a kid from a terraced house in Armley. He had decided she would be Nellie from that time on, a good sensible name, and her mother had had no more sense than to go along with his decree. It was then that the little girl had started to think of herself as Maisie, although to her family, her teachers and the children at school, and her neighbours – almost everyone, in fact – she was known as Nellie Jackson. Only her mum, occasionally, called her Maisie, when she remembered that that was what she preferred, and when Sid was nowhere around. One blessing, she supposed, was that she was not called Nellie Bragg, as she might have been. Her step-father had never suggested that she should have the same name as the rest of the household, probably because he considered her to be of little importance. And the dislike was mutual.

'You're always going on about not being able to make ends meet,' Sid was saying now, 'although God knows why. Yer've got yer charrin' job, 'aven't yer?' There was barely enough left over when he had paid his nightly visit to the pub down the road, or his dinnertime visit if he happened to be on late shift, thought Maisie, but she knew her mother would not have the courage to say so; or to remind him that she was forced to go out to work because he left her short of money.

'I would miss her,' said her mother. 'She's my little girl. Of course I know you've never taken to her...'

'I've never said that...'

'You don't need to, Sid. It's quite obvious you don't like her, and the child knows it, I'm sure she does.'

'Huh! All the more reason for her to go then, if she hates me so much...'

'I didn't say she hated you,' replied Lily. (But I do, thought Maisie, I do, I really do...)

'She's quite a pretty little thing, I suppose,' said

Sid, to Maisie's surprise. 'An' I know our Percy thinks so. I dare say the lad'll miss her, but he'll have to get used to her not being there, same as you will.'

'Percy hardly ever bothers to speak to her,' replied Lily. 'The child might as well be a fly on the wall for all the notice he takes of her.'

'Oh, you'd be surprised,' said Sid. 'I've a feeling he's rather taken with her.' He laughed, a nasty sneering laugh, just like the one Maisie had heard Percy make when he crept into her bedroom at night.

He knows! she thought. Her step-father actually knew what Percy was doing to her when the others were fast asleep, his hand over her mouth so that she did not cry out. Percy had threatened her that she would get a good belting, worse than any she had ever had, if she were to tell, if not from his father then from Percy himself. It sickened her to think that Sid might even have been egging him on, and now was laughing about it.

'But she's only a kid, ain't she?' Sid continued. 'My lad'll have to wait till she's grown up a bit, eh, Lily?'

Lily did not answer that. 'I don't see the need for her to be evacuated,' was what she said. 'We're not even at war yet.'

'Bloody close to it. Only a matter of days, they're saying.'

'Aye, well, that's as may be. If we lived in London, happen I could see the sense of it. But not up here in the north of England…'

'Don't talk so bloody daft! Liverpool'll cop it

when Hitler starts dropping 'is bombs, an' Manchester an' all.'

'But we're in Leeds. I can't see as there'll be much danger here...'

'Then that shows how stupid you are, don't it? It's a big city, ain't it? So is Bradford an' Hull an' York. An' there's factories an' mills an' munition works an' God knows what else. Look 'ere; the Government's started this evacuation lark, and Nellie's school says as how they're going...'

'They won't all be going, Sid...'

'Give over butting in, will yer? Nellie's going and that's that. What's the matter with yer? Don't you want her to be safe?'

'Of course I do, but if she's in danger staying here, then so are our Joanie and Jimmy, and me an' all. And you and Percy.'

'Yeah...well; we can't all go running off, can we? We're doing vital work, me and our Percy, at t' mill.'

'There's nothing to stop me going though, is there, Sid? Me and the little 'uns. They won't let kids under school age go on their own, but they're encouraging mothers and babies to get away as well as schoolchildren.'

'What the hell are you talking about, woman? Who's gonna look after me and t' lad if you go gallivanting off into t' countryside? No; you'll stop here. Somebody's got to keep the 'ome fires burning. So that's settled, right? An' I don't want to 'ear no more about it. Now, you go an' gerron with yer washing up, and I'll fetch me ciggies from upstairs. I'm going down to t' pub...'

At the sound of her step-father getting up from his chair, Maisie scuttled silently up the stairs and into her bedroom. She leapt into bed and pulled the covers tightly around her, closing her eyes and feigning sleep. It was doubtful that he would come in and look at her... Him, Sid, her mother's husband. She could never think of him as her father and never, in all the four years he had lived with them, had she called him Dad or Daddy; she had managed to get away with calling him nothing at all. But he might cast a glance at his own two children, Joanie and Jimmy, fast asleep in the double bed at the other side of the room.

Fifteen-year-old Percy had a room to himself, little more than a large cupboard really, but he had flatly refused to share a room with two 'snivelling smelly brats' as he put it. He had had the larger room to himself at first, when Sid had married Lily Jackson and they had come to live there. It was only right, as he was by far the older of their two children, Sid had decreed, and Lily, even then, had not had the courage to argue with him. So Maisie had slept in the box room, not much caring where she was, only knowing she was unhappy and all mixed up inside herself since those two awful bossy males had taken over their household.

Now she was back in the bigger room again, so that Percy could have the privacy he demanded, but it was very much changed from the time she had slept there four years ago. Percy, in fact, was quite right when he declared that Joanie and Jimmy – half-brother and -sister both to him and to Maisie – were smelly brats. So they were. Jimmy, at two years old, was still wearing nappies, and Joanie, one year older, still wet the bed frequently. Maisie knew that her mother had a difficult job trying to keep up with the washing. It was often skimped on, the sheets being dried hastily and put back on the bed just as they were, making the whole room stink of stale urine, or worse, at times.

Her mother was a different person since she had married Sidney Bragg. Maisie was well aware of the change in her, although it had come about gradually. She often wondered what had happened to the pretty happy lady with the curly brown hair and laughing eyes whom she remembered from the time when she, Maisie, had been a very little girl. The person she lived with now was slovenly and careworn with lank greasy hair, and all the sparkle had gone from her silver-grey eyes. They did not chat and sing and laugh together as they had used to do. It even seemed, at times, as though this person that her mother had changed into did not love her little girl any more. And then, occasionally, Maisie would catch a glimpse of the old mummy in a smile or a kiss or a sudden hug, and she would tell herself that her mother must still be the same person deep down, beneath all her cares and anxieties.

The bedroom was shabby now and not very clean. The net curtains hung in tatters at the windows; neither they nor the faded draw curtains had been washed for ages, but, from what Maisie had gathered, they would soon need to be replaced by blackout blinds. The wallpaper was dirty and hanging off in places where the two younger children had pulled at it. It had been drawn on, too;

a scribbly mess of red and blue wax crayon that would not come off. Maisie had been taught, as a little girl, to take care of the few possessions she had and she would never have dreamed of scribbling on the wallpaper. But Joanie and Jimmy, it seemed, could get away with all sorts of dreadful behaviour. Joanie ran wild in the street with the neighbours' children, with Jimmy usually not far behind her, and Maisie knew they were regarded as a couple of ruffians with their dirty faces and habitually running noses.

They were big children for their age, but then Sidney Bragg was a giant of a man, over six feet in height and hefty with it; and Percy was of a similar build. The children had inherited, too, the straw-coloured straight hair and pale blue eyes of both Sidney and Percy; and Maisie, whenever she looked at them, could see no resemblance to either herself or her mother. Which was, no doubt, the reason that she could not like her half-sister and -brother very much.

Sid went downstairs again without entering the bedroom, to Maisie's relief, and soon afterwards she heard the door banging; he was off on his nightly visit to the pub. She relaxed her tensed-up limbs and thought hard about what she had heard. She knew about the evacuation scheme, of course. They had been told about it at school. They had been back only a few days since the long summer break, but already some of the kids had got their cases packed, awaiting the signal that it was time to go. Maisie had taken the official letter home that they had been given at school, but her mother, after giving it a cursory glance, had shoved it behind the wooden clock on the mantelpiece, where the few items of mail they received always ended up. She had been pleased to hear her mother say, a few moments ago, that she would miss her, and Maisie knew that if she were to be evacuated, then her mother would be the only person she would miss at all. But she knew, also, with a tiny stab of guilt, that she would not miss Mummy nearly as much as she would once have done, when she had been the happy and bubbly young woman of her memory.

What odd words they were that had recently come into their language. Evacuation, evacuated, evacuee... Maisie said them over to herself several times to get used to them. And she would be an evacuee. Where would they go? she wondered. And how would they get there? On a train or on a bus? Or a charabanc, as they were sometimes called. Maisie remembered, in what seemed to be the dim and distant past, going on a 'chara' once with her mum and dad to a place called Scarborough, by the sea. She vaguely recalled the castle up on the hill – they had stayed near there in a boarding house – and she had made sand pies on the beach and paddled at the edge of the sea; and Daddy, with his trousers rolled up to his knees, had paddled too, holding her hand, whilst Mummy had sat in a deck chair. That was the only holiday she could remember. Since her mother had got married again and had the babies – it had seemed no time at all before the house was full of babies and bottles and nappies – they had not been anywhere together, not even for a day. Maisie had been on Sunday School outings to Kirkstall Abbey and to the grounds of a big house called Temple Newsam, but those places were only a few miles away and the trips were only once a year. And just lately she had not been to Sunday School at all; she had been too busy helping her mother with the babies and the endless washing.

Yes; Scarborough, she mused… Wouldn't it be just great if they were to go there; she and the rest of the kids from her school? Probably not all of 'em though. It was quite a big school and no doubt a lot of the mums and dads would not want their children to go away. Not like Sid, whom she knew could not wait to get rid of her. Well, she could not wait, neither, to get away from him and his horrible son. She made up her mind, in that minute, that if Percy came to her room that night, then she would scream out and wake everybody up. She had nothing to lose; she would be far away from them all in a few days time, with a bit of luck.

She pushed the thought of Percy to the back of her mind again; the memory of him mauling at her beneath the bedclothes; touching her legs and other, more private parts, that she knew you shouldn't let anybody touch, and his wet red mouth slobbering all over her. She shuddered, and concentrated instead on how nice it would be to get away. It might not be to Scarborough, of course. She knew that was quite a long way. Perhaps it would be to the countryside. There were lots of lovely villages in Yorkshire. Her dad had lived in one called Grassington before he had moved to Leeds to find work. And it was then that he had met her mum, when they had worked at the same woollen mill.

She closed her eyes, thinking of the black-and-white cows in the meadows, munching at the grass and the golden buttercups, the white mayblossom in the hedgerows, and, above it all, the sun shining from a clear blue sky. It had always been a gloriously sunny day, or so it had seemed, on those infrequent trips to the countryside. Here in Leeds, particularly nearer to the city centre, the sky was more often grey than blue, the sun obscured by the smoke from the chimneys of the myriad factories and mills.

How lovely it would be to live in the countryside with woods and fields all around, instead of rows and rows of red-brick houses which all looked alike, thought Maisie. But would she, perhaps, find it all too quiet? said a small voice inside her. This, after all, was her home. She had known nothing else but this humble house surrounded by factory chimneys and built almost in the shadow of Armley Jail. The only green she saw was in the nearby cemetery, and across the main road, near to where the posher people lived, there was a park. The kids from Maisie's area, though, were not encouraged to play there. They were chased away by rival gangs whenever they ventured near and fights sometimes ensued. Maisie had learned to keep to her own neck of the woods.

She would miss her mum, she told herself now, feeling ashamed that she had thought, for a moment, that she might not do so. But perhaps her mother would be able to come and visit her, if she was not too far away. And, she reminded herself again, it would he heaven to get away from those other two, her step-father and Percy. And maybe, by the time she returned from wherever she was going, a miracle would have happened and they would no longer be there... But what she had in mind she was not quite sure.

She made herself think of pleasant things – of woods and fields, trees and flowers – and at last she fell asleep. But thoughts of the dreadful Percy and the fervent hope that he would not disturb her that night were not far below the surface of her dreaming.

Lily, also, was thinking of her step-son, Percy, and the remarks that her husband had made.

Sid, after fetching his cigarettes from upstairs, had gone out immediately to the Rose and Crown down the road. He would not be back until after closing time and, if he followed his usual procedure he would expect – or, more likely, demand – what he called his marital rights, whether she happened to be awake or asleep. Lily was usually awake, waiting for his lumbering steps on the stairs, or sometimes the sound of him stumbling and crashing around, if he had had too much of a skinfull. If that was the case, she would breathe a sigh of relief. It meant that he would be incapable of making love to her, although his abuse of her could in no way be credited with such a name. There was nothing in his almost nightly routine that resembled love, or even tenderness or respect, nor had it done for almost as long as she could remember. Sometimes he didn't even make it up the stairs, then she would find him crashed out on the sofa in the morning, his clothes and the cushions stained with his own vomit.

What was that remark he had made? Lily pondered, as she sat by the burnt out embers of the fire; that Percy had taken quite a fancy to Nellie – or Maisie, as she liked to be called – but that he would have to wait until she grew up a bit. Over my dead body! she thought with feeling. It wasn't the first time she had heard Sid hint that the lad was taking an interest in the little girl, but she had, until now, not taken a great deal of notice. As far as she was concerned the two of them – step-sister and step-brother, as they were in actuality – ignored one another as much as was possible and their dislike seemed to be a mutual thing. Now she began to wonder. She recalled Sid's sneering grin and the sardonic gleam in his pale blue eyes when he mentioned his son and her daughter; and, she recalled, she had seen the selfsame mocking expression on Percy's face, too. And it was true that Maisie did, at times, appear afraid of the lad. Lily had sometimes seen her cast nervous glances in his direction, unaware she was being noticed.

But why, then, had the child not said something, if the boy was tormenting her...or worse? Or had she, Lily, become so apathetic, so bogged down with her own concerns that she had failed to notice that her daughter might be in danger? Suddenly, a paroxysm of anger seized hold of her. If he ever lays a finger on my little girl, then – God help me! – I will kill him, she vowed.

She stared unseeingly into the faintly glowing cinders, then, as her rage subsided a little she began to consider – as she had done so many times before – however she had come to be in this pathetic and parlous state. Married to a husband for whom she had no feeling whatsoever other than contempt and, sometimes, fear; with two toddlers who resembled him, rather than herself, in all ways, and for whom, to her shame, she found it hard at times to summon up any maternal feelings; a step-son who treated her with indifference; and a house which had become a prison rather than a home, and a not very clean one at that. Set against all this, of course, was her first born child, Eleanor May, whom she and Davey had loved so very much. Lily still loved the child – of course she did – but she seemed to have lost her, gradually, as all her anxieties and hardships threatened to submerge her. And now, if she allowed her to go away as an evacuee, she would lose her completely.

She knew it was futile to look back, remembering the few happy years she had spent with Davey, then cursing her foolishness in getting married again. She had been desperately unhappy and lonely after Davey had died, as the result of influenza turning to pneumonia – it had happened so suddenly – and she had found herself in dire straits, too. She had been obliged to go out to work to pay the rent, taking Eleanor May with her, as the child was not then old enough for school. She had gone cleaning at some of the posher houses near to the park, and it was on one lunchtime break that she had met Sidney Bragg.

Such a tall, swarthily handsome man he had been, well built, with yellowish hair and rather prominent blue eyes; and how pleasant he had seemed. He had taken a fancy to the young widow, and he had been friendly towards her little girl, too, which had pleased Lily. She had soon learned, as he continued to meet her each day in the park – he was between jobs, he told her – that he was a widower, seventeen years older than herself. Lily was twenty-three at that time. His two eldest children had 'flown the nest' as he put it, and now there was only himself and his younger son, Percy, living in temporary lodgings. He led Lily to believe he had owned his own house; it was only later that she learned he had been evicted from a property, very similar to the one in which she lived, for non-payment of rent.

She could not have explained to anyone how, or why, it had happened, and so quickly, too. But she had married him, and he and his son had moved in with her and Eleanor May; soon to become Nellie, and destined to become a drudge, which was what her mother had very soon turned into.

Sid managed to find a job in another woollen mill – she was to learn, also, that he had been sacked from his previous employment, although she never knew why – as did Percy when he left school. Lily, in less than two years, had two babies, as well as a growing girl, to say nothing of two males who could eat whatever she put in front of them twice over, and then ask for more. She found it hard to make ends meet, particularly as a large share of Sid's weekly wage went into the coffers of the Rose and Crown. She was forced to go out cleaning again when the children were old enough to take with her, sometimes to the annoyance of her employers. But they found that Lily Bragg was a hard worker who took a pride in making the furniture and paintwork, the glass and silverware in the houses of her affluent clients gleam with care and attention.

So much so that her own home, of which she had once been so proud, had deteriorated. Lily was often too tired and dispirited to give the place more than a cursory wipe with a duster or floor cloth. The furniture and wallpaper, the carpets and curtains all became shabby and soiled, but there was never enough money to buy replacements. Nor did Lily feel any incentive to do so.

A glance in the mirror, something she seldom bothered to do, told her that she looked older than her twenty-eight years. She had put on weight since having the babies and no longer had the slim waistline and hips of which she had used to be so proud. Her dark hair was already greying slightly at the temples and it no longer curled alluringly as it had done when she was younger. It hung now in greasy strands to her shoulders, or sometimes she pinned it back with a few kirby grips. It was such a palaver to wash her hair at the kitchen sink, which was why she did not now do so as often as she knew she should; although it had never seemed any bother to keep her hair clean and shining when Davey was alive, she recalled. She was still meticulous, however, about keeping her body and face clean, and she had a strip-wash by the sink every day when Sid and Percy were out of the way. And once a week, again making sure the menfolk were nowhere about, she took the zinc bath down from the nail on which it hung outside the back door. She then filled it with buckets of water from the kitchen tap, plus a few kettlefuls of boiling water heated on the open fire, and luxuriated in a long soak, washing herself well all over with pink carbolic soap. This was when the two little ones and Nellie had gone to bed.

The children shared a bath on another night of the week. Nellie used the water first – she was by far the cleanest of the three of them – followed by her two siblings. This was the only time during the week when Joanie and Jimmy could be said to be really clean. The rest of the time it was an uphill struggle to keep their noses wiped and their bottoms clean or to wash their continually grubby hands and faces.

Fortunately the house had an outside lavatory with what was known as a tippler system, flushed by water that had been used previously in the house. This was a vast improvement on Lily's childhood memory of the Corporation 'dirt cart' coming once a week to empty the night soil and the ash-pit. She longed at times, pointless though she knew it was, for a proper indoor bathroom and lavatory, such as the ones in the houses she cleaned; with gleaming white tiles and a tablet of lavender-scented soap in a shell-shaped dish; that, indeed, would be luxury beyond measure.

What Sid and Percy did about their ablutions she neither knew nor cared. She guessed they visited the public baths occasionally; but Sid washed and shaved every evening when they had finished their meal, standing over the kitchen slop-stone splashing and puffing, and cursing whenever he cut himself with his open razor. The sight of him in his grubby vest with his braces dangling down revolted her.

Thinking of him now, Lily found herself wishing that she, too, could get away from it all; escape to the countryside, or wherever, with Nellie. Poor Nellie – Maisie – tried her best, her mother knew, to keep herself nice and clean. But many of the children in her school lived in far worse conditions than did her own family, so it probably didn't matter too much to her if she was rather less than sparkling bright. And just recently the poor lass had caught head lice from the girl she sat next to in class. Lily had been forced to cut her dark hair very short, and she knew she had not made a good job of it either. It stuck out from her head in uneven spikes and Sid had laughed tauntingly and told her she looked like a hedgehog. Lily knew, though, that nothing could detract from the child's true loveliness. Maisie had an inward beauty that shone from her deep brown eyes and lit up her rosy complexioned face when she smiled. Her smiles, however, had been all too rare of late. Lily found her thoughts returning again to Percy. Yes, she vowed, if I ever find him touching my child I will kill him; I really will...

No sooner had the thought formed in her head than the door burst open and her husband entered the room. He was far earlier than she had expected; she liked to be in bed, feigning sleep, if possible, before he came back from the pub.

'You're early,' she said bravely, trying to force a smile to her lips. He was not as drunk as he usually was; in fact he seemed quite sober.

'Aye, so I am. Pleased to see me, are yer?' He leered at her, but she looked away, not answering.

'Get yerself upstairs then...my Lily of Laguna.' He gave a sardonic laugh. That was what he had used to call her when they were first married; a term of endearment that she hadn't heard on his lips for a long time. 'I thought we'd have an early night.'

She glanced at him apprehensively, thinking she might see a glimmer of affection in his eyes, but, as she had feared, there was nothing there but lust and a mocking smile.

'Where's...where's Percy?' she asked.

'Why? What's it to you?'

'Nothing...I just wondered if he had got his key, that's all.'

'Of course he's got his key, you silly cow. But he won't be needing it. He's going home with his mate, young Bertie, and he'll be staying there the night, so he says. They're three sheets to the wind already, the silly young divils.' Sid laughed good-humouredly. Under-age drinking did not worry Percy, nor, it seemed, did it bother his father or the landlord.

'Put t' bolt on t' door and get yerself movin', lass. Ah'm as randy as a dog on heat tonight...'

Lily did as she was bid. Her little girl would be safe for tonight at least, but as for herself... She dreaded what was to come, knowing that, tonight, Sid was not likely to be hindered by his customary inebriation. The thought of escaping from everything was becoming even more tempting.

Chapter Two

'We're goin' tomorrer,' said Esme, the girl who shared a double desk with Maisie. 'You know – on that evacuation thingy. I'm dead excited, me. I can't wait to gerraway, can you?'

'How d'you know we're going?' asked Maisie. 'They haven't said so yet, not definitely. Anyroad, I don't know whether I'm going or not. Me mam hasn't made up her mind.'

'I 'eard two o' t' teachers talking in t' yard at playtime,' replied Esme. 'Aye, it's right. We're goin' in t' mornin'. You'd best tell yer mam to make up 'er mind quick, or else you'll be bombed to blazes. That's what me dad says. Old 'Itler, he can't wait to start droppin' 'is bombs on all t' cities.'

'Esme Clough and Nellie Jackson, stop that talking at once!' yelled Miss Patterdale, their teacher. 'Have you finished writing out the list of spellings on the board?'

'No, Miss.' Both girls shook their heads.

'Then get on with it, and in silence. I've told you all, I don't want to hear a sound.'

Maisie put her dark head down and resumed her task. She didn't want to talk to Esme Clough anyway. She was the one who had given her nits, but Miss Patterdale had not seen that as any reason to separate the pair of them. Several of the children in the class had head lice. Maisie didn't like Esme very much. The girl was a cheat and a telltale and, because of that, was not popular with a lot of the girls – and the boys as well – who had their own code of honour. You didn't try to get others into trouble, nor did you snitch at other kids' answers. Maisie was surprised that Miss Patterdale had not cottoned on to the fact that Esme frequently copied the answers to her sums, not because Esme was a 'thickie', to use the common idiom, but because she was too lazy to think for herself.

Or maybe Miss Patterdale was not a very good teacher... Maisie had sometimes seen her reading a copy of Woman's Weekly behind the teachers' desk whilst the class was occupied in composition or sums. She was sure that this was 'not on', and she had once seen the teacher quickly cover the magazine with the class register when Mr Ormerod, the headmaster, had unexpectedly entered the room.

'I 'ope she's not goin' with us, the miserable old cow!' Esme ventured another whispered remark under cover of the desk lid, to which Maisie just gave a brief nod. It was a good job Miss Patterdale had not noticed, or Esme might have got the cane.

Maisie, in point of fact, agreed with Esme. She hoped, too, that their own class teacher would not be going with them to...wherever they were going. Maisie had already made up her mind that she would tell her mother that she wanted to go. She did not want to miss out on the adventure, as well as her desire to get away from the two awful menfolk in the house. She felt worried, though, about what Esme had said about the bombs. If her mother was left behind then she would be in danger, and so would the little 'uns, Joanie and Jimmy. Still, Esme was known to exaggerate; more than that, she told whopping big lies sometimes, so it might not be as bad as she made out. Anyway, they still hadn't been told definitely that they were going tomorrow. That might well be another of Esme's yarns.

At the start of the afternoon session, however, all the classes were summoned into the school hall where the headmaster, Mr Ormerod, told them that the evacuation scheme was to be put in force the very next day. Those children whose parents wished them to go were to be at school by half-past eight, with their luggage, of course, and then they would be taken by bus to Leeds City Station.

'Where are we goin', Sir?' piped up one of the smallest boys on the front row. Maisie thought he was very brave. It was not done to shout out like that in assembly, especially to Mr Ormerod, who, at six feet tall, with a beaked nose and a glowering expression, was not someone to mess around with.

However, it seemed that today might be an exception, because the headmaster actually smiled. 'That I can't tell you, laddie,' he replied, 'because I don't know myself. All will be revealed to you in due course. Now...will you all return to your classrooms, quietly please. Any talking about this can wait till playtime...'

Maisie's class was normally subdued, under the eagle eye of Miss Patterdale who did not allow talking in lesson time. Only occasionally, when the children were engaged in more recreational pursuits, such as drawing – very seldom painting, because Maisie guessed their teacher would think that too messy – or sewing (or raffia work for the boys) they might be permitted to talk very quietly. This afternoon was one of those occasions, it being Friday and a time for a slightly more free and easy mood. Miss Patterdale had placed a few brightly coloured dahlias in a vase on her desk and instructed the children to make a drawing of them, which they could then colour with the pencil crayons. This was quite an event; very rarely did the crayons leave the big tall stock cupboard at the back of the room. But this, apparently, was a day on which to relax the usually strict environment of the clasroom; to enable the children to forget what was to happen on the following day, maybe.

Esme continued to say, to all around her, that she just couldn't wait to go. Some of the boys, too, seemed very excited about the adventure that lay ahead.

'Hey, 'appen we'll go to Blackpool,' Maisie heard a lad called Billy say to his mate. 'It's dead good there. There's a bloomin' big tower, miles 'igh, and sticks o' rock, and fish and chips you can eat in t' street. I went there once wi' me mam and dad.'

'Course we won't go to Blackpool,' scoffed Arthur. 'Don't talk so daft! It's bloomin' miles away. Anyroad, you can eat fish and chips 'ere. You don't 'ave to go to Blackpool to do it.'

'Aye, but me mam says it's common to eat in t' street. It's different when yer on 'oliday.'

'Quietly now,' said Miss Patterdale, but without

her usual severity. She appeared to be in a thoughtful mood, staring out of the window at the uninspiring view of the concrete playground and the stunted bushes that grew around it in the barren earth.

Maisie, too, was quiet and thoughtful. She had found out at playtime that Dorothy, the girl she was most friendly with, was not going to be an evacuee after all. If things got bad, she said, then she and her mum might go to a place called Skipton where her uncle had a farm. And Sheila wasn't going, nor was Beryl. Joyce was going, but Maisie was not particularly friendly with her; she was just one of the crowd she sometimes played with.

She glanced across the classroom to where Joyce Randall was sitting. She shared a desk with Audrey Dennison, a girl whom Maisie did not know very well. Audrey was what Maisie thought of as 'one of the posh kids'. She lived in a semi-detached house across the main road, on the fringe of the park, in a much more salubrious part of Armley than the one in which Maisie lived. It was the area where her mother went cleaning, and she was glad that Audrey's mother was not one of the ladies that she 'did' for, or Audrey wouldn't half look down her nose at her, Maisie. At least, she suspected that she might – most of the kids in that locality thought they were 'it' – but she had to admit that Audrey might be different. She seemed nice enough, but there was an unwritten rule that there were two quite separate entities, those who lived near the park, and those who lived in the shadow of the jail, and seldom did the twain meet.

Audrey Dennison was a quiet and diligent girl who was nearly always 'top of the class'. Maisie's group of friends tended to dismiss her, and others of her ilk, as 'clever clogs'. But Maisie was a clever girl, too; she worked much harder at her lessons than did most of the children in her particular crowd, simply because she enjoyed doing so. Most especially she loved reading, and writing compositions. Once or twice she had nearly made it to the top of the class, but had been just pipped at the post by Audrey. Very shrewdly, Maisie had come to the conclusion that Miss Patterdale had wangled this with a slight jiggery-pokery of the marks. Audrey Dennison was something of a teacher's pet because she was so quiet and polite…and clean; much more worthy of her position as top pupil than Nellie Jackson, who sometimes had too much to say for herself and was, moreover, an untidy scruff of a girl. But this, in all fairness, was not Audrey's fault, thought Maisie, and she had often wished that she might get to know her a little better.

She watched the girl now. Audrey was not making any attempt at the drawing of the flowers, but was sitting very still and quiet, with her hands in her lap. She was a pretty girl with pale golden hair which she wore in a neat page-boy bob. Her skin was pale, too, almost like porcelain, with a pinkish tinge to her cheeks, like a china doll, Maisie thought. But she knew that was not entirely fair to Audrey because china dolls with their big blue eyes looked vacant, quite stupid really, and Audrey certainly didn't. She had blue eyes, but they were full of intelligence and eagerness most of the time. Sometimes, however, they seemed to hold a trace of sadness. Maisie could not see the girl's eyes now, but as she observed her secretly, she saw Audrey lift a hand to her eyes as though she were brushing tears away. Then, as though suddenly aware that she was being watched, she glanced across the room and her eyes met those of Maisie. Audrey looked at her, so very sadly, for a moment, then she gave a wan fleeting smile and looked away again.

Maisie's heart went out to her. She did not know for sure what was the matter, but she guessed that Audrey was to leave her home the next day, as an evacuee, but that, unlike Maisie, that was something she was not looking forward to at all.

'Mum, they're going tomorrer,' Maisie shouted as soon as she entered the house that afternoon. 'You know – them that are going to be evacuees. We have to be at school by half-past eight in the morning... Can I go with 'em, Mum?'

Lily looked at her in surprise. 'You really want to go, do you, Nellie?' The girl nodded. 'Well then, that's quite a relief I must admit, because I'd decided meself that it's best for you to go. I thought happen you might be upset, though?'

'No, why should I be?' retorted Maisie. 'I can't wait to get away from here...' Then, aware of the sad look that had appeared so suddenly in her mother's eyes, she hurried on to say, 'I mean...I shall be sorry to leave you, Mum. I shall miss you...and Joanie and Jimmy,' she added as an afterthought. 'Where are they, anyroad?' She glanced around the untidy living room strewn with their somewhat meagre selection of toys – building bricks and battered cars and one or two ragged looking dolls – but there was no sight or sound of the children.

'Upstairs, both of 'em; having a sleep, I hope,' replied her mother. 'From the sound of it they must have dropped off. They came in as black as the ace of spades, both of 'em, yelling 'cause a big lad down the street had chased 'em. Jimmy had fallen down and grazed his knee; he didn't half make a hullabaloo. Anyroad, I gave 'em both a quick wash – just a lick and a promise, mind – and left 'em to play nicely with their toys. Next minute they were chucking bricks at one another, so I says, 'Right – upstairs, the pair of you…''

Maisie, in all honesty, would not be too sorry about leaving those two little brats, but she knew she must pretend that she would. 'Mmm…I shall miss 'em,' she said, somewhat half-heartedly, 'but I shan't miss Percy and…and Sid,' she went on, 'not one little bit.'

Lily sighed. 'No, I know that, love. I know you haven't been very happy just lately, and I'm sorry. There isn't anything you want to tell me, is there…about Percy, or…anything?'

'No, why should there be?' Maisie answered quickly; too quickly because her mother gave her an odd look.

'Are you sure?' she asked.

'Yeah, 'course I'm sure. I just don't like him, that's all.' There was no point in telling her mother now because she was going away the next day and she wouldn't need to see Percy or Sid ever again; well, not for a very long time at any rate. 'What made you change your mind, Mum, about me going?' She decided to change the subject. 'I thought you didn't want me to go.'

'How did you know that? We hadn't even talked about it, Nellie, because I didn't even want to think about you going away and leaving me.'

'I heard you and Sid talking about it last night,' said Maisie. 'I sat on the stairs, listening. He can't wait to get rid of me, I know that.'

'Oh, Nellie, you silly girl! You know what Sid has said about you earwigging. It's a good job he didn't catch you.'

'I made sure he didn't.' Maisie grinned. 'Why did you change your mind though? Is it because of what he said? Because he said I had to go?'

'No, not really...' said Lily. Then, 'No, of course not,' she repeated, more firmly. 'If I wanted you to stay here, then I would make sure that you did. I just think it might be for the best at the moment. Like I said before, I know you haven't been too happy.'

Whilst they had been talking Maisie realised that she would, in fact, miss her mother very much. She had seemed, in the last few moments, much more like the person she remembered from a long time ago; loving and caring and wanting to talk to her little girl.

'I shall miss you though, Mum,' Maisie said again. Then she looked away as tears started to mist her mother's eyes, making them appear silvery-grey, as she remembered them, not lacklustre and careworn as they had been so often of late.

'Yes, I know,' said Lily, sniffing a little. 'But don't worry, love. I'll be able to come and see you. I could come on a day trip, happen, and bring the little 'uns with me. They'd like that. Anyroad, what are we worrying about, eh? This 'ere war hasn't started yet, and if it does, then it might not last for very long, eh? Cheer up, Nellie. Let's go and put a few things together, shall we? I've made sure you've got a clean vest and liberty bodice and knickers to take with you, and a couple of pairs of socks. They're a bit holey, though, so happen I'd better darn 'em tonight...'

'Mum,' Maisie interrupted. 'You keep on calling me Nellie and you know I don't like it. It's what they call me, Sid and...Percy. You did say you'd try to remember...and now I'm going away I've decided that that's what I'm going to be called. I shall tell everybody me name's Maisie. I hate Nellie, I really do! I hate it!'

'Very well, love. I won't forget.' Her mother smiled, then she put an arm around her and kissed her cheek. 'That's what Daddy used to call you, didn't he? Maisie, my little mayflower... Oh, come on, love; let's get upstairs and sort yer things out, or else we'll both be crying, and that'll never do, will it?'

Lily led the way up the narrow staircase between the living room and the kitchen. The carpet was threadbare, worn into holes in parts, and the wallpaper was greasy and peeling off in places, especially where it had been helped along by grubby little hands. 'Those two little demons are quiet, aren't they? But I don't suppose it'll be for much longer. They'll be waking up, the pair of them and then they'll...' Lily stopped dead on the threshold of the children's bedroom.

'Oh! Oh...you little devils! I thought you were too quiet. Just wait till I get hold of you! I might have guessed you weren't asleep. Joanie, Jimmy, come 'ere, you naughty pair!' The room was full of feathers, greyish white feathers, fluttering in the air and clinging on to every surface where they could land; carpet, counterpane, the tops of the dressing table and cupboard, and on the clothes and in the hair of the two children who were trying to disappear under the double bed. An empty pillow case lay on the floor, a pile of feathers, those that had not already been scattered by grasping little hands, lying at the side of it.

'Come 'ere, come 'ere, you little devils!' Lily yanked them, one at a time, from under the bed, pulling roughly at their arms and then laying into them, shaking them and trying to smack their bottoms whilst they danced and yelled and pulled away from her. She did not make a habit of smacking her children, although oftentimes they deserved it. She was usually too weary and dispirited to do much more than threaten them and tell them they were naughty; even now she was hitting out at them mainly through despair and frustration and sorrow. Her beloved eldest child, Maisie – whom she was now realising she loved far more than she loved these two terrors put together

– was going away in the morning, to goodness knows where and for goodness knows how long. This was the very last straw. How could they do this to her?

Her blows held little weight and after a minute she let go of Joanie and Jimmy, collapsing on to the bed and burying her head in her hands. 'Whatever have I done,' she moaned, more to herself than to anyone else, 'to deserve a pair of little horrors like these two?' The pair of horrors were not crying or making any show of trying to do so, nor did they even look cowed or repentant; they were grinning impishly at one another and at their big sister. But Maisie was just as horrified at their behaviour as was her mother.

'Just wait till your dad comes home and I tell him what you've done,' Lily was saying, but not very convincingly. Maisie knew that this was an idle threat. Sid, more than likely, would just laugh or would find a reason to blame their mother rather than the children, that was if she even bothered to tell him at all.

'Come on, Mum,' she said. 'I'll help you clear it away. I'll get the dustpan and brush, an' I'll give this bed cover a good shake in t' backyard. That should get rid of most o' t' feathers… Just look what you've done, you two!' Maisie turned on her brother and sister. She had never been able to summon up much affection for them, but now she almost felt as though she hated them, just like she hated their father and elder brother. 'Just you sit there, the pair of you!' She plonked both of them roughly on their bottoms in a corner of the room, 'and don't you dare move an inch until we've got rid of all this mess!' She wrinkled her nose. Jimmy, as usual, smelled very unpleasant. 'And you need yer nappy changing, Jimmy, but you'll have to wait. An' I just don't care. You're a wicked boy, and so are you, Joanie, a very naughty little girl.'

She scowled at them and, for once, they did not grin back at her. Jimmy stuck out his lower lip and glowered at her, whilst Joanie stuck out her her tongue as far as it would go. Poor Mum, thought Maisie. She began to feel very sorry at the thought of leaving her mother behind with these dreadful children. Sid did not give her any help with their upbringing, except to yell at them occasionally or give them what he called a 'clip round the ear 'ole'.

A thought struck her as she and her mother struggled to brush away the feathers that had stuck fast to the carpet and curtains. She had heard some of the kids in the playground saying that their mothers were going with them on this evacuation thing, but only those with babies and young children. Those of school age were considered old enough to go on their own. Perhaps her own mother could go. Maisie was sure that she, too, would be only too happy to leave Sid and Percy behind. It would mean taking Joanie and Jimmy of course, but maybe they might not be so badly behaved if they got away from this neighbourhood. There were a few older kids – older than Joanie and Jimmy, that was, but still not old enough for school – who ran riot in the streets, and it was from them that the 'Bragg brats', as they were sometimes called, had learned many of their unruly ways.

'Mum, why don't you come with us tomorrer?' she said. 'They'd let you go, y' know, 'cause you've got two little 'uns. And they might learn to behave themselves if they got away from here.'

Lily gave a deep sigh. 'Don't imagine I haven't thought about it, love, because I have. It would be heaven... But Sid won't hear of it. No; he's adamant that I have to stay here and look after him...and Percy. An' I suppose he's got a point. He's my husband when all's said and done, and we can't all go swanning off dodging our responsibilities... Don't you dare mention it to him, Nellie – I mean Maisie,' she went on, as Maisie continued to look at her thoughtfully. 'He'd go barmy, he would really. He nearly went off 'is 'ead when I said before, casual like, that perhaps I could go an' all. No, love... Let's just hope and pray that things turn out for the best. Happen those two'll learn to behave 'emselves when they start school.'

'That's a long time yet, Mum...'

'Aye; I know that, Maisie...' She turned away, shaking her head sadly. 'Come on, laddie; let's be 'aving you. Let's get this mucky nappy off.' She picked up Jimmy who was sitting sullenly in the corner – at least he had stayed put – and plonked him on to the bed. 'Maisie – go and put the kettle on, there's a good lass. And happen you could peel a few spuds. Those two'll be home before I can turn round.'

Tea was late, inevitably, and Sid was not best pleased when he had to wait for several minutes whilst Lily and Maisie set the table and dished up the meal. Maisie usually had her tea – bread and jam, more often than not, as she had had a cooked meal of sorts at midday – before the menfolk came home, but this day was an exception. With all the commotion she had not had time to eat, so she sat at the table with her mother, Sid and Percy to eat the hastily prepared meal of sausages, chips and Heinz baked beans. Lily, at her wit's end with the younger two, had bundled them into bed when they had eaten their jam butties.

Sid coughed and spluttered when he had swallowed a mouthful. 'What the 'ell's this?' He spat out a half-chewed morsel of sausage on to his hand. 'That's a feather, woman! A bleedin' feather! 'Ow the 'ell did that get there? I might have choked to bloody death.'

'Oh dear...' Lily began.

'Don't blame me mum,' said Maisie. 'It's not her fault. It was Joanie and Jimmy. They took all t' feathers out of a pillow and chucked 'em around, didn't they, Mum?'

'And you had no more sense than let 'em?' scoffed Sid, giving his wife a withering look. 'You stupid, brainless woman...'

'I thought they were asleep, Sid. They were so quiet.'

'You let 'em run rings round you. You 'aven't a bloody clue 'ow to look after 'em, and they're grand little kids.'

'They're very naughty,' retorted Maisie, the thought that she would be leaving the next day giving her courage. 'And it's not me mum's fault. She does her best.'

'You speak when you're bloody well spoken to,

Nellie Jackson!' Sid gave her a vicious look. 'It's nowt to do wi' you, so keep out if it, you interferin' little brat, or you know what you'll get... What's she doing here anyroad, 'aving her tea with us?' He scowled at Lily.

'She's going away tomorrow, Sid,' said Lily quietly. You know – we talked about it and I decided to let her go. So we've been getting her things together.'

'Oh, so you've seen sense at last, 'ave yer?' said Sid. 'Not afore time.'

'Good riddance to bad rubbish,' mumbled Percy through a mouthful of food. Maisie noticed, nonetheless, the way he leered at her from under his eyelids. And her mother noticed too. 'So we're celebratin', are we, wi' sausage and chips?' He laughed uproariously.

Maisie tossed her head, not deigning to answer. Only one more day and she would be rid of them. She looked with loathing at Percy, and at Sid, with tomato sauce dribbling down his chin. Despite his initial comment, he had scoffed all his meal, without choking. He wiped his forearm across his mouth and burped loudly. Maisie gave an inward shudder. Only one more day, she thought again. But poor Mum... However would her mother manage when she, Maisie, had gone and left her?

◆

Maisie's belongings, such as they were – knickers, vest, liberty bodice, two pairs of socks, recently darned, a shabby nightdress that was way too short for her; plus her toothbrush and flannel and her beloved, but battered, teddy bear – were all packed away in a black leatherette bag that Lily sometimes used for shopping. When Sid and Percy had gone out her mother had locked the door, filled the zinc bath tub and placed it on the hearthrug in front of the fire, and Maisie had emerged from the hot water cleaner than she had felt for a long while. She had gone to bed early, but she knew she would not be able to sleep, not for a while, at any rate. Her stomach was all churned up, partly with excitement, but mainly with anxiety. In fact, she was more than anxious; she was scared almost out of her wits that Percy would come into her bedroom that night. She knew she must keep awake, even if her eyelids grew heavy. She was frightened, but she knew she must try to be brave. And if he came, then she would be ready for him.

Lily, too, had retired to bed before either of the menfolk returned from wherever they had gone; Sid to the Rose and Crown, most likely, but she was not sure where Percy spent his evenings. Lily knew she would not be able to sleep, and she had made sure she was armed and ready...for whatever might happen. She hoped and prayed that nothing would, but if it did, then that lad would get what he deserved, and more.

When she had been in bed for a while, half an hour or so, she guessed, she heard the back door open and close again, then footsteps on the stairs. She could tell by the slight cough he gave, clearing his throat, that it was Percy and not her husband. She lay, still as a stone, but when she heard his footsteps pause, she guessed he was listening outside her bedroom door. She made herself snore, just a little, catching her breath at the back of her throat, then she started to breath heavily and evenly as though she were deep in slumber. She heard him give a chuckle and she could imagine the sneering grin on his podgy florid face. All her senses were alert, every nerve straining as she waited, fearful and yet certain what his next move would be.

Maisie heard him pushing open her bedroom door, then creeping across to her bed. He did not waste any time. He yanked off the bed cover and the thin sheet that covered her, staring down at her slim figure in the too short nightgown. She knew she had outgrown her nighties ages ago and had started wearing her knickers as well in bed, because she was, instinctively, a modest girl. She pulled at her nightdress now, trying to cover the tops of her legs. She looked up at him with wide frightened eyes as he leered at her, his prominent blue eyes gleaming lasciviously in the semi-darkness and his thick lips wet with saliva.

'Hello, Nellie,' he whispered. ''Ow about a kiss for yer big brother? And 'appen a bit more, eh, 'cause yer goin' away tomorrer, ain't yer? I shall miss yer, Nellie. I've enjoyed out little…sessions.'

She was terrified, but she did not struggle any more than she had usually done as he lay down beside her, lowering his nasty slobbering mouth on to hers. Let him think that she was too scared to shout out, as she always had been in the past. She felt his hand touching her unformed breasts, then stroking her legs and pulling at her knickers. It was then that she did what she had always wanted to do, but had never dared to do before. She pushed him away with all the strength she could muster, at the same time bringing up her knee and punching him hard in whichever place her knee could reach.

'Get off me, you filthy beast!' she yelled at the top of her voice. 'Mum, Mum...come quick! Help me...'

She saw Percy writhing on the floor at the side of the bed. He was clutching at himself, at that private part of him, but she had not known which bit of him she had punched. 'You stupid little bitch!' he shouted. 'What d'yer want to do that for? I was only kissin' yer and...y'know, like I've done before. I thought you liked it.'

'Well, I don't! I hate you! I hate you!' Then she stared in amazement as her mother burst into the room. Something was gleaming in her upraised hand, and Maisie realised with horror that it was a pair of scissors with long sharp blades. Lily dashed across the room, thrusting the points downwards at the cringing cowering figure on the floor. He had stopped writhing around now, and was staring up at her in fright.

'Don't! Don't! I never meant it...' he cried.

'Mum, stop it! You mustn't!' Maisie leapt from the bed and knocked the scissors from her mother's hand just before they reached their target. They clattered on to the floor, but as they fell, the sharp points grazed the lad's arm, drawing a trickle of blood.

'Look what you've done, you bloody fool!' he yelled. 'I'm bleeding! I'm gonna tell the police. You tried to kill me, you ravin' loony...'

None of them had heard the footsteps coming up the stairs, but suddenly Sid Bragg was there in the doorway, the jowls of his big red face quivering with anger, his slavering mouth spitting out words of venom. 'What the 'ell's goin' on 'ere? You crazy brainless woman!' He kicked out at Lily who by this time had collapsed on the floor, his foot landing with force in the pit of her stomach. She cried out, doubling up in pain as he struck out again, this time with his fist, delivering a heavy blow to her temple. 'Try to kill my son, would you, you wicked scheming bitch? The lad's right. We'll get the law on to you. You want lockin' up...'

'Stop it! Stop it!' cried Lily 'He was molesting my little girl. Goodness knows what might have happened if I hadn't come in.'

'I weren't,' retorted Percy. 'It weren't like that, Dad. I were kissin' 'er, that's all. I've done it before an' she likes it. She's never tried to stop me before. I were only 'avin a bit of fun.'

'You're a bloody liar, Percy Bragg!' It was the first time Maisie had ever used such a word, but she could not contain herself. 'He said he'd beat me up, an' that he would an' all...' She jerked her thumb in the direction of Sid, '...if I told anybody. He did...all sorts of horrid things, but I didn't dare tell. Not till now. But I'm goin' away tomorrer so I don't care any more.' Suddenly it was all too much for her and she burst into tears.

Lily was at her side at once, her arms around her, stroking her spiky hair. 'Never mind, darling. It's all over now. He won't be able to hurt you again.'

'Huh! I reckon she encouraged him,' sneered Sid.

'She'll 'ave led 'im on, the little tart. I allus knew she was trouble, that one. Well, thank the Lord she's going tomorrer…and as far as I'm concerned you can go an' all.' He poked Lily roughly in the back. 'D'you hear me? You clear off an' take them two with you.' He gestured towards the other side of the room. 'Me an' our Percy, we can manage on our own wi'out an 'ouseful of loony women.' He stalked out of the room and Percy followed him.

'I never did nowt,' he mumbled in a sullen voice. 'I only touched 'er. I never…— 'er.'

Lily was shocked that he should use such a word in front of her daughter and herself. But thank God Percy hadn't…done that, she thought, if he was to be believed, and she guessed that that much was true.

The two younger ones had woken up now, disturbed by all the commotion and were both sitting up in their bed.

'Want a drink…' said Joanie.

'Me an' all…' said Jimmy.

'All right,' sighed Lily. 'I'll get you a drink, then you must go back to sleep.'

She decided she would spend the night in Maisie's bed. She could not bear to share a bed with Sid and, from what he said, he would not want her there. She guessed, though, that his words were all bravado and that, come the morning, he would have changed his mind about her going. He would not let her get away that easily.

Chapter Three

It had been a glorious summer, one of the best in living memory. War was the last thing on the minds of many of the inhabitants of Great Britain as the mellow, sunny days of August gave way to September. Hadn't they been promised peace, only last year, by the Prime Minister, Neville Chamberlain, coming back from Munich waving his scrap of paper and proclaiming that it was 'Peace in our time'? And 'the war to end all wars', as it had been called, had ended only twenty years before. It was well nigh impossible to think that there might soon be another one.

Yet, as the summer faded, momentous events were taking place in Europe and, eventually, even those who had continued to bury their heads in the sand were forced to wake up to the fact that the threat was real.

Patience Fairchild, the wife of the rector of St Bartholomew's church in the little market town of Middlebeck, high in the northern Yorkshire Dales, was not one who had ignored – or had pretended to, as many did – the dire warnings. She and her husband, Luke, always endeavoured to keep abreast of the times. Indeed, Luke maintained that a 'man of the cloth', such as he was, should keep himself informed about what was going on in the country and the wider world outside his own small parish. Some clergymen tried to live a purely spiritual existence, leaving problems they knew they could not deal with themselves in the hands of God, believing, in the fullness of time, that all would be well. But Luke was a man of action, as well as a great believer in the power of prayer. Very soon, within the next day or two, their small town and the surrounding area would be host to dozens, possibly scores of evacuees. At the moment they were not sure of the actual numbers, nor would they be until the trains carrying the children arrived at the station.

There was to be a meeting that night in the rectory to discuss plans for the part that Middlebeck would play in the evacuation scheme. And so, on the evening of Friday the first of September, Patience was busy setting out all the chairs she could muster from various parts of the house, in the spacious lounge. This was where meetings were very often held; not only those appertaining to church life, but to school and village life in general as well. She counted on her fingers as she went through, in her mind, the people she expected to be present that evening. Miss Foster, the headmistress of the school, and her other two members of staff; the squire, Archie Tremaine and his wife, Rebecca; representatives from the WVS, possibly three or maybe more; the two church wardens, Mr Allbright and Mr Carey; Miss Thomson, the undisputed spokeswoman of the church council; and herself and Luke, of course.

Fifteen cups, saucers and plates should be more

than enough, she decided as she moved into the kitchen to get out the second-best willow pattern china, which came out for every meeting. She had been busy all morning, baking cakes and shortbread biscuits. As though some sort of a party was about to take place, she thought, instead of a gathering of village folk to discuss their plans as they stood on the brink of what might prove to be the most cataclysmic event in the history of the world.

Patience had never been convinced by Chamberlain's assurance of appeasement. Neither, it seemed, were the more sceptical members of the Government as plans for re-armament and the compulsory conscription of young men were put into force. And long before that, all schoolchildren had been issued with gas masks and had been given practice in emergency drill. The adults had now been provided with them as well; hers and Luke's lay at the bottom of the wardrobe in their cardboard boxes. Please God, may we never have to use them, prayed Patience. She remembered her father returning from the last war, suffering from the effects of mustard gas and he had since died as a result of his injuries. War was a truly dreadful, horrific experience, and Patience, in her bleaker moments, was tempted to question in her mind why God allowed such things to happen. But she did not voice her uncertainties aloud or try to discuss them with her husband. It was one of life's imponderables and such questioning could drive one mad.

There had been little doubt as to the outcome when, earlier that year, German troops had marched into Czechoslovakia, in direct contravention of the Munich agreement. It was useless for the Government to tell people not to panic-buy, as there was plenty of food available. Many folk, at last waking up to reality, had begun to do just that. It was then announced that conscription was to be extended to include menfolk up to forty-one years of age. Patience had said a silent prayer of thanks. Luke was forty-two, but, even so, she knew she would have to struggle hard to dissuade him from joining up.

And now, on that very day, the first of September, 1939, there had come the news, on the wireless and in the newspapers, that Germany had invaded Poland. The blackout restrictions had been enforced and the evacuation of children had already begun. There were plans to evacuate millions of them. And the inhabitants of Middlebeck were to play their part.

~

'They're arriving tomorrow,' announced Muriel Hollins, who was not only the Chairman of the local Women's Institute, but also an active member of the Mothers' Union at St Bartholomew's church. And recently, she and others of her ilk had joined the growing ranks of the Women's Voluntary Service. The membership of the WVS was, at first, essentially upper and middle class, and the women in their green tweed suits, red jumpers and unbecoming felt hats were the object of ridicule in some circles. The members, so far, had done little more than preside over church fetes and open bazaars and sales of work. But now that war was imminent thousands of women were joining its ranks to help in whatever capacity they could on the Home Front. And the chief task at the moment was their organisation of the evacuation scheme.

Patience had enrolled as a member as well, but on this warm late summer evening she had decided not to wear her uniform, but had put on a favourite light rayon dress with white spots on a pale green background. She noticed that Muriel and her two stalwart helpers, Jessie Campion and Ivy Spooner, were wearing the full rig-out of green and red. They all looked far too hot, although they had discarded their jackets by now; but not, however, their hats, which they seemed to regard as an inalienable badge of office.

Muriel's face, in particular, was as beetroot red as her jumper as she told the meeting of the plans to be put into action the next day. 'Tomorrow, probably towards midday, as far as we know; those will be the ones from the Leeds area. And some more are expected in the afternoon, from Hull.'

'Good gracious! Two lots?' queried Miss Amelia Thomson. 'How do they expect a village like Middlebeck to accomodate such a large number of evacuees?'

'We really don't know how many there will be until they arrive.' Mrs Muriel Hollins cast a disdainful look at the speaker. 'But we can be sure they will not send us more than our quota. And Middlebeck is no longer classed as a village, Miss Thomson. It has grown extensively over the last few years. There is the new estate, and all the outlying farms. And everyone – and I do mean everyone –

will be expected to take an evacuee; more than one if possible.'

Miss Thomson looked away hastily from the eagle-eye of Muriel Hollins, shaking her head and pursing her thin lips, and fiddling with the crochet-work gloves on her lap. 'Well, I am sure we will all do what we can, but some of us are not as young as we used to be. I have already said that I will help with the meal when they arrive, handing round sandwiches or…whatever you are going to give them.'

'Thank you, Miss Thomson. I am sure your help will be much appreciated,' said Muriel dismissively.

There was not much love lost between the two women, as most of the folk assembled there realised. Miss Thomson resented the fact that Mrs Muriel Hollins was a leading light in the Mothers' Union – not actually the enrolling member because Patience Fairchild, as the rector's wife, was awarded that honour – whereas she, because of her spinster status, could not take an important role in MU affairs. But to make up for that, Miss Amelia Thomson had made sure, over the years, that she was a force to be reckoned with on the Parochial Church Council.

Patience, sensing that the hackles of these two ladies were beginning to rise, decided she must try to avert any unpleasantness. She glanced around the room, her warm smile embracing them all. Patience had the flair for making everyone feel welcome and appreciated, and they liked and admired her for it.

'All your efforts are appreciated,' she said, 'every one of you, and my husband and I do thank you for taking the trouble to come here this evening. Now...we have decided then, have we, that the Village Institute would be the best assembly point?' There were nods of agreement.

It had been suggested at first that the evacuees, on arrival, should be taken to the church hall, where church functions and the Sunday School of St Bartholomew's took place. The church, however, was situated at the furthest end of the town from the railway station. The procession of newcomers, therefore, would have to pass the Village Institute, which stood half way down the High Street, so it made sense for this to be the chosen venue. Moreover, this building was the home, primarily, of the Women's Institute and, latterly, of the WVS, the two organizations having become almost synonymous.

'Yes, I think we are all agreed on that,' said Muriel. 'I have already been asking round our ladies and I have the promise of sandwiches – egg and cress, potted meat, and sardine – and scones and cakes. And Jessie and Ivy here have promised to make iced buns, haven't you, dears? And to be responsible for making the tea. We have some large enamel pots that we used for our meetings, but we don't really want to use our best china tea service. There wouldn't be enough of it anyway.'

'There are plenty of plain white cups and saucers, and plates, too, in the church cupboard,' said the rector. 'We use them for Sunday School parties and concerts and suchlike. I can make arrangements for them to be transported to the Institute.'

'Oh, thank you so much, Rector,' said Muriel,

clasping her hands together and beaming. 'That would be most kind of you.'

'Jessie and I have been thinking,' said Ivy Spooner, cautiously. The two of them were always rather in awe of their chairman, as were most of the ladies of the WI. 'Might it not be better to give them orange juice. I mean...some children are not very partial to tea. It's...just an idea.'

'Hmm... It seems to me that they should be grateful for whatever they are given.' Miss Thomson raised her eyebrows behind the wire-framed spectacles which were perched on the end of her nose. 'When I was a child we were not allowed to pick and choose.'

Muriel Hollins ignored her, turning to her two helpmates from the WI. 'Thank you, Ivy, and you too, Jessie. What a splendid idea! Of course kiddies prefer orange juice, don't they?'

'Think of the expense though,' muttered Miss Thomson. 'You will have to make sure it is well diluted then it will go further.' She sniffed audibly. 'I don't suppose children from backgrounds like theirs will know the difference anyway.'

'Never mind the expense,' broke in Rebecca Tremaine. She was the wife of the man who was generally regarded as the squire, by virtue of the fact that he was the largest landowner in the area. 'I will be only too pleased to contribute half a dozen bottles of orange squash, or however many you think you well need.'

'Splendid! Splendid!' Muriel clapped her hands in delight. 'That is really most generous of you, Mrs Tremaine.'

'You will need tea as well, though,' that lady reminded her. 'There will be adults to cater for as well as children. Their schoolteachers and...am I right in supposing there will be mothers, too, and some babies and children under school age?'

'Yes, that's quite right,' replied Muriel. 'But, as I've said, we are not sure of the numbers.'

'Hang on a minute,' said Thomas Allbright, one of the churchwardens. 'All this business of sandwiches and cakes and orange squash and what-have-you...it sounds as though it's going to be a real old bun feast. But won't they already have had their dinner or whatever? Won't they bring sandwiches with 'em, to eat on the train?'

'Mebbe not,' said his opposite number, Albert Carey. 'It's nobbut a hop, skip and a jump from Leeds, is it? Relatively speaking, I mean. They won't be more than a couple of hours on the train, if that. They'll not need sandwiches. Of course, the ones from Hull will have further to come; I'll grant you that...'

'Thank you, gentlemen, for your observations,' said Muriel, 'but it's all immaterial. We want to provide a meal, whatever the cirumstances, to make them feel welcome. Yes, they may well have brought their own lunch, or maybe not. You see, it's doubtful whether any of the evacuees will know where they are going until they actually arrive. They will have no idea whether they are embarking on a long journey or a short one.'

'Why ever not?' asked Mr Allbright.

'Security reasons.' Muriel nodded importantly. 'The fewer people who know the destination the better, just in case important information is leaked and gets into the wrong hands.'

'It sounds a funny sort of how d'you do to me,' said Mr Carey, scratching his bald head. 'Very hit and miss. It's to be hoped the engine driver knows where he's going.'

There was a slight ripple of laughter. 'Oh, I reckon he'll have inside information, Albert,' said Archie Tremaine. 'Now, about the business of accommodating all these children, Mrs Hollins. How do you propose to allocate them?'

'That's tricky,' said Muriel. 'We have been giving it some thought, and we think the best way to do it is to invite people to come to the hall and...well...to choose their own children.'

A few people nodded, but Miss Foster, the headmistress of the school who, so far, had said very little, spoke up. 'What about the poor little mites who are left, though? The children at school love to choose sides when they are playing a game, and it's always the unpopular ones who are left till last. I always feel so sorry for them.'

'Yes, that's true,' agreed Jean Bolton, one of the other teachers; and her colleague, Shirley Sylvester, nodded her agreement. 'It's the ones you don't really notice who don't get picked, or perhaps they can't run very fast.'

'It's not something I would advise for housing the evacuees,' said Miss Foster. 'On the other hand...I must admit that I can't think of any other way of doing it.'

'You are right, Miss Foster,' said the squire. 'As always, you are right.' Miss Charity Foster, now nearing her retirement age, had been the headmistress of the village school – now rather more than a village – for as long as most people could remember. She was much respected for her fairness and her genuine love of the children in her care.

'I think we can rely on most of our fellow villagers, however, to be fair and to play the game,' Archie Tremaine continued. 'Of course I know the farmers amongst us will choose big strong lads. Well, nobody could blame 'em for that.'

'Now, wait a minute, Archie,' broke in the rector. 'I don't think we can regard the evacuees as unpaid labour, can we? They are supposed to be under our care and protection.'

'Sorry, sorry…' Archie held up his hands. 'I think you misunderstand me. You are right, of course, Rector. I only meant…once they have settled in, the older lads might enjoy helping with odd jobs around the farm. Don't forget that a lot of the farm hands will be called up to serve their country in the armed forces.'

'And they are already sending land girls to the farms,' said Jessie Campion. 'The WLA has been re-formed.'

'Thank you, thank you… We are getting away from the main issue,' interrupted Muriel. 'The allocation of the children…?'

'Quite right, quite right,' said Archie, rubbing his hands together. 'Well, my wife and I have been talking things over, haven't we, Becky? And we know only too well that we have much more room at our place than most other folk. So, what we propose is that we should take the women with the babies and small children, as many of them as we can fit in. As you may know, my wife was a nurse before she married me, and she has brought up our three children; so I think she knows what she's about.'

'Splendid!' cried Muriel again. 'I'm sure we are all very pleased to hear that, Mr Tremaine. Thank you, Mrs Tremaine. We must all try to put our talents to their very best use.'

The two church wardens volunteered, on behalf of their wives, to take two evacuees each. They were middle-aged couples whose children had grown up and left home. The squire and his wife, also, had two children who had married and moved away, but they had a son as well, Bruce, who would soon be returning to his boarding school.

'And we will, of course, be taking some children ourselves,' said Muriel. 'Myself and Jessie and Ivy here; in fact the majority of our members have agreed to do so. That includes your two mothers as well, Joan and Shirley.' She smiled at the two younger women who were teachers at the school.

'There is a spare bedroom at the schoolhouse,' said Miss Foster. 'I realise, though, that it might be rather different for me. I would willingly accommodate two children, but...would it be fair to them? They might not like the idea of living with a teacher, especially the headmistress, and who could blame them?' She smiled. 'So...how would it be if I were to have one of the teachers instead? They are sending some teachers with them, aren't they?'

'We believe so,' said Muriel. 'Thank you, Miss Foster. That is an admirable solution...'

There was a silence during which everyone tried not to look at Miss Amelia Thomson, the only person who had not volunteered to take any evacuees. Eventually, it was Muriel Hollins who glanced at her, a determined look on her face and her eyebrows raised questioningly. Miss Thomson, appearing flustered, dropped her gloves on the floor then stooped to pick them up. Mrs Hollins was still regarding her solemnly, her pencil poised at the ready. 'Now Miss Thomson,' she said. 'What about you? I am sure you must have room for at least one child.'

Miss Thomson cleared her throat. 'Daisy lives with me now, you know. She moved in when things became too much for me.' Daisy was her maid-of-all-work who had been employed by her – some would say slaved for her – ever since she left school at fourteen. Ten years later the young woman was still there, but now 'lived in' rather than to-ing and fro-ing each day from her home at the other end of the village. 'And I have to keep a room vacant for when my sister comes to visit me...'

Miss Thomson's words faltered under the steadfast gaze of her opponent. 'Er...very well, then. Perhaps I might see my way to taking a child. Just one, mind; that's all I could manage. And...it must be a little girl... Girls are so much easier to cope with,' she added in an undertone.

'Splendid!' boomed Muriel, slapping her hand on her thigh. 'I knew everyone would come up trumps. Thank you, Miss Thomson. Thanks to you all, indeed, for volunteering. And you good people, of course, will be allowed first choice; the pick of the bunch, one might say.'

Patience frowned a little, but did not say anything. This picking and choosing – and rejecting – sounded rather like the sort of thing that went on every Wednesday in the animal market at the back of the market hall, when cattle and sheep were bought and sold. The children who were coming did not deserve to be treated like that, but she supposed there was no other way but to let people have their choice. She glanced uneasily at her husband, and it was Luke who spoke up.

'I thought we had agreed that there wasn't to be too much of that sort of thng? They are all God's children, even though they may not all be blessed with pretty faces or strong limbs. And some of them may be from very unsatisfactory homes… I am sure I do not need to remind you all to treat them kindly and with the respect due to them.'

Muriel Hollins coughed pointedly. 'You may be sure we will all do our best, Rector, in these…er…difficult circumstances.' She did not take kindly to even the slightest criticism, but Patience knew that, under the bossiness and the determination to have her own way, she did have what was termed a 'heart of gold'. Whereas Patience had never had the same feeling about Miss Amelia Thomson. She was generally regarded as a bitter and parsimonious old maid, and Patience was already beginning to feel sorry for any child unlucky enough to be selected by her. She broke in hurriedly.

'Yes, as you say, Muriel; I am sure we will all do our best...Miss Foster...' She turned to the headmistress. 'What are the plans for schooling? We are going to find ourselves – at a rough guess – with double the number of children we have already, aren't we? And there is no way they will fit into our existing school.'

The school, which had originally been entirely under the control of St Bartholomew's church, had been started over a hundred years ago when Middlebeck was still a village, as a one-class school. As the village had expanded and more children had been born it had soon increased to two classes, one for the children up to the age of eight or nine, and the other for those pupils who would remain there until they left at the age of thirteen.

But now the education of children was starting to be taken more seriously. The Education Act of 1870 had made school attendance for all children compulsory, and since then things had moved on apace. There were now three classes at St Bartholomew's school, an extension having been built to accommodate the rising numbers; Infants, aged five to seven; Lower Juniors, aged eight and nine; and Upper Juniors, aged ten and eleven. At the age of eleven the children now went either to the senior school at the other end of the town – built when the town expanded, and catering for outlying villages as well as Middlebeck – or, for those who had passed a Scholarship Examination, to the High School further afield.

St Bartholomew's School was now aided financially by the Local Education Authority, but it was still the rector of the church and the headmistress who made most of the decisions.

'That is very true, Mrs Fairchild,' said Miss Foster. 'Our small school is bursting at the seams already. I have heard that some authorities are proposing part-time education; that would be the local children in the morning and the evacuees in the afternoon, or vice versa. But it's not something I'm in favour of myself.'

'It would please the kiddies, though, wouldn't it?' laughed Albert Carey. 'Only half a day at school! They'd be tickled pink.'

'Precisely,' said Miss Foster, smiling. 'They would also be running wild and getting up to all sorts of mischief. They have had quite long enough away from school already. I think we should establish a routine for our own children and our visitors as soon as possible. Routine; that is what is important to help them with the problems that they are sure to face. That's one thing; another, of course, is love and care...' She stared into space for a moment before continuing. 'I have already given this matter some thought. And I suggest that we make more use of the church hall, with the rector's permission, of course. We could fit two classes in there, with some sort of a partition down the middle.'

'Excellent! I was about to suggest it myself,' agreed Luke. 'And the same goes for the Village Institute, perhaps? That is not under my jurisdiction, of course, but maybe you good ladies might allow the school to use it?' He looked at Muriel and her chums. 'It's quite a distance from the school, I know, but we just have to do the best we can.'

This was agreed upon and there followed a discussion about furniture. Card tables would have to be used as desks for the time being. There should be sufficient chairs, however, and school equipment would have to be shared out fairly, but Luke was sure that a grant from the Education Authority, as well as the Church, would be forthcoming.

Should the evacuees be taught separately? was a point for discussion. Some, including Miss Thomson, thought that they should. Others were in favour of integration, so that the children could get to know one another, and as this was Miss Foster's view this was what was decided. It was agreed, though, that as this would require a good deal of organization, the children should be given two extra days holiday. School would recommence on Wednesday, the sixth of September instead of on the Monday.

Dusk had fallen as they had been discussing plans and partaking of the refreshments that Patience had provided. It was time to light the two standard lamps which stood at either end of the lounge and cast a rosy glow through their pink shades. But before that could be done the blackout curtains must be drawn, because blackout restrictions had been enforced that very day. This was the signal, it seemed, for all the visitors to depart. They all remembered that they had their own arrangements to see to at home. Patience could hear their comments as they put on their hats and coats.

'Confounded nuisance it is! But I left it all to the wife...'

'I got some really strong black cotton material at the market; only sixpence a yard...'

'I've covered my landing window with black paper. It makes it gloomy upstairs, but it might not be for long, eh?'

'Goodnight, Patience, dear. Goodnight, Rector...'

'Thank you for the supper. But we've done a lot of good work as well, haven't we?'

'Indeed we have,' agreed Patience. 'Thank you all for coming...'

'Goodnight everyone. And God bless you all,' added Luke.

He stood at the side of his wife, his arm around her, as she drew the red plush curtains, now lined with black, against the windows. Such a peaceful scene, thought Patience. She never tired of the view from the lounge window, across the village green to the greystone school and the schoolhouse towards which Charity Foster was now making her way. At the top side of the green, marking the end of the little town, stood the church, parts of it dating from the fifteenth century, and the graveyard with its ancient lichened stones. And to her left from where she was standing, the High Street led down through stone-built houses to the shops, the market square, the Village Institute and then to the railway station in the valley. Behind the church, but out of sight from the front of the house, was a rippling stream, a tributary of the river which ran through the dale; and on top of the hill that rose behind the church tower were the ruins of Middleburgh Castle, standing out black and gaunt against the darkening sky.

'It's so peaceful. How very tranquil and lovely it all is,' breathed Patience. 'I can't bear to think about what trials and dangers may lie ahead.'

'None of us know, my darling,' said Luke. 'But God is our refuge and strength, a very present help in trouble...' he added quietly. He did not often quote from the Bible, fearing it made him sound solemn and sanctimonious, but Patience knew that was from one of his favourite psalms. 'But that does not mean that we can stand back and do nothing,' he went on. He looked heavenwards. 'I have the feeling that He is going to need all the help He can get, from all of us.'

Chapter Four

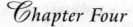

There was only her mother sitting at the kitchen table when Maisie went downstairs the following morning. She had left the two little ones having a pillow fight, laughing and screaming and bashing one another around the head, as if they hadn't already caused enough trouble with pillows the day before. The remains of toast and the used cups and plates indicated that Sid and Percy had already gone to work, to Maisie's great relief. Her mother glanced up, giving a sad and weary smile. One eye was puffed up and her face darkened by a bruise all down one side, and Maisie guessed her body must be bruised as well from the kicking Sid had given her.

'Are you alright, Mum?' she asked anxiously. 'They've gone, have they, Sid and...Percy?'

Lily nodded. 'Aye, they've gone... And, yes, I'm all right. As right as I'll ever be, I suppose.' Maisie noticed that her mother winced as she reached across the table for the teapot. 'Here y' are, love. Have a cup of tea – it's still quite fresh – and there's some toast left. An' I'll go and get them two terrors out of bed. We'd best be shaping ourselves if you're to be at school in less than an hour.'

'All of us, Mum; not just me,' Maisie reminded

her. 'You're coming an' all, aren't you? And our Joanie and Jimmy.'

'No, I'm afraid not, love,' said Lily, and Maisie could see a tear forming in the corner of her eye. 'We're not coming with you.'

'But Sid said, last night…'

'Oh aye; I know what he said last night, but he's changed his tune now, hasn't he? I knew he would. I've to stay here and look after him…and Percy.'

'But you can't, Mum! Not after what's happened. You know what he's done to yer, an' he'll do it again. And Percy an' all; he'll be dead mad after you going for him like that…'

'I wouldn't have killed him, love. I know I felt like it…but I'd never have had the guts. I haven't got the guts for anything, not any more. He's knocked it all out of me.'

'Then get away, Mum. Don't take any notice of what he says. Just…go.'

'How can I?' Lily sighed. 'He'd only come after me.'

'He won't know where you've gone. It's all a big secret.'

'He'd find out – you know what he's like. No, love – I'll have to stay put.'

'Then I'm staying with you…'

'Oh no, you're not!' Lily thumped her fist on the table. 'That's one thing I'm certain of. You're going Nellie…Maisie, I mean.' She shook her head sorrowfully. 'I don't want to lose you – of course I don't – but you've got to give yourself a chance. There's not a hope in hell for you if you stay here…' She stood up. 'Come on, now; eat your breakfast an' we'll get moving. I'll make a few sandwiches for you to eat on the train...'

An hour later Maisie and her mother with the two youngsters, bundled hastily into the pram – fed, but not yet washed or fully dressed – joined the ranks of children and parents, mostly mothers, at the school hall. Maisie was provided with a label on a string which she was told to put round her neck. Her teacher, Miss Patterdale, had already printed on it, Eleanor May Jackson (Nellie). Maisie intended, as soon as she got the chance, to cross out the name Nellie and substitute Maisie. She hoped, in passing, that Miss Patterdale had not changed her mind and decided to go with them. They had been told that she was one of the teachers remaining behind.

The teacher also handed her a carrier bag, which Maisie immediately opened and looked inside. 'That's not for you,' snapped Miss Patterdale. 'It's emergency rations for two days, to be given to...whoever takes charge of you when you arrive. And it has to be handed over complete, so just think on!'

Maisie had already glimpsed a small bar of chocolate along with the tins – corned beef, pilchards and evaporated milk, she had made out at a glance – and the packet of Ryvita and carton of tea; her sharp eyes had missed nothing. There was little chance of the chocolate arriving at its destination, and she guessed all the other children would be of the same opinion. So shucks to you, Miss Patterdale! she thought.

Eventually all the children were shepherded out, by the two teachers who were to accompany them, on to the pavement outside the school where a big double-decker bus was waiting to take them to the station. It turned out that there was not as many as had been, originally, anticipated. One or two of the mothers, indeed, changed their minds at the last minute.

'She's not going. It's no use; I can't do it,' one woman was heard to utter, with tears in her eyes; and off she marched with her little girl, obviously relieved, trotting along beside her. A couple of others followed suit.

Maisie had noticed Audrey Dennison in the school hall, being fussed over by an elderly lady; her gran, Maisie assumed, wondering fleetingly where her mother was; she did not know anything about the girl's background except that she was rather posh. Audrey was crying, and Maisie would not have been surprised if the lady with her, whoever she was, had decided to take her home again. But no; this did not happen. Audrey tearfully boarded the bus, one of the first to do so, although there were still tears in her eyes and in the eyes of the woman waving goodbye to her.

'Cheerio then, Maisie love,' said her mother, giving her a hug and a quick kiss on the cheek. 'Be a good girl, won't you? Well, of course I know you will... And write as soon as you get there. Let me know where you're staying.'

'I will. 'Course I will, Mum,' said Maisie. 'Mum...you will be OK, won't you? I mean...I don't have to go.' She could see that her mother was upset, trying desperately hard not to cry, so Maisie knew that she mustn't do so either. Mum looked scared and bewildered too, as well she might, being left behind with Sid and Percy and those two naughty children to contend with. She had put a headscarf on, pulling it down over her forehead and across her cheek to hide the worst of the bruising, but the purplish patch was still visible and told its own story; although most folk that morning were too concerned with their own troubles to worry about other people's.

'Yes, you do have to go,' said Lily decidedly, 'especially now…with Percy and everything. But try to put it all to the back of your mind, love, OK? Forget about him…and have a good time in the country. I expect that's where you'll be going. And we'll come and see you very soon; me and Joanie and Jimmy. Wave tara to your sister, you two…'

The youngsters waved mechanically, Joanie shouting out, 'Tara, Nellie…' Then her mother quickly turned the pram around and headed for home.

It did not take long to reach Leeds City Station. They all trooped out again, on to the forecourt of the station where Miss Mellodey, one of the teachers, counted them. '…forty-five, forty-six; yes, that's right.' Although it was hardly likely that any of them would have disappeared on the journey between Armley and the city centre. In a separate little group were the four mothers, with two toddlers apiece, plus a baby in arms, who had chosen to join the party.

'Come along now, boys and girls; find a partner and follow me,' said Miss Cousins. She led the way and Miss Mellodey went to the back of the crocodile to deal with any stragglers, followed by the mothers and babies.

They were a motley assortment of children, ranging in age from six to eleven. Most of them were wearing navy-blue gaberdine raincoats, some stiff with newness and reaching to well below their knees, others shabby and too short for their wearers; Maisie's was in the latter category. The boys wore serge trousers and grey woollen socks, mostly concertinaed round their ankles. Some wore their school caps and others woollen balaclava helmets, in spite of the warmth of the late summer day. Similarly, some of the girls looked hot and uncomfortable in knitted pixie hoods, but Maisie had taken hers off and shoved it in her bag. They were laden like pack-horses; not only did they have a bag or a suitcase containing their own belongings, but also the carrier bag with the supply of food, and the obligatory gas mask in its cardboard box, slung over one shoulder.

Maisie was partnered with a girl she only knew by sight as they made their way through throngs of people, then through the barrier and on to the platform. The girl was from the top class and chose to ignore Maisie; so she kept her eye on Audrey Dennison who was two in front of her. She decided she would sit next to her on the train, if she could. There were only six of them from their particular class in the end, three boys and three girls, and she was determined not to get lumbered with Esme Clough. She had had enough of her at school, and it went without saying that you didn't sit near the boys unless you were forced to do so.

She stared at the busy scene that surrounded them. The station was a large one with lots of platforms and trains frequently arriving and departing. Maisie remembered coming to this station once before, when she and her mum and dad had been going on a rare visit to York. It had been busy then, she recalled, and as a little tot of about three or four she had been quite overwhelmed by the crowds, but today it was worse; jam-packed with people pushing and shoving their way through the milling throng with large suitcases, bags and haversacks. Many of them must be holidaymakers returning from a visit to the seaside or the country, maybe, back to the security of their homes before they found themselves at war. At least, this was what she heard Miss Cousins remark to her colleague.

'Yes...' Miss Mellodey replied with a sigh. 'I'd rather be staying at home too, but I decided I'd better do my bit and volunteer to go with the children. There's not much left for me in Armley now Bill has joined the RAF...'

Bill must be her boyfriend, thought Maisie. Fancy that! Somehow you never thought of teachers having boyfriends. Miss Mellodey was very pretty, though, with dark curly hair and blue eyes and a nice friendly smile. And she supposed she was not all that old either, certainly not as old as Maisie's mum. Maisie liked her although she didn't know her very well. She taught the younger children, seven- and eight-year-olds, but maybe in the new place, wherever it was, she might be lucky enough to get Miss Mellodey as her teacher.

She moved away from her position near the two teachers in case they should think she was earwigging, but they did not appear to have noticed her. There were a lot of servicemen waiting on the platforms too; soldiers in khaki uniforms, and RAF men – like Miss Mellodey's boyfriend – in blue with huge kit-bags humped over their shoulders. And the war hasn't even started yet, mused Maisie.

Their group was waiting near a comparatively quiet siding where a train was already standing. There was another group of children further along the platform. They looked older, but it was obvious that they were evacuees as well. They were waiting for the man in charge to tell them when they could board, Miss Cousins announced to them shortly, in her booming voice. She was the top class teacher, red-faced and horsey looking, and the younger children were somewhat in awe of her, although many of those in her class said how much they liked her. The teacher said that they didn't need to stick closely to their partners now, as they had done when they were making their way through the station; they could move around and chat to one another, provided they did not go away from this part of the platform.

Maisie edged nearer to Audrey Dennison who was standing on her own away from the rest of the children. She stood out from the others, too, in the way that she was dressed. Her coat was obviously her best one, what was usually termed a Sunday coat. It was maroon with a neat little black velvet collar and cuffs, and she was wearing a matching fairisle beret on her shining fair hair, knitted in shades of maroon, grey and blue, and very pretty it was too. She had black patent leather ankle-strap shoes on her feet – how Maisie had longed for a pair like that! – and white ankle socks. And her gas mask was not housed in a cardboard box, like those of the other children, but had its own posh case of blue leatherette. She looked as though she was dressed for a party, not in readiness for war.

'Hello Audrey,' said Maisie. 'Can I come and sit with you, on the train, I mean? I'm on my own an' all, like you are.'

Audrey looked at her in surprise, but whether she was pleased or not Maisie could not tell because she still looked sad. She had stopped crying, but it seemed as though smiles were still a long way off. 'Why?' she asked. 'Why d'you want to sit with me?'

'Because...because I want to, that's all,' said Maisie. 'Because...well, I like you.'

'Do you?' said Audrey. 'Do you really, Nellie? I didn't think you did.'

''Course I do,' Maisie persisted. 'Why shouldn't I?'

'Because...well, at school you never bother with me, do you? And some of your lot, they laugh at me and call me clever clogs and teacher's pet an' all that. And they say I'm posh and stuck-up.'

'Well, I don't think so...not really,' said Maisie. 'An' I never say all them things about you...I thought you looked lonely, see.'

'I am, a bit,' agreed Audrey. 'None of my special friends have come.'

'Mine neither,' said Maisie. 'I saw you were upset when you were saying tara to that lady. Your gran, is she?'

'No.' Audrey shook her head. 'That's my mum.'

'Gosh! Is it? But she's dead old, i'n't she?' Then Maisie put her hand to her mouth as she realised what she had said. For some reason ladies didn't like you to say they looked old; and Audrey might think she was being rude although she was only speaking the truth. 'I mean…she's a lot older than my mum.' She knew that her own mum was not yet thirty, but she knew, too, that Lily looked much older because of all the heartache she suffered with Sid and Percy and the two brats.

Audrey nodded. 'Yes,' she replied. 'My mother is rather elderly. She was forty-five, you see, when I was born, so was my dad.' Maisie did a quick calculation. Gosh! That meant that Audrey's parents were…fifty-four! 'They had been married for a long time before they had me,' she added, in an old-fashioned sort of voice. 'Mum said they had almost given up hope of ever having any children and she said that I was…a little miracle.' She smiled, rather shyly.

'Why have they made you come away then?' asked Maisie. 'I'd 've thought they'd want you to stay with 'em, being the only kid, like.'

'Oh, they're worried about me being safe,' said Audrey. 'They worry about all sorts of things, Nellie, you've no idea. They're terribly fussy.'

'But you didn't want to come, did you?'

'No, of course I didn't…but I'm feeling a lot better now.' Suddenly she smiled quite cheerfully. 'Thanks for coming to talk to me, Nellie. And I'll sit with you on the train. It's taking them a long time, isn't it, to let us get on?'

'Hang on a minute, Audrey,' said Maisie. 'D'you think you could give over calling me Nellie?'

'Why? It's your name, isn't it?'

Maisie shook her head. 'Not any more. That's what me step-father calls me…and his son, Percy. An' I hate it, just like I hate them an' all. So I've decided I'm going to be Maisie from now on. That's what me real dad used to call me, and me mam…when she remembers. Have you got a pencil in that posh bag of yours?' As well as the other items of luggage that belonged to her, Audrey also had a nice fawn shoulder bag, the sort that grown-up ladies used, slung across her chest.

'I think so,' said Audrey. 'What d'you want it for?'

'Give it us here an' I'll show you.'

Audrey undid the zip and rummaged in the bag, drawing out a lace-edged hanky, a purse, some photographs, and, from the very bottom, a newly sharpened pencil which she handed to her new friend.

Maisie pulled the string with the offending label over her head. She scribbled out the word Nellie, completely obliterating it, and wrote Maisie underneath it in large letters. 'There,' she said. 'That's me name now. An' here's your pencil back.'

Audrey giggled. 'It's a good job Miss Patterdale isn't here. I bet she'd 've gone on calling you Nellie.'

'So she would, just for spite,' replied Maisie. 'She didn't like me. She liked you, though, didn't she? 'Cause you're clever and pretty and you always do as you're told.'

'I didn't like her, though,' said Audrey, with more

spirit than Maisie had ever heard her use before. 'Not one little bit...an' I thought she was dead mean to you sometimes...Maisie. You're just as clever as me, you know... P'raps even cleverer,' she added with an admiring look at the girl who had befriended her and whom she was beginning to think of as a real chum. 'And I like your new name. I think it's much nicer than Nellie, honest I do.'

'Hey up,' said Maisie, getting hold of her arm. 'Look at that fellow talking to the teachers. I think we might be going.' An important looking man with a peaked cap and gold buttons on his jacket was nodding and pointing towards the train. At the same time there was a loud snort and a hiss of steam from the large engine at the front. Grey clouds of smoke were drifting back along the platform as the two teachers started to usher their charges on to the train and into separate compartments. It was a corridor train, fortunately, so they would be able to keep an eye on the children, and there were toilets, too, at each end of the train, which was handy.

'Come along now, boys and girls. Quickly now...and quietly please! Don't push; there's plenty of room for everyone...'

Maisie sat in a corner near the window with her new friend next to her. There was a mother with two young children on the opposite seat, and four small boys from a different class whom the girls did not really know although they had seen them in the playground. The toddlers started at once to climb on the seats, jumping up and down. They reminded Maisie of Joanie and Jimmy and she was surprised to find herself feeling a little bit sad.

'Stop it, you two! Sit down and behave yerselves!' said their mother, but they took about as much notice of her as the two terrors at home took of Lily.

Maisie stole a sideways glance at Audrey as the train gave an extra loud hiss and bellow, and the guard with his green flag walked past their window. And then slowly the train started to draw away from the platform. Audrey had gone all quiet and sad looking again. Maisie took told of her arm.

'We're off!' she said. 'I'n't it exciting?' Although, if she were truthful, she was feeling a tiny bit sick inside and her voice sounded all feeble and wobbly.

Audrey nodded. 'Yes…I s'pose so…I don't really know…' She gave a loud sniff and turned her head away. In a few minutes, though, during which they sat in silence, she seemed to recover herself. She opened her shoulder bag and started to search around in it again.

'Mummy gave me some barley sugars,' she said. 'They're very good for you when you're travelling. Daddy always has some in the car; they stop you from feeling sick.' She had found the paper bag which she handed to Maisie. 'Would you like one…Maisie?'

'Gosh, ta!' said Maisie, whose taste usually ran to aniseed balls or pear drops on the odd occasions her mother bought sweets.

Audrey then offered the bag to the lady on the opposite seat, which, Maisie knew, was the polite and proper thing to do. 'Would you like a sweet, and your little boy and girl?'

'Oh, no thanks, lovey,' said the lady. 'You keep

'em for yerself. But what a kind little girl you are to ask. They're too big anyway, for Billy and Brenda. We don't want 'em choking, do we? Although I feel like throttling them meself at times,' she added in an undertone as the kiddies continued to roll around, this time on the floor. 'I'll give 'em some chocolate in a minute to keep 'em quiet.'

Audrey put the bag away again, having no intention of offering her sweets to the boys. They didn't appear to be taking much notice anyway. They were involved in a loud conversation, more of a shouting match, about how many trains they had been on in their lives, and the places they had visited. Scarborough, Filey, Bridlington, Blackpool; even somewhere called Skegness, and the Isle of Man. They sounded like experienced travellers to Maisie, but when she heard the names of London, Paris and Rome she guessed they might be showing off. More likely they had been learning capital cities in a geography lesson.

She hadn't been on a train for ages. She sucked her sweet – you couldn't talk anyway with such a large sweet in your mouth – and gazed out of the window. They had soon left the city centre and the rows and rows of houses and factories behind and were in the country. How quiet and peaceful it all looked after the noise and bustle of the big town and the crowded station. Maisie feasted her eyes on the lush greenness of the fields and trees and vast stretches of hillside. There were sheep grazing on the slopes of the hills near to large boulders of rock. Maisie knew that these were limestone, the stone from which these hills, the Pennines, had been formed millions of years ago. So long ago that you could not take it in; they had learned that at school.

She knew, too, about the art of drystone walling, a craft passed down through the generations of Yorkshire farming folk, and here the fells were criss-crossed with drystone walls. The lonely cottages and farmhouses were also built of greystone, but there were splashes of colour too from the golden gorse bushes and the purple sweep of the heather, now starting to turn brown in places with the changing of the season. In the far distance she glimpsed a ruined castle on a hill.

When they had passed through the station at Skipton – Maisie recognised that name – Miss Mellodey came into their compartment to check that everyone was all right.

'Hello, boys. OK, are we?' she asked. 'That's good.'

'Yes, Miss Mellodey,' they chorused. Maisie guessed they were in her class, or had been last term.

'Now, let me see...I've noticed you two girls at school, of course, but I don't know your names. You are...Audrey. Hello, Audrey. And you are...' Miss Mellodey looked carefully at the label. '...Maisie. Hello, Maisie.' She smiled at both the girls in turn; her lovely blue eyes were so warm and friendly that Maisie was quite taken aback. All she could do was nod and whisper a tiny little, 'Hello...'

'Please, Miss Mellodey; she used to be called Nellie,' chimed in Audrey, to Maisie's great surprise. 'That's what we always called her, but she's decided that she wants to be called Maisie instead.'

'Shurrup, you!' Maisie dug her elbow into her new friend's side, and not too gently either.

Miss Mellodey laughed. 'Well, I think she's quite right, don't you, Audrey, to choose her own name?' She turned to Maisie, then glanced again at her name tag and nodded. 'Eleanor May. Yes, I see. They're both such beautiful names. It's a shame to shorten it to Nellie. But Maisie is…just right.'

'Thank you, Miss Mellodey,' breathed Maisie. At that moment she felt as though she would have done anything, anything at all for this lovely kind-hearted lady. She would be her willing slave for evermore.

'Please miss, can we eat our butties?' asked one of the boys. 'We're starving!'

'Yes, I don't see why not.' Miss Mellodey smiled again. She was a very smiley sort of person. 'In fact I suppose it might be a good idea for you all to eat your sandwiches, if you've brought any. It may not be all that long before we arrive.'

'Why, where are we going, Miss?'

'Aw go on, tell us…' The boys started up a barrage of questions.

'Is it Scarborough, miss?'

'Is it Blackpool, miss?'

'Don't be such a barmpot, Bobby! 'Course it's not Blackpool! Blackpool's miles away, in t' other direction, i'n't it, miss?'

'Yes, that's right,' agreed the teacher. 'We're heading north, and Blackpool's just as far as you can go to the west… I don't suppose there's any harm in telling you now – I've only just found out myself – that we're going to Middlebeck.'

'Middlebeck? Where the heck's that?'

'It's a little market town in the northern Yorkshire Dales,' said Miss Mellodey. 'I must admit I've never been there myself, but I'm sure it will be a very nice place, surrounded by this lovely countryside.' She waved her hand at the view through the window.

They were now passing through a somewhat stark landscape of high bare hills, more grey-brown than green, lacking in trees and the verdant pasture land they had seen earlier. 'Er...not quite like this, of course,' she added hurriedly. 'It's rather lonely and bleak up here, isn't it? There used to be lead mining in this area in the olden days. But Middlebeck is in a nice fertile valley, so I'm told. And it's a market town, so I'm sure there will be a lot of shops.' She nodded confidently at the lady with the toddlers, then at the rest of the occupants of the carriage, 'townies' all of them. 'Now...I'd better go and see how the others are faring. That's right; eat your sandwiches, and let me know if you have any more questions. I'll answer them if I can.'

'She's real nice, isn't she?' said Maisie to Audrey. 'D'you think we might be in her class when we get to...where did she say? Middleton?'

'Middlebeck,' corrected Audrey. 'Yes, we might be. That'd be great, wouldn't it?'

'Hey, she's our teacher, not yours,' said the boy called Bobby. 'Ain't she, Colin?'

'Aye, thass reight,' replied Colin. 'She teaches the

ones as 'ave just come up from th' Infant School. So you've 'ad it, you two.'

'Wot's it matter, anyroad,' said another of the small boys. 'Hers just a teacher, and teachers is all bossy an' bad tempered and thinks they knows it all.'

'Miss Mellodey ain't like that!' retorted Bobby. 'You know you like 'er, Jack. She were dead nice with yer that time you wet yer pants in t' classroom.'

'Shurrup!' yelled Jack as the other boys all fell about laughing. 'Shurrup, the lot of yous! I were ill, weren't I, an' I 'ad to go 'ome. I never said I didn't like her. She's all right; not bad for a teacher. Anyroad, never mind 'er...I'm gonner eat me butties, like she said we could.'

'We'll just have to wait and see,' whispered Maisie to Audrey.

Both girls took their sandwiches wrapped in greaseproof paper out of their bags.

'What've you got?' asked Maisie, peering at her friend's neatly cut triangles with the crusts taken off. 'Gosh! Them's fancy! Me mum used to cut 'em like that when I had a party. But that was ages ago...' Birthday parties were now things of the past, back in that far-away time when her daddy had still been with them. Bread was now invariably cut in thick doorsteps and spread with dripping or margarine and a smear of jam.

'I think they're salmon,' said Audrey, looking carefully at them. 'Yes; salmon...and some egg and cress as well... Would you like one, Maisie?'

'Ooh, I wouldn't mind,' said Maisie. 'Ta very

much. I tell you what; I'll swap you one of mine for one of yours.'

'Oh, all right then,' said Audrey, although she was looking rather dubiously at the thick sandwiches with the crusts left on and the jam oozing out of the centres. 'Er, no...I don't think I will after all, thank you. I'm not really all that hungry.'

'OK; suits me,' said Maisie cheerfully. 'I 'spect I can eat 'em all. Ta for the salmon one; it's yummy!' She licked her lips appreciatively. 'Me mum makes me eat the crusts. She says they make yer hair curl.' She fingered her spikey dark crop. 'But it's not true, is it?'

Audrey shook her head. 'No; I don't suppose it is. It's just one of those things that mums say. I've heard mine say it too, sometimes...' She was starting to look sad again, so Maisie nudged her.

'Here, have a crisp,' she said. 'No; take an 'andful. We can share 'em.' That was something that she, Maisie, had found in her bag and that Audrey did not have. A packet of Smith's crisps. Maisie was particularly fond of them. She dug her hand in the packet now and drew out the tiny blue paper screw of salt. She sprinkled it over the crisps then shook the bag vigorously.

There was silence in the compartment, apart from the crunching of crisps, as everyone ate their sandwiches, at the same time looking out of the window at the changing scene. The bleak landscape gradually gave way to pleasant pasture land again, where sheep and cows were grazing. There was a river running through the valley, quite near to the railway track and, in the distance, a waterfall tumbling down a gully between two hills. They passed near to the ruins of what Maisie guessed was an old abbey where, in the olden days, monks had used to live.

Then the signs of life became more abundant. A cluster of farm buildings, a row of greystone cottages, their gardens ablaze with colourful flowers, a stream where boys were fishing, smoke coming from the chimney of a small factory; and then there were more and more houses and streets as they drew near to a town.

At last there was an extra loud hiss of steam and a gigantic bellow from the engine, then a screeching of brakes as the train gradually slowed to a halt. It stopped with a jerk. There on the platform was a black and white sign which said MIDDLEBECK, and standing by it a guard with a green flag and another important looking man, like the one in Leeds, but with rather less gold braid on his uniform.

'Come along now, everyone. We're here!' shouted Miss Cousins. 'Hurry up now and get off the train. Just the ones from Armley, of course; the others are staying on. Now make sure you've got all your belongings because this train's going further north...' With the kids from the other schools in Leeds, thought Maisie, as noses were pressed against the windows and dozens of pairs of eyes watched the Armley lot alight from the train.

'Now – stand in twos on the platform, then we can count you. Do try to stand still, and stop fidgeting! Yes, I know you've been sitting down a long time, but we're here now... And here are some people to welcome us. How very kind...' Miss Cousins put on a posh voice as she stepped forward to greet two ladies wearing green suits and hats who had just arrived on the platform.

'How do you do? I am Miss Cousins, and this is my friend and colleague, Miss Mellodey...'

Maisie and Audrey looked at one another, trying to smile, but a little worriedly. They were miles from home in a place they had never heard of before. But they had, each of them, made a new friend that day. Instinctively and simultaneously they reached out and clasped hands, holding tightly to one another.

Chapter Five

Patience Fairchild noticed the two little girls as soon as they entered the hall, one dark and one fair, clinging tightly to each other's hands as though they would never want to let go. Her heart went out to them at once. Poor little mites! Although not so little, she guessed; maybe nine or ten years old. She and Luke had already decided they would have an evacuee, a girl, preferably, to live with them. Maybe they could have two, these two... In some ways two would be easier than one. A single child might be lonely, especially so far away from home.

Immediately came the thought that they had decided last night at the meeting there was to be no picking and choosing...or rejecting. Although human nature being as it was, a certain amount of that was sure to go on, Patience reflected. It might look bad, though, if the rector's wife were to step in and lay claim to two pretty little girls. She realised she would have to 'hold her horses' so to speak, but she would keep a watchful eye on the two friends all the same.

Patience had elected to stay at the Village Institute and help with the making of the tea and orange juice and setting out the food. Rector's wife or no, she did not mind how she 'mucked in', and people admired her for this. It was Muriel Hollins and her second-in-command, Jessie Campion, the VIPs of the WVS, who had gone along to the railway station to meet the children and teachers from the train. Patience, like the rest of the women, was wearing her uniform of green and red that day. The weather was still warm – God was blessing them with an Indian summer, as though to counteract their tribulations and anxieties for the future – and the red jumper felt hot and clingy. A splash of colour, though, in the rather bare and dismal room. The WVS ladies looked like so many cheerful robin redbreasts as they bobbed about, seeing to the needs of the children and the adults accompanying them. Patience would have like to pull off her green felt hat, shaking free her hair, but all the other women appeared to be keeping them on, so she decided she must do the same.

There were sixty or so newcomers altogether, she estimated, including the teachers and the women and younger children under school age; who now, free from the constraints of prams and their mother's arms were, for the most part, charging wildly around the room.

It was at that moment that Muriel Hollins clapped her hands and raised her voice above the hubbub. 'Ladies, please! Those of you who have young children, will you please keep them under control? We cannot be held responsible if there is an accident with boiling hot tea. Make them sit down, please! There are lots of lovely things to eat.'

The women, in the main, did as they were requested, chasing after the infants and then holding them firmly on their laps. Although

Patience did hear one woman complaining, 'Oo the 'ell does she think she is, tellin' us what to do? I'd like to see 'er with an 'ouseful of kids.' Patience reflected that Archie Tremaine's wife had volunteered to take the women with the small children. Poor Rebecca! she mused. I hope she realises what she is letting herself in for.

A long trestle table had been set out down the centre of the room and covered with an assortment of cloths, some gingham, some plain white, some flowered; they were normally used on the small card tables for afternoon tea. The children and mothers, and the toddlers on knees, were soon tucking into the sandwiches the women of the WVS, to give them their due, had prepared as carefully as they would for their own families. Egg and cress, salmon paste and sardine; they were going down very well. There were, also, some with mashed banana, now turning into a gooey brown mess, and some 'jam butties' with a bright red substance oozing from the sides, but these were very popular with the children.

They had soon gulped down the orange juice, which had proved to be a winner, holding out their cups for more, like Oliver Twist, some saying 'please' and 'thank you', and others not bothering with such niceties. The mothers, likewise, drank thirstily the dark brown tea, a much needed pick-me-up to face their new life in strange surroundings.

All the children had been persuaded to take off their headgear; the boys their school caps or balaclava helmets and the girls their pixie hoods

and woollen berets. But they kept their coats on –
mainly navy gaberdine mackintoshes – and many
still had their gas masks slung around their necks,
with their labels. This little detail affected Patience
more than anything. Poor little kiddies; being
labelled as though they were on sale at a market.

She kept her eye as she circled the table, offering
sandwiches and cakes, on 'her' two little girls. It
was the dark one who was by far the more
animated of the two, chattering away and trying to
draw her friend into conversation. The fair-haired
one seemed much more timid; probably the little
lass was feeling very lost and homesick, thought
Patience, and the dark-haired little girl was doing
her best to cheer her up. Her heart went out to them
both again.

There were other differences between them, too,
that she could not help but notice. The little blonde
girl looked like a model child out of a picture book
or a film; not exactly Shirley Temple, though,
because her hair was smooth and sleek, not done up
in ringlets like the child star's. She was very clean
and tidy, even after the train journey; clearly a child
who was mindful of how she looked, and behaved
as well. Her clothes, too, would have cost a bob or
two, thought Patience; her mother, obviously, had
dressed her in her best coat and shoes for the
journey to unknown territory.

The little dark-haired girl was a complete
contrast. Her spiky hair looked as though it had
been cut with a knife and fork, as Patience's mother
had used to say, and her clothes might very well
have come from a jumble sale. But Patience could

see beyond that. The child's face was lively and alert, with a good deal of sympathy in her deep brown eyes as she tried to coax her friend to talk and smile a little. Chalk and cheese they seemed to be, but it was, no doubt, a case of opposites being attracted to one another. Patience guessed at the little dark one's depth of character; and, though more that a trifle unkempt, she did not appear neglected. Her cheeks were rosy and she was not thin and scrawny as deprived children often were. Patience imagined there was someone at home in Armley who cared for her, although she felt, intuitively, that the little girl had not had an easy life.

She realised she could not go on thinking of them as 'the dark one' and 'the fair one', so she went over to chat to them and discover their names.

The dark-haired girl looked up and smiled. 'Hello...' she said, just a shade warily as Patience smiled down at her.

'Hello,' said Patience. 'I've been watching the two of you. You are good friends, aren't you? I've come to find out what you are called.'

'I'm Maisie and she's Audrey,' said 'the dark one', pointing at the other girl. 'Yes, we are friends, aren't we, Audrey? We've decided we're going to be 'best friends', but we weren't, not till today. We're in the same class, y'see, but we didn't sit near to one another so we didn't know one another very well. But we do now, don't we, Audrey?'

'Yes,' said the other girl. She glanced up at Patience and, recognising kindness and understanding in the grown-up's manner, she began to smile a little. 'She's going to be my best friend...Maisie is. She used to be called Nellie; that's what we all called her at school, but she's going to be Maisie now... It's a nice name, isn't it?' she added shyly.

'Shurrup you!' retorted Maisie. 'What d'you want to go and tell her that for?'

Patience laughed. 'Well, I can't say I blame you, my dear. Maisie is a lovely name...and so is Audrey.' She peered at the name tags. 'Eleanor May Jackson, and Audrey Dennison. Well, I'm very pleased to meet both of you. And I'm Mrs Fairchild. Patience is my Christian name. Perhaps we will get to know one another better and...'

Maisie interrupted. 'All you ladies, you've all got green hats and red jumpers on. Do you belong to some sort of club or summat?'

'You could say that,' smiled Patience. 'We belong to the WVS – the Women's Voluntary Service. We've all volunteered, you see, to do what we can to help the war effort... Although we're not really at war at the moment,' she added, feeling a little guilty at having mentioned the word. But the child, Maisie, was obviously a realist.

'But we're going to be, aren't we,' she said. 'That's why we've all come here, isn't it, 'cause there's going to be a war?'

'I'm afraid so,' replied Patience. 'It seems very much like it... I think we all look like jolly robin redbreasts in our red jumpers, don't we?' she said, in an attempt to lighten the conversation.

'Mmm...p'raps you do,' said Maisie. 'Them hats, though; they look like the hats those posh girls wear; you know, in Angela Brazil books.'

Patience laughed. 'Yes, you're right; so they do.' She remembered the Angela Brazil school stories with fondness, from her own girlhood. She had revelled in them, and they were still widely read, although a little old-fashioned by now, she would have thought. 'Do you read those stories, dear?'

'Oo yes, I love 'em,' said Maisie. 'You read 'em an' all, don't you, Audrey?' Her friend nodded. ''Course, they're all about posh kids,' Maisie went on. 'Rich kids that go away to school an' all that, but they're dead good. Me mam has a few what she had when she was a girl and I've read 'em hundreds of times. And sometimes they let us take books home from school. I like Enid Blyton an' all, and I've read 'Black Beauty' and 'What Katy Did'... I wish somebody 'ud write stories about ordinary kids, though, like me.'

She's a discerning child, thought Patience. She was already noticing the class structures and the differences they made. She, Patience, had wondered, too, when she was growing up why many things, literature in particular, always seemed geared to the upper classes. Maybe a war would succeed in levelling out the status quo... This little Maisie must be a clever child, though, to be reading and understanding books such as those at her age.

'I'm pleased you like reading,' she said, 'both of you. You never feel lonely if you can lose yourself in a story... How old are you?' she asked. 'Let me guess. Nine?...or you might even be ten.'

'You're dead right!' It was Audrey who answered, rather to Patience's surprise. The little girl had livened up considerably. 'We're both nine; well, we're nearly ten, aren't we, Maisie? We're in the Third Year Juniors, you see, Standard Three. I shall be ten in December.'

'Aw, will yer?' said Maisie, looking a little crestfallen. 'I didn't know that. It's not fair! You're older than me!'

'And when is your birthday, Maisie?' asked Patience.

'Not till May. May the first. That's why me mam and dad called me May, y'see... But I didn't know she was older than me...'

'It doesn't matter, silly!' said Audrey.

'No...I s'pose it doesn't. But I look older than you, don't I?'

Patience was distracted from the friends' minor altercation by the sight of Miss Amelia Thomsom approaching, an earnest expression on her sallow thin-featured face. Patience felt her heart sink. She remembered the woman saying, though a shade reluctantly, that she would take an evacuee, a little girl she had specified, to live with her. They had not actually got round to sorting out the living accommodation yet, as the children were only just finishing their meal; but Patience was kicking herself for not having jumped in immediately and asked the two little girls if they would like to come and live with her. Immediately upon that thought came another. How would it look if she, the rector's wife, were to lay claim to these two little girls who happened to appeal to her? There would be a good deal of bickering and back-biting and talk of favouritism. But she feared she could guess what was in Miss Thomson's mind. The woman was looking appraisingly at the girls, but particularly, Patience thought, at the one called Audrey. She forced herself to smile, saying, 'Now, Miss Thomson...I think they are all enjoying their meal, aren't they? Thank you so much for coming to help us today. We really do appreciate what you are doing.'

The older woman did not answer her. Instead, she addressed her remark to Audrey, fixing the little girl with her gimlet eyes and leaning down to look more closely at her. 'You seem to be a nice little girl,' she said. 'Very clean and presentable. I'm rather fussy about who I invite into my home, but I think that you might do very nicely. Would you like to come and live with me...' She peered at the name tag. '...Audrey? What do you say?'

The child stared at her open-mouthed and wide-eyed. Patience could see a glimmer of fear there in her blue eyes, which was not surprising. Even her husband, the rector, found himself pussy-footing around Miss Thomson at times, for fear of provoking her displeasure. Her autocratic bearing and her almost black piercing eyes that seemed to bore right into one's mind, were enough to scare any child, particularly a timid one such as Audrey. But Patience did not believe there was any real malice in the woman. Miss Thomson was a God-fearing woman and she would do her duty, as she saw it. Audrey, she felt sure, would not be ill-treated were she to go and live there. Would she be welcomed though, or understood? The woman had had little or nothing to do with children.

'Come along, Audrey,' Miss Thomson was

saying. 'What's the matter? Has the cat got your tongue? I'm asking you if you would like to come and live with me. Not that you have any choice really. I have decided…'

Patience could not help herself. 'Now just wait a minute, Miss Thomson,' she said. 'We haven't started to sort out, yet, where the children will be living. They are only just finishing their meal. I think you are being a bit hasty…'

'Oh, you do, do you?' The woman's steely black eyes were magnified by the spectacles she wore, and Patience felt herself begin to quail a little. 'And what were you doing, then, if you were not staking your claim? I have been watching you talking to this child for the last ten minutes or so. But I had already picked her out as being suitable for me.'

'Don't you remember us saying at the meeting last night that there was to be no selecting…or rejecting?' said Patience, although she was aware that she was on very shaky ground.

'I don't know about that, but I do distinctly remember Mrs Hollins saying that the helpers were to have the first choice,' Miss Thomson retorted. 'Not that I have much time for the woman, and she's been more bossy that ever since she became one of the bigwigs of the WVS. But she's in charge of this evacuation scheme when all is said and done, and she definitely said…'

Patience could see that Audrey was looking very worried and tears were forming in her big blue eyes. 'Don't cry, dear,' she said, patting her shoulder. 'We'll sort something out, don't you worry.'

'Yes, you'd better stop that,' said Miss Thomson.

'I'm not sure that I want a crybaby.'

'She's not a crybaby!' chimed in Maisie. 'She wants to stay with me, that's all. We've decided. We're going to stay together. So if she's got to go and live with this old lady, then I'm going an' all.'

Patience had noticed Miss Thomson bristle at being referred to as an old lady and she suppressed a smile. Clearly Maisie was a child who called a spade a spade, as Yorkshire folk were inclined to do.

'Oh no, no; that's quite out of the question,' the woman said. She glanced witheringly at Maisie. 'I have room for only one evacuee. And I would not want to take you anyway. You are a very rude little girl, interrupting like that when grown-ups are talking. I was always told that little girls should be seen and not heard.'

'I'm sure she didn't mean to be rude,' said Patience. 'She's just trying to stick up for her friend, aren't you, dear? They've been together all day, looking after one another, and it's understandable that they don't want to be parted. So it might be better, Miss Thomson, if you were to decide on another little girl…?'

'So that you can have this one, I suppose?' She cast Patience a frosty look; but she did at least have the sense to lower her voice before making her next remark. 'I must say, Mrs Fairchild, that they seem to be rather an unsavoury lot of children. Most of them are not what you could call clean and tidy – positively scruffy, some of them – and their table manners leave a lot to be desired. But that little girl, Audrey, has obviously been well-brought-up. No, I am afraid my mind is made up. This is the child that I want.'

Maisie's eyes were narrowed and she was scowling, staring at the woman with dislike. It was more than likely that she had heard the remark about the children being scruffy and, moreover, the woman seemed bent on taking her new best friend away from her. Patience knew that Maisie would not really want to go and live with Miss Thomson, even if the woman wanted her, but it had been generous of her to offer to go with her friend. Poor Audrey was looking very perplexed and she glanced up at Patience pleadingly.

Patience was in a quandary. She felt she ought to dissuade Miss Thomson against taking such a timid little girl; more than that, her gut feeling was to put her arms around the two children and say, 'No, you selfish old woman! They are coming with me!' But she knew she could not say, or even hint at what she felt. She, more than anyone, as the rector's wife, had to behave with propriety. It was only children who could get away with speaking their minds; and it seemed that Maisie was one who was inclined to do just that. She only hoped that the child had not made an enemy of Miss Thomson, who certainly would not be dissuaded from taking Audrey.

Patience sighed inwardly, but outwardly she smiled encouragingly at the two children, and then a little less fulsomely at Miss Thomson. 'Very well then, Miss Thomson,' she said, and then, as Audrey gave a little start and edged closer to her, 'It's all right, Audrey dear. Everything is going to be fine. Miss Thomson will take care of you...and I'm going to take care of Maisie. She can come and live with me and my husband.' To her relief and pleasure she saw Maisie's face light up with a smile of delight, which, just as quickly, vanished.

'But...what about Audrey?' she said. 'I told you...we want to be together.'

'Ah well,' said Patience, 'what you don't know is that Miss Thomson and I are very close neighbours. We live very near to one another, don't we, Miss Thomson?' The woman nodded briefly, moving her lips in a slight semblance of a smile.

'Yes, we do. Right opposite one another.'

'I live at the rectory next to the church,' explained Patience. 'My husband is the rector there, you see, and Miss Thomson lives just across the green. I can see her house from my front windows. And next door to Miss Thomson's house is the school you will both be attending. So you won't have very far to go to school, will you?'

'No...I s'pose not,' said Maisie. The two girls were regarding one another anxiously, Audrey biting her lip hard in an effort not to cry and Maisie still frowning a little.

'You will be able to see one another every day,' Patience continued, smiling brightly and trying to sound full of optimism. 'And not just at school. You can come across to the rectory, Audrey, and have tea with Maisie sometimes. And we have a nice big garden you can play in. Miss Thomson has a lovely garden, too, and I'm sure she will let you play in it.'

'Perhaps,' said Miss Thomson, but sounding not at all sure. 'I am very proud of my rose bushes, though, and my flower beds. I don't want them trampling on, and neither will Wilfred. He takes a great pride in his work.' Wilfred was the gardener who went twice a week to tend the gardens at the front and rear. It was true that they were a delight to the eye. He also went, rather less frequently, to tend the rectory gardens; Luke and Patience were not quite as fussy about immaculate lawns and tidy borders as was their neighbour. 'I suppose you might be allowed to play on the lawn at the back occasionally,' the older woman conceded. 'I will have to see... So is that settled, Mrs Fairchild? I will take Audrey and you will take...the other one. I suppose we had better go and inform Mrs Hollins. I see she has her list in front of her.'

Mrs Muriel Hollins and her assistant, Mrs Jessie Campion had now seated themselves at a table at one end of the room with official looking papers in front of them. Other WI ladies, those who were less high-ranking, were now clearing away the empty cups and plates and moving into the kitchen to tackle the washing-up. Several people from the town of Middlebeck and the outlying farmland had now come into the hall, after hearing the news that the evacuees had arrived. Patience noticed a couple of farmers from the outskirts of Middlebeck. As she might have known, the two men made a beeline towards a group of boys, the oldest and sturdiest of the evacuees – possible farmer's boys in the making? – although none of the children could be more than eleven. The women who had entered the hall, some with children of their own, were looking around somewhat apprehensively, their eyes fixing first on one and then on another of the children sitting at the tables. Then, some of the WI helpers from the kitchen, no doubt realising they were missing out – and after all, hadn't they been told that they could have first pick? – came dashing out to lay claim to the children they preferred.

Yes, it was as Patience had feared. In spite of their best endeavours, it seemed as though there was no other way to sort out the accommodation for these children than to let people choose for themselves. What about the ones who were left at the end, though, the ones to whom no one had offered a home? It had been suggested at the meeting that they should be taken round from door to door in the village until they were all housed. Everyone who had room in their home was obliged to take one evacuee or more, but no doubt all sorts of excuses would be forthcoming. And Patience guessed it would be those with the grander houses who would offer the most resistance. Miss Thomson herself was a case in point. She had ample room for two, three or even four evacuees in that mansion of hers, but maybe it was better left as it was. No doubt one would be all she could cope with.

Patience, holding Maisie by the hand, and Miss Thomson, shepherding a reluctant Audrey, still clinging to her friend, went to inform Mrs Hollins of their decision.

'Come along, Audrey,' said Miss Thomson briskly. 'Let go of your friend's hand now, dear.' At least she had called her 'dear' thought Patience. 'We are going back to my house now. I think I have done my share, Mrs Fairchild. I was here early this morning so I would like to go now and get…er…this little lady settled into her new home.' She actually smiled at the child, a little frostily, but at least she was making some effort.

'Can we go now an' all?' asked Maisie. 'Can we, Mrs…what did you say you were called?'

'Mrs Fairchild,' smiled Patience. 'Yes, I dare say we could go as well. I really ought to stay and help with the washing-up, but maybe, under the circumstances…'

'Yes, you run along, dear,' said Mrs Hollins, always eager to keep well in with the rector's wife. 'There are plenty of folk to help out here, and you will want to get back to the rector. Actually, I thought he might have popped in to see us all today?' She looked questioningly at Patience.

'My husband is away on business,' she replied, 'or else he would have been here, I assure you. He has a very important meeting today.' But she had no intention of telling Muriel Hollins that Luke had gone to see his Bishop. Even Patience was not altogether sure what they would be discussing, but she surmised, knowing her husband as she did, that he would be asking how best he could serve his King and Country in the war which was now inevitable.

As they left the Village Institute and came out into the main street, Archie Tremaine was busy shepherding a flock of women and small children into his shooting brake. Behind him was his wife, Rebecca, assisting the remainder of them into their saloon car, as there were too many to fit into one vehicle. Mrs Tremaine was one of the few women in the little town who drove a car; she was often to be seen rolling majestically along the High Street in their sturdy black Ford Prefect.

'Oh look, Audrey,' cried Maisie, stopping and pointing. 'There's that lady that was in our carriage, an' her little boy and girl. Yoo-hoo...' She waved to them as the little lad pressed his nose against the shooting brake window and the tiny girl on her mother's lap stared around in bewilderment. 'Hello Billy, hello Brenda. That's what you called 'em, i'n't it? I don't know your name though, Mrs...'

The young woman laughed out loud. Patience was learning that Maisie had that effect on people and she suspected that life would never be dull with this little girl around. 'I'm called Mrs Booth, Sally Booth,' replied the woman. 'It was clever of you to remember the names of these two scallywags. And you are Maisie and Audrey, aren't you?' She ruffled her little boy's hair. 'Come on, Billy. Sit down now, there's a good lad. You're muckying up the man's nice clean window.' She turned to the girls again.

'You've got two nice ladies to look after you, I can see. And what about us, eh? Ridin' in a posh car as though we're gentry or summat. Talk about swanky! I can see we're goin' to 'ave a rare old time 'ere. I'll look out for you both. Tara then... See yer...'

'Come along, come along,' said Miss Thomson brusquely. 'We haven't time to stand here chatting, especially to these sort of...' She became aware of Patience looking at her with slight annoyance. 'Well, we haven't time, that's all. I have a lot to do at home, and so has Mrs Fairchild, I'm sure. Good-day to you, Mr Tremaine, Mrs Tremaine.' She nodded at the two of them, then set off at a brisk pace up the main street.

Patience raised her eyebrows and Archie Tremaine grinned. They all knew Miss Thomson and her innate snobbishness. 'Thank you both for all your help,' she said. 'We appreciate it very much.' Then, in a quieter voice, 'You will have your hands full, I can see, but I'm sure you and Rebecca will be able to cope beautifully. I must dash...or else the fat will be in the fire! Bye for now. Come along, girls.' She seized hold of their hands and the three of them hurried along to catch up with Miss Thomson.

The woman sniffed audibly as they came near to her, looking down her long thin nose disapprovingly. 'You two girls go on ahead,' she said, 'then we can see what you are up to, while I have a talk to Mrs Fairchild. Go along now, we haven't got all day.'

'Yes, you'll be quite safe,' added Patience. 'There are no big roads to cross and we will be right behind you.' She smiled encouragingly at them, pointing ahead. 'This is Middlebeck High Street. Our little town is nowhere near as big as Leeds, of course, but it's a nice friendly little place. I'm sure it will soon begin to feel like home...'

<hr>

The High Street sloped up gently, passing rows of stone-built houses on each side of the road. They opened straight onto the pavement and had no gardens, and the short streets leading off had similar houses, not unlike the one Maisie lived in, in Armley. Very soon, though, the houses gave way to shops; a butcher's, a newsagent's, an ironmonger's, a couple of shops with various garments for ladies and children in the windows, then a familiar name, a Maypole grocery store. The road then widened out to form a small square, at one side of which was a large building with a stone plaque over the door stating that it was the Market Hall. And there, in the square, was an assortment of stalls with gaily striped awnings, selling fruit and vegetables, cheeses, eggs and butter, boiled sweets, brightly coloured materials...

The girls' footsteps slowed down, and Maisie started to think that maybe Middlebeck would not be such a bad place after all. She wrinkled her nose. 'I can smell cheese, and fish an' all... Ooh, this is dead exciting, i'n't it, Audrey? And look...look what's over there!' Her eyes had alighted on a familiar looking red-fronted store opposite the market Hall. 'Woolies! They've even got a Woolies! It's only a little 'un, though, not like the big 'un on Briggate.' Maisie had not often visited the large Woolworth's store in Leeds, but she remembered it as a wonderland of colour and all sorts of exciting things to buy.

'We haven't time to stop and look at the market today,' said Patience, before Miss Thomson had a chance to stick her oar in. 'But you'll be able to come here another time and buy something with your spending money. The stalls are here every Saturday, and Wednesdays as well, but the Market Hall is open all the time. Come along then; we haven't much further to go. Look, you can see the church there, right ahead at the end of the street.' She pointed to the building with a small tower where a Union Jack was flying, some two hundred yards away. 'And that's the rectory to the right, and the school on the opposite side. Now, best foot forward; we'll soon be there.'

'She's real nice, isn't she?' said Maisie as they ran ahead to get out of earshot of the grown-ups. 'I'm glad I'm going to live with her...but I wish you were coming an' all.'

'So do I,' replied Audrey, looking at her friend so very tragically. 'I don't like my lady, not one bit. And she hasn't even told me her name.'

'Miss Thomson,' said Maisie. 'That's what I heard Mrs Whotsit call her. Mrs...Fairchild; that's a funny name, isn't it?'

Audrey didn't answer. She had not said much at all, leaving all the talking to Maisie as they walked up the High Street.

'P'raps that old lady won't be so bad when you get to know her,' Maisie went on. 'I 'spect she lives in a big posh house with servants an' all that. You'll be treated like...like Princess Elizabeth, I bet you anything.'

'But I want to come with you,' whimpered Audrey. 'I don't like it here at all. I want to go back home...'

To Maisie's horror her friend was starting to cry again. 'Oh, don't cry!' she begged. 'Give over, Audrey! Don't start crying again, or she really will be mad at you. You know what she said before, that you were a crybaby.'

'I can't help it,' wailed Audrey. 'I don't like her...'

Maisie seized hold of her arm. 'See here... Just shurrup! Stop crying right now! It'll be all right, honest it will. An'…an' if it's really awful, then you tell me, an' I'll tell Mrs Fairchild, an' she'll do summat about it. I know she will… But you're going to be OK; honest, Audrey.'

Already Maisie was starting to look to the lady who had taken her under her wing with trust and an immense liking. She was kind and friendly, and pretty, too, with dark gingery hair, all short and curly, and nice greeny-brown eyes. Maisie knew she was lucky to have been chosen by her, and she felt quite dreadful that Audrey could not be with her. That was why she was trying so hard to cheer her up.

Audrey took a deep, deep breath, dabbed at her eyes with a lace-edged hanky she took out of her pocket, and, to Maisie's relief, she had stopped crying by the time they reached a row of much bigger houses, next to the squat greystone building which was obviously the school. Miss Thomson stopped at the iron gate of the end one.

'This is my house,' she said. 'Say goodbye to your friend now, Audrey, and I'll go and ring the bell for Daisy to let us in. Come along now; quick sharp…'

Maisie was dying to ask who was Daisy, but she knew she mustn't. Anyway, she guessed that Daisy would be the maid. Probably there was a whole tribe of maids. It was a big house, standing on its own, not joined on to another one. There was a tidy lawn in front of it edged with neatly trimmed rose bushes, and in the centre a bed of bright flowers in fiery colours of red, orange and yellow. Maisie thought they were called dahlias.

Audrey turned and waved forlornly as she

reached the glossy black-painted door. She did not shout goodbye. Maisie guessed she was too choked up to trust herself to open her mouth. Oh heck! She hoped her friend would not start yelling as soon as she got inside.

'Tara, Audrey,' she shouted, waving cheerily. 'See yer...see yer soon...'

Then the door was opened by a plumpish young woman dressed in black with a white apron and cap. Maisie knew she had been right; Daisy was a maid. Then the three of them disappeared into the hall beyond and the door shut behind them.

Chapter Six

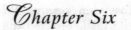

The garden surrounding the rectory was a complete contrast to the one that encompassed Miss Thomson's house. Neither Patience nor Luke was keen on the formal, spick and span type of garden favoured by their neighbour. They did not have the time to indulge too much in horticulture, or have the wherewithal to employ a gardener, other than very occasionally. They made sure that the lawns at the front and rear were kept tidy; people visiting the rectory must be given a good impression. Otherwise, their garden was a riot of perennial flowers and bushes that seeded themselves year after year and needed little tending. Marigolds, lupins, marguerites, golden rod, rambling roses, honeysuckle and a variety of heathers; and instead of a formal neatly trimmed privet hedge there were lilac and fuchsia bushes, spiky berberis and holly, and a laburnum bush which leaned gracefully over the front gate, a riot of cascading yellow blossoms in the springtime.

On the other side of the path was a rowan tree, and it was this that Maisie noticed as soon as she came through the gate. She stopped, gazing with delight at the abundance of bright red clusters of berries nestling between the pretty fern-like pale green leaves. 'Gosh! That's lovely!' she exclaimed. 'I don't think I've seen one of them trees before. What's it called?'

'It's a rowan tree, sometimes it's called a mountain ash,' replied Patience. 'My husband and I planted it when we came to live here ten years ago. It was just a little sapling then, but see how it's grown. I'm glad you like it. It has given us a good deal of pleasure, watching it grow.'

'I like your garden,' said Maisie. 'It's all cheerful and busy, like, isn't it? All them flowers falling over one another. I like it better'n her garden, over there.' She gestured with her thumb over her shoulder, in the direction of Miss Thomson's. 'I say, Mrs...er...Fairchild, Audrey will be all right, won't she, with that old woman?'

'I'm sure she will, Maisie love,' replied Patience. 'Her bark is worse than her bite. Have you heard that expression?'

Maisie nodded. 'I think so.'

'It means that she appears stern and forbidding, but underneath she's...well, she's not so bad. She'll look after Audrey well enough, but don't you worry; and Daisy is there as well, of course.'

'Daisy's the maid, is she?'

'Yes... She's a nice lass. She lives there all the time now, so she'll keep an eye on Audrey. The trouble is, Miss Thomson has never had a great deal to do with children. She has never married, so she has no children or grandchildren of her own. But Audrey is a lovely little girl. I'm sure she will be just fine when she's settled down.'

'What about you?' asked Maisie now, quite out of the blue it seemed to Patience, although she supposed it was an inevitable question. 'Have you got any little boys or girls?'

'No...no, I'm afraid we haven't,' replied Patience, inserting her key in the lock and opening the door, then closing it behind them. She was somewhat taken aback by the forthright question. An adult would have been more tactful, but children she knew, were apt to speak 'straight from the horse's mouth', as the saying went; and this child seemed to be more than usually outspoken. Not cheeky or disrespectful, though, Patience had already decided. Her bluntness would no doubt be explained when she divulged more about her family history. Patience realised that, as yet, she knew nothing whatsoever of her background, but she would ask her about herself in a little while. The main thing now was to familiarize the child with her new surroundings.

Maisie was staring around, a look of surprise and awe on her face, although Patience knew her home to be quite an ordinary, run of the mill, clergy house. It was spacious, to be sure, but at the moment it was badly in need of decorating, and it was not always as warm as it might be, especially when the winter winds howled around the hilltop house. She knew, too, that the carpet on the stairs and in the hall was shabby; a new one had been on the agenda until the imminence of war had made most people look again at their priorities. But it was clear that the little girl was impressed by the high coved ceiling and the rather splendid oak balustrade.

Patience felt she had answered the girl too

abruptly. After all, Maisie was not to know that she and Luke badly wanted a child; that they had been hoping and praying for one ever since they had married and come to live here ten years ago, but to no avail.

'No, dear,' she said now. 'There are no children living here; I wish there were... But you are here now, aren't you? And I'm going to show you all around our house; where you will be sleeping and where we have our meals... Take your coat off, dear, and give me your bag to carry upstairs.'

'Can I go to the lav, please?' asked Maisie as they went upstairs. 'I 'spect you've got one inside, an' a bathroom an' all, haven't you? We haven't, y'see. The lav's down the yard, but we've got water what flushes it, and me mum keeps it nice and clean. Well, her and the lady next door; we have to share it. The houses where me mum goes to clean have got posh bathrooms though. I thought you would have one...'

Patience smiled to herself at her chatter. What a friendly and appealing little girl she was. 'Yes, our bathroom is here,' she said, pushing open the first door at the top of the stairs. 'You go and make yourself comfortable and wash your hands, and then come in here. This will be your bedroom.' She pointed to a door across the landing.

The bathroom was really posh, all gleaming white tiles with black edges, a huge bath with feet like a lion's claws, and a lavatory with a polished wooden seat and lid, and a chain with a matching handle on the end. There was even a tablet of fresh sweet-smelling soap on the wash-basin, not that awful pink carbolic stuff that they used at home, and a fluffy white towel for Maisie to wipe her hands on. And another big towel hanging on a rail which, she supposed, was for when you had a bath. Gosh! Wouldn't it be lovely to soak in a bath like that, and have nice clean water all to herself. Friday night was bath night, and Maisie had only just had one, but she hoped that Mrs Fairchild would let her have one soon.

This was just the sort of bathroom that Maisie had often heard her mother say she would like. Poor Mum... She felt a pang of sadness come over her for a moment. It had been an exciting day – a little bit frightening as well, at times – but she had had Audrey to look after, and then so many things had been happening that she had scarcely had time to think about all she had left behind in Leeds. Her mother, and her naughty little brother and sister. And... She shook her head, pushing the thoughts of them, those two awful males, away. No, no! She was not going to think about them, not ever again.

Her thoughts returned to the present very quickly when she set eyes on the bedroom that Mrs Fairchild had prepared for her. Well, not for her in particular, she realised, but for one of the evacuee children. The lady had not known until they all arrived who would be coming to live with her; but Maisie was so very very glad that she was the one who had been chosen.

It was not a very large room but, to Maisie, it was beautiful, the most beautiful room she had ever seen in her life. It was all blue, as blue as the sky on a summer's day. Pale blue walls, a blue floral carpet on the floor, a bit threadbare in parts, but there was a woolly blue rug near the bed which covered up a worn patch. The curtains were a bright design of blue and sunshine yellow. It was a pity about the horrid black-out blind that she could see at the back, but she knew it was what they called 'regulations', another big word that had come into use recently. On the bed was a plump blue silky eiderdown, a little bit frayed and faded, but Maisie thought how comfy it would be to snuggle underneath it. And sitting on top of it was a teddy bear, almost identical to the one that was hidden away in her bag, except that Maisie's was worse for wear, having put up with a lot of rough treatment from Joanie and Jimmy, despite her instructions to leave Barney Bear alone.

There was a little dressing table with a blue gingham frill all round it, just like she had seen in story books, but never anywhere else, a small oak wardrobe, and a white-painted set of bookshelves. When she had stared around for several moments she dashed over to the books which filled the shelves. 'Ooh! You've got Angela Brazil, loads of 'em,' she cried. 'And there's some I haven't read an' all.'

'Yes, I didn't think it would take you long to find those,' smiled Patience. 'You told me you liked them, remember? You are very welcome to read any of the books; they were mine when I was a girl, and I can't bear to part with them. No Enid Blyton's though; she hadn't started writing when I was a little girl, but there are lots of old favourites... Anyway, come along now, Maisie; let's get your things out of your bag. We'll put them on to the bed, shall we? And there is my teddy bear, see, waiting to welcome you.'

Patience wondered, as she said it, about the appropriateness of the remark. Maisie seemed to be a very mature little girl in some ways – probably having had to grow up before her time, she surmised – and might consider she had outgrown such things as teddy bears. However, she was glad to see the child's face light up with pleasure.

'I've brought my teddy bear an' all,' she said, pulling out a somewhat battered and threadbare creature from the black bag. 'See, this is Barney Bear. Can he sit there with yours? He was yours, wasn't he, Mrs Fairchild, when you were a little girl?'

'Yes, he was,' replied Patience. 'Actually, though, my bear is a 'she', not a 'he'. I know we always tend to think of teddies as being boys, but I always thought mine was a girl. I called her Betty.'

Maisie grinned. 'That's good, isn't it? Barney and Betty. They can keep one another company. And Barney's sure to feel a bit lonely at the moment. 'Course I should have known yours was a girl. He's – I mean she's – got a pink ribbon on, hasn't she?'

'Yes, so she has. We will have to find a blue ribbon for Barney.' Patience was pleased that the little girl could still find delight in such things as teddy bears, even to the extent of giving him a real personality. No doubt Maisie, too, like the teddy bear, was feeling a bit lonely, despite her chatter.

'Your Betty is cleaner than Barney Bear,' she went on, 'an' he must be much older. But my little brother and sister have been chucking him around, y'see. I've told 'em not to, but they take no notice. They don't take no notice of me mum neither. They're real naughty, Mrs Fairchild...' She paused for a moment. 'I don't know how me mum's going to manage...'

Without you to help her? thought Patience, but she did not say so. She felt she was beginning to guess at the picture. 'I think most little brothers and sisters can be tiresome,' she said. 'Don't worry, dear. I'm sure your mum will be able to manage very nicely. You are sure to miss her, though, and the children as well, and your...your dad?' The child had made no mention of a father, and she now shook her head vigorously.

'I haven't got no dad, not a proper 'un anyway. He died a long time ago, when I was little.'

'Oh dear; I'm sorry to hear that,' replied Patience. She guessed she would have to tread carefully here. Maisie had clammed up, her mouth set in a grim line and her eyes were sad now instead of filled with enthusiasm as they had been a little while earlier. Patience feared for a moment that she was going to start crying. That was bound to happen, though, she supposed; sooner or later there were sure to be tears of homesickness and bewilderment at the strangeness of her surroundings. And it sounded, too, as though there might be a step-father, maybe not a very sympathetic one, in the picture.

'Now then, let's sort out your things, shall we, and put them away in the wardrobe.' She opened the door of the single wardrobe in the corner. 'There are shelves at the side, see, for your underwear and your bits and pieces.'

'I haven't got very much,' said Maisie. 'Me mum can't afford to buy me many new clothes, what with Joanie and Jimmy and everything. She got me that jumper and skirt at a jumble sale, and these things what I've got on I wear for school. Me gymslip's a bit short, but me mam said it 'ud have to do for a while.' She spoke matter-of-factly, not in any complaining way. She was obviously used to their situation of near-poverty.

It was true that she did not have many possessions, not with her at least, and it was doubtful that there would be much more at home in Leeds. The items of underwear – knickers, vests, liberty bodice and a nightdress – were clean enough, though a trifle grey and dingy looking, and the two pairs of grey socks were darned quite neatly. Apart from that the only clothing was a blue jumper and a grey skirt; the garments from the jumble sale, no doubt. The skirt looked as though it would be too long, in contrast to the gymslip that the child was wearing which came to way above her knees. Then there were a few ragged handkerchieves, a toothbrush and a comb, a pair of wellingtons which appeared to have done much service, and a pair of plimsolls which were equally worn. And, at the bottom of the bag, a few copies of Enid Blyton's 'Sunny Stories'.

'Very good,' said Patience, although, in truth, it was not good at all. It was sad to see the little girl's meagre selection of worldly goods laid out on the bed. 'Now, you put them where you want to, on the shelves, and I've got a nice padded coat hanger to hang your gaberdine mack on.' The coat smelled a little of grease or chip fat, and Patience guessed it had spent most of its time hanging on a peg in the hall – if there was one – or on the kitchen door.

'Shall I leave you for a few minutes, Maisie, while you get used to your new room?' asked Patience.

Maisie nodded. 'Mmm...I think so.'

'Very well, dear. Come downstairs when you are ready, and I'll show you the back garden and everything, and then in a little while we'll have our tea.'

'All right,' said Maisie. She smiled, a little pensively. 'I'll...I'll come down in a minute or two.'

It was clear that the child was overwhelmed by all the happenings of the day and needed a little breathing space to sort herself out. Poor little lass! Patience tried to put herself in the same position and realised it was just too awful to contemplate, being snatched away from all that was familiar and brought to live amongst strangers. She and Luke would have to try very hard to make her feel welcome and wanted.

～

Maisie took a deep breath. She could feel tears pricking at her eyelids again, as they had done a little while ago when Mrs Fairchild had mentioned her dad. It had made the thought of Sid – and Percy – come into her mind, and she had been trying to blot them out altogether. She blinked hard, then walked over to the window, framed by the pretty blue and yellow curtains. The small room she was in was situated over the front door, and it looked out over the front garden and village green, across to the school.

'Oh...how lovely!' She gave an involuntary gasp of delight as she stood and drank in the view, her depressing thoughts, for the moment, fading into nothingness. It all looked so beautiful from up here; so quiet and green and peaceful. Mrs Fairchild had told her that the stretch of grass in front of the house was the village green. They still called it that although Middlebeck was now more of a small town than a village. She had not mentioned the stone cross that stood in the middle, but Maisie knew it was a war memorial and that it was there to remember all the men who had been killed in the war, just over twenty years ago. She could see their names carved into the plinth in black letters.

The school looked cosy and friendly, she thought, surrounded by a little wall and low iron railings; nowhere near as big as the one she attended at home. She wondered how the teachers would find room for all the evacuees that had arrived, but that was their problem. The children had been told they had a few days extra holiday whilst they sorted it all out. There was a little greystone house across the school yard, but in the same grounds, and she guessed that the Headmaster – or Headmistress? – might live there; she knew they sometimes lived at the schoolhouse in country places. She hoped he – or she – would be nice and kind. Mr Ormerod at the school in Armley had been a rather a frightening sort of person and Maisie had kept out of his way as much as possible. Not that he knew her name, or any of the others, apart from the boys who were always in trouble. He was a disciplinarian who had ruled the roost from his little room upstairs.

Next door to the school was the big house where Audrey had gone to live. Maisie looked hard at the windows, but she could see no sign of her friend. There was another storey above the first floor. A little pointed attic window peeped out from under the roof, but that, too, reflected back nothing but blackness. The garden was neat and trim and precise, just like Miss Thomson herself, bounded by an immaculate privet hedge. The black front door with a knocker in the shape of a lion's head looked grim and forbidding. Maisie could not imagine herself going and knocking there to ask if she could see Audrey. But she was sure Mrs Fairchild would find out for her how her friend was faring. It was strange; she had hardly known Audrey Dennison, even yesterday, and now she was her best friend. What was more, she could feel that they were going to be best friends for always.

Her eyes wandered to the top side of the green where, behind a low stone wall, was the church. It was built of grey stones, as were all the buildings, and it looked as though it was very old. The tower was crenellated, like a castle, and there was a Union Jack flying from the top. There were flags on all sorts of buildings at the moment, all fluttering bravely, 'to show old Hitler we are not afraid of him', Maisie had heard her mother say. There were gravestones in the chuchyard, ancient stone ones, mostly, with green moss growing on them and leaning at odd angles towards one another, although here and there she could see larger marble ones in the shape of a cross and one with a praying angel. This was the church that Mrs Fairchild's husband was in charge of. She had called him the Rector, but Maisie supposed that that was just another name for a vicar; that was what they called the one at home... But she hadn't been to Sunday School for ages, not since Joanie and Jimmy arrived.

Behind the church tower, in the distance, she could see a range of hills, dark against the blue of the sky. On top of one of the hills she could see what she thought were the ruins of a castle, or it might be an abbey. She remembered visiting Kirkstall Abbey, near Leeds, a long time ago, and she knew there were lots of other ruined abbeys and castles to be seen in Yorkshire. Who could tell what wonders were to be found in that unseen countryside which lay behind the church. It was all so lovely, and it would be hers to explore in the next few days and weeks, with Audrey, she hoped.

She gave a sigh, partly of wonder at the beauty of the scene she was viewing through the window, but also partly of – what? Homesickness, anxiety about her future and Audrey's and of those she had left behind? Maisie could not sort out in her mind exactly how she was feeling, but she knew she just had to get on with it. She went downstairs to find Mrs Fairchild.

❦

'I think you could call me Aunty Patience, don't you?' said Patience whilst they were eating their early evening meal. 'Mrs Fairchild sounds so formal. That is...if you would like to? Or just Aunty, perhaps?'

'Ooh yes, please,' said Maisie, swallowing the meat and potato that was in her mouth before answering. Obviously she had been taught some table manners. 'I'd like that. I haven't got any real aunties. Me mum hasn't got any sisters, or brothers neither. And I don't think me dad had any. I call the lady next door Aunty; she's Aunty Kate, but me mum hasn't got any other proper friends. Yes...I'd like to call you Aunty. I say, this cottage pie's dead good...Aunty Patience.' She grinned. 'Is that what you call it, cottage pie? Me mum makes it sometimes...but it's not as good as this,' she added after a slight pause.

Well, I'm sure the woman does her best, thought Patience. 'I call it shepherd's pie,' she replied. 'It's made with lamb instead of beef, but it's more or less the same. I'm glad you like it, dear. I thought you would be hungry after such a busy day.' She had prepared the meat and onions before leaving home that morning, topping it with potato and cooking it to a satisfying crispness when they returned.

'And there's apple pie to follow – apples from our own back garden – and custard. Do you think you can manage some?'

''Course I can!' said Maisie. She was thoughtful for a moment, then she said, 'Aunty Patience, do you think Audrey will be having a nice tea like this?'

'I'm sure she will,' said Patience, convincingly, she hoped. 'I've told you, Maisie, your friend will be fine. You mustn't worry about her. I'll make sure you see her tomorrow.'

'All right then...' Maisie tucked into the apple pie

with gusto, pausing only to say, 'What about your husband then, Aunty Patience? What shall I call him?'

'Oh, I don't really know.' Patience deliberated. 'Uncle Luke is rather a tongue-twister, isn't it? Most people call him Rector...but he'd rather be called just Luke. We'll ask him when he comes home, but it will probably be tomorrow before you see him.'

She knew that Luke intended to call and see a friend of his after he had concluded his meeting with the Bishop, a fellow he had been at college with who was now a vicar in the town of Richmond, not too far distant. He would arrive back later that evening, but Patience guessed that the little girl would be in bed by that time. Already the strains of the day were beginning to show in her tired face and one or two barely supressed yawns.

'Is a rector a sort of vicar?' asked Maisie. 'That's what we call him at home... But we don't go to church no more,' she added with her engaging honesty.

'Yes, sort of,' replied Patience. 'Vicars in the country parishes are usually called rectors.' The explanation would suffice. In times long ago the tithes paid by the parishioners all used to go to the incumbent of the parish, as part of his stipend, and the ones who were paid in that way were known as rectors. So it had been at St Bartholomew's, but those days were long gone.

'Now, I'm going to leave the washing-up, Maisie, so that you and I can have a little chat. You can tell me all about yourself and that little brother and sister of yours. And we have that important postcard to write to your mother, haven't we?' Each evacuee had been given a postcard, ready stamped and addressed, with instructions to send it home as soon as possible with details of their present address and the name of the person who was now in charge of them.

'You can write this on your own, can't you, dear?' asked Patience as they sat by the fire in the sitting room. 'I'll write the address if you like, and you can tell your mum that you are being looked after by the Reverend – just put Rev for short – and Mrs Luke Fairchild.' She glanced at the front of the card. 'I see your mother is called Mrs...Bragg. Is that right?'

The girl nodded, and Patience noticed that once again the light had gone out of her eyes. 'That's his name. And the little 'uns an' all, Joanie and Jimmy, they're called Bragg. 'Cos they're his kids, y'see. But it's not my name, though. I'm Maisie Jackson.'

'Yes, that's right. Of course you are. So this man...he's your step-father?'

'S'pose so.' She shrugged. 'He's called Sid, Sidney Bragg. I don't call him Dad or anything...I don't want to talk about him.'

'That's all right, dear. We won't talk about him. You just write and tell your mum whatever you want. That you have arrived safely...just a nice chatty little note. She'll feel a lot better when she has heard from you.'

Despite her assertion that she did not want to talk about her step-father, Maisie went on to say, 'He's got a son an' all, called Percy. He lives with us.'

'Your step-brother?' said Patience gently.

The child nodded. 'S'pose so,' she said. Then, just as quickly, she shook her head vehemently. 'No, no he's not! He's not me brother, not any sort of brother, and Sid's not me dad. I hate them! I don't want to talk about them, Aunty Patience…'

'It's all right, my dear.' Patience went over to sit on the settee next to the little girl and put an arm round her. 'We won't talk about anybody or anything, not until you want to. OK? But when you feel you want to tell me about…anything, anything at all, then I'll be here, Maisie.' Instinctively she kissed the girl's cheek, and felt her give a start of surprise.

'I'll just finish this card to me mum,' she said, recoiling a little as though embarrassed by the display of affection. Patience smiled and patted her arm.

'And I'll go and make you a drink of cocoa. That will be lovely and soothing before you go to bed.'

Maisie wrote, 'Dear Mum, I am staying with a nice lady in a big house. She says I can call her Aunty Patience. Her husband is the vicar, but I haven't seen him yet. I hope you are alright and Joanie and Jimmy. With love from Maisie. This is my address.'

And at the bottom Patience added, Rev and Mrs Luke Fairchild, 1, Church Square, The High Street, Middlebeck, North Yorkshire.

⌐——

'She's a dear little girl,' said Patience to her husband, later that evening. 'Well, not so little really. She's nine, going on for ten, but more like twenty in her head from some of the things she says.

I can tell she's had a pretty rough time of it, although she's not very forthcoming at the moment.'

'Give her a chance,' replied Luke. 'It must be so bewildering for all of them. Everything went off according to plan, did it?'

'Yes, it all ran pretty smoothly...' She told him about her day, and Luke told her that he had had a long and candid talk with the Bishop. He was honest with her, too, telling her what she had suspected all along; that he had told the Bishop that it had been in his mind to join up and serve in the army again.

He had done so in the previous war, serving as a second lieutenant in the Shropshire Light Infantry. He had not been in the thick of it all on the battlefields of the Somme, having served instead in the Middle East. Nevertheless, the brutality, the horrific sights he had seen, even so far away from the main conflict; and, above all, the futility and the sheer waste of that unneccesary war had affected him deeply. He had been unable to settle down to his former employment as a bank clerk in his home town of Shrewsbury. He knew that the God he had always believed in was calling him to serve Him more fully. He had been accepted for training at a theological college in 1920; then it was during his first appointment, as a curate in a Birmingham parish, that he had met Patience. The couple had fallen in love almost at once. They had married in 1929 and then moved immediately to the town of Middlebeck where he was to take up the living as priest in charge of St Bartholomew's.

They had been almost ideally happy in the little north Yorkshire town, such a contrast to the grime and clamour of a large city. The only thing to mar their happiness slightly was their disappointment that no child, as yet, had been born to them. Luke felt the frustration just as much as did Patience, but it had not been allowed to spoil their deep love for one another nor the way they worked together as a team.

'And what was the Bishop's answer,' Patience asked him now, 'about serving in the army again?' She held her breath waiting for his reply. To her relief he grinned at her and shook his head.

'An unconditional no,' he said. 'That was his answer. He says my place is here; right here in my own parish.'

'What a sensible man!' said Patience. 'Of course you must stay here. You have already served in one world war, Luke, and that is enough in any man's lifetime.'

'So it is,' replied Luke. 'The Bishop said that as well, that I have done my share of service to my King and Country. But there will be many thousands, my dear, who will be joining up for the second time. The words on many people's lips are that the last war was supposed to be the war to end all wars...and look at us now, on the brink of another one.' He looked regretful for a moment, before going on. 'I have no doubt, if I were to enlist again, that my place here would be easily filled. There are any amount of retired clergymen who would be willing to take up the reins again. And I would be able to act as a padre this time, to the soldiers...'

'I thought you had made up your mind to stay here,' said Patience fearfully.

'So I have; really I have. But I can't sit around on my...er, backside...excuse the expression, darling.'

Patience laughed out loud. 'Do you ever?'

'No...no, I don't. But what I mean is, I could join something here. You know; fire fighting, or there is sure to be some sort of local civil defence scheme for the men to join, like you have joined the WVS. I want to be seen to be doing my bit.'

'You will do that by keeping up the morale of your parishioners,' said Patience. 'The young men will be joining up, and there will be wives and mothers, and girlfriends, who are feeling sad and worried. And don't forget we have this influx of evacuees... To be honest, Luke, I am wondering if I should have taken more than one child. Maisie's little friend, Audrey, was taken by Miss Thomson across the road.'

'Heaven help her then!' said Luke, smiling a little. 'The child, I mean.'

'Yes, quite... They didn't want to be separated, and I would have had them both, but Amelia Thomson was persistent.'

'So I can imagine,' said Luke. 'I was only joking, though. I'm sure the little girl will be all right there.'

'That's what I told Maisie; she was really worried about her. Maisie's a grand little lass, Luke. Rather neglected looking though. Her clothes are shabby and worn, but I get the impression that her mother does her best. She's certainly clean enough, but I suspect she's had head lice recently, poor kid.'

'I should imagine that's par for the course, isn't it,

with evacuees, if they're from a poorer sort of home?'

'Possibly. I haven't asked her too much about her home life as yet. But she shut up like a clam at first when I mentioned her step-father. Then the next minute she burst out with a tirade about how she hated him, and his son. I was quite worried, Luke.'

He shook his head sadly. 'I dare say some of these children come from dreadful homes. But you are just the right person, my darling, to show her that she is loved and cared for. I'll go up and have a peep at her in a while, when I've finished my cup of tea. You put her in the little front room, did you?'

'Yes...' Patience smiled. 'She seemed to think it was wonderful, but I know that it's ready for decorating, and for a new carpet. She went off to bed happily enough, and when I popped in a little while later she was fast asleep.'

'God bless her,' replied Luke. 'We will make sure she feels wanted here, for as long as she stays. But let's hope and pray that this war doesn't go on for as long as the last one did...'

Chapter Seven

Mrs Fairchild – Aunty Patience – kissed her gently on the forehead. 'God bless, Maisie,' she said. 'Have a nice sleep and don't worry about anything. See you in the morning. Goodnight dear.'

'Goodnight...' said Maisie as she snuggled down between the sheets and the warm blankets.

It was dark in the room because Patience had pulled down the blackout blind and drawn the curtains, and just as no light could be seen from outside, so none could enter the room through the window. She had left the bedroom door slightly ajar and an arrow of light from the landing filtered into the room.

'Shall I leave this light on for a little while, dear?' called Patience.

'No...it doesn't matter,' replied Maisie from beneath the bedclothes. 'I'll be all right, honest. You can switch it off.'

'Very well, dear. But if you need to go to the bathroom the switch is just outside the door.'

'OK,' said Maisie. 'Thank you...Aunty Patience.'

It was almost totally dark after the light had been turned off, but Maisie was not afraid of the dark. It was not the dark she had feared at home, only what had happened from time to time under cover of darkness. But she was safe here; she did not need to be frightened any more. Even the thought of the war that everyone said was coming did not frighten her as much as the thought of Sid and Percy, particularly Percy. But they were many miles away in Leeds, and she was here in Middlebeck with a nice kind lady who was a new aunty to her.

Maisie's head was a jumble of thoughts. So much had happened that day that she could not separate them. Her mother and the two children and her home in Armley seemed so very far away, but it was them she was thinking of just before she went to sleep. She said a little prayer inside her head, as they had taught her to do in Sunday School, a long time ago. 'Please God...take care of my mum...and Joanie and Jimmy too,' she added, because she knew she should. Then her eyelids closed and she drifted off to sleep

She was awakened, not by a sound, but by a faint beam of light coming through her door. She stirred dazedly, not remembering where she was, but then she became aware that there was someone there in the room with her. She lifted her head from the pillow, looking towards the doorway. There was a person standing there. In the half light, half dark she could make out the shape of a male figure, tallish, with broad shoulders and fair hair. He smiled and took a step towards her.

Maisie sat bolt upright. It was him! It was Percy! He had come to get her. She gave a piercing scream which made the figure stop dead in his tracks. 'No! No!' she yelled. 'Go away! Go away! Don't come near me. Just...go away...' She was more terrified than she had ever been in her life, but as she cowered away from him she still continued to stare at the person who had entered the room, as though she was powerless to look away. And then, suddenly, the light of reason returned and she began to remember where she was. She was not at home in Armley. She was at her new home, far away from Leeds and...and it was not Percy. It could not possibly be Percy, or Sid.

'Ohhh...' Her breath escaped in long drawn out sigh and her whole body sagged with relief. 'You're not Percy. I thought you were Percy. Who...who are you?'

By this time Patience, hearing the screaming and shouting, had arrived on the scene. She dashed into the bedroom and over to the child, taking in her arms the limp and crumpled little figure. 'It's all right, darling. You're quite safe. It was just a bad dream.' At the same time she turned to her husband. 'Luke! I told you not to wake her up. Poor little girl; she was frightened to death. You should have had more sense.'

'I didn't mean to,' said Luke. 'I'm sorry. I didn't even put the light on. I only opened the door, and she started yelling. I suppose I must have startled her, and she thought I was...somebody else.' He went towards the bed and gently touched the little girl's shoulder.

'I'm Luke,' he said. 'Patience's husband. And you've come to live with us, haven't you, Maisie? I'm sorry if I frightened you. I can see now that it was very silly of me. I'm sorry, Maisie...'

'It's all right.' Maisie looked at him searchingly. 'I thought you were Percy. But you're not. Of course

you're not. You're nothing like him...' Then she
began to tremble uncontrollably. She buried her
head against Patience's shoulder, and the tears – the
long overdue tears, for not one had she shed since
leaving home – began to flow. 'Oh, Aunty Patience,'
she cried. 'I really thought it was Percy, that he'd
come to get me again. I didn't know where I was,
an' I thought it was him. I was really frightened...'

'I know you were, darling, but you're quite safe
now.'

'It wasn't a dream...I thought it was real, that it
was Percy...' She began to sob, impassioned sobs
that shook her whole body. Patience held her close.

'That's right, dear. You have a good cry. It's not
babyish to cry, Maisie. We all need to cry sometimes.
And there is nothing to fear here, nothing at all.' She
motioned to her husband. 'Now, Luke is going to
make us a nice cup of tea – with lots of sugar in it,
please, Luke. And you and I will sit here and drink it
before you go off to sleep again. And you can tell me,
if you would like to, what it is that is worrying you.'

Patience listened with increasing horror and alarm
as the little girl poured out her story of what had
happened to make her so frightened. She found it
hard to imagine the child going through such a
dreadful experience. But thank God she had
managed to get away from it all and that she was
safe here for the duration. It seemed as though the
evacuation scheme – the outbreak of war, indeed –
was proving to be far from an ill wind for children
like Maisie.

Patience heard how the man called Sid, Maisie's step-father, had 'belted' her from time to time; and her mother, too, had had more than the occasional thumping and black eye. The 'little 'uns, our Joanie and Jimmy', however, had usually managed to escape his wrath, 'because they're his kids, y'see,' Maisie told her, an' they look just like him an' all; they don't look anything like me mum.'

'But...they are your mother's children, aren't they?' she enquired carefully.

'Oh yes, 'course they are. I remember them being born. Soon after he came to live with us she started having babies...but I hope there won't be any more.'

It was the lad called Percy, though, of whom Maisie was the most scared, terrified out of her wits. No wonder she had screamed on seeing a strange figure in her bedroom.

'He started coming into my room, Aunty Patience, when the little 'uns were asleep, an'...an' he'd get into bed with me and make me do all sorts of things – awful things. I knew it was wrong and I didn't like it. But he said he'd beat me up, or his dad would, if I told on him.'

Patience was appalled. Had the child been badly molested? she wondered; interfered with in a serious way. But she hesitated to ask outright. Besides, she doubted she could find the words to phrase such a question.

'He made me kiss him, an'...an' touch him,' Maisie went on, as though a dam had burst inside her and the story, in all its awfulness, had to pour out of her. Patience knew that it was cathartic, part of a healing process that the child had to go through, and that she must listen and help if she were able. 'An'...an' he touched me an' all, me legs an'...an' places what I knew was wrong.'

Patience held her close. 'Did he...did he do anything else, Maisie? Really...hurt you, I mean?'

Fortunately the child seemed to grasp her meaning. Patience guessed that she had already learned the facts of life, or had guessed at them. She shook her head decidedly.

'No, he didn't do...what you have to do to get babies,' she said. 'I know what that is, y'see, Aunty Patience. One of the big girls at school told me.'

'Oh, I see,' said Patience, feeling slightly relieved and speaking hurriedly before the girl went on to explain, possibly in more graphic detail. 'But what this boy did was very very wrong and I'm glad you've told me about it. What about your mother, though? Does she still not know about...what was happening to you? I really think she ought to know, Maisie...' There were younger children in that house, she was thinking. They sounded a couple of terrible tykes, that Joanie and Jimmy; nevertheless, they were vulnerable.

'Oh, she knows about it now,' said Maisie. 'I screamed, y'see, and shouted out when he came into me room the last time – last night it were – an' I kicked him hard an' all. Then me mum came dashing in. I think she must've guessed there was summat going on, 'cause she'd got a pair of scissors in her hand and she tried to stab Percy.'

'Good gracious!' breathed Patience. This tale was going from bad to worse.

'But I shouted at her that she hadn't to kill him. I knocked the scissors flying and they cut Percy's arm a bit, but he weren't really hurt. He yelled though; you should've heard him! An' then Sid came in – he'd just got back from the pub – an' he punched me mum and kicked her in the stomach, an' she had a black eye this morning. An' her side was hurting an' all where he kicked her. She didn't say it was, but I could tell.

'An' I'm dead worried about her now, Aunty Patience, left behind with him. She was going to come with me, and the little 'uns. Sid told her last night she had to clear off, but then he changed his mind and said she had to stay and look after him and Percy. I tried to make her come, but she said she daren't.'

Patience felt almost too shocked to speak. Maisie had cried intermittently during the telling of the story, every word of which Patience believed to be true. But she seemed calmer now, as though, having unburdened herself and shared her troubles with a grown-up, she could relax a little and transfer some of the problem on to someone else. Her next words bore that out.

'Aunty Patience, d'you think, p'raps, if you wrote to my mum you could make her see that she'd be safer if she came here? Safe from the war, when it comes, and from Sid an' all. I'm scared of what he might do to her.'

'I'll see...' replied Patience, knowing that it was an evasive remark. 'I'll talk it over with Luke, and we'll see if there is anything we can do to help your mother. Try not to worry about it any more tonight, dear. Drink this last drop of your tea, and take this little tablet. It will help you to go back to sleep.' She gave her an aspirin tablet, broken in half, which the child swallowed obediently. Her eyelids were drooping already and Patience felt that she would sleep soundly now till the morning.

'Goodnight, dear,' she said again. 'God bless...and thank you for telling me about all the things that were worrying you. A trouble shared is a trouble halved. That's what grown-ups say sometimes; it helps when somebody else knows about it. Night night now; sleep tight.'

'Mind the bugs don't bite!' countered Maisie with a little grin. 'That's what my mum says sometimes. G'night, Aunty Patience.'

I hope bed bugs were not another problem in that unhappy household, thought Patience as she went downstairs again. It sounded as though the woman, Mrs Bragg, tried to do her best for her own three children, but that she was ineffectual when it came to dealing with her brute of a husband and his perverted son. For that was what the lad must be to molest his young step-sister in that way.

She repeated the sad story to Luke who was shocked, but not altogether surprised. 'Unfortunately this sort of thing does happen, and not always just in the poorer homes,' he said. 'Sometimes it might be abuse of the children by a step-father, or even a natural father on occasions. But these things are not often talked about. They are swept under the carpet, probably because the mother is too ashamed to speak out, or she may not even know. Thank God this little girl has got away, for the time being… But I admit, my dear, that – like you – I feel at a loss to know what we can do about the mother's situation back home. The police still tend to look upon these occurences as domestic problems and don't want to get involved.'

'Thank goodness the child wasn't raped,' said Patience. 'That was what I feared when she was telling me, but it seems that the lad was just…amusing himself. Ugh! The thought of such a thing, and that dear little girl…'

'Yes…I must try to win her confidence,' said Luke. 'I should imagine she is not very keen on the male sex at the moment.'

'She has mentioned her dad, her real dad, and it sounds as though she was very fond of him. He died when she was only a tiny girl.'

'And then her mother made a disastrous marriage,' remarked Luke. 'Why do women do these things, I wonder? For security, I suppose, for somebody to lean on. No doubt he sweet-talked her, poor woman…'

'I know we can't interfere, Luke,' said Patience. 'But they will be running trips, I'm sure, for mothers to visit their children who are evacuated. Perhaps, if we could get Maisie's mother to come here, then we could have a chat to her.'

'That sounds like a good idea,' said Luke. 'But we seem to be overlooking the fact that the war hasn't even started yet.'

'It's inevitable, though, isn't it? The Prime Minister is broadcasting to the nation at eleven o' clock tomorrow…and I'm sure we all know what he is going to tell us.'

Luke nodded. 'Yes, I was unsure what to do about the morning service. I think it would be best to cut it short, then everyone can be back in their own homes for eleven o' clock. I doubt if there will be much of a congregation tomorrow, anyway. And what about Sunday School, my dear?' Patience was in charge of the Junior department.

'I think we will carry on as usual in the afternoon,' said Patience, 'for those who want to attend. It will be better if we act as normally as possible. And no doubt there will be some of the evacuees there as well. I shall take Maisie along, and I expect Miss Thomson will want Audrey to go. They'll be glad to see one another again, those two, Maisie and Audrey. Oh dear! I can't help wondering how little Audrey has gone on. She's by no means the tough little customer that Maisie is.'

'Maisie has needed to be tough, God bless her,' said Luke. 'It sounds as though Audrey is from an altogether different background. But they all belong to somebody, and I'm sure that most of the folk of Middlebeck will make them welcome. Now, come along, my darling; bedtime, I think. It's been a long and hectic day, and we are going to need all our strength for tomorrow...'

When the door closed behind them Audrey found herself enveloped in the comfortable arms of Daisy, the maid.

'Oh, the poor little lamb!' Daisy cried. 'Isn't she sweet? Have you come to live with us then, luv? What's your name?'

The welcome was such a surprise to Audrey after the standoffishness of Miss Thomson that she burst into tears.

'There now, look what you've done!' scolded an irate Miss Thomson. 'Put her down, Daisy, you stupid girl! The last thing we want is her crying again. I thought she'd got over that.' She prodded at Audrey's arm, but quite gently, saying in a voice that was not really harsh or unkind, 'Do stop it, child. I've told you I can't do with crybabies. You're going to be perfectly all right here, Audrey. Daisy will look after you.'

'Audrey – is that your name?' said the plump rosy-cheeked young woman. She crouched down in front of the child still holding her arms. 'Let's have a proper look at you then, and let's wipe those tears away. ''Ave you got an 'anky?' Audrey produced the lace-edged one from her pocket. 'Ooh, that's posh, ain't it?' said Daisy, dabbing at her cheeks. 'Now, don't cry no more.'

Audrey found herself looking into a pair of blue eyes, rather prominent ones, a shade lighter than her own, and when the young woman smiled, which Audrey was to find she did quite often, she revealed a mouth of large uneven teeth with a gap at the top side. Her hair was short and dark and a little bit wavy and on top of it she wore a white cap to match her stiffly starched apron. Audrey was aware of a smell of musky perfume and another faint, sort of greasy, cooking smell. But she felt she had met somebody who would be kind to her, who might even be a friend.

Miss Thomson sniffed audibly several times, a

sign, Audrey had already guessed, that she was a little bit annoyed. 'Stop fussing, Daisy, for goodness' sake! She's called Audrey; Audrey Dennison; it says so on her label, although she doesn't need to go on wearing it now. You can take her upstairs and show her where she will be sleeping. Show her where the bathroom is and everything, and make sure she puts her clothes away tidily. Then you can make a start on the meal. What are you preparing today, Daisy?'

'Liver and onions, Miss Thomson. I've gorrit braising in th' oven already, an' I'll mash some spuds to go with it.' So that was what she could smell, thought Audrey.

'Potatoes, please, Daisy,' said Miss Thomson reprovingly. 'And – I-have-got-it-braising-in-the-oven,' she added precisely. 'How many times do you need telling? Try to speak correctly, girl.'

'Oh aye; I keep forgetting. Sorry, Miss Thomson.' Daisy grinned. 'And rhubarb crumble for afters.'

Miss Thomson sniffed again, but this time it seemed to be a sniff of satisfaction. 'That sounds very good. And just for today, while we have a visitor, you may eat in the dining room with me, Daisy. Just this once, mind; after that…we will have to see. Off you go now, both of you. Make sure Audrey washes her hands and face, although I don't think she will need reminding. She seems a very clean and tidy little girl, not like some of them that were there. That's why I chose her, because I thought she might fit in here with me.'

'OK then, Audrey luv. Give us yer bag and I'll show you what's what. Just foller me.' Daisy led the way up the stairs to the first floor landing.

There were several doors opening off it and Audrey paused, thinking that one of these rooms would be her bedroom. Through a partly open door she could see a double bed covered with a green satin eiderdown and a massive wardrobe with a carving of curlicued leaves on the front.

'That's 'er Ladyship's bedroom,' said Daisy. 'And this 'ere is the bathroom.' She pushed open a door to reveal a bath cased in mahogany and a large wash basin. 'An' a separate lav next door. Do yer want to go, luv?' She opened the next door.

'Perhaps I will in a minute,' said Audrey, feeling a bit shy. 'Which is my room then?'

'Oh, it's not down here,' said Daisy, although there were three more doors not opened. 'You and me, we're up in the Gods. Come on; up the wooden hill we go.'

She led the way up a narrower staircase carpeted, not with the rich red carpet of the lower floors and landing, but with a coarse brown matting. 'Here we are, up in the attic. That one's mine and this is yours. It ain't so bad, though. We've gorra great view from up here, all over t' place.'

Daisy pushed open the door and they entered a small room with a sloping ceiling and a little window that poked out of the roof. Audrey put her shoulder bag and gas mask case on to the bed, on top of the white woven counterpane, and went over to the window. As Daisy had said, it was a great view overlooking the front garden and the green, and beyond to a range of hills; and across the green was the rectory where Maisie had gone to live.

'That's where my friend, Maisie, has gone,' she said pointing. 'Over there.'

'What, in the rectory?' said Daisy. 'Oh, she'll be OK with the Rev and Mrs Fairchild; they're real nice. Lucky thing, eh? You'll be all right though, an' all. I'll look after you, Audrey. Now, tek off yer coat and let's get all yer stuff into t' wardrobe. And there's a little chest of drawers, so you'll have plenty of room. And, like I said, the bathroom's on the floor below, and the lav. But there's a potty under yer bed in case you want to go in the night. Them stairs is a bit dangerous, like, in the dark.' She lifted the white counterpane to show a chamber pot with a design of pink flowers.

'Oh...I don't usually...' said Audrey, feeling embarrassed.

'Don't worry about it, luv,' said Daisy cheerfully. 'I'll empty it in t' morning. I use one an' all when I have to.'

'I think I'll go now, to the proper toilet, I mean,' said Audrey.

'OK; off you pop then. I'll be putting this stuff away...'

Audrey had got over her tears now. She still felt bewildered, though, and she knew if she started to think about her mother and father back in Armley she would start to cry again, so she tried to concentrate on what was happening in this new place; she could not yet think of it as her home. She knew she was lucky to be staying in such a nice big house. She still wasn't sure about Miss Thomson, but Daisy, the maid, was nice and friendly. She thought she might have had a bigger bedroom, though; perhaps one of those on the first landing. She had a nice big bedroom at home, all to herself, with much posher furniture and carpets than in the small bedroom here. Audrey was used to her creature comforts, unlike Maisie, her new friend. She had not known much about Maisie until today, but Audrey guessed that she had had to share a bedroom with her little brother and sister and, also, that their lav would be in a shed at the bottom of the garden.

'Righty-ho then,' said Daisy when Audrey returned to the bedroom. 'Let's get back downstairs.'

They went into a large kitchen at the back of the house. Miss Thomson was nowhere to be seen. 'I've already peeled the spuds – sorry, I mean potatoes,' laughed Daisy, 'so I'll just put 'em on to boil. She's always trying to get me to talk proper is her Ladyship, but I don't allus remember. It's hard work anyroad, trying to talk posh.'

'She's not really a Lady, is she?' asked Audrey. 'You know – like Lords and Ladies?'

'No, of course she isn't, but she'd like to be. She's not so bad though, old Amelia, when you get to know her. I give as good as I get, y'see, so she's 'ad to get used to me. I know how far I can go with her though; so far and no further. I've been with her for ten years, ever since I left school. I've lived in for the last couple o' years.'

'Are you the only maid?' Audrey went on to ask. 'My friend, Maisie, she said she bet Miss Thomson had loads of servants.'

Daisy laughed. 'Oh, no doubt she'd like to, like it

was in the olden days. But times change, don't they? And now there's only me. I'm the maid of all work, you might say. But I'm also the 'ead cook and bottle washer; I can please meself what I do a lot of the time. I'm not complaining. Here – make yerself useful. You can lay the table in t' dining room if I find you the knives and forks and spoons. She says I can dine with 'er tonight, and that's a turn up for the book, I can tell yer. I'm usually on me owny-own in 'ere... Here y'are; here's the cutlery, that's the proper word, ain't it? And the table mats are in that there drawer...'

Miss Thomson was somewhat surprised at the way Daisy had taken the evacuee girl under her wing. The young woman was used to children, of course, being the eldest of a large family. But she had not had much to do with them since she had come to live in, only visiting her home, at the other end of the village, on her day off. She had declared, also, that she was glad to get away from the youngest two, eight-year-old twins who were reputed to lead her mother no end of a dance.

As for her, Amelia Thomson, she had had no dealings at all with children, not since her own long ago childhood. Her father had been the manager of a woollen mill down in the valley, and his shares in the company, through his friendship with the owner, had enabled him to buy this house in Church Square. Amelia, the youngest of four children, two boys and then two girls, had lived there all her life. Her brothers had married and moved away; so had her sister; and when her father had retired and her mother had fallen ill it had been taken for granted that Amelia should be the one to care for them both. She had never gone out to work, except in the office at the mill on a part-time basis. She remembered the days when they had employed a trio of maids, as well as a cook, and a seamstress who came in to help her mother with the household linen, although they had never aspired to a butler.

At least she, Amelia, had been left the house after the death of both her parents. Her brothers and sister had agreed that that was only right, as they all had homes of their own plus a goodly share of their father's capital.

Amelia was not poor, not by any means, but she watched the pennies carefully. She knew, although she seldom admitted it, that her maid, Daisy, was a veritable treasure. She did the cooking, washing, cleaning and shopping single-handedly, with scarcely a grumble. Occasionally Miss Thomson employed Daisy's mother, Mrs Kitson, to help out with a bit of the rough work, especially at spring cleaning time, and Sid, the gardener was needed to keep the grounds in perfect order, just as Amelia's father would have wished.

She knew, however, that Daisy was long overdue for a raise in her wages. Amelia had a plan. There was no reason at all why her maid should not take complete charge of the evacuee girl, if she was to make it worth Daisy's while; a few more shillings a week, maybe. And, of course, there would be an allowance for taking an evacuee, so she would hardly be out of pocket. Daisy had already shown a certain fondness for the child, and it really would be better that way. She, Amelia, would hardly ever need to see the little girl, except perhaps on Daisy's day off. But she would deal with that problem when it arose...

Chapter Eight

Maisie stared around the church at the huge stone pillars; at the stained glass windows with the morning sunlight filtering through them, making dappled pools of colour, red, blue, green and gold intermingling on the stone-flagged floor; and at the large wooden cross at the front of the church over what she thought was called the altar. It was quite a while since she had been inside a church and her recollections were hazy. There was a blue velvet cloth on the altar, embroidered with gold letters, fancy ones which read IHS, and in the middle was a smaller silver cross and a pair of silver vases filled with autumn flowers; michelmas daisies, vibrant dahlias, and chrysanthemums in glowing shades of orange, deep crimson and yellow.

She was sitting with Aunty Patience in a pew near the front of the church which, she guessed, was reserved for the rector's family. But Luke did not have a family, only his wife, Patience. She had met Luke again at breakfast time this morning, and when she saw him she had felt unusually shy, and silly because she had mistaken him, the night before, for that awful Percy. He had been very kind to her. He said how pleased he was that she had come to live with them and that he wanted to be her friend. If she had any worries at all she was to tell him, or Patience, about them, so that was good to know. He said, too, that she should call him Luke; it didn't matter about the uncle bit, and he didn't really like being called Rector or Reverend. She did not feel frightened any more, nor worried either, except for that niggling little anxiety about her mum which would not go away.

They had had a lovely breakfast of bacon and eggs, and warm toast spread with real butter, not marg like they had at home. And then, a little later, Patience had said they were going to church, so Maisie had put on her navy gaberdine mack, the only coat she possessed, and her pixie hood. Aunty Patience had said she would be too hot in church in a pixie hood, so she had given her a red beret to wear, setting it at a jaunty angle on top of Maisie's dark hair. It was a little bit too big, but it was a lovely bright colour and Maisie felt very pleased and proud as she sat next to her new aunty.

She knew she looked rather shabby, though, at the side of Patience, but Maisie was quite used to that. Patience was wearing a green costume with a white silky blouse underneath, and a little white straw hat with a green ribbon round it. Maisie thought she looked lovely.

She turned at the sound of footsteps coming down the centre aisle, and she nudged Patience as she saw Miss Thomson, Audrey and Daisy, the maid, sitting down in the opposite pew. 'There's Audrey,' she whispered. 'Can I go and say hello to her?'

'Wait until afterwards, dear,' said Patience, 'when the service is finished. Then perhaps you can have a few words with your friend.'

Maisie watched as the three of them bowed their heads, saying a little prayer. It looked as though Audrey was quite used to going to church as she seemed to know just what to do. Then Miss Thomson settled herself into her pew with her black gloved hands folded neatly in her lap. Maisie leaned forwards and flapped her hand to attract Audrey's attention; and Audrey, catching sight of her friend, gave a gasp of pleasure and waved her hand in return. Only to receive a look of displeasure and a slight dig of rebuke from Miss Thomson. The woman turned and looked disapprovingly at Maisie; but the maid, Daisy, sitting at the end of the pew nearest to the aisle, turned her head slightly and grinned, then she gave a broad wink. Maisie didn't dare to wink or even grin back, not with that dreadful Miss Thomson watching, but she decided that she liked Daisy very much. Audrey would be OK, she was sure, if that nice plumpish young woman with the beaming smile had anything to do with it.

The organ, somewhere up high above the choir stalls, had been playing quietly; then, suddenly, it began to play more loudly, and a door opened at the front of the church. First of all a man came out, holding a sort of long pole in his hand, and following behind him came Luke, and then a choir of men and women, boys and – Maisie was surprised to see – a few girls, some no older or bigger than herself. The men and the boys were wearing white gowns over their ordinary clothes, and the ladies and girls wore blue cloaks and had little square caps on their heads. They all processed round the church, to the back and then down the centre aisle, passing near to Patience and Maisie.

They took their places in the choir stalls, the children at the front and the men and women at the back, and Luke, in his black gown, went up the steps into the pulpit. The hymn they were singing was 'Onward Christian Soldiers'. Maisie remembered it from her Sunday School days, and they sometimes sang it at day school as well, in morning assemblies. It was one she enjoyed singing because it had such a rousing tune that made you feel you wanted to march along in time to it. She didn't understand all the words though, and it said the word 'hell' twice, which sounded rather dreadful, she thought, to sing in church. It was a word that Sid was always using, amongst other words which were even more awful.

Maisie had a clear ringing voice and she kept in tune perfectly. Patience looked at her fondly and smiled, and Maisie smiled back feeling, suddenly, very happy. She saw Luke glancing at her, too, from his place in the pulpit high above their heads, a quirky little grin playing round his lips. Shyly, she smiled back at him, then quickly lowered her eyes again to her hymn book.

When the hymn came to an end Luke said 'Let us pray', and they all sat down again, bowing their heads. Patience knelt on a flat cushion which was underneath the pew, so Maisie did the same. There was quite a lot of standing up and sitting down, so Maisie followed Patience and did exactly what she was doing, following the words of the service carefully in her red prayer book.

'I am sure you will all be pleased to hear that my sermon will be very short this morning,' said Luke, when the congregation had settled down and everyone was looking at him expectantly. 'Only five minutes,' he added with a grin, and a polite little ripple of laughter ran round the church.

'But we all know the reason for this,' he continued, his face taking on a much more sober expression. 'I realise that all of you, as well as my wife and I, want to be home by eleven o' clock to hear what our Prime Minister has to say to us. We can all guess, alas, what that will be. My dear friends...we stand on the brink of what may turn out to be a long and bitter struggle, but we must believe, in the end, that right will prevail...'

He talked about trusting God, and saying your prayers, and helping one another...and Maisie kept her eyes on his face all the while, thinking how stupid she had been to mistake him for Percy. Luke was handsome. He had fairish wavy hair, turning a little bit grey at the sides, shining bluey-grey eyes that looked so kind and understanding, and a sort of noble face – like pictures she had seen of kings and lords in history books – with a rather longish nose and a wide mouth. Kings usually looked solemn though, but Luke smiled a lot, and his eyes smiled too, as well as his mouth.

Today, though, was a serious sort of day and Luke, the rector, was suitably grave and dignified. They sang another hymn, 'O God Our Help in Ages Past', and when the choir had processed round the church again it was time to leave. Luke stood at the door, shaking hands with everyone. Not with his wife, though; that would have been silly, Maisie thought, but she noticed that he had a special extra loving smile for Patience.

Maisie pulled at her hand. 'Aunty Patience, can I go and talk to Audrey now, please? Look – they're going.' Miss Thomson, Audrey and Daisy were already walking briskly down the path, with Audrey casting appealing backward glances at her friend.

'Yes, of course,' replied Patience. 'Come along dear, quickly. We'll both go and have a word with them. Miss Thomson...' she shouted, but not too loudly, quickening her footsteps to catch up with the trio. 'Could you spare a minute, please? Maisie wants to say hello to Audrey.'

Miss Thomson turned sharply, casting a slightly disapproving look at Maisie before answering. 'Yes, I suppose so. It will only have a to be a minute, though. We have left a joint of beef in the oven, and Daisy still has the potatoes and vegetables to see to. Go along then, Audrey.' She gave her a little nudge. 'Go and say hello to your...er...friend.'

'Hello...' said both girls together, feeling a little ill at ease. They grinned unsurely at each other.

'Are you OK then, with...her?' whispered Maisie, gesturing slightly with her thumb.

'Yes, I'm OK; honest, I am,' Audrey whispered back. Maisie was relieved to see that she was not crying and she looked perfectly normal. 'Daisy's looking after me. She's real nice...'

And that was all there was time for because already Miss Thomson was fussing and fidgeting with her gloves and bag. 'Come along now, Audrey, and you, Daisy...'

'There is Sunday School as usual this afternoon, Miss Thomson,' Patience said, before they disappeared down the path. 'Perhaps you would like to send Audrey along? Maisie will be going with me.'

'Of course,' said the woman with a haughty look at the rector's wife. She smiled condescendingly. 'There was no need to remind me. I should hope I know my duty.'

The wireless set belonging to the Fairchild household was a posh affair, as big as a small cupboard, with a pattern of a sunray on the front and lots of knobs, not at all like the little crackly thing that Maisie's family had in Leeds. Luke had taken off his jacket and he looked rather odd in his white shirt with a black vest on top and his official clerical collar. He twiddled a few knobs and they all sat down in the comfortable sitting room to hear the Prime Minister's broadcast. Maisie knew he was called Neville Chamberlain and she had seen pictures of him in the newspapers; an old man, he looked to her, with a kind but worried face and a little bristly moustache.

His voice, as he started to speak, sounded sad and flat. He said something about Berlin – that was the capital of Germany, she knew – and Poland, and words that Maisie did not properly understand. But she knew only too well what he was talking about when he said, '...this country is now at war with Germany.'

Even though they had known what was going to

happen Patience gave a little gasp and Luke, sitting next to her on the settee, took hold of her hand, stroking it gently.

'Now may God bless you all,' said the Prime Minister at the end of his speech, and he used exactly the same words that Luke had used in his sermon only half an hour before. 'I am certain that the right will prevail.'

Patience wiped a tear from her eye. Then she smiled sadly. 'Come along now, Maisie. I'll find you an apron and you can come and help me in the kitchen. I've made a nice big trifle for after our dinner, and it would be such a help if you could put the nuts and cherries on the top...'

———

Sunday School was at half-past two in the hall at the rear of the church. There was a smaller room behind a partition where the Infants met, but the Juniors, the department of which Patience was in charge, met in the main room. First of all they sang a hymn, 'Loving Shepherd of Thy Sheep', and Maisie noticed that the lady playing the piano, very loud and boldly, was one of the WVS ladies who had met them at the station the day before. It was the rather bossy one, the one who had seemed to be in charge, but today she was not wearing her red jumper and green hat. She had a hat on, though, with her tweedy costume, a brown one with a sticky-up feather like Robin Hood.

'Thank you, Mrs Hollins,' said Patience; then she said a prayer and they all said 'Amen' before dividing up into their classes and sitting down in little groups around the room. There were about six or eight in each group and they sat in a circle of chairs with the teacher at the front. Patience had a group of the oldest girls, ten and eleven years olds. The sexes were strictly divided, but Maisie noticed that most of the teachers were women. She was a little disappointed that she wasn't with Aunty Patience, but she was delighted that Audrey was put into the same group as herself. Their teacher was another of the WVS ladies, who introduced herself as Mrs Spooner.

'We are very pleased to welcome our visitors from Leeds and from Hull,' she said, 'and we hope they will be very happy in Middlebeck, don't we, girls?'

'Evacuees,' whispered one of the local girls to the girl next to her, at the same time pulling her mouth down in a grimace.

Mrs Spooner frowned. 'They are our friends, Gertrude,' she rebuked her, 'and we are all going to make them feel very welcome here.'

The lesson for the afternoon was the parable of the Good Samaritan. The girls took it in turns to read a verse each from the Bibles that Mrs Spooner handed out to them. Maisie was pleased, in view of what that rather rude girl had said, that the evacuees fared very well. Both she and Audrey read their verse without faltering, and so did the other newcomer, a girl of the same age as them from Hull; she was called Ivy Clegg. The three of them exchanged pleased little smiles, but when the girl who had spoken disparagingly about them faltered over her verse they were sensible enough not to giggle or even to let on that they had noticed. But Maisie thought to herself, 'Serve her bloomin' well right!' She had already discovered when Mrs Spooner called out the names on the register that the unpleasant girl was called Gertrude Flint. She was a thin scrawny looking girl with stringy pigtails that stuck out on either side of her head because her hair was really too short to plait.

Mrs Spooner asked them questions about the story, which they all appeared to have heard before, then she explained that Jesus was pleased when people tried to help others, especially those who might not be close friends or neighbours. 'And we are all going to make a special effort,' she said again, 'to be good friends to Maisie, Audrey and Ivy, and all the others who have come to live in our little town.'

She handed out sheets of paper and boards to rest them on and put a box of pencils and coloured crayons on a chair in the middle; the lesson always ended, they were to learn, with the drawing of a picture to illustrate the story. There were drawings of the previous weeks' stories mounted and pinned up on the walls around the hall. Maisie could make out Daniel in the Lion's Den, Noah's Ark, Moses and the Burning Bush, and Moses parting the Red Sea. It was obvious that was what it was because the water round his feet was a brilliant scarlet colour. But now, it seemed, it was the turn of the New Testament.

Mrs Spooner didn't seem to mind if they talked whilst they were occupied with their art work, so Maisie took the opportunity to ask Audrey if she really was all right with Miss Thomson.

'I've been dead worried about you,' she said. 'She looks like an awful old witch to me, like the one in Hansel and Gretel.'

'Don't be silly,' said Audrey. 'She's not as bad as all that. She isn't going to fatten me up and eat me. Actually, I've not seen her all that much. I told you, that nice maid, Daisy, is looking after me. We had our meal with Miss Thomson last night, Daisy and me, because it was a special occasion, Miss Thomson said. It was liver and onions and mashed potatoes, real tasty, like my mother makes it. Daisy had made it...and then afterwards I helped her to wash the pots. Well, she washed and I dried them.

'And then I told Daisy I had to write that card to my parents, so she helped me with it. Well, she didn't help all that much because, actually, I don't think she can spell all that well; she said she wasn't much of a scholar. But she told me the address and I wrote it down. And then this morning I didn't see Miss Thomson until she said it was time to go to church. Daisy says old Amelia – that's what she calls her behind her back – expects her to go to church with her every Sunday, but she has to get the meat in the oven before they set off; Daisy, I mean, not Miss Thomson. So I helped her to clear away again after dinner. We had ours in the kitchen, Daisy and me.'

'And...what about Miss Thomson?'

'Oh, she dines in the dining room all on her own. She has all her meals in there and Daisy has hers in the kitchen. I expect she thinks I'd rather be with Daisy; I suppose I would, really... What about you then? D'you like it in your place with that rector and his wife? She's a pretty lady, isn't she? And he's real handsome I think.'

'He's nice as well,' said Maisie. 'Real friendly. He says I've to call him Luke,' she added proudly. 'I'm glad you're OK though, Audrey.'

'Well, yes…I am,' her friend answered, a shade doubtfully. 'I'd rather be with you, like we said we would…but I'm OK. And we'll see each other at school, won't we? Perhaps before that.'

One of the other girls, a local girl, had been half listening to the conversation and she joined in now. 'You'll be coming to our school, won't you? We might be in the same class; I hope so.' She turned to the other evacuee, the one from Hull. 'And you an' all, Ivy. It is Ivy, isn't it?'

'Yes, I'm called Ivy Clegg,' said the quietly spoken girl. She had straight carroty-coloured hair held in place with kirby grips.

'And I'm Doris Nixon. Wouldn't it be great, eh, if the four of us were in the same class? We don't know yet who our teacher is going to be. They've had to do a lot of sorting out with you lot coming. We might even get one of your teachers instead of one of ours. That'd be a nice change.' Doris was a plumpish girl with flaxen hair tied in bunches with red ribbons, rosy cheeks and a little snub nose. Maisie was not surprised when she told them that her father was a farmer. She certainly looked as though she had her share of creamy milk and butter.

Gertrude Flint, at the other side of the circle, was whispering behind her hand to the girl next to her, a spiteful look in her eyes. The other girl nodded and grinned and they both started giggling.

'That will do, Gertrude,' said Mrs Spooner. 'It is very rude to whisper.'

'Take no notice of her,' said Doris in a quiet voice. 'She's always causing trouble at school, and her friend – that's Norma Wilkins next to her – she's nearly as bad.'

'Collect the papers up, please, Doris,' said Mrs Spooner. 'I can see there are some very good illustrations there, in spite of all the chattering!' She laughed. 'But I don't mind that. I'm pleased to see you all making friends.'

'Some of us...' murmured Gertrude Flint, but Mrs Spooner pretended she hadn't heard.

Patience was standing at the front of the hall again as it was time to sing their final hymn.

'There's a Friend for little children
Above the bright blue sky,
A Friend who never changes,
Whose love will never die...'

Maisie knew that was Jesus. She had never given him much thought except as a baby at Christmas time, and then there was that terribly sad Easter story. But if He really was up there, above the bright blue sky, looking after everyone, then there could be nothing to be afraid of...could there?

⸺

'You are very welcome here, my dear,' said Charity Foster to the young woman who was to be one of her fellow teachers, Anne Mellodey. 'I want you to make yourself at home. We will take our meals together, of course, if that is agreeable to you; but if there are times when you want some privacy, then I will understand. I have become very used to living on my own, but I'm sure we will get along splendidly together.'

'Yes, so am I, Miss Foster,' said Anne. 'Thank you again for offering to accommodate me. This is a lovely cosy room, and I am thrilled with the view from my bedroom window. It's such a change to see hills and green fields and the blue sky, after the factory chimneys and the smoke of Leeds. Still...' She could not help giving a little sigh. 'It's home, and I know my parents will miss me, just as I will miss them.'

But Anne was feeling already on the second day of her stay in Middlebeck that she would grow to be very fond of Miss Foster. A kindred spirit, she thought, this neat little woman, no more than five foot in height, with her kindly smile and all-seeing brown eyes, and her copious grey hair drawn into a bun at the back, but escaping in curling tendrils around her face. She was relieved that her colleague from Armley, Dorothy Cousins, had been billetted elsewhere; in point of fact with Jean Bolton, one of the local teachers, and her mother and father. Anne found her colleague, Dorothy, more than a trifle bossy and very much inclined to 'know it all' from the lofty height of her twelve years' teaching experience, where as she, Anne, had been a teacher for only four years.

'Yes, you are sure to miss your family at home,' said Miss Foster gently, 'but when the new term starts we will all find ouselves very busy; and there is a good deal of organizing to be done before then, of course. There is nothing like hard work, is there, Miss Mellodey, to take one's mind away from problems? I am wondering though, dear…if I may call you Anne? Seeing that we are going to be living together…'

'Of course you may, Miss Foster,' replied Anne. 'I would be delighted. Miss Mellodey sounds so formal.'

'A pretty name, though,' said Miss Foster, smiling. 'You should be musical with a name like that. Are you, I wonder?'

Anne laughed. 'Yes, just a little. Well, I know what I like; nothing too highbrow.'

'And you must call me Charity,' said the headmistress.

'Oh, are you sure…? I wouldn't have presumed…'

'No, I know you wouldn't, my dear. That is why I am suggesting it. I do like to hear my baptismal name now and again, but hardly anyone ever calls me by it any more. Over the years I've become Miss Foster, the schoolmistress. Of course, that is only right and proper in school. I wouldn't dream of allowing my two young teachers to call me by my Christian name, and I only use theirs on rare occasions, when we are away from our work. But it is rather different with you… Now, are you going to tell me something about yourself, Anne dear? Might there be…someone else at home in Leeds, as well as your mother and father?' Her brown eyes were alive with interest, and Anne guessed that Charity Foster, as well as being a very perspicacious lady, might also be the tiniest bit nosey. Still, Anne supposed, as the village schoolmistress, she was sure to know pretty well everything that was going on around her.

'Yes, I have a fiancé,' replied Anne, smiling a little coyly. 'Actually, Bill and I only got engaged a couple of weeks ago.' She looked down at her left hand, twiddling with the crossover ring of three small diamonds that Bill had placed there so lovingly. Maybe Miss Foster had already noticed it? 'We have been friendly for more than two years, and we both knew that...well, that we would get married sometime, in the not too distant future. But then...the war was imminent and Bill couldn't wait to join the RAF. He was a cadet in his last year at school and he's been a member of the ATC ever since. He wants to be a pilot and I'm quite sure he will be accepted for training, with his background, and he is so keen. So...we decided to get engaged.'

'And was he a teacher, like you, dear?'

'Oh no; Bill went to university, whereas I just went to training college for two years. He is a chartered accountant – was, I should say – in partnership with an older man. But he will be able to go back to it when...when this lot is all over. Bill is twenty-four, the same age as me.'

The poor young things, thought Charity, thinking back to the years of the Great War, as it had been called, 1914 to 1918, and the loss she had suffered because of it.

'He was born and bred in Leeds, same as me,' Anne continued. 'In Headingley, though; a rather more salubrious area than where I lived. I'm from

Armley, on the other side of the city. I managed to get a teaching post at a local school when I left college, so I've always lived at home, apart from my college days in Bingley. Bill and I met through mutual friends. We hit it off straight away...'

She stared into the fire that Charity had lit in the morning and then built up after they had had their tea. Now the flames flickered in the hearth, radiating a comforting warmth and a glow that lit up the chintz covered settee and armchairs, the oak-beamed ceiling, and the shelves on either side of the fireplace, crammed to overflowing with Charity's books, ornaments and vases of autumn flowers. Much of the room was in semi-darkness, the only other source of light being a red-shaded standard lamp which stood at the back of the room. But Anne found the firelight and the dim lamplight to be friendly and restful.

'He's stationed somewhere in East Anglia now,' she continued. 'We're not sure when we will be able to see one another...' She turned her eyes towards her hostess, before her thoughts became too dismal. 'Anyhow, that's enough about me. What about you, Miss Foster...er...Charity? I mean, how long have you lived here?'

'Oh, it seems like for ever.' The older woman smiled reminiscently. 'I'm sure some of the people in the village – I should say town – regard me as quite as institution here. Actually, it is getting on for twenty years. Just after the war, it was, when I came here. I am almost sixty years old now. I should be thinking about retiring in a few years' time, but I'm still very fit and active. And now...well, of course I can't even think about giving up. We all have a very important job to do.'

'So you have been teaching – how long? – about forty years?'

'Yes, that's right, Anne. Forty years, ever since I was twenty years of age. Teachers were not allowed to get married in my day, you know. Well, that is not strictly true; you could get married, of course, if you wished; but what I mean is that, if you did so, then you were obliged to give up your post. So that is why...' Charity, also, now stared thoughtfully into the fire.

'I had a fiancé,' she continued quietly after a moment or two. 'We were quite a lot older than you, my dear, Jack and I, but there didn't seem to be any particular hurry for us to get married. I had elderly parents, and my teaching career, and the money I was earning was a great help to the family budget. Jack and I, we intended to get married at the end of the war. We loved one another very much. I know it might not seem so, waiting for so long, but we did...but...he didn't come back.'

'Oh; I'm so sorry,' breathed Anne.

'There were so many thousands who didn't come back. I was only one of many who had lost a loved one; and I was nearly forty years old. Well and truly on the shelf.' She gave a wry little chuckle. 'Too old to find anyone else; besides, so many of the younger men had gone. Not that anyone would have compared with Jack... Then my parents both died, within a few months of one another, and I had the chance of this post, high up in the Dales. It seemed like the other side of the world to me – I had lived in Sheffield all my life – but I came for an interview, and I had the feeling at once that I could be happy here. When they offered me the post I was delighted. And I have been happy, very contented indeed. I think of myself as a real country lass now. It's a grand place to bring children up, with the fields and woods all around and the clean fresh air. There is a certain amount of industry, down in the valley, but nothing to compare with the big towns.

'I hope your stay here will be as happy as mine has been – not as long, of course – and... circumstances permitting. I know, for all of us, that the future is very uncertain.'

'And what about the schooling arrangements?' asked Anne. 'We won't all fit into the school building, will we?'

'No, but we have the promise of other quarters; the church hall and the Village Institute. We should be able to accommodate six classes without any difficulty... We are meeting in the morning, as I told you; myself and my two teachers, you and your colleague, and the teacher from Hull. Then we can decide who is going where and about the dividing up of the various groups of children. I feel it would be better to integrate rather than to segregate the boys and girls. It will make for greater harmony and understanding and that is what we all want to achieve.'

'Yes, I agree,' said Anne. 'It will help them all to make friends...' And then, unable to help herself, she gave a tremendous yawn. 'Oh, I'm so sorry. How rude of me!'

'Not at all, Anne,' laughed her companion. 'That

is just how I feel myself. I'll go and make us a nice cup of cocoa... No, you stay where you are,' she added, as Anne made to rise to her feet. 'And I think it might be a good idea for us to take it up to bed with us. It has been a long and tiring day...and an eventful one too. It will help us to sleep, and we must be bright and fresh for tomorrow...'

And for all the tomorrows, thought Anne. Yes, September the third, 1939, had been a day that no one would ever forget.

Chapter Nine

'Now Maisie,' said Patience on Monday morning. 'You have two whole days before you start school. I think it would be a good idea for you to have a little wander round and about; explore the countryside and get to know the place. You won't get lost if you don't go too far. And if you keep your eye on the church tower and the flag you will know where to head back to. What do you think? Would you like to do that?'

Maisie nodded. 'Yeah, that'd be great. I don't want to go on my own though. What about Audrey? D'you think that Miss Thomson 'ud let her go with me?'

'I was just about to suggest that,' said Patience. 'When you're ready you can go and knock on the door and ask if Audrey might come out for a little while. I shall want you back for your lunch anyway, at half-past twelve. I'll lend you an old watch of Luke's in case you can't see the church clock.'

Maisie hesitated. 'I don't like to go and knock over there. That Miss Thomson – I don't think she likes me very much. She'll happen tell me to go away.'

'Of course she won't,' said Patience. 'How about if I come with you? She won't tell me to go away, will she?' She smiled mischievously and Maisie grinned back.

'No, I s'pose not. Actually, it might be that maid, Daisy, what comes to the door, mightn't it? And she's real nice. Audrey said so at Sunday School. Anyway, it's Daisy what's looking after Audrey, not Miss Thomson, so p'raps I wouldn't see her at all... I don't really want you to go with me, Aunty Patience, 'cause that'd be babyish, wouldn't it?'

'Yes, perhaps so, dear,' Patience answered a little vaguely. It was the previous remark that she had latched on to. 'Did you say that Daisy was looking after your friend? Not...all the time surely? What did Audrey say?'

'Well, she said, like, that she had her breakfast and her dinner with Daisy, in the kitchen. They had a meal in the proper dining room when Audrey first got there, but Miss Thomson said that was a special occasion. But Audrey's all right, Aunty Patience, better'n I thought she would be. She likes Daisy and she has a little bedroom up at the top of the house, under the roof, like what Daisy has. And she can see our house from there.'

Patience smiled to herself at Maisie's use of the possessive pronoun. It was clear that already she was beginning to feel at home. But she did not like the sound of what was happening across the square. It seemed as though Miss Thomson might well be dodging her responsibilities to the girl to whom she had offered to give a home. Still, Daisy was a sensible young woman and maybe the child would feel more at ease with her. Maybe that was Miss Thomson's idea, to help the little girl to feel more at home with someone who was so much nearer to her own age. Patience was always anxious to give everyone the benefit of the doubt. But an attic bedroom, when there were rooms unoccupied on the first floor? She, Patience, had always thought it was bad enough for Daisy to be shoved away up there when, after all, she ran the house single-handedly. But Audrey as well?

However, she smiled at Maisie. 'I'm glad your friend is settling down. She was a bit upset, wasn't she, when you first arrived? And you were such a good sensible girl looking after her the way you did. Now, put your coat on; I don't think you will need your pixie hood or your beret this morning. The sun is shining and it doesn't look like rain.'

'Where shall we go then, me and Audrey? D'you mean behind the church and up to that castle on the hill?'

Patience laughed. 'Don't try to go so far this morning; it's quite a long way, much further than it looks. Luke and I will take you there another time. If you go through the churchyard and out of the gate at the back there's a little lane that leads to the farm. It's the one where Doris lives; you met Doris Nixon at Sunday School yesterday, didn't you? There are fields and woods and a little stream. You'll enjoy it and you will be quite safe if you don't wander too far.'

It was with a slight feeling of apprehension, though, that Patience watched the girl run off across the green to the house on the opposite side. She guessed that Maisie was quite used to fending for herself and finding her own way around in Armley, and she knew that she had already experienced far more of the darker side of life than a child of her age should have to. But here she was in strange surroundings, so different from what she had known in the city. A safe environment, though, Patience told herself. Middlebeck was a peaceful little town where, by and large, the inhabitants looked out for one another, and there was scarcely any crime, certainly not of a violent nature. And it was better, Patience was sure, for the newcomers to find their own feet; to get their bearings in the unfamiliar territory and to make new friends, knowing that they had a safe haven to return to at the end of each day. She only hoped that all the children had settled down as well as Maisie appeared to have done.

She watched surreptitiously from behind the curtains as Maisie knocked at Miss Thomson's front door. As she had anticipated, it was opened by Daisy. After a few moments, during which Maisie was left standing outside, Audrey joined her. She was dressed, not in her best maroon coat, but in a gaberdine raincoat similar to Maisie's, but much neater and smarter. They both waved to Daisy – Miss Thomson was nowhere in sight – then they strolled across, arm in arm, like a couple of middle-aged friends, to the church gate.

Patience moved away from the window. She was due to go to a WVS meeting in a short while to discuss any problems which might have arisen concerning the evacuees, although it was early days as yet. She knew there was a stock of clothing there, donated by the villagers whose children had outgrown their various garments. She would see if there was a good warm coat that would fit her little girl, and possibly another jumper and skirt and some underclothes, and the child really needed another pair of shoes. The ones she was wearing were very scuffed and down at heel...and what she could not find in the parish collection she decided she would buy or make herself. Patience felt a warm glow inside her at the thought of having a child in the home for whom she could buy a nice shiny pair of shoes, or knit a bright red jumper.

The sun was shining brightly, but it was quite low in the sky. The gravestones cast long shadows across the grass and the path through the middle of the churchyard.

'It was OK for you to come with me, was it?' asked Maisie. 'Miss Thomson didn't make a fuss about it?'

'I haven't seen her this morning,' said Audrey. 'She's not got up yet. Daisy says she's caught a chill or something, so she's staying in bed. Daisy wants me to go back at twelve o' clock though, to help her with the dinner. She's showing me how to peel potatoes. I haven't ever done it before.'

Maisie stared at her in surprise. 'Haven't yer? I used to do it all the time at home, I mean, ever since me mum married 'im, Sid, and she had the little 'uns. Still...I s'pose you wouldn't have to do the spuds, would you?' She remembered now how she had always thought Audrey was a posh, spoiled kid, until she had got to know her.

'Daisy calls them spuds,' Audrey said now,

giggling a little, 'but Miss Thomson says she has to say potatoes.'

'And don't you mind helping, like?' asked Maisie.

'No; it's quite good fun,' said Audrey. 'Daisy says I have to think of her as a big sister, sort of.'

Maisie was quiet for a while. It was rather odd, she thought, that Audrey, the one from the posh home should be helping out with the jobs in the kitchen, whereas she, Maisie, was doing no such thing. She had helped to clear the table that morning, but then, she remembered with a stab of guilt, she had sat reading her Sunny Stories whilst Aunty Patience did the washing-up. Patience, in fact, had shooed her out of the kitchen because she wanted to get on with some jobs. But she had made her own bed, as she always did, of course...

They went through a little iron gate behind the churchyard, which led into a leafy lane. There were cart tracks along the lane, but it was quite dry as there had been no rain for some considerable time. There were berries in the hedges, big fat orangey-red ones, and some smaller darker red ones that Maisie did not know the names of – neither did Audrey – but they both recognised the purple glistening blackberries.

'Shall we pick some?' said Maisie.

'D'you think we ought to? They might belong to somebody. We might get into trouble. Anyway, we've nowhere to put them, have we?'

'No; 'course we haven't. Silly me! I tell you what, Audrey. Aunty Patience says this lane leads to a farm, the one where Doris lives. You remember

Doris at Sunday School. She was dead nice to us. We might see her. And we can ask her if we can pick them berries.'

'But we still won't have anywhere to put them...'

'Oh no... Well, never mind, eh?'

They climbed over a stile, and there, ahead of them, they could see a farmhouse. It was built of yellowish-grey stones and had a grey tiled roof and tiny windows, and in the cobbled yard at the front they could see brown hens running around and pecking at the ground. As they drew nearer they could hear them clucking, and there was their friend, Doris, from the previous day, waving to them and running towards the big gate which separated the farmyard from the lane.

'Hello you two,' she said, climbing on to the five-barred gate. 'Are you going exploring? Shall I come with you, or else you might get lost.'

'I don't think we would,' said Maisie decidedly. 'But you can come with us, if you like... Yeah, that'd be great, Doris,' she added, more enthusiastically.

'Can we pick those blackberries?' asked Audrey.

'Yeah – them berries over there. Can anybody have 'em, or do they belong to you?'

'Of course they don't,' said Doris. 'If they grow in the lane, then they're for everyone. Part of God's bounty, that's what me dad says. Hang on; I'll go and get some bowls and then we can go blackberrying. My mum was saying she wanted some to make a blackberry and apple pie. And happen your ladies 'ud like some an' all.'

She didn't invite them into the farmhouse, not

that time, but she opened the gate and they stepped into the farmyard. Audrey looked warily at the hens, as she tried to dodge out of their way.

'They won't peck at yer, don't worry,' said Doris laughing. 'You have to be careful of the geese sometimes. They're a bit fierce, but they're not here at the minute. Just wait here. I won't be long...'

She came out of the farmhouse a few moments later carrying three enamel bowls. She gave one each to Maisie and Audrey. 'There y'are. Me mum says you can bring 'em back another time.'

A smallish lady was standing at the door. She had dark brown hair in a roll around her head, a style popular with a lot of the women of her age, and she wore a snowy-white apron over her black dress.

'That's me mum,' said Doris, waving to her as they went through the gate, so Maisie and Audrey waved as well. Doris's mum smiled and waved more vigorously. 'She's busy making cheese,' Doris went on, 'or else I would have asked you in. You can come another time. Me mum said she was glad I had made friends with you.'

'Didn't you have to take any evacuees?' asked Maisie.

'No, 'cause we haven't got very much room. I've got two big brothers, y'see, who work on the farm. Joe and Ted they're called. Joe's fifteen and Ted's fourteen; he's not long been left school, our Ted. Me mum's glad they won't have to join the army, 'cause they're too young.'

'And what about yer dad?' asked Maisie.

'What about him? What d'yer mean?'

'Well, might he have to go and join the army?'

'No, I don't think so. I don't think farmers have to go. I heard me mum and dad talking about it. Anyway, he's nearly forty and that's quite old.'

Maisie's thoughts returned, momentarily, to Armley. How old was Sid, she wondered? She was not sure, but probably he was older than Doris's dad. She was hoping he might be called up, then her mother would have a bit of peace, although that would mean she was left on her own with Percy, and that might be even worse...

'Come on,' said Doris, breaking into her thoughts. 'We'll go along this lane an' I'll show you round our farm.'

'What about the blackberries?' asked Audrey.

'Oh, there's loads more up here. There'll be plenty for all of us.'

There were three horses, two brown and a dapple-grey one, grazing in a field, and in the next field there was a herd of cattle.

'Look at all them cows,' exclaimed Maisie, standing still and gazing over the hedge.

'You've seen cows before, haven't you?' said Audrey. 'You must've done.'

''Course I have,' retorted Maisie a little crossly. 'Loads of times. But not as close to as this.'

Doris laughed. 'They're not cows,' she said. 'They're bulls. Actually, they're bullocks; that means young bulls. Don't you know the difference between cows and bulls?' Doris was not mocking her; her question was quite sincere. But Maisie was not one who liked to admit defeat.

''Course I do,' she replied. 'But...there's not all that much difference, is there?'

'Well, the cows give us milk,' explained Doris, 'so they have udders at the back, underneath their tails. You have to pull 'em to squeeze the milk out. But me dad's just got some new milking machines so they won't have to do it all by hand.' Maisie was looking puzzled, but she nodded as though she understood perfectly. Doris pointed over the hedge. 'If you look at them bullocks you can tell that they're different from cows. 'Cause they're males, see.'

Maisie looked, feeling rather silly. She had known, of course, that milk came from cows and she had a vague idea about the milking. But she could see now that the bulls were different. They didn't have udders; there, at the back, they had something else, because, as Doris had said, they were males.

'Yes...I know,' she replied quietly, then, to change the subject. 'What else does yer dad have, besides cows and bulls?'

'Sheep, over there on the hills.' Doris waved her arm casually. 'And hens – you've seen them – and geese and turkeys. And he does a bit of arable farming an' all... Growing crops,' she explained as the girl's faces were rather blank. 'Potatoes and beetroot and brussel sprouts.'

'And have you got pigs as well?' asked Audrey.

'Mr Tremaine looks after the pigs mostly,' replied Doris. 'He's the squire.'

'What's that mean – the squire?' asked Maisie.

'Well, he owns the land, does Mr Tremaine. I think that's what being the squire means. Me dad works for him. He's what they call a tenant farmer.'

'So your farm...it belongs to this chap you call the squire?'

'Yeah, that's right; Mr Tremaine. But me mam and dad call him Archie. He doesn't mind; he's real nice and friendly. He rears the pigs and he farms some of his own land around his house. I'll show you if you like; he won't mind.'

Doris opened another gate, a small one for pedestrians at the side of a big iron gate beyond which stretched a long driveway. At the end of the drive was a large greystone house, much bigger than the farmhouse where Doris lived. It had a centre doorway and on each side were six windows, three upstairs and three downstairs, perfectly balanced, like a drawing in a story book. There was a neat lawn at the front with a flower bed all round it, but Doris led the way to the back of the house where there was a garden which was on two levels; she called it the terrace garden. Beyond that there was a tennis court, and an orchard with apple, pear and plum trees.

There were two young men gathering the crop of ripening reddish-brown apples and one of them shouted out to Doris as they were going by. 'Hi there, little Doris. D'you want an apple?' He threw one down to her which she caught deftly. 'An' here's another couple for yer mates.'

'Ta very much, Andy,' she called, picking them up from the grassy floor and handing one each to Maisie and Audrey.

'Don't get into mischief now,' shouted Andy. 'And watch them wopsies. They're a dratted nuisance just now.' He flapped his hand at the insects buzzing round him. 'Cheerio then. See yer...'

'Bye, Andy... He means wasps,' she told her friends. 'It's just his little joke, like he always calls me little Doris. I wish he wouldn't, but he's known me ever since I was a little kid.'

'Does he work for your father or for the squire?' asked Audrey.

'He works for Mr Tremaine, him and the other one, Bert. But I 'spect they might soon be called up, then Daisy Kitson'll be real upset. She's going with Andy. I've seen 'em sometimes, kissing an' that, behind the hedge, but I don't let on.'

'Daisy?' queried Audrey. 'D'you mean...Miss Thomson's maid?'

'Yeah, that's right. Oh, I forgot; you live there, don't you? Hasn't Daisy said anything, like, about her boyfriend?'

Audrey shook her head. 'No, not yet.'

'Oh well, I s'pose she has to keep quiet about it. That Miss Thomson, she's dead strict. I've heard me mum say that Daisy isn't supposed to have followers, not in the house at any rate.'

'Followers?'

'Young men – you know. Andy Cartwright's her young man, an' she meets him when it's her day off. That's when I've seen 'em... Anyroad, ne'er mind about them, eh? Let's pick some o' these blackberries. Come on, Audrey, what's up? Are you scared of getting prickled? See, I'll hold the branch down, then you can reach.'

The three girls were busy for several minutes, picking the purple glistening berries from the branches and popping them into their bowls.

Audrey grew braver, reaching out further to the topmost branches until her bowl was more than half full.

'Mmm...yum, yum!' said Maisie as she put a succulent berry into her mouth then licked her lips. She reached for another one.

'Don't eat too many,' said Doris, 'or else you'll get belly ache...and you mustn't eat any other sort of berries, you know,' she added, a trifle bossily. 'You might get poisoned. It's summat we learn, living in the country, but folk from the town don't always know.'

'We're not stupid!' retorted Maisie. 'Are we, Audrey? Of course we know you can't eat 'em... Anyway, what are they called, them big orangey ones? Look, them birds are having a rare old feast.'

'They're rose hips,' replied Doris. 'Wild roses grow there in the summer time. And those dark red ones are the berries of the hawthorn bush. Hips and haws, we call 'em.'

Maisie was quiet for several moments as they wandered further along the lane. She stopped every now and again to pluck another cluster of berries, gazing in awe at the beauty all around her. The trees growing behind the hedge were just beginning to change colour, the edges of the leaves tipped with yellow and brown, and a few already falling to the ground. She was loth to show Doris how ignorant she was of country matters. A tree was just a tree to Maisie, or had been until now. She could tell the difference between an oak and a sycamore, though, many of which were growing in the lane. And there, hiding amidst the branches, were the twin seeds of the sycamore trees, like little aeroplanes, and acorns, too, nestling behind the curly oak leaves. They had learned about 'seed dispersal' at school in so-called nature lessons, but it had not meant very much to them, brought up in the smokey streets of Armley. The trees in the park, near to where Audrey lived, were quite lovely, Maisie supposed, although she had never really given them much thought. And they certainly did not glow with the brilliance of these trees here, growing freely and in splendour as God had intended them to do.

She noticed a spider's web in the hedge, glistening with droplets of dew, so different from the dusty cobwebs that hung from the dark corners of their rooms at home. A little stream rippled and gurgled between the hedge and the field and she heard a blackbird singing his heart out from a nearby bush. But when a grey squirrel leapt from the branches of a tree and scuttled across the path in front of her she cried out in delight. 'Oh look, a squirrel! I've never ever seen one of them before, only pictures of 'em.' She didn't mind admitting it. 'Isn't he lovely?'

'They can be a nuisance,' said Doris, a shade reproachfully. 'They strip the bark off trees, you know, and they pinch birds' eggs from the nests. Still, they are rather sweet to look at, I suppose. The red ones are nicer, but you don't often see them.'

Audrey had wandered off in front of the other two and now she stood in the middle of the lane, looking into her bowl which was almost full. Suddenly a black and white dog appeared, from out of nowhere, or so it seemed. It came bounding towards her, its tail wagging and its pink tongue lolling out in delight. She stood transfixed as the dog leapt up at her. It pawed and sniffed and jumped all round her, barking excitedly, whilst she, terrified, backed away. Then the bowl flew out of her hands and its contents rolled away across the lane, many of her precious berries trampled under the feet of the exuberant dog.

'Go away! Go away!' she yelled, falling over her own feet in fright and ending up in a heap on the ground. Then she burst into tears.

The next minute a boy came running from around the corner where the lane forked. 'Prince, Prince! Come back here! Oh, you dreadful dog, just look what you've done... I'm very sorry...er... Miss.' He went towards Audrey, holding out his hand to help her to her feet, but she just sat there and stared at him. 'He wouldn't mean to hurt you. Prince wouldn't hurt anybody. He's just playful, you see. He wants to make friends. Here Prince, here boy...now, sit!'

The dog obeyed, but Maisie dashed forward in Audrey's defence. 'You ought to look after him better'n that,' she shouted. 'He frightened my friend to death, and look, she's gone and lost all her blackberries. Come on, Audrey. Get up! See, that naughty dog's sitting still now.' Audrey scrambled to her feet, still with one eye on her attacker. 'An' I'll give you some of my blackberries,' Maisie went on, 'and so will Doris, I 'spect... But he should be on a lead.' She wagged her finger crossly at the strange boy not caring, at that moment, that he was older and bigger than she was.

An amused look crept across his face, and Doris,

at his side, was smiling too. 'This is Bruce,' she said. 'Bruce Tremaine. You know, the squire's son – Mr Tremaine that I was telling you about. That's Maisie and that's Audrey,' she continued, pointing to her two friends. 'What Bruce says is right, though. Prince won't hurt you, but he gets a bit excited sometimes. He's a collie dog – you know, a sheepdog. He's real good at rounding up the sheep, isn't he, Bruce?'

'So he is,' said the boy. 'And I'm really sorry that he frightened you…Audrey.' Then he nodded at Maisie, with a twinkle in his eye. 'Yes…Maisie, you are quite right. I should have had him on a lead. As a matter of fact, I have one here, in my pocket.' He patted at the short tweed jacket he was wearing. 'But he likes to have a run and I wasn't expecting to meet anyone. You two – you are some of our visitors, aren't you, from Leeds…or are you from Hull? I'm very pleased to meet you both. I hope you are settling down and that you will like living here.'

'We're from Leeds,' said Maisie, a little grumpily and determined not to say any more. She hadn't forgiven him for the dog frightening Audrey like that, although she had to admit that he seemed quite a decent sort of boy, as boys went, and he had called them visitors and not evacuees, which was a point in his favour. The dog, too, he seemed OK now he had settled down. Maisie tended to steer clear of boys, especially of ones who were older than herself. If she was honest, she was scared of them lest they should turn out to be like Percy. But this boy, well, she could tell at a glance that he could not be more different.

For a start, he was posh. He spoke much posher than Audrey did, or even Patience and Luke. He had no trace of what Maisie knew to be a Yorkshire accent, the way most people spoke when they came from anywhere in Yorkshire. She knew he must be a few years older than she was – say thirteen or fourteen years old – because not only was he taller, but he wore long trousers. Boys of Maisie's age wore short trousers and they did so until they were getting on for twelve years old and went on to the senior school. He was a good looking boy, too, she admitted to herself a little grudgingly. His hair was dark whereas Percy's was a sort of mucky blond colour – why did she have to compare every lad she met with Percy, she wondered? – and she thought his eyes were brown; dark anyway, and warm and kind, and he had a round cheerful face and rosy cheeks.

'I am really sorry that Prince frightened you,' he said again to Audrey, who had not spoken as yet. 'Here, give me your bowl and I'll gather some more berries for you. We'll have this full in two shakes of a lamb's tail... Where are you off to anyway, Doris?'

'Oh, just here and there,' she replied. 'I'm showing them around yer father's land. I know he won't mind. And on the way back we'll perhaps see me dad. I know he's got a field to plough this morning.'

'I'll come with you then,' said Bruce... 'Here boy, here. Now...stay!' Prince trotted over to him obediently and he fitted a lead to his collar. 'He might not like it, but I can't have him scaring our new friends. We've got a houseful, you know; mothers with their babies and toddlers. I heard one of them saying to her friend that it was as good as a holiday.' He laughed. 'Better, in fact, because she hadn't got the old man with her.'

Maisie thought again about her mother. She, too, would love it here in the countryside... But she was also listening, though pretending that she wasn't, to Bruce.

'When do you go back to school, Bruce?' Doris was asking him.

'Oh, the middle of September. I have almost two weeks left yet. Then I will be home for half-term, round about the fifth of November. Although I don't suppose there will be any bonfires or fireworks this year, worse luck. I expect we will be having some new boys at school. I've heard that there is a whole school being evacuated from somewhere near Hull, but goodness knows how they will find room for them all.'

Maisie gathered that he was away at boarding school for most of the year, like those girls she had read about in the Angela Brazil books. Billy Bunter, she supposed, was the boy's equivalent, although she hadn't read any of those. Neither had she met anyone before who went to a boarding school.

They crossed a field and came to a pond where ducks and geese were swimming around, then to a paved area inside a gate. 'This is where our pigs live,' said Bruce. 'Do you want to see them, girls? Doris is quite used to them, but you might find it a bit...you know...whiffy.' He wrinkled his nose.

'Yes, please,' said Audrey.

'Yeah...I don't mind,' said Maisie.

Bruce swung back the big wooden gate. 'Mind your feet,' he said. 'It's rather messy. You should really have your wellingtons on. Anyway, you'll remember the next time you come, won't you?' He smiled at them, and Maisie actually found herself smiling back a little.

She nodded, but she couldn't remember whether her mum had packed her wellingtons or not. She thought not, because they were shabby and a bit small for her. The ground was muddy, but only in parts, and there were places where straw had been put down so she tried to place her feet there. Audrey was not managing too well, tip-toeing around very carefully. It was a good job, though, that she had sensible lace-up shoes on today and not her fancy ankle-strap things. Even so, she was looking in some dismay at the splatters of mud on her white socks. It didn't matter about Maisie's knee length grey ones; they were full of darns anyway.

There was a wall round the pig pen and a little house at the back, and on a carpet of straw lay a huge fat pig, the biggest one Maisie had ever seen. She could not remember, in fact, ever seeing a pig at all, except for dead ones hanging up in butchers' shops. And sucking away at the pig's stomach were six or seven tiny little piglets. No – eight, she decided as another one suddenly ran out of the house at the back. There were so many she could not count them all.

'That's Ruby, our prize sow,' said Bruce. 'I shouldn't get too close, Maisie, if I were you,' he added as Maisie leaned right over the wall. 'She might think you are wanting to steal her babies.' At that moment the sow gave a loud snort, looking at her visitors with a malevolent eye. Maisie laughed, whilst Audrey jumped and took a step backwards.

'Doesn't it pong?' said Maisie, holding her nose. 'You were right, Bruce, about it being stinky.' She had used his name, for the first time, without being aware of it.

'That's rude, Maisie,' said Audrey. 'I don't suppose they can help being a bit...er...smelly.'

'That's right,' said Bruce. 'It's a smell you get used to after a while. It's just a pig smell; it's not because they're dirty. Actually, pigs are very clean animals, and they only roll in the mud when they get too hot... Isn't that so, Dad?' he said as a man came in through the gate.

'What's that, Bruce?' said the man.

'Pigs aren't dirty animals, are they? I was just telling our visitors about them.'

'Aye, that's right, lad,' he said. Maisie recognised him as the man she had seen two days ago with all the women and children getting in the shooting-brake. Of course, he was the squire, Mr Tremaine. He looked just like she imagined Bruce would look when he was a man, with the same kind brown eyes and cheerful ruddy face, although his hair was nearly all grey. To her surprise, though, he did not speak nearly so poshly as did his son.

'Hello, you lasses,' he greeted them. 'I'm glad you've brought your new friends to see us, Doris. I'm going to shoo you out of here though, now, 'cause there's work to be done. Off you go.'

He entered the pig pen though a little door. 'Hey up!' he said as he tipped the bucket he was carrying into a trough. Out fell a mass of potato peelings, carrot tops, bits of swede and turnip, all mixed up together in a sludgy gooey mess.

'Come on,' said Bruce. 'I'll show you the rest of the estate, then you can go and see Doris's dad.'

'Aye, he's over yonder,' said Mr Tremaine, waving his arm vaguely. 'Cheerio, girls. Nice to meet you. Come and see us again.'

'Bye, Mr Tremaine,' called Doris, and 'Bye...' said the other two, not knowing him well enough yet to use his name.

They went past fields where crops were growing. 'Potatoes, beetroot, carrots, swedes, brussel sprouts,' said Bruce. 'We supply the local shops, and the market, of course.'

They had gone in a full cirle and when they arrived back at the big house Bruce said goodbye to them. 'I won't invite you to come in today,' he explained. 'Mother's got her hands full at the moment with all our guests, and I don't think she would be too pleased. Another time, though.' He smiled cheerily. 'Goodbye for now, girls. See you soon.'

'He's nice, isn't he?' remarked Audrey as they walked away.

'Yeah...he's OK,' said Maisie. 'Dead posh though, isn't he?'

Doris laughed. 'I suppose so. He's started talking like that since he went to boarding school. But he's not stuck-up or anything. He's still just Bruce... Look, there's me dad; over there in that field.'

Mr Nixon was guiding a plough, pulled by two brown horses. Maisie guessed they were the ones she had seen earlier that morning. She watched, fascinated, as the blades of the plough turned over the soil, making a deep straight furrow in the earth. He stopped when he reached the end of the field nearest to the lane, but it was clear that he did not have much time to stop and chat. He spoke kindly enough, though, to his daughter and her friends.

'Finding yer way around, are you, girls? Aye, you'll soon settle down 'specially when school starts again. Run along now, Doris, there's a good lass. And tell yer mam I'll be wanting me dinner prompt at half-past twelve. You best'd go and give her a hand, hadn't you?'

'Yes...I suppose so,' said Doris to his retreating back. She looked put out that her father had not spent more time with her.

Just as Bruce resembled his father, so Maisie thought that Doris looked like hers. Mr Nixon was large and fair-haired, with blue eyes and a snub nose, like his daughter's, but which seemed too small for the rest of his plump face. Maisie did not think he looked as friendly and kind-hearted as Doris was, but it was probably because he was busy.

They had come into sight of the church tower again, and the clock said ten minutes to twelve. Doris left them with a cheery wave. 'Tara, then. See you at school on Wednesday. Hope we're all in the same class, eh? Keep yer fingers crossed.'

'Bye, Maisie,' said Audrey when they reached the village green. 'I'll have to go now and help Daisy with the dinner. Perhaps I'll see you later. Or...tomorrow, maybe.'

'Yes, I 'spect so,' said Maisie. 'Look, there's Daisy at the door.'

Audrey had lost some of her cheerfulness as they got near to the house. Maisie thought her friend had enjoyed herself this morning, apart from the incident with the dog. Now she looked a bit miserable again, although she did keep saying that Daisy was kind to her. Maisie wished they could both be together, as they had planned. But quick on the heels of that thought came another one. It was really rather nice to have Aunty Patience all to herself.

Chapter Ten

When all the children had been sorted out, Infants and Juniors, local children and those from Leeds and Hull, Maisie and Audrey found, to their relief, that they had been put into the same class. An added bonus was that their friend from the farm, Doris Nixon, was with them; also the girl from Hull, Ivy Clegg, whom they had met at Sunday School. But the greatest delight of all, especially to Maisie and Audrey, was that their teacher was to be Miss Mellodey, the one they had admired back in Armley and who had been so kind to them on the train journey.

Instead of the original three classes, there were now six classes of school children in Middlebeck. Three of them were in the school itself, two in the church hall, not very far away, and one, for the oldest children, the ten and eleven years olds, in the Village Institute at the other end of the High Street.

Miss Mellodey's class consisted of boys and girls of nine and ten years of age, the third year Juniors, or Standard Three, as it was called. During the following school year, when they went up to Standard Four, those children would be sitting for the Scholarship Examination. But there was plenty of time, as yet, to think about that. Who could tell where they might be in a year's time? The war

might well be over; they could be back in Leeds or
Hull. The children knew, as did the grown-ups, that
they could not look too far ahead. 'One day at a
time...' Maisie had heard those words spoken by
both Patience and Luke. She knew that the future
was uncertain, but the present, for her at least, was
a very happy one.

At school she had her three good friends, Audrey,
Doris and Ivy, as well as her beloved Miss
Mellodey. Their class was held in the main school,
right opposite to the rectory and next door to where
Audrey lived with Miss Thomson, so it was very
convenient for both of them. Miss Mellodey, also,
lived very near, at the schoolhouse with the
headmistress, Miss Foster. The headmistress was in
charge of an Infant class – as well as being in overall
charge of the school – and this class of younger
children met in a classroom which had been built
on to the main building, jutting out into the
playground at the back.

Maisie's classroom and the one next to it were
really one enormous room divided into two by a
wooden and glass partition. In the other half was a
class taught by Miss Bolton, who was one of the
local teachers. The system worked well enough
most of the time, except when the other class
recited their tables; one three is three, two threes are
six, three threes are nine, and so on. Or chanted
verses of poems they had learned by heart...

'I wish I lived in a caravan,
    With a horse to drive, like a pedlar man...'
But Maisie guessed it was equally distracting for the
younger children in the other half of the room when

her class repeated their tables. Except that they were doing much more difficult ones; eleven times and twelve times, they were learning now. The school was much more old-fashioned than Maisie's school back in Armley, but she had decided very quickly that she liked it much better. It was cosier and had a more friendly feeling.

She had been surprised to see that there was a fireplace in the room, although there was no fire burning in it because the weather had been very warm for the time of the year. It was surrounded by a large sturdy fireguard. How comforting it would be, she thought, to feel the warmth of a fire whilst learning your lessons.

On the wall at the front of the room, near to the teacher's large blackboard perched on an easel, there was a photograph in colour of King George the Sixth and Queen Elizabeth and, on the other side, a map of the world showing, in red, the tiny islands of Great Britain and the parts of the world over which Great Britain ruled; the British Empire. There had been little else of interest to look at, at first, but as the term progressed Miss Mellodey began to pin up the children's paintings and drawings and some coloured pictures from a teacher's magazine which she bought each month. There was one of rice fields in China and another of a tea plantation in India; they were learning about harvests in other countries across the seas as well as the more familiar Harvest Festival at home, the time of which was drawing near.

The windows were quite small and high up, almost impossible for the children to see out of, unless they were very tall. Miss Mellodey explained to them that, in the olden days, children had not been encouraged to gaze out of windows; they had to keep their minds on their work and day-dreamng was frowned upon. But it did not matter too much because the view from the windows was a familiar one of the village green and the church, or, at the back, of the school playground. Besides, Miss Mellodey took them once a week for a nature walk through the lanes and fields nearby. She taught them the names of the different trees and wild flowers and birds they saw, and they watched the scene around them gradually changing from summer to autumn.

Miss Mellodey's desk stood on a little raised platform at the front of the room from where she had a good view of what all the children were doing. Not that she was strict or given to bouts of shouting, like Miss Patterdale had been. All the same, her pupils obeyed her, mainly because they liked her so much.

There were large wooden cupboards with glass doors around the walls, where the exercise books and some dusty ancient-looking volumes were kept, but Miss Mellodey had soon added her own collection of story books; *Peter Pan*, *The Wind in the Willows*, the fairy stories of Grimm and Hans Anderson, *Treasure Island* and *Gulliver's Travels*. The children soon began to look forward to Friday afternoon as the highlight of the week, for it was then that Miss Mellodey would read to them from a favourite book. It was *The Wind in the Willows* at the moment, and she really made the characters of Ratty, Mole and Mister Toad come alive by speaking in their different voices.

But before that, on Fridays, they all had to tidy their desks, throwing out any rubbish that had collected there during the week, and polishing their own desk lid with a scrap of material and a dab of polish put on by the monitor. The desks were double ones, old and scarred with scratches and pen-knife carvings of intials of bygone pupils. There were two ink-wells and a groove along the top where they could rest their pens. The children of Standard Three were just learning to use pens and ink instead of pencils. They did 'real writing' too, instead of printing, but Maisie and Audrey had already learned that in Standard Two back in Armley.

Maisie's desk partner was not Audrey – Miss Mellodey had thought it was better to mix them up so that they could get to know one another better – but Ivy Clegg, the girl from Hull, and they soon got on together very well. Audrey was in the desk next to them with Doris Nixon, and the four of them became firm friends.

Her previous life in Armley sometimes seemed very far away and unreal. She remembered to say a prayer each night for her mother and her little brother and sister, with Aunty Patience prompting her; but there were times during her busy new life in Middlebeck when she almost forgot about them. Her mother wrote to her every week, and she wrote back; but although Lily kept saying she would come and see her and bring Joanie and Jimmy, she did not make a definite date for her visit. Neither did she mention Sid or Percy, except to say that Maisie hadn't to worry about her because she was all right.

Maisie was a little surprised, as the weeks went by, that Audrey's mother did not come to see her either. Audrey said it was her father who had written to her, telling her that her mum had not been too well and had had to stay in bed for a while, but that she was now 'on the mend' and hoped to see her soon.

One day in every week, usually on Wednesday or Thursday, when it was Daisy's day off, Audrey came across the road to have her tea with Maisie. Patience always cooked them something tasty, like sausages and mash, or bacon, beans and chips, knowing that Audrey had only had a sandwich lunch, eaten on the school premises.

There was no school kitchen as there was in some of the bigger town schools, because all the children lived near enough to go home at lunchtime. If they – or their parents – chose, however, they could take sandwiches with them to eat at school, saving their little bottles of 'school milk' to drink then rather than at the mid-morning playtime. The teachers each took a turn at looking after the 'sandwich eaters' and supervising their play afterwards in the school yard.

Patience had insisted that Maisie should go home each day for a cooked meal, especially as the school was so near. Sometimes Luke dined with them, or if he was busy on church business he would just have a snack and he and Patience would dine together later in the evening. At all events, Maisie was enjoying nourishing food and was already putting on weight and looking much healthier than she had when she first arrived.

Patience had assumed that Audrey, also, would go home – if, indeed, the little girl regarded it as 'home'? Patience wondered about that – but she learned, to her surprise, that the child was taking sandwiches, made each morning by Daisy.

'Your friend is quite happy, is she, living over there with Miss Thomson?' she sometimes enquired of Maisie.

'Yes…she's OK,' Maisie always answered. 'In fact she likes it much better than I thought she would, Aunty Patience.'

Patience did not wish to pry too much or to put the idea into Maisie's head that Audrey might be unhappy. According to Maisie, the little girl had settled down and although she did not see very much of Miss Thomson, she was quite happy because she had Daisy as her companion. All the same, Patience was a little disturbed by the situation and knew she must keep an eye on what was happening across the road.

Maisie, also, was concerned about her friend. There were things that Patience did not know about because they happened at school. She and Audrey had always been amongst the cleverest children in their class in Armley, the ones to come top or nearly top in exams, and in the weekly spelling and mental arithmetic tests. But here, in Miss Mellodey's class, it seemed as though Audrey was falling behind.

Maisie had soon realised that the girls and boys

from Leeds and Hull were, on the whole, slightly more advanced in their scholastic achievements than their counterparts in Middlebeck. For instance, they could already do proper joined-up writing and they were further on with their arithmetic and reading. Not all of them, of course – some of the Middlebeck children were clever – but Maisie and Audrey had soon shown themselves to be the bright stars of Standard Three. Miss Mellodey had made no comment about this, which Maisie thought was right and very fair of her.

But Audrey had obviously not learned the spellings for the last test and she had only got seven out of ten which, for her, was a very poor mark. And in a mental arithmetic test, which was something you could not learn in advance, she had done even worse. Neither did she seem concerned that she, Maisie, had got ten out of ten in both tests. Audrey looked tired and sometimes her pale face looked even whiter because of the grey shadows beneath her eyes. And Maisie had noticed, but had not commented upon, the grime underneath her friend's finger nails. Audrey, though, had seen her looking at them and had quickly hidden her hands behind her back.

'Yeah, they're mucky, aren't they?' she said with an ashamed little smile. 'It's with washing the spuds. I do 'em to help Daisy...'

Maisie guessed that Audrey was doing too many jobs to help Daisy. She knew, for instance, that she often made her own sandwiches in the morning and quite regularly washed up after eating her evening meal, still taken with Daisy in the kitchen. And another thing she had noticed was that Audrey was starting to talk like Daisy, whereas she, Maisie, following Patience's example, was speaking much more correctly.

But she had not admitted her fears about Audrey to Aunty Patience. She kept telling her that her friend was all right. She felt a little bit guilty about that...but it was so nice living in the rectory, just herself, with Luke and Patience. It made her feel rather ashamed of herself...but she did not want to share them, not even with Audrey.

Anne Mellodey was happy in Middlebeck, as happy as she could be, that was, away from her beloved Bill. He wrote every week, sometimes more than once, telling her that he loved her, that he was missing her and counting the days until they could meet. He was not sure when that might be, but he hoped he might be able to get a forty-eight hour pass to coincide with her half-term break from school. Then maybe he could come to Middlebeck to see her? He hoped she could find him somewhere to stay? She hadn't broached the subject with Miss Foster – Charity – yet, but she hoped her colleague would allow him to stop at the schoolhouse. Sleeping on the settee downstairs, of course; or if Charity considered that that was not really the right thing to do, then there would surely be someone in the little town who had a room to spare.

Bill said very little about his training; it was an official secret, she supposed. But reading between the lines she gathered he was looking forward to the time when he would have his wings and pilot his own plane. Anne dreaded this happening and prayed continually that there would be an end to the conflict before this should take place.

There was certainly no sign, in the north Yorkshire countryside, that the country was at war, nor even, she gathered from her letters from her mother, in the busy cities. The German bombs that everyone had anticipated would fall from the skies as soon as war was declared had not materialised. The autumn of 1939 was being called the 'Bore War'. The people of Great Britain had lived with the threat of war hanging over them for so long that there was, now, nothing more than a feeling of anti-climax.

There were petty irritations to endure though, the chief one being the blackout; but folks who lived in the country were well used to the darkness and to finding their way around the lanes with the aid of a torch. Anne did not often go out at night, only occasionally to meet her friend, Dorothy Cousins, the other teacher from Armley. Dorothy had become more of a friend rather than just a colleague, as the two of them had been thrown together in this new experience. For the rest of the time she was content to stay at home of an evening, enjoying the restful company and the words of wisdom of her new friend, Charity, or listening to their favourite programmes on the wireless. They both enjoyed 'It's that Man Again' with Tommy Handley, usually known as ITMA, Monday Night at Eight, and Garrison Theatre. It was not a very exciting life, she sometimes thought, for a young woman of twenty-four, but Anne was of an optimistic disposition, determined to make the most of this new challenge. She knew she was only one of thousands who had been forced to leave their homes and loved ones in these uncertain times.

In some ways it was good to be away from the confines of her home in Leeds. She had been happy enough living with her parents; however, as an only child, she had been starting to feel their care and protectiveness of her rather stifling, especially since she had met Bill. Apart from her two years away at college – and, even then, she had been only a matter of a few miles away, in Bingley – this was the first chance she had had to spread her wings a little.

She had always enjoyed teaching, and she was finding that being in charge of this class of children from both the town and the country was very rewarding. She could not help feeling gratified that the pupils from Armley could more than hold their own with the rest of the class. In some subjects, indeed, they were further advanced – a matter for self-congratulation – but she had the wisdom not to make any comment about this, either to the children or to the teachers at Middlebeck.

She knew that, in many things, the town children had a great deal to learn; and so had she. Until coming to live here Anne had had little notion about such things as animal farming or the growing of crops, or about the wealth of beauty and wonder to be found in the countryside that surrounded them, there in Middlebeck. The weekly nature rambles that she had instigated were as much for the benefit of Anne herself as for the children. They

did not realise – or maybe the brightest of them did?
– that she was only one step ahead of them, having
swotted up the night before about the names of
flowers, trees and birds. It was a good ruse to say,
when unsure, 'Now, can anyone tell me the name of
this tree?' (or plant, or flower). There was always
someone who knew for certain; and so Anne, along
with her pupils, was gradually learning the lore of
the countryside and to appreciate the joy of living
there.

Something she knew would long remain in her
memory was the celebration of the Harvest Festival
in the parish church of St Bartholomew's. Anne had
not been a regular churchgoer at home, although
she had been confirmed and had attended
occasionally with her mother on such occasions as
Easter or Christmas. But in Middlebeck it appeared
that it was considered the correct thing for the
school teachers to do, especially as the school was
still partly governed by the church. Charity
attended morning worship each Sunday and so
Anne, as a matter of course, started to go along
with her.

There was something about the interior of the
little church that made you feel reverent and
respectful as soon as you entered. The stone arches
and pillars, the dark oaken pews and pulpit, and the
subtle hues of the stained glass windows were all
redolent of a bygone age; indeed, parts of the
church, Anne had been told, dated from the
fourteenth century. It smelled faintly musty, but not
unpleasant, and the chill emanating from the stone
walls – how cold it must have been in days gone by!

– was relieved by the gentle warmth which came up through the grilles on the stone floor. You could not help but be aware of the aura left behind by thousands and thousands of past worshippers in this small place, and the feeling was strangely humbling.

The Reverend Luke Fairchild was just the right rector for such a church, so Anne thought. He could relate both to the young and to the not so young in his parish. His sincerity and the love of the God he served radiated from him, but he was aware, too, of the day-to-day worries and fears of his flock, especially in the present uncertain times. They all knew they could go to him with their problems, both great and small.

At Harvest Festival time the church was ablaze with colour and full of the rich ripe fragrance of fruit, vegetables and flowers, the harvest of the fields and gardens, which completely masked the usual musky, slightly dusty, ages old aroma. Apples, red, green and russet; oranges and yellow grapefruit; pears, plums, purple damsons, and bunches of grapes, both black and green, filled every window ledge and corner. There was a cornucopia of fruit of every kind at one side of the altar, and at the other side an enormous sheaf of corn. The abundance of flowers – late roses, michelmas daisies, dahlias, chrysanthemums and wild flowers from the hedgerows – overflowed from vases, pots, bowls and even jam jars. The children brought their own gifts – some large, in baskets done up with ribbons, some small, maybe just a couple of apples or pears – and laid them on the chancel steps. The congregation sang,

> 'Come ye thankful people, come,
> Raise the song of Harvest Home...'

They had much to be thankful for, the rector reminded them. God was merciful and bountiful and He would always provide for them... But they knew, certainly the more perceptive adults amongst them did, that in a year's time the situation might be very different. The war was in its infancy, but already there were rumours of rationing, and of digging up precious flower gardens for the cultivation of vegetable crops. And in many hearts the joyousness of the occasion was tinged with sadness and a fear for what the future might hold.

Anne had noticed, as teachers do, the friendships that were forming in her class, particularly amongst the girls. Girls were always more clannish than boys, forming little cliques of like-minded souls, whereas boys were more free and easy, making friends with – or sometimes fighting with – anyone who happened to take their fancy. A foursome that had developed was that of the two girls from Armley, Maisie Jackson and Audrey Dennison, the local girl, Doris Nixon, and Ivy Clegg, a rather shy girl from Hull. It was for this reason, because she had sensed the shyness of Ivy, that Anne had suggested she should share a desk with Maisie. She had met Maisie and Audrey on the journey from Leeds and had been touched by Maisie's care of her new friend; she was pleased, now, that they were in her class. Audrey seemed happy enough sitting next to Doris, the pleasant good-natured girl from the farm. An interesting foursome, each of them differing both in looks and personality, but finding in one another qualities they liked and that made them want to be friends.

Anne was not quite so happy about another foursome which had formed. She tried hard to like all the children equally and to have no favourites, but teachers were only human. Besides, teachers learned to pick out instinctively the ones that might be the 'bad apples in the crop'. And it was amazing how quickly such girls – and they were usually girls, not boys – discovered one another. She had noticed Esme Clough back in Armley, a troublemaker who picked on the younger children in the school yard and who, according to some other members of staff, was a cheat and a telltale. But Anne preferred to find out such things for herself rather than listen to staff room gossip. Esme had soon become pally with two local girls, Gertrude Flint and Norma Wilkins, although Norma seemed to be in thrall to her more dominant friend. This trio had soon been joined by a girl called Paula Jeffries, one of the Hull evacuees.

For some reason – although, as Anne knew, there did not always need to be a reason – this quartet seemd to dislike the other four girls. She had seen the 'Gertie foursome' – which is how she thought of them, Gertrude Flint seeming to be the leader – jeering and pointing at the 'Maisie foursome' in the playground; and there were nudges and snide glances exchanged – which Anne, so far, had chosen not to comment upon – whenever one of the others, usually Maisie, did well in a class test.

Ivy Clegg had a little brother, Timothy, who was in the Infant class, taught by Miss Foster in the annexe classroom. He was a dear little boy, but rather an unprepossessing one. He had pale sandy hair like that of his sister, spindly legs and bony knees, and wire-framed spectacles from which his pale blue eyes looked out like a frightened baby owl. Fortunately, he had been housed with Ivy at the home of a gentle elderly couple and his big sister did her best to look after him, but he did not appear to have made any friends, so far, at school.

He tried to cling to his sister at playtimes, but Ivy, understandably, wanted to play with her own friends, and she would sometimes tell him to go and play with his own classmates and leave her alone. Anne noticed one such incident when she was on playground duty.

Ivy and her three friends were playing a skipping game; two of them were holding the ends of the rope and the other two were taking turns at jumping in and chanting,

'Jelly on a plate, jelly on a plate,
   Wibble wobble, wibble wobble, jelly on
   a plate...'

They had just got to the 'sausage in a pan' chorus when Timothy appeared, running towards Ivy who was holding one end of the rope. He cannoned into her and made her drop her end.

'Oh, look what you've gone and done,' she cried. 'Do go away, our Timothy. You're spoiling our game. An' it's my turn to skip an' all. See, there's a little boy over there who's on his own. Go and play with him.'

'Don't want to! I want to stay with you,' said Timothy, sniffing, then wiping his sleeve across his damp nose.

'Aw, let him stay,' said Maisie. 'He's not doing any harm. Let him watch.'

'No! He'll only spoil it,' replied Ivy.

The other four girls, led by Gertie Flint, were watching the incident with interest.

'Aw, diddums!' said Gertie. 'Isn't he sweet? I wish I had a little brother like that. I wouldn't be nasty with him, would you Esme?'

'No,' said Esme. 'Would I heck as like! You come and play with us, Timothy.'

'Yeah, you come 'ere, an' I'll give yer one o' my pear drops,' said Paula, the girl from Hull. 'Yer sister's dead mean, i'n't she, telling yer to go away.'

'But we'll let yer play, Timothy…'

The little boy looked uncertain for a moment, then he shook his head. 'No…don't want to,' he said.

The foursome went away shrieking with laughter, and Anne, who had guessed that their gesture of friendliness was not sincere, decided to intervene. 'Come along, Timothy,' she said. 'Let the big girls finish their skipping game. We'll go and talk to that little boy, shall we? He's all on his own.'

Timothy looked up at her, then he smiled shyly and put his hand into hers. 'He's called Peter,' he said.

The little ones sometimes liked the security of holding the teacher's hand at playtime. The school yard could be a noisy and intimidating place to children of a more nervous disposition, although, usually, they quite soon became used to the din and often boisterous behaviour. Peter was another lonely little boy that Anne had noticed. Perhaps the two of them just needed a little encouragement to make friends.

'Do you two know one another?' she asked, stooping down to talk to the dark-haired, rather plump little boy. 'I expect you do.'

'Yeah...we're in Miss Foster's class,' replied Peter. 'He's a 'vacuee...' He pointed at Timothy, 'but I live 'ere. I've only just come back to school, though. I've been ill, y'see, and there's all different kids in our class now. We've all been mixed up, like.'

'That's so you can get to know one another,' said Anne. 'Perhaps you and Timothy could be friends. What do you think about that?'

The two little boys looked at one another seriously for a moment, then Peter nodded. 'Aye, p'raps we could,' he said.

Timothy nodded too, but a little unsurely. 'Yes...all right,' he said.

'Come on, Timothy,' said Peter. 'Come over 'ere an' I'll show you summat. I've got a reight big conker in me pocket. D'yer want to see it?'

Timothy nodded again, and as he was starting to smile a little Anne decided to leave them to it. But she sensed that the situation might need watching. Little Timothy Clegg was just the sort of child who attracted the attention of teasers and bullies, and his big sister was not one who would find it easy to defend him. But she was reluctant to say anything to Miss Foster lest the older teacher should think she was interfering. After all, the two little boys in question were in her class and were, largely, her responsibility.

But it was Charity who mentioned the incident, and not Anne. Charity had been watching the playground scene from her classroom window, as she often did. 'You've worked wonders with little Timothy Clegg,' she said, as they were having their evening meal. 'I saw it all through the window.' She laughed. 'Yes, I'm an old busy-body, aren't I?'

'I think I'm the busybody, not you,' replied Anne. 'I hope you didn't think I was sticking my nose in. They are your pupils.'

'Not at all, dear,' said Charity. 'Timothy has been rather a problem. I put him to sit with a local boy, Joey, and asked him to look after him, but they didn't seem to hit it off at all. I think Joey thought he was a 'softie'. So then I put him with a rather fussy little girl – you know the type; a motherly little soul – but that wasn't much better; but I didn't want to move him again. Anyway, he and Peter Harris came running in as thick as thieves, and I thought, 'Yes! This is it.' I don't know why I hadn't thought about it before. Peter's been off with bronchitis; he suffers with his chest, poor little lad, and he's a bit of a loner as well. So, we've had a move round – again – and now they are sitting together, as happy as Larry. Thank you, my dear. Do you know, sometimes one can't see what is right under one's nose... Now...' Charity's eyes twinkled. 'Didn't you say you had something to ask me, Anne? Might it be something to do with that young man of yours?'

She listened quietly, smiling to herself; then, rather to Anne's surprise, she agreed that Bill could stay for the night when he came to Middlebeck. And he would not need to sleep on the settee as she had a camp bed for such emergencies. He was due to come in a fortnight's time, the first weekend in November.

Chapter Eleven

'Audrey, will you do summat for me?' asked Daisy. 'A big favour, like...'

It was a Saturday morning in mid-November and the two of them were washing up the breakfast pots.

'Yes, I s'pose so. What is it you want then?' Audrey guessed it might be peeling the potatoes or scrubbing the carrots whilst Daisy went to the grocer's down the High Streeet, which she often did on a Saturday morning. But she didn't usually ask, taking it for granted that Audrey would perform her usual chores; she certainly wouldn't refer to it as a big favour.

'Well, it's a bit – what shall I say? – difficult, like. You know, Audrey, don't yer, about my 'intended'...' That was how Daisy often referred to Andy Cartwright, her young man who farmed for Mr Tremaine.

'Yer boyfriend? Yes, course I know him,' replied Audrey. She had met him on the day when Doris had showed her and Maisie round the estate, and she had seen him several times since then when he came to call for Daisy on her half day off. He always waited outside, though; Miss Thomson would not allow him to set foot inside the house.

'Well, he's been called up, has Andy. He's got his

papers an' he's got to go on Monday. I'm seeing him tonight, after I've finished here.'

'So you want me to finish off the pots so you can get off early? Is that it? Yeah…I don't mind, Daisy. But I don't want to get into trouble with Miss Thomson. Does she know you want to go out?'

'She can't stop me, can she? I can do as I like, so long as I've done me work here. No…it weren't acksherly about the washing-up. It's summat more important than that. You know how I've always to be in by half-past nine, don't yer? Even when it's me proper day off she insists I get in early. Then she makes a great to-do about locking t' door and making sure the bolts are on an' all that…'

'Ye…es,' said Audrey, a shade doubtfully. She was always in bed by that time and usually asleep. If Daisy was going out for the evening, which she was allowed to do occasionally, then Miss Thomson made a great concession by allowing Audrey to sit with her in the dining room at the back of the house, the only room, apart from the kitchen, where there was a lighted fire. Audrey much preferred to be in the kitchen with Daisy; it was always warm in there with the coals constantly glowing in the big black range; the rest of the house was decidedly chilly now that autumn was here.

'Well…' said Daisy. 'What I want you to do is this. When Miss Thomson's gone to sleep – you'll know she's asleep 'cause you'll hear her snoring – I want you to sneak down and pull the bolt back on the front door…then I can stay out late, y'see. Don't worry; I'll push it back when I come in. She'll never know… What's up? Don't yer want to do it? She'll not find out, not if we're dead careful.'

'But it doesn't make sense, what you're saying,' replied Audrey. 'She'll know you're not in when she locks up, won't she? She never locks the doors, neither the front or the back, until she's heard you come in. That's what you told me...'

'Aye, that's right, but I'm going to be real crafty, like. I shall come in through the back door and shout goodnight to 'er, like I always do – she never gets up off her backside to say goodnight back to me anyroad – an' then I shall sneak off out again. She'll think I'm upstairs in me little room, but I won't be. I'll be with Andy. I can't leave him at half-past nine, not when he's going away on Monday, an' I shan't see him again for God knows how long. Please, Audrey; you'll do it won't yer? Just for me. Aw, go on, please...'

Audrey knew that Daisy was not 'the sharpest knife in the drawer'; that was an expression she had heard her mother use and she understood perfectly what it meant. Daisy did not always apply a great deal of common sense to what she said, and this idea, to Audrey, appeared to be full of holes.

'But...how will you get in?' she said. 'It's not just the bolt, is it? The door's locked with a key. And you haven't got a key...have you?'

'Ah, that's where you're wrong,' said Daisy, grinning. 'There's a spare one, you know...'

'But she'll notice if you take it. Anyway, how would you get hold of it? D'you know where she keeps it? No...' Audrey shook her head emphatically. 'It won't work. She probably keeps it in her handbag.'

Daisy laughed. 'That's where you're wrong, see. She keeps it in a little tray on 'er dressing table. An' I borrowed it one day when she were out at her whist drive. I knew she'd be gone ages, so I went down to t' cobblers in t' market hall – he cuts keys as well as mending shoes – an' he made me another as fast as anything. So now I've got me own key, and old Amelia knows nowt about it.'

'But...you know how she makes me go to bed at nine o' clock? An' I don't know what time you'll be coming in, do I? I might've gone to sleep...'

'Yer don't have to wait till just before I come in, silly! It'll be late anyroad.'

'Why? Where are you going? What are you going to do?'

Diasy grinned and tapped at her nose with her forefinger. 'Mind yer own business, kid,' she said, but not unkindly. 'Never you mind what I'll be doing... You want to know where I'm going? To Andy's probably. His mam'll make us a fire in t' front room, but I daresn't stay out all night or else t' fat really would be in t' fire. I'll come back...oh, about one o' clock, I reckon. It's just so as Andy and me can have a bit more time together.'

Audrey looked solemnly at her. She liked Daisy a lot, even though the young woman made her do a lot of jobs around the house – well, not exactly forced her to, but more or less expected that she would – and she wanted to do something to help her. It was real romantic, she thought, Daisy wanting to see her young man for the last time before he joined the army.

'Are you going to say yes, then?' asked Daisy.

'Please, please, Audrey! I'll be ever so quiet when I come in, and old Amelia sleeps like a log. She'll be dead to the world till I wake 'er up with 'er cup of tea in t' morning. I'll have to make sure I'm up meself, mind.' She giggled. 'I'll only get four or five hours at t'most if I set my alarm for six, like I usually do. Still, ne'er mind, eh? It'll be worth it.'

Audrey started to smile a little unsurely, her blue eyes wide as she considered the audacity and the possible dangers of Daisy's plan. But it was so romantic, just like something you read in a book. 'All right,' she said. 'I'll do it for you, Daisy.'

The young woman flung her arms round her. 'Gosh, thanks kid! You're a little luv, honest you are.'

'I shall have to keep awake meself though,' said Audrey. 'I shall read under the bedclothes with me torch. I do sometimes when I can't get to sleep. And then I'll creep down and listen outside Miss Thomson's door to hear if she's snoring.'

She giggled a little, too, beginning to be caught up in the excitement of the plot; but part of her was scared and somewhat unwilling because she knew that it was deceitful. Audrey had always been taught to behave correctly and not to tell lies; and this was just as bad as lying. It was being sneaky and dishonest and she knew that her mother would not like it at all. Neither, she suspected, would that nice Mrs Fairchild who looked after Maisie. Audrey liked Mrs Fairchild and she thought Maisie was very lucky to be staying there with her and the rector; he was lovely, too. She had to try very hard to hide her feelings of envy for her friend's situation; but she knew that, back home in Armley, Maisie had had a pretty rotten time with her awful step-father and -brother, so she did deserve some happiness now. And she, Audrey, had not fared too badly... Daisy had said she had to think of her as a big sister, and that was very nice; she had always wished she had a sister or a brother.

'You're sure it'll be OK, aren't you?' she asked now. 'I mean...nothing'll go wrong?'

'No, how can it?' said Daisy. 'Don't worry; it'll be OK. Look, I'll let you off peeling t' spuds this morning, seeing as 'ow you're going to 'elp me. Off you go now and see young Maisie. Not a word though, mind, not to anyone...'

'No, of course not,' said Audrey.

She put on her coat and woolly hat and walked across the village green, deep in thought. She was remembering that last weekend, when she and Maisie, together with their other friends, Ivy and Doris, had been shopping in the High Street, they had met Miss Mellodey, arm in arm with a handsome airman. The couple had just been coming out of Woolworth's and Miss Mellodey had stopped to speak to them and not hurried away as though she hadn't seen them, as Audrey guessed some teachers might do, especially if they were with their boyfriend.

'Hello girls,' she had said, smiling happily at them. 'This is my fiancé, Bill. Bill, this is Audrey, and Maisie, and Ivy, and Doris; four of my very special girls.' She had actually told him all their names, and he had smiled and said, 'Hello there;

I'm very pleased to meet you all.'

Miss Mellodey's blue eyes had sparkled with delight and with what Audrey – and the other girls, talking about it afterwards – had decided was 'the light of love'. Maisie said she had read that somewhere in a book, and they all thought it was dead romantic. They had felt so glad for Miss Mellodey, but sad as well because they knew Bill had only come to see her for a short while, and then he would be going back again, learning to fly an aeroplane or whatever he was doing. When they had gone back to school after the half-term holiday Audrey had fancied that their teacher had looked a bit unhappy, but she was just as pleasant and kind to them as ever.

And Daisy was another young woman who would soon be saying goodbye to the young man she loved. Yes…Audrey nodded to herself. Maybe it would not be so very wrong to help her.

—

Every Saturday, usually in the afternoon, the four friends would meet in Middlebeck and have a little wander around the market or their favourite store, Woolworth's. It was getting dark now, though, by teatime, as winter was fast approaching. The market stalls packed up early and the shops closed because they were not allowed to let any lights shine out into the darkness. For fear of enemy aircraft, everyone said, although there was still no sign of them anywhere in the country. So the girls had started to meet in the morning instead of the afternoon. They were all allowed a small amount of pocket money, often referred to as 'Saturday pennies'. To Maisie's surprise – and to Audrey's too – her friend, Audrey, had been allowed some spending money from the normally stingy Miss Thomson. It was one of the high spots of the week, to all of them, as they deliberated whether to buy liquorice shoelaces, or aniseed balls, or pear drops; or maybe some new hair slides or a sixpenny book or toy from Woolie's.

The twice weekly market – it was held on Wednesdays as well as Saturdays – was a real delight. The farmers and market gardeners from the surrounding area gathered there to sell their produce. There were fruits and vegetables of different varieties, and gaily coloured flowers, many of them specially grown in hothouses. The pungent aroma of ripe apples, cabbages, onions, large Jaffa oranges – those were from overseas, of course – and musky mop-headed chrysanthemums scented the air.

But it was the sweet stalls that appealed to the girls, and week after week they watched the lady at the homemade toffee stall breaking the slabs of treacle and butterscotch toffee into small pieces with a little silver hammer; or cutting the delicious fudges into bite-sized chunks. But the trouble was that you didn't get very many pieces in two ounces or for a precious threepenny bit. They found that their money went further at the other woman's stall. She had tiny scented floral gums in jewel-bright colours – there were dozens of those to the ounce; dolly mixtures, jelly babies, sherbert lemons, humbugs, Yorkshire mixtures – too many varieties to count them all – and penny chews of all kinds of flavours. The bright pink spearmint was Maisie's favourite and this was what she opted for that day; a spearmint chew and a sherbet fountain with a stick of liquorice to dip into it.

'Come on, what are you going to choose?' she said to Audrey when she had given her own pennies to the stall lady. Her friend was dawdling around and she seemed very quiet that morning, as though she had something on her mind.

'Er...I'll have the same as you I think,' said Audrey. She often fell in with Maisie's ideas.

'Well, hurry up then. The others are waiting for us.'

'I'll have one of them, and one of them,' said Audrey, pointing at the sweets and handing over her money; but she appeared to be taking very little interest in her purchases.

Ivy and Doris had gone over to the toy stall where there were all kinds of items for only a few pence, as well as much more expensive toys, like model trains and dolls and teddy bears. There were tiny celluloid dolls, complete with a bath – although those were really for very little girls; packets of marbles, whips and tops, skipping ropes, puzzles with silver balls that you had to get into the holes, yo-yos, colouring and magic painting books... After staring, mesmerised, for several moments Ivy chose a kaleidescope that you could peer into and watch the changing patterns, and Doris a skipping rope with shiny red handles. And Maisie found she had just enough money left to buy a little notebook with a picture of a dog – she thought it looked like Bruce's dog, Prince – on the cover and a tiny pencil tucked into the spine. She loved the thrill of writing on the first page of a new notebook.

'Are you going to buy something else, Audrey?' she asked. 'You've got some money left, haven't you?' To Maisie, money was there to be spent, when you were fortunate enough to have some.

'No; I think I'll save it till next week,' said Audrey, carefully putting her purse back into her shoulder bag.

Whatever is the matter with her today? thought Maisie. Something was up, that was for sure. Perhaps she would tell her, Maisie, when they had parted from the other two; because Audrey was still her special friend.

Doris's mother had a stall there, too, selling farm produce; homemade cheese and butter, jams, marmalades, pickles and chutneys, and new-laid eggs. The crumbly pale yellow cheese had a distinctive tangy odour and Maisie always sniffed appreciatively when they drew near to the stall. They usually went there last and had a chat with Mrs Nixon, between customers, because the stall was a very busy one. And then Doris sometimes stayed there to help her mother, as she said she was going to do that morning.

Maisie had been entrusted with the task of buying a few items from this stall. Patience had a weekly order at a little local grocery store, in preference to the larger Maypole shop; but she liked to patronize the Nixons' market stall as well, especially as Mr and Mrs Nixon were parishioners of St Bartholomew's church, Walter also being the leading baritone singer in the choir.

'Aunty Patience wants half a dozen eggs, please,' said Maisie, 'and half a pound of best butter and six ounces of cheese.'

'Of course, mi'dear,' said Mrs Nixon, smiling at her. 'Six big brown eggs, new laid this morning. Be careful you don't break 'em, mind.' She put them into a cardboard container and popped them into the wicker shopping basket that Maisie was carrying. 'And here's your butter...' That was already packaged in greaseproof paper. 'An' I'll cut you a nice piece of cheese.'

Maisie watched with interest as the wire cutter sliced into the huge round slab of cheese and Mrs Nixon cut off a triangular portion. She placed it on the scales. 'There we are now. A good guess, or as near as makes no difference. Six and three quarter ounces to be exact, but I'll just charge you for six, like Mrs Fairchild said.'

'Thank you very much,' said Maisie. 'I love your eggs. We have 'em for breakfast on Sunday morning with bacon and fried bread.'

'Mmm...yum yum!' exclaimed Doris. 'You're making me feel hungry already. What's in our butties for lunch, Mam?'

'Cheese and pickle, and home-cured ham,' replied her mother laughing. 'It's a wonder you're not as big as an elephant the amount you manage to put away! Honestly, girls, she eats us out of house and home.' Doris, indeed, did look very well fed and she had put on quite a few pounds since Maisie had first met her. She resembled her father who was large and fair-haired with a florid face, and not her mother at all. Mrs Nixon was thin and wiry and dark-haired, but she had muscular arms with all the work she did on the farm.

'You'd best make the most of it, all of you,' Mrs Nixon went on, 'because we don't know how soon they will start putting stuff on ration. We've heard rumours and it's sure to come, sooner rather than later. And then t' Government'll step in I suppose and tell us what we have to do with our eggs and butter and meat an' all that. Aye; I reckon we'll all be issued with ration books afore long... But there's no point in you young lasses worrying yer heads about it all. Let us grown-ups do the worrying, eh? You try to enjoy yerselves while you can.'

She beamed at them, and Maisie decided that she liked Mrs Nixon very much, far more than she liked Doris's dad. She had only met him a few times, but he always seemed to be shouting, not always because he was cross, but because he had a loud voice and liked to make himself heard, as he did when he was singing in the church choir; you could hear his voice above all the other men. Maisie thought he was impatient and short-tempered too, and she wondered how he treated his wife; because he reminded her, just a little bit, of Sid. She hoped that he did not behave towards Mrs Nixon anything like as badly as Sid did with her mum. She thought that Doris's mum, Ada, sometimes looked tired, the same as she remembered Lily, her own mother, had used to look. But it was probably because she worked so hard on the farm and had to get up very early in the mornings.

Mrs Nixon had said that they had to let the grown-ups do the worrying, but children often worried about things as well. She, Maisie, was still anxious about her mother and was still waiting for her to come on a visit to Middlebeck, as she had promised she would. And something was certainly troubling Audrey that day...

'Off you pop now, you three,' said Mrs Nixon. 'Doris is going to stay and help me, and you'd best be getting home for your dinners, hadn't you? Cheerio then; see you again soon...'

Ivy lived in the opposite direction from Maisie and Audrey, so they said goodbye to her and set off for their homes in Church Square. Audrey was still quiet, shuffling along instead of walking briskly, and staring distractedly down at her feet.

'What's up?' asked Maisie. 'I know there's summat the matter, 'cause I'm your friend, aren't I? And best friends always know when there's something wrong, don't they?'

'Oh...it's nothing much,' replied Audrey.

'Are you upset about your mum not coming to see you? I am, a bit, about mine,' said Maisie. 'She keeps on saying she'll come, and then she doesn't.'

'No, it's not really that,' said Audrey. 'I was upset when me dad said she was poorly, but he says she's feeling a lot better now, and she'll come up here before Christmas if she can manage it.'

'What was the matter with her? Do you know?'

'No...they don't always tell us everything, do they, grown-ups?'

'Not always, no...' But if Maisie thought there was a problem she was like a dog with a bone. 'Well, what is it then, if it's not your mum that you're worried about?'

'You're dead nosey, you, aren't you?' said Audrey, grinning a little. 'I'm not supposed to say, 'cause it's not my secret, y' see; it's Daisy's... Oh, I don't suppose it matters. I might as well tell you, so long as you promise not to say anything to Mrs Fairchild.'

''Course I won't,' said Maisie. 'Cross my heart and hope to die... Come on, what is it?' Her eyes were as big as saucers as she began to imagine a really romantic explanation. 'What's Daisy goin' to do then? Is she goin' to elope and get married to that Andy from the farm?'

'No...not exactly,' said Audrey. 'I think they will get married though, sometime, 'cause she calls him her 'intended'. No; she wants to stay out a lot longer with him tonight, so she wants me to unbolt the door...' She explained about the front door and the lock and the extra key, and about Miss Thomson's insistence on the bolts being on, whilst Maisie listened, goggle-eyed.

'Gosh, that's dead exciting!' she said. 'It's like summat that you read about in books. Y'know; those girls at boarding school that are always having adventures. But this is more serious, like, isn't it, 'cause it's grown-ups, not kids? An' have you said you'll do it?'

'Yes; she's been real kind to me has Daisy. I didn't like to say no. She'll be in awful trouble, though, if Miss Thomson finds out, and so will I.'

'You'll not get found out,' said Maisie convincingly. She was quite enthralled by the secrecy and daring of it all. She knew, of course, that she was not the one having to take the risks.

Audrey was quick to remind her of that.

'It's all right for you, isn't it? It's me that has to do it... And I'm dead scared, Maisie, honest I am.'

'You'll be OK,' said Maisie. 'Just act ordinary, like, or Miss Thomson might guess there's summat going on.'

'I don't usually see her in the evening, but I'll have to sit with her tonight, I suppose, while Daisy's out,' said Audrey thoughtfully. 'I'll read me book and keep quiet. She never talks to me very much anyway, so she p'raps won't notice anything.'

They had arrived at the village green and Audrey paused at Miss Thomson's gate. 'Keep your fingers crossed for me, Maisie,' she said, looking pleadingly at her friend.

'Yeah, 'course I will,' said Maisie. 'See you tomorrer. You can tell me all about it at Sunday School. Tara then. See yer...'

———

Audrey, lying wide-awake in her little bed, heard the back door opening, and her heart missed a beat as she heard Daisy's voice. 'Hello there...I'm back,' she was calling. She was shouting extra loudly which, no doubt, would not please Miss Thomson, but it was to let Audrey, at the top of the house, know that she was in – and soon to be out again – through the back door. She imagined Daisy now, popping her head round the dining room door and telling Miss Thomson that she would go straight up to her room; that was what she usually did when she came in. Audrey, in fact, did hear clumping footsteps on the stairs, and then they ceased suddenly. She visualised Daisy creeping down again silently, then through the kitchen and out of the back door, closing it stealthily. That part of the plan must have gone all right because there were no more sounds for several moments.

Then there was the noise of the bolts being put into place on the front door, and Miss Thomson's footsteps, much quieter than Daisy's, climbing the stairs. Then came the sound of the cistern flushing, and after that all was quiet.

Audrey had imagined that it would be hard to keep awake. She glanced at her little bedside alarm clock that she had brought with her from Armley. It was a quarter past ten. She was usually fast asleep by this time, but tonight she was feeling too agitated even to think about sleeping. There was a fluttery feeling of butterflies dancing in her tummy and she was sure her heart was beating extra fast and extra loud. Maybe when she had done the deed she would settle down again.

She had been trying to read, with a torch beneath the bedclothes. It was not likely that Miss Thomson would check to see if she was asleep. She had never done so before, but there might always be a first time. But even the exploits of Elinor Brent-Dyer's Chalet-girls failed to hold her interest tonight. The adventure that she and Daisy were embarking upon was filling her mind to the exclusion of everything else. She switched off her torch and just lay still in the darkness, letting the seconds and the minutes creep by. Time went very slowly, she realised, when your mind was not occupied with the busyness of all the things that filled your life in the daytime.

When she switched on her torch to look at her clock again it was still only twenty minutes to eleven. She decided to wait, if she could contain herself, until eleven o' clock. By that time she was sure Miss Thomson would have gone to sleep.

When eleven o' clock at last arrived she stole out of bed. The cold made her shiver, so she put on her red woolly dressing gown, fastening the girdle tightly around her, then she slid her feet into her furry bedroom slippers. Making scarcely a sound, apart from the soft pad of her footsteps which no one else could possibly hear, she crept down the stairs. It was pitch dark so she was forced to use her torch, but she shielded it with her hand lest it should shine into Miss Thomson's door, which was always left a little ajar. She felt that her heart almost stopped beating as she heard a stair creak; it must always have done so, but she had never noticed it before. She stood motionless for a second or two before venturing further.

But as she reached the first floor landing she knew she was safe because she could hear a noisy snoring sound coming from Miss Thomson's bedroom. She almost laughed out loud, partly with relief and partly in amusement. There was something very funny about people snoring. How Maisie and she would giggle together if her friend were with her. Miss Thomson was making so much noise it was a wonder she didn't wake herself up. Thinking of Maisie made her wish desperately that her friend was with her at that moment. Maisie would be brave and cheerful and think it was a great adventure. But Audrey plucked up all the courage she was capable of and crept down the flight of stairs that led to the hallway.

She felt she could use the torch quite safely down there. There was no way that its beam would reach up the stairs. Kneeling down by the front door and holding her torch in her left hand she shone the light on the bolt. Then, with her other hand she began to pull it slowly back. It was stiffer than she had imagined, and to her horror the last inch or so shot back with a loud clatter. She held her breath, listening intently, but there was no sound from upstairs. Thank goodness! She breathed a sigh of relief. There was only the top bolt to do now, then she could escape upstairs again to bed. The rest would be up to Daisy.

She shone her torch on to the top bolt and reached up towards it. She stood on her tiptoes and stretched her arm as far as it would go...but she could not reach it. Oh no! Whatever was she going to do? She hadn't even considered the possibility that she was not tall enough. She had grown quite a lot lately, but it was no use; there was no way she could reach the bolt. She stood there in a quandary. Unless...

In the dim light from the torch she saw the two chairs standing one on either side of the monk's bench, where Miss Thomson kept her spare bedding. They were heavy old-fashioned chairs with carved backs and plush seats, but she had never seen anybody sitting on them. If she could stand on one of them, then she could easily reach the bolt.

Still holding her torch in one hand she started to

drag a chair across the hallway. It didn't make a noise on the carpet, thank goodness, but she needed both her hands to get it into place. She put the torch on the floor so that it shone upwards, then she pulled the chair up behind the door. She picked up the torch again – she would need it to see the bolt – then took a big step up on to the chair. She was not sure what happened next. She was being very very careful and as quiet as a mouse, but the chair began to wobble. Her dressing gown girdle had somehow got tangled round the back of the chair and as she stepped up she caught her foot in a fold of her gown. The torch dropped from her hands and fell on to the carpet. Then the chair toppled over and Audrey crashed to the floor with the heavy chair on top of her. She was not hurt; only shocked and dismayed and very very scared.

As she might well be, because before she could get to her feet the hallway was flooded with electric light and a white nightgowned figure appeared at the top of the stairs.

'What on earth is going on down there? I was frightened out of my wits. I thought we had burglars... Whatever are you doing, Audrey? Why is that chair out of its place? Get up child! Get up at once and answer me.' Miss Thomson certainly did not look scared out of her wits. Indeed, she looked a frightening figure herself – enough to scare any burglar – as she advanced down the stairs, her face set in grim lines and her black eyes, curiously magnified by her spectacles, fixed menacingly on Audrey. Her hair was encased, incongruously, in a bright pink hairnet, which might have softened the forbidding image she presented, but to the terrified little girl it did not do so.

Audrey scrambled to her feet, trying to pick up the chair as she did so. Miss Thomson grabbed hold of it and pushed it back into its rightful place by the bench, but she made no attempt to help Audrey. In fact she seized hold of her and shook her hard.

'What are you doing? Come on, girl; answer me. I can tell by the look on you face that you are up to no good.' Audrey said the first thing that came into her head.

'I'm...I'm sorry, Miss Thomson. I thought...I thought I heard a noise, and I came down to see what it was. And then I noticed you hadn't bolted the door, so...so I was climbing up to do it...and I fell. I'm ever so sorry...'

'Stop lying to me, girl! Of course I bolted the door. I always do.' Miss Thomson glanced upwards. 'Yes; it's in its place just as usual.' Her glance fell to the one at the bottom, and her eyes narrowed to slits as she grabbed hold of Audrey's arms again, shaking her roughly.

'What...on...earth...is...going...on...here?' She stopped for a moment, her face as red as a turkey cock and her breath coming in short pants with the exertion of her assault on the child. She stared venomously at her. Then, as she suddenly realised what was going on, 'Daisy!' she exclaimed. 'Where is Daisy? Answer me, girl!'

'I...I don't know, Miss Thomson,' stammered Audrey. 'I expect...I think she's asleep in bed. I don't know where she is, honest.' She was gabbling now, not thinking what she was saying. She was more frightenend than she had ever been in her life and she could feel the tears overflowing from her eyes and running down her cheeks. Miss Thomson raised her hand and slapped her hard across the face, so hard that she went reeling across the hallway.

'Liar! You little liar!' she yelled. 'You're all alike, you evacuees. I might have known no good would come of it, having one of you brats from Leeds. You are aiding and abetting that maid of mine, aren't you? Aren't you?' she thundered, as Audrey did not at first answer. Then she nodded dumbly.

'Yes, I knew it! Where is she? Tell me now. Where is she?'

'With...with her boyfriend, Andy, I think. I didn't mean to do anything wrong. I was just helping her. She wanted to see him, 'cause he's going away to join the army...' Audrey burst into tears, then buried her face in her hands, sobbing as though her heart would break.

'You can stop all that snivelling!' said Miss Thomson coldly, not a shadow of pity or understanding showing on her face. 'Go on now; get off back to bed.' She pushed at her roughly. 'We'll decide what to do about you in the morning. You are not staying here with me any longer, that's for sure. I have no time for girls who are cheats and liars. And I shall deal with Daisy too. That young woman's days are numbered. I have never heard anything like it. Staying out till all hours with some man! I will not have such carryings-on in my household...'

Audrey guessed that Miss Thomson was now

talking to herself. Still sobbing intermittently she stole back up the two flights of stairs. She was shaking all over and her face was stinging from the slap she had received. Never before had she been slapped like that and she felt shocked and humiliated. And what about poor Daisy? What would happen to her? She would blame her, Audrey, too, for it all going wrong.

She crept beneath the bedclothes and eventually, after what seemed a long while, her crying and sobbing ceased. In the midst of all her fear and unhappiness, and guilt, too, about the awful thing she had done, there was a faint glimmer of hope. Miss Thomson had said she didn't want her to live there any more. Perhaps, now, she might be able to go and live with Maisie...

Chapter Twelve

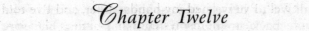

Soon after they had finished their breakfast on Sunday morning Patience opened the door – at an extremely loud knock – to find an irate Miss Thomson and a very subdued looking Audrey standing on the step. The moment Audrey set eyes on Patience she burst into tears.

'Oh dear, oh dear! Whatever is the matter?' cried Patience, putting a comforting arm around the little girl. 'Come along in, Audrey dear, and you as well, Miss Thomson, then you can tell me what is wrong.'

Miss Thomson bristled as she stepped into the hallway. 'You don't need to start all this snivelling again, Audrey. It cuts no ice with me, and it won't with Mrs Fairchild either, when she knows what a naughty girl you have been. Take no notice of her, Mrs Fairchild; it's just a plea for sympathy, and she doesn't deserve any.'

'Why? Whatever has she done?' asked Patience. The little girl was looking up at her pleadingly, tears brimming over in her lovely big blue eyes. Whatever crime she had committed Patience was sure it could not be as bad as all that. Instinctively she stroked the child's golden hair, in spite of the older woman at her side looking daggers at them both. 'I'm sure we can sort it out, whatever it is. Can't we, Miss Thomson?'

'Well, I've washed my hands of her, and I've told her so.' Miss Thomson's cold and pitiless glance at the child made Patience realise – as she had, in her heart, felt all along – that this woman was not a fit person to be in charge of such a sensitive little girl or, indeed, of any child. 'She will have to be billeted elsewhere. I knew it was a mistake for me to take an evacuee in the first place.'

'I must agree with you there, Miss Thomson,' said Patience, grimly. How callous of the woman to use such words as billet and evacuee in front of the child. 'I can see now that you are not at all suited to looking after children.'

'Now wait a minute; that's not fair,' retorted Miss Thomson. 'I have done my best. I have tried to do my duty, only to have it all flung back in my face – by her...' She pointed a witch-like finger at Audrey, '...her and that wanton maid of mine.'

'Daisy?' Patience frowned. 'Whatever...? How does Daisy come into this?' She shook her head in bewilderment. 'Come into the sitting room, Miss Thomson,' she said, opening the door to that room. 'And you, too, Audrey, love.' She ushered them in, at the same time raising her voice and shouting up the stairs, 'Luke...Luke, could you come here for a moment, dear? We seem to have something of a problem.'

But before Luke could answer the summons, Maisie suddenly appeared on the scene. She dashed into the room, going immediately to her friend's side and putting an arm around her.

'Audrey! What's up? Has summat gone wrong? I was in the kitchen and I heard her going on – Miss

Thomson I mean...' She jerked a thumb in the woman's direction, 'and I guessed what had happened...'

'Yes! I might have known you would have something to do with this!' interrupted Miss Thomson, pointing her crooked finger now at Maisie. 'Yes, the pair of you and that shameless maid of mine, you cooked it up between you, didn't you?'

'No! I never knew nowt about it, not till Audrey told me,' yelled Maisie. 'You've no business to go blaming me...you awful old woman!'

'Maisie, be careful now...' said Patience in a warning voice, but Maisie appeared not to hear.

'I've not done nowt,' she went on. All her endeavours to speak more correctly, more like Patience, and to be polite, flew out of the window as she tried to defend herself. 'And it weren't Audrey's fault neither,' she said, realising she must stick up for her friend as well; Audrey appeared to be in deep trouble. 'She was only trying to help Daisy...an' I think she was very brave,' she added stoutly.

Audrey nodded. 'It was nothing to do with Maisie, Miss Thomson,' she said, more calmly now that her bosom friend was with her. 'I only told her 'cause I was scared, an' I couldn't keep it all to myself.'

'Would somebody please tell me exactly what we are talking about?' said Patience, who was by now completely mystified.

Luke, entering the room at that moment, also had no idea what was taking place, but he sensed a crisis of some sort – quite a minor one, though, he intuited – and he gathered that Miss Thomson was at the centre of it.

'Miss Thomson,' he said, in his usual cheerful and welcoming voice. 'Good morning to you. I understand there is a little problem? Now, why don't you and I go into my study, then you can tell me all about it? I have a good half hour before I need to get ready for Morning Service, and the needs of my parishioners always come first.' He smiled graciously at her. 'We will leave my wife to sort out the girls. I sense we are all getting a little…overwrought, maybe?'

Miss Thomson pursed her lips and silently followed him out of the room.

'Now,' said Patience, breathing a sigh of relief and sitting down thankfully in an easy chair. 'Perhaps we can get down to some straight talking. Sit yourselves down, you two.' They perched on the settee opposite her, looking at one another apprehensively. 'And, for goodness' sake, tell me what on earth has been going on.'

Audrey started the story – she had stopped crying by this time – then Maisie joined in, and together they managed to explain about Daisy and the plan with the door and the bolts, and how it had all gone wrong. A storm in a teacup, was Patience's verdict. She felt very angry with Amelia Thomson for overreacting as she had done and frightening Audrey so badly. For it all came out; how the woman had shaken her – 'till my head was nearly coming off,' said Audrey – and had slapped her face, such treatment as the well-brought-up and cherished little girl had never before suffered in her life. Patience could not entirely overlook the fact, however, that Audrey had been mite deceitful, although undoubtedly led on by Daisy and unable to resist the young woman's pleas.

'Oh dear! What a tale of woe,' said Patience, shaking her head and smiling at Audrey, but not without a faint air of reproach. 'You know it was wrong, though, don't you, Audrey, to try and deceive Miss Thomson like that?' The little girl nodded. 'But I do realise that Daisy is the one most to blame,' she continued, 'and she certainly should not have involved you in her devious plans.'

'But she couldn't've done it without me,' said Audrey, 'and Andy's joining the army. She's real upset.'

'That's understandable,' said Patience, her heart going out to the foolhardy young woman, whose desire to be with her boyfriend Amelia Thomson would not countenance at all. One would have thought the woman would have stretched a point for once and let her maid stay out till...half-past eleven, maybe? But probably Daisy had thought it wasn't even worth asking. 'But it was still very wrong of Daisy to deceive her employer. What happened? Do you know? Did Miss Thomson wait up till she came in?'

'I don't think so,' replied Audrey. 'I think she must have pulled the bolts back so that Daisy could get in.' At least the woman had some heart, thought Patience. 'I didn't sleep very well, y'see, and I heard Daisy come upstairs and go into her room, but Miss Thomson wasn't shouting or anything. Not till this

morning, and then she really went mad at Daisy. I
would have warned her it had all gone wrong, but
she woke up before me and I never got the chance.
And Daisy wouldn't say nothing when I had me
breakfast with her except, 'It's not your fault, kid.'
She kept on saying that. She looked as though she'd
been crying, and then Miss Thomson told me to
hurry up and put my coat on, and we came over
here.'

'I see,' said Patience, nodding gravely. 'What did
you say just then, Audrey? That you had your
breakfast with Daisy? Is that what you usually do?'

'Oh yes, I have all my meals with Daisy,' said
Audrey. 'I hardly ever see Miss Thomson. It's Daisy
what looks after me. Although I can look after
meself really,' she added. 'Getting washed and
bathed and everything. I wash me own hair now,'
she added proudly. 'Me mum used to do it, but now
I do it meself. Daisy lets me use her Amami
shampoo.'

'Daisy is very kind to you then?' said Patience
smiling.

'Oh yes; she's lovely,' said the little girl. 'Just like a
big sister.'

'But she helps her with the work, don't you,
Audrey?' said Maisie. 'Washing up and peeling
spuds – I mean potatoes – and cleaning the silver
an' all that.'

'Do you, Audrey?' asked Patience. 'And does
Miss Thomson know about it?'

'I 'spect so,' said Audrey. 'I don't really know.'

'I told you before, Aunty Patience,' said Maisie.
'Don't you remember? About Daisy looking after

Audrey an' Miss Thomson doing nowt...I mean nothing.'

'Yes, I know you did, dear,' replied Patience thoughtfully. 'I know you mentioned it, but I didn't realise you meant all the time...' This was far worse than she had anticipated. The child was being used as an extra servant in that household, no matter how kind Daisy was to her, and the sooner that situation came to an end the better.

'But Miss Thomson says I've got to go and live somewhere else,' said Audrey. 'You heard her, didn't you? She doesn't want me there now, and I don't suppose she'll want Daisy neither.'

But Patience could not imagine the woman letting her 'maid of all work' go, no matter how displeased she was with her. Genteel ladies like Amelia Thomson did not take kindly to such lowly tasks as cooking and washing and cleaning. And it would, more than likely, be Daisy who would decide she had had enough.

'Don't worry about Daisy,' said Patience. 'She's quite a sensible young woman – although she's behaved very foolishly over this – and she'll soon sort herself out. I've know Daisy a long time and she'll take it in her stride, whatever happens. But it's you that we are concerned about, isn't it, my dear?' Patience did not even have to stop to consider, though, the solution to the problem; it was obvious, and was what she had really wanted all along.

'Would you like to come and live here?' she asked the child, 'with Luke and me, and with Maisie, of course? There is another bedroom you could have, unless you and Maisie would like to share. That might be fun. And we would love to have you…wouldn't we, Maisie?' She looked across at the other little girl. But to her surprise Maisie's face did not immediately break into a beaming smile.

'Yes…' she said quietly, just smiling a little bit. 'That would be lovely.'

'Oh, Mrs Fairchild, can I really?' exclaimed Audrey. 'Oh, thank you. It's…it's just wonderful. It's just what I wanted, but I never thought it would happen. Oh, I can't believe it!'

She burst into tears again, but Patience knew that this time they were tears of excitement and happiness rather than sadness and worry. She also knew that it might appear to Miss Thomson – although she did not really care, if she were honest, about that woman's feelings – as though Audrey was being rewarded for her wrong doing. She knew that the bitter old woman must be seen to be mollified to some extent.

'Now, stop crying,' said Patience. 'Just settle down and we'll think about what we are going to do. I intended taking both of you – you and Maisie – when you first arrived, seeing that you were such good friends. But I had to give way to Miss Thomson because she was so determined that it was you that she wanted. I'm sorry, for her sake, that it hasn't worked out. I suppose she has done her best…' She crossed her fingers tightly, something she had done every since she was a child when she knew she was telling a lie; well, a white lie at any rate.

'But she is not used to children, so maybe she thought it was for the best, letting Daisy look after you some of the time.' Although, from what the girls had said, it sounded as though the maid had had complete charge of Daisy. 'However, Audrey...' Her face took on a more solemn aspect. 'What you and Daisy did was wrong. I know Daisy was mostly to blame, but I think you should apologise to Miss Thomson; tell her you are sorry for being so deceitful.'

Audrey nodded slowly. 'Yes, of course I will. My mum always told me to say I was sorry to people if I had done something naughty. But supposing... supposing she changes her mind and says that it's all right, and that I can go on living there? I don't really want to, Mrs Fairchild.'

Patience smiled. 'Don't worry about it.' She did not think it was very likely. She guessed that Amelia Thomson was using this misdemeanour as an excuse to get out of something she had never really wanted to do. 'Leave it to my husband and me. We'll sort it out... Oh, I think they're coming back now.'

Luke entered the sitting room, all smiles, followed by a serious, but no longer angry looking Miss Thomson. 'All sorted,' he said, sitting down on the settee next to the girls. 'Do sit down, Miss Thomson.' He motioned towards the easy chair and the lady sat down, appearing, Patience thought, a trifle reconciled.

'We have had a good chat,' he went on, 'and Miss Thomson has agreed that she might have been a little...hasty; and that, possibly, she overreacted. But it was a great shock to her, being woken up suddenly and thinking that her house was being burgled. Anyway…she has something she wants to say to Audrey.'

Patience caught sight of the look of apprehension on the child's face. Oh dear! She hoped that Miss Thomson was not going to ask her to stay with her; the woman could be most persistent.

However, 'I am sorry that I hit you,' the woman said, a little guardedly. She cast a quick glance at the girl, then looked down at her gloves and handbag, held precisely on her lap. 'It was wrong of me…and I know I shouted at you, perhaps more than I ought to have done. It was Daisy's fault, in the main, and she has had the decency to admit to it.'

'It's all right, Miss Thomson,' murmured Audrey. 'I want to say I'm sorry as well. It was wrong an'…an' I shouldn't have listened to Daisy. I should've said no. I'm sorry…if I've been a nuisance to you.'

Miss Thomson shook her head a little impatiently. 'You haven't, not really. I know you are a good well-brought-up girl. I could tell that when I first saw you. That is why I chose you. It's just that…I am not used to children and so…' She looked across at Luke, who continued the speech for her.

'And so…Miss Thomson and I have decided it would be better if Audrey came to live here with Patience and me, and Maisie, of course. I don't need to consult my wife first, because I know that she will agree with me wholeheartedly. Isn't that so, my dear?'

Patience smiled conspiratorially at Audrey, whose beaming smile reached nearly from ear to ear, then she turned to her husband. 'Great minds think alike, Luke. That is what we had already decided. Audrey will come and live here with us. In fact, I think she had better stay here now, then she can come to church with Maisie and me.' She nodded across at her husband. 'Time is creeping on, my dear.'

'Quite so.' Luke stood up. 'If you will all excuse me, I have some things to attend to before the morning service. I am pleased it has all ended happily. Thank you, Miss Thomson.' He inclined his head graciously towards her.

The lady rose to her feet. 'Thank you too, Rector. I will arrange with Daisy to bring your things across, Audrey. After morning service shall we say, Mrs Fairchild? And I must have a little talk to Daisy. I may have been rather impulsive... But I am sure she will not really want to leave me. Daisy knows on which side her bread is buttered...' She was talking almost to herself as Patience showed her out of the front door.

It sounds as though Amelia is having second thoughts about losing her treasure of a maid, she thought, as she watched the woman cross the village green to her house. It was most likely that she had dismissed Daisy and was now wondering what on earth she would do without her. Well, that was one problem that was between Daisy and Miss Thomson. She, Patience, had quite enough on her plate at the moment. There was a shoulder of lamb to put in the oven before they set off for church, and two little girls to see to instead of one. Maisie was abnormally subdued, but Audrey, quite on top of her own little world, did not seem to have noticed.

After the church service had finished Patience busied herself with the lunch preparations, enlisting Maisie's help in setting the table, whilst Audrey went across the green to assist Daisy in moving her belongings. Patience wanted to have a little chat with Maisie, on her own. She placed the potatoes in the oven to roast around the lamb joint, and diced the carrots and swedes ready for boiling, then she went into the dining room where Maisie was setting out the wooden mats and the cutlery.

'Four places today, Maisie,' she said. 'Have you remembered? Yes, I see you have; good girl. It's exciting, isn't it, having your friend, Audrey, to come and live with us? It's what you always wanted, isn't it?'

The girl looked up at her and nodded silently, then a tiny frown appeared between her eyebrows and she pursed her lips tightly together. Patience went across and put her arm around her. 'But, somehow, I get the impression that you are not quite as thrilled about this as you might have been at one time. Am I right?' She felt Maisie nod again.

'Then won't you tell me all about it, dear? What is worrying you? I promise that I won't say a word to anyone, not even to Luke. I don't want you to be unhappy, not about anything.'

Maisie was silent for a moment, then she said, quietly, 'I thought I wanted Audrey to come and live here. I did at first. An' I do now, really, I suppose. But...it's been so nice, Aunty Patience, hasn't it? Just you and me and Luke. An' I thought I was a bit special, like, an' so I stopped thinking about Audrey coming here, 'cause I liked it just on my own. I was never special at home, y'see. Me mum was always so busy with the little 'uns, an' she was always tired. She never had time for me... But you have, Aunty Patience. An' I've been real happy here.'

'Of course you are special, Maisie,' said Patience, giving her a hug. 'You always will be, to me and to Luke, and to your mum as well. You mustn't think like that about her, my dear. You've told me about...your home, and I know your mother is sometimes not very happy. But you are special to her, because you were born out of the love that she and your father shared. Do you understand that, Maisie love? I think you do...'

'Yes...' Maisie nodded. 'But I haven't seen her for ages, and it's getting hard to remember her and the kids.'

'She has promised to come and see you before Christmas, hasn't she? And I'm sure she will, very soon...' Please God, let it be true, thought Patience, in a fervent little prayer. Lily Bragg had been promising for so long that she would come.

'Try to be happy about Audrey coming here,' Patience continued. 'Luke and I...we have grown to love you, Maisie. But the amazing thing about love is that there is always more than enough to go round. There will be some to spare for Audrey, and we will learn to love her, too. And we will all be happy together; I feel certain of it. Now...do you feel any better?'

'Yes, I think so,' said Maisie. 'Yes...yes, I do. But...Aunty Patience; you know how you said me and Audrey could share a room? Well, I've got used to my own little room now, an' I like being there on my own. I had to share with Joanie and Jimmy at home, an' I hated it. An' I think Audrey'll want her own room an' all. It's nice to have your own little place, isn't it?'

'Very nice,' agreed Patience. 'Yes, Maisie; I understand perfectly. Audrey can have the room at the back that overlooks the garden. When we've had our lunch we'll find some clean sheets and blankets and get the bed made up. Oh, here are Daisy and Audrey coming in. Off you go and give them a hand. And show Audrey which bedroom she will be having. The room at the back, next to the bathroom; that will be Audrey's...'

———

Maisie, feeling a little better about everything, went into the hallway where Daisy and Audrey were carrying various bags and parcels across the doorstep. Luke had appeared, too, from the sitting room, looking much more informal than he had a little while ago, now in his shirt sleeves and black vest, topped by his clerical collar.

'I'll take the heaviest bag for you,' he said, 'and this one as well.' He picked up the bag and a paper carrier full of books. 'Come along, Audrey. Let's go and find your room. I think Maisie knows which one it is, don't you, Maisie? Then I'll leave all you young ladies to get on with things. A very big welcome to you, Audrey. We are very pleased to have you here with us.'

'Thank you,' mumbled Audrey, going rather red and obviously quite overcome with emotion, too much so to look at Luke. But she cast a covert glance at Maisie, and the two friends smiled knowingly at one another.

Yes...Maisie nodded to herself. She had realised that she felt tons better now. Aunty Patience had a way with her of smoothing out the rough patches. She supposed Audrey, too, would soon be calling her Aunty Patience...?

'This is going to be your room,' she said when they reached the upstairs landing, pointing to the door next to the bathroom. She felt pleased that Patience had put her in charge.

'I thought you and me might be sharing a room,' said Audrey. 'Aren't we going to? Mrs Fairchild said...'

'Oh, it was just an idea,' replied Maisie airily. 'My room's only got one bed in it, y'see, so I would have to move. Besides...I like it on me own,' she added truthfully, 'an' I thought you would an' all, Audrey. Anyway, it's what Aunty Patience and I decided would be best.'

'Yes, that's right,' agreed Daisy. 'There's nowt like a bit of privacy. There'll be times when you want to be on yer own, kid. You make the most of it, Audrey.'

'Audrey nodded. 'OK; I don't mind. Actually, I've never shared a room and I thought it might be fun, but I'm sure this will be very nice.' She went across to the window. 'Oh yes...' she said, eagerly, as she looked out. 'What a lovely view of the back garden. And look...I can see the chimneys of the big house. It's the one where the squire lives, isn't it, and Bruce? And look at the hills in the distance... Oh yes, I like it. It's lovely.'

'It is indeed,' said Daisy, standing next to her and giving her a hug. 'You've fallen on yer feet all right, kid.'

'Yes, it's a very nice view,' said Maisie, in a matter-of-fact voice. But her room was at the front; she had a view of the village green and she could see all the comings and goings further down the High Street. Admittedly, Audrey's room was a little larger than hers. There was enough room for two single beds, but her eagle eye noticed that it was quite sparsely furnished. A wardrobe, a dressing table (rather a plain one; it didn't have a frill round it like the one Maisie had), and an empty bookshelf. It appeared a little gloomy, too, because the back of the house faced north and did not get the advantage of whatever sun there might be until much later in the day; which meant scarcely at all in the wintertime.

Maisie realised she was being rather spiteful, comparing Audrey's room unfavourably with her own, and being secretly glad that it was not as nice. To make amends she said, 'Come on, Audrey. Let's put all yer books on the shelf, then it'll make it look more cheerful, like.' Audrey had brought several books with her from Armley and had bought some more, from a second-hand stall on the market, with her spending money. 'And I expect Aunty Patience will lend you a few ornaments and vases and things. And perhaps a nice bright cushion like she gave me. Now, let's put your clothes in the wardrobe. See...you've got three drawers an' all for your underwear and stuff.'

Maisie's organising abilities came to the fore, and the three of them were just getting the last garments away when Patience appeared. 'It's looking more like home already,' she remarked, looking at the books on the bookshelf with Audrey's little alarm clock, and her teddy bear sitting on the bed which, at the moment, was covered with a dreary looking grey blanket. 'This room's a little bit drab, I know. It's ready for decorating, but then so are a lot of the rooms. But I've got a nice jolly counterpane, all coloured stripes and zig-zags, and that will brighten your bed up no end. And we'll put a blue blanket on the other bed to make it look more cheerful. I've just put some clean sheets in the airing cupboard, so after we've had our dinner we'll get it made up and I'll put a hot water bottle in.'

'I'd best be getting back now,' said Daisy. 'I've got to see to t' dinner. There's a piece o' beef in th' oven, but I've still got all t' veg and t' gravy to see to. Old Amelia...er, Miss Thomson,' she amended at Patience's sharp glance, although if she had observed her more closely she would have seen a definite twinkle in that lady's eye. 'Miss Thomson'll have to make the most of it, 'cause it'll be me last Sunday, all being well.'

'What do you mean, Daisy?' asked Patience. 'I know Miss Thomson dismissed you, but I thought that was just her reaction, on the spur of the moment. I understood that she had asked you to stay on?'

'Oh aye, she asked me all right,' said Daisy, 'but I said no. Not on your life! I'm not going to stay there no longer being treated no better than a bloomin' slave. She'll have to find another skivvy, won't she?'

'Yes, maybe she will,' replied Patience, 'if you mean what you say. But you have been getting quite a lot of help recently, haven't you, Daisy?' She looked at her quite sternly. 'From what I gather, Audrey has been helping with many of the household chores, and that is not what was intended for these children who are our guests. They are not supposed to be used as extra servants. Maisie helps me now and again with little jobs and she makes her own bed, and I shall expect Audrey to do the same. But no more than that. What you have been doing, Daisy, was quite wrong. Whether Miss Thomson knew about it or not, I am not sure.'

'She turned a blind eye,' said Daisy. 'She did when it suited 'er. Other times she had eyes like a bloomin' 'awk. I'm sorry, Mrs Fairchild, honest I am. I know Audrey weren't supposed to help, like, but I were so tired sometimes and she didn't seem to mind. Y'see, Miss Thomson asked me if I'd look after her – Audrey, I mean – when she first come here, when t' war started. She said would I take charge of her, like, an' she gave me a bob or two extra in me wages. So I thought, aye why not? She's a grand little lass. An' we got on well, didn't we, kid?'

'Yes, we did,' replied Audrey. She turned to Patience. 'Like I told you, Mrs Fairchild, Daisy was kind to me. Don't be cross with her, please.'

'Very well, we will say no more about it,' said Patience. 'But I had no idea, Daisy, that Miss Thomson had delegated the charge of Audrey to you. That was certainly not right...' It was, indeed, a revelation. Amelia had certainly opted out of her resposibility. What a nerve, handing the child over to her maid! It was fortunate that Daisy was a kind and good-natured young woman at heart. It could have turned out so much worse.

'What do you intend to do though, Daisy?' she asked. 'Are you going to look for another position? I should think carefully if I were you. I know Miss Thomson is a bit of a tartar, but you might do worse. I could have a word with her; I would try to explain that she expects far too much of just one person.'

'No, me mind's made up,' said Daisy decisively. 'I were thinking about it before all this, an' now I know for sure what I'm going to do…I'm going to join the ATS.'

Patience gave a little gasp. 'Well, that is a surprise!' she said. The two girls looked at Daisy in amazement, Maisie with a knowing glint in her eyes as well.

'Is that so you can be near yer boyfriend?' she asked.

Daisy laughed, shaking her head. 'No, it ain't; not really. I don't suppose we'd be sent to t' same place anyroad. No…I reckon all us young women'll be expected to do our bit afore long if this war goes on. So I might as well join up sooner rather than later.'

'But…what about Miss Thomson?' asked Audrey.

'What about her?' laughed Daisy.

'Does she know what you're going to do?'

'No, not yet. But she soon will. And what she's going to do about it is her look-out, not mine…'

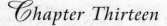

Chapter Thirteen

Lily missed her eldest child more and more as the days and the weeks went by. She kept promising herself – and promising Maisie as well – that she would go on a day visit to the little town of Middlebeck. But already it was mid-November and she still had not been to see her daughter. She felt rather guilty about it, but it was partly circumstances that had prevented her from making the journey.

Joanie had caught chickenpox; not badly, but it had forced her to keep the child in for a while. And then, inevitably, Jimmy had gone down with it as well. During the few weeks when the pair of them had not been able to run wild with the other children of the neighbourhood she had made a determined effort to make them behave themselves, and, also, to get them thoroughly clean and tidy and to encourage them to stay that way. They had been scrubbed clean, once their spots had receded, their hair washed and trimmed, and they had both had a selection of new clothes – at least, newish, from the church jumble sale – and sturdy shoes from a second-hand shop to replace their down-at-heel sandals.

Jimmy, who would be three years old in January, had finally dispensed with nappies, to his mother's great relief, and with this achievement he had seemed, suddenly, to become a little boy – a much more lovable one – and not a whining baby. Joanie had just turned four years old and she, too, had stopped wetting the bed. Lily was convinced that her earlier lapses had occurred because, in her own childish mind, she was competing with her baby brother for attention. Now, to Lily's amazement, she finally seemed to be making headway with both her young children.

She had known she must get the upper hand with them before going to see Maisie. She would, of course, have to take the children with her. There was no question of her leaving them behind with Sid. He would not want to look after them, much as he reminded her that they were his children, and neither would she consider asking him, even for one day. The husband and wife hardly spoke to one another now.

It sounded to Lily as though Maisie had done really well for herself with her lodgings in Middlebeck. A reverend gentleman, of all things, and his wife, a woman called Patience who, from Maisie's letters, seemed to be quite a paragon. Lily felt rather envious of her on occasions, at the same time being relieved that her daughter was in good hands and was so obviously happy there. Maisie did write in her letters that she missed her, which touched her very much. Occasionally she made mention of her younger sister and brother, although Lily guessed this was more out of duty than true concern. But she never referred to either Sid or Percy.

Lily had realised, to her shame, that she could not take two scruffy badly behaved children to visit what she thought of as Maisie's posh guardians up in north Yorkshire. Not only would she, Lily, feel ashamed of them, she knew that Maisie would as well, and she did not want to let her eldest child down. She knew only too well that she had allowed herself to become dispirited and careless of her appearance, trapped as she was in a hopeless marriage. And so, as well as taking her two little ruffians in hand, Lily had made an effort to sort herself out as well. She did not want to arrive in Middlebeck – if she ever managed to get there – looking dowdy and shabby and middle-aged. She treated herself, out of her 'charing' money to a fashionable dark red coat, only a little worn at the collar and cuffs, from the second-hand shop, and a perky little hat with a feather on the brim to match. Her new jumper and flared skirt, also a pair of black patent leather shoes with only a slight crack in them, came from a jumble sale. All this finery, though, did not look right with the thick lisle stockings she normally wore. And so she spent a precious two shillings on a pair of pure silk ones. The local draper's shop had recently had a small allocation, which the proprietress told her would be the last for goodness knows how long.

Her hair had not been cut for ages. Lily could not afford to have it cut properly at a hairdresser's, but then neither could most women that she knew. Occasionally, if it became too straggly she lopped the ends off herself. Most of the time now she bundled it into a sort of roll around her head, which was a little tidier than having it hanging loose, but was not very becoming.

The only person Lily could really call a friend was her next door neighbour, Kate Smedley. Kate was a few years younger than Lily and, so far, was childless. She worked part-time at a local greengrocer's shop and her husband, like Lily's menfolk, worked at the woollen mill.

'I'll cut your hair for you,' she said one day when Lily was complaining that she could no longer manage it herself. 'You've got nice hair, Lily. It's a shame to scrape it back like that. It looks as though it would curl if you would let it.' Lily remembered a time when she had been proud of her shining dark hair with its natural wave, and Davey had admired it, too. 'What about next Saturday afternoon?' said her friend. 'I expect your fellers'll be going to t' football match, won't they, like my Fred? So we'd have the house to ourselves. That is if you would like me to?'

'Of course I would,' said Lily. 'That's real kind of you, Kate. Your hair always looks lovely.' Kate's fair hair was worn in a page-boy style which almost reached her shoulders. It looked as though it might need constant attention, but there never seemed to be a hair out of place.

'Me mam cuts it for me,' said Kate. 'She always has done, ever since I was a kid. An' I've got a special shampoo that I got from Woolie's. It makes it all nice and soft and easy to manage. There's a drop left in t' bottle so I'll let you have it. Next Saturday then, at your place? You could come to me, but you don't want to be going out with wet hair.'

'Er...yes, all right then,' said Lily. If they got started early they would have finished before Sid and Percy got back. Sid would not be best pleased to walk in on a hairdressing session, although the chances were he would not be rude to Kate. He had an eye for a pretty woman, but Lily knew that she no longer fell into that category. Nor did she care what Sid thought about her, but she wanted to look attractive again, if that were possible, for her own sake and for Maisie's. 'I'll wash it meself, first, shall I?' she said. 'Then you can cut it, and set it up for me, if you like.'

'I'll do me best,' said Kate. 'When I've done you'll look just like Betty Grable. Oh no, she's a blonde, isn't she? Well, Paulette Goddard then, or somebody. Anyroad, you'll look just like a film star.'

So the following Saturday afternoon Lily washed her hair thoroughly, over the kitchen sink, with Kate's Vinolia shampoo, then Kate set it into curls with kirby grips, all over her head. She sat close to the fire to let it dry whilst Kate, making herself at home in the kitchen, made a cup of tea for both of them.

'How are things?' asked Kate, as they drank their tea. 'Still the same, is it, between you and Sid?'

'Yes, I'm afraid so,' replied Lily. 'Well, that's not true; I'm not really afraid so, because I just don't care. He leaves me alone, and that suits me fine. I cook his meals and wash his clothes an' everything, and the lad's as well; what else can I do?' She shrugged. 'We're still husband and wife, I suppose, but it's only in name. But there's nowt I can do about my rotten marriage, so I just keep meself to meself. I look after the kiddies, an' I've got me cleaning jobs which gets me out of the house. Not much of a life, I know; but I'm going to see my Maisie soon, up in north Yorkshire. I've made up me mind this time; I'm really going to make an effort and go.'

'Then just make sure that you do,' said Kate. 'It'd do you no end of good, and she'd be thrilled to bits to see you... About your Sid, though; don't you think he might be...well...finding his pleasures elsewhere, if you know what I mean?'

'Oh, I know what you mean all right,' replied Lily. 'Aye, most probably he is, but why should I care? He means nowt to me; neither him nor his lad...' She stopped, realising that she had said enough. She had confided in Kate to a certain extent, but her friend did not know the whole of the story.

After ordering her to clear off and take the kids with her, on the night that she had attacked Percy, Sid had subsequently changed his mind and demanded that she should stay in Armley. To her immense relief, however, since that night he had not attempted to come near her. After spending a couple of nights in his bed, as near to the edge as she could move away from him, she had decided to take a bold step. She moved into the room that the two youngsters occupied, and slept in the bed vacated by Maisie. She had half expected ructions from Sid, but he had made no comment whatsoever. He had scarcely spoken to her from that day to this, save to issue orders or hurl abuse at her, or to tell her, when he felt inclined, that he was going out. Percy, too, ignored her, but that was only what she had expected.

She knew it was no sort of a life that she was living. Indeed, she was not living, in the true sense of the word, only existing from day to day. But she felt freer in her mind now that she was not suffering from her husband's physical torments, and it was a relief to know that her daughter was far away from the clutches of her devilish step-brother. Lily had begun to hope, although it seemed a forlorn hope at the moment, that one day this wearisome existence of hers would come to an end and, even though the country was now at war, better times might lie ahead for her and the children.

Kate knew nothing of how Percy had abused her daughter. Lily was too ashamed to admit this to anyone. All Kate knew was that Sid had hit her, Lily, the night before Maisie's departure – the evidence had been there only too clearly, in her bruises and swollen eye – and that Lily had finally decided that she would put up with no more and had vacated his bed. She felt that what Kate had suggested was true; Sid had found someone else to give him what he wanted. If he cleared off then it would suit her just fine. But Sid, she guessed, wanted both the cake and the ha'penny.

Kate went home in a little while, not wanting to be still there when the men arrived back, and she had her husband's tea to get ready. As far as Lily knew, the two of them, Fred and Kate Smedley, had a reasonable enough marriage. At least the young woman did not complain, only that she would like a child and that none, alas, was forthcoming.

When her hair had dried Lily pulled out the kirby grips, then she brushed and combed it into gentle waves which curled attractively – at least, she thought they did – over her forehead and ears. She actually smiled at her reflection in the mirror over the sideboard. She looked, now, more like the woman she had been when she was married to her beloved Davey. She sighed. One thing was certain; Sid would not notice her changed appearance. And, even if he did, he would not make any comment.

———

Before Lily had had a chance to find out about the times of the trains to north Yorkshire, or had decided on which day she would go, she had a visitor.

On the following Monday afternoon, soon after she had returned from one of her cleaning jobs, she opened the door to see a middle-aged woman standing there. She looked familiar. Lily was trying to recall who she was, whether it was, in fact, someone that she ought to know, when the woman spoke.

'Mrs Jackson? You are Maisie's mother, aren't you? I've seen you with her at school now and again, although she used to be known as Nellie, didn't she...?'

'Yes, that's right,' said Lily, suddenly remembering who this woman was. 'She's called Maisie now, though – that's what she liked to be called – and, yes, I'm her mother. But I'm not Mrs Jackson, not any more. I'm Mrs Bragg.'

'Oh dear! I'm sorry; I didn't know that.' The woman looked flustered at her mistake, although it was an understandable one to make.

'There's no reason why you should know, is there?' said Lily, smiling at her. 'You're Audrey's mother, aren't you? My little girl and yours have got quite friendly, I've heard, since they went up to Middlebeck.'

'I believe they have... Yes, I'm Mrs Dennison...'

Lily recalled how she had first seen her outside the school, saying goodbye to a little fair-haired girl who had been in tears. Lily had taken her to be the child's grandmother, but she had learned, in letters from Maisie, that the woman was, in fact, her mother. Moreover, Maisie and the tearful girl, Audrey, had since then become close friends. They were in the same class in the school in Middlebeck and lived very near to one another. Lily had seen Mrs Dennison once or twice when she had been out on her cleaning jobs. She lived in one of the semis in an avenue where Lily worked, but this was the first time they had spoken together.

'I was wondering, Mrs...er...Bragg, if you were thinking of going to see your little girl?' asked Mrs Dennison. 'I've been ill, you see, so I've not been able to go yet. But now I really must make the effort because I've just heard that she's been moved to a new place.'

'Yes, actually I am thinking of going...' Lily suddenly remembered her manners. 'Come in, Mrs Dennison,' she said. 'How rude of me to keep you standing on the doorstep...' At the same time she was hoping frantically that the living room was not too untidy, although since taking herself and the children in hand, she had been trying to do the same with her house. She could do little about its shabbiness, but she could, at least, make more effort to keep it reasonably clean and tidy.

And so Mrs Dennison, seeing Lily's home for the first time, entered a room where a cheerful fire, surrounded by a sturdy fireguard, was burning in the shiny black range. A few clothes were airing on a clothes horse, but there were no longer rows of greyish nappies drying, as there had been in the past. Two blonde-haired children were playing together on the rag hearth rug, building towers of wooden bricks and then knocking them down again with squeals of glee.

'Hello,' said Mrs Dennison, smiling at them. 'That's a good game, isn't it? And what are your names?'

'I'm Joanie an' he's Jimmy,' said the girl, pointing unceremoniously at her brother before continuing with the game.

'Not too noisy, now,' said Lily, hoping they would take notice of her. 'This lady and I want to have a chat. Do sit down, Mrs Dennison…' She hastily moved a newspaper and two toy cars from the armchair which sagged the least and the woman sat down.

She did not look at her surroundings – at the threadbare carpet and the faded wallpaper and the ragged net curtains, clean because they had recently been washed and 'dolly-blued', but rather holey – for which Lily was very relieved. She seemed, in fact, to be occupied with her own thoughts.

Glancing at her more closely Lily could see that she was not as old as she at first appeared to be. In her mid-fifties, Lily surmised – she could not be much more than that to be Audrey's mother, unless the child had been adopted? – although one could take her, at a first glance, to be well into her sixties.

She looked pale, too; an unhealthy paleness, not one just caused by the lack of sunshine, and rather weary. Her clothing did nothing to relieve her pallor. Her coat was an unbecoming dark brown, as was her hat, with the brim pulled low over her forehead. It was obvious, however, that both items, as well as her shining brown leather brogues, were expensive. No jumble sale or second-hand clothing for Mrs Dennison, mused Lily, and probably not for Audrey either. She recalled that the girl had been dressed, on that September morning, as though she was going to a party, whereas all the other children had been clothed in their usual school attire.

'Now, Mrs Dennison,' said Lily, sitting down in the opposite chair, the one in which the springs had almost gone. 'You were telling me about Audrey. What were you saying? That she had been moved to a new place...? I'm Lily, by the way. That's what I like to be called, not...Mrs Bragg.'

'And I'm Edith...' The older woman smiled a little, and when she did so she appeared to shed a few years. 'I'd be pleased if you would call me Edith. When you get older you find that fewer and fewer people use your Christian name. Of course, I don't like too much familiarity. Younger people should show respect... However, as I was saying, it appears that my Audrey has now gone to live at the rectory, with a Mrs Patience Fairchild and her husband; he's the rector, of course. It was the lady, Mrs Fairchild, who wrote to tell me. She sounds a lovely person, and I believe your daughter, Maisie, is already living there?'

'So she is,' replied Lily. 'Yes, she's very happy there. But she hasn't said anything in her letters about Audrey being there.'

'I gather it's only just happened,' said Mrs Dennison. 'I don't know a great deal about it, except that they all thought it was for the best that Audrey should move. Apparently the lady she was living with, Miss Thomson, was elderly and not really able to cope with an evacuee... Oh dear! I do so hate that word! And I do hope my little Audrey wasn't unhappy there or ill-treated. We hated sending her away, Alf and me, but we thought it was the best thing to do, especially as we knew that I had to go into hospital. Oh dear, oh dear! It has worried me so much, and now that I've heard that they've moved her...' She looked at Lily appealingly, her pale blue eyes starting to brim over with tears.

'I'm sure she's fine,' said Lily. 'If she had been unhappy she would have said so, wouldn't she?'

'I don't know. She might not have wanted to worry me. She knew I wasn't well, although we didn't tell her everything...'

'But I'm sure my Maisie would have said summat...er...something. She tells me all the news, and she said they're having a real good time up there in Middlebeck, her and Audrey, and two other girls they've met. They've joined the Brownies at the church, and they like their teacher at school. And I get sick of hearing about how wonderful this Mrs Fairchild is.' She laughed. 'Aunty Patience, Maisie calls her. So if your Audrey has gone to live there, then everything's fine, isn't it? Try not to worry about her.'

Edith Dennison nodded, a little unsurely. 'Yes, you're right. But I shan't be satisfied until I've seen her for myself and I've found out what's really behind this move. I'm thinking of going next Saturday if there's a through train to Middlebeck. Well, even if I have to change trains, I'll still have to go. I've left it too long.'

'And so have I,' said Lily decidedly. 'Far too long...' She felt guilty; she hadn't got the legitimate excuse that she had been ill as had the other woman. 'Listen...Edith; I'll find out about the trains, shall I? It'll save you the trouble. Then we'll go together up to Middlebeck, how about that? Of course I shall have to take these two scallywags with me...'

'Yes, of course you will,' said Edith. 'I'm sure their big sister will be pleased to see them. Good as gold, aren't they, bless them?'

Lily took a deep breath and hid a wry smile. 'They're not so bad, sometimes,' she replied. 'They have their moments.'

'Don't they all?' said Edith, fondly. 'Alf and I regret at times that Audrey is an only child. We would have liked to have more children, but it wasn't to be. We'd been married for nine years before Audrey came along. We'd given up hope because I was forty-five. And then...well, there she was. It seemed like a miracle. But of course I was too old to have any more. You have to count your blessings, though, don't you, Lily? I always try to tell myself that.'

'Yes...I suppose you do,' said Lily.

⸺

The following Saturday morning the two women, with Joanie and Jimmy, met at the bus stop in Armley as they had arranged, to catch a bus to City Square. They were to board a train soon after eight-thirty, one that would take them through the moorland and the dales, northwards to the little town of Middlebeck.

The late November morning was chilly and misty, so the children were bundled up like Eskimos in woollen coats, hats and mufflers. They were so excited, though, at the idea of going on a 'puffer train', as Jimmy called them, that they did not appear to be feeling the cold. Lily was, however. It seemed to seep into her very bones and she guessed it would be colder the further north they went. She had an extra jumper on underneath her red coat, which she had been determined to wear, but she had decided against the patent leather shoes and silk stockings, opting instead for her comfy flat shoes and thick lisle stockings to keep out the cold.

Edith was clad in the brown coat and hat she had worn the other day, but with a fox fur around her shoulders. This attracted curious looks from the children, until Edith invited them to stroke it.

'What is it?' asked Joanie. 'Is it real?'

'Will it bite?' asked Jimmy.

'No,' laughed Edith. 'It won't hurt you. It's a fox; at least it was, once upon a time…' She didn't go into any more detail and the children seemed satisfied at that.

They were behaving very well that morning and Lily felt quite proud of them, for almost the first time in their lives. Not since they had been babies had she felt so much affection for them. She had the old pushchair with her, the one she had used when Maisie was a baby, which was rather worse for wear by now. Jimmy still rode in it when he was tired. That was when he usually started whining, and Lily did not know how far they might have to walk to the rectory when they left the train at Middlebeck station.

Mrs Fairchild had written – not to Lily, but to Mrs Dennison as it was she who had written to tell her of the proposed visit – to say that she would meet them off the train when they arrived, which should, all being well, be soon after ten-thirty.

The journey was not a long one. The place where the girls were now living was in the same county, but in the north rather than the west riding. Yorkshire was the largest county in England, as Lily remembered being told, with some pride, in school geography lessons. It was often referred to, also, as 'God's own county', although it was possible, thought Lily, that inhabitants of Lancashire or Westmorland, for instance, might say the same about their county.

Lily was Yorkshire born and bred, and proud of it, although she had not seen a great deal of the county apart from the environs of Leeds and

Bradford. A long time ago she had visited the lovely little village of Grassington, in Wharfedale, where Davey had been born and had lived until coming to Leeds to work. She had been to Scarborough, too, and she had fond memories of the lively seaside resort on the east coast where she and Davey and Maisie had once spent such a happy holiday. But she had never visited the part of Yorkshire for which they were now bound. She had heard that parts of the county, away from the grime of the industrial cities and mill towns, had some of the loveliest scenery of anywhere in England.

When the train arrived, only fifteen minutes late, from its starting point much further south, it was crowded – with servicemen from all three of the armed forces and civilians on weekend trips – but not so crowded that they were obliged to stand. Lily feared at first that this might be so, but a good-natured RAF recruit – who looked no more than sixteen – stood to let her have his seat, and then nudged his pal, who did the same for Edith. The two lads helped her to fold up the pushchair, leaving it in the corridor with the piles of kit-bags and suitcases, and the rest of the people in the compartment budged up to make room for the two women and children. Jimmy sat on Lily's knee and Joanie knelt by the window, eagerly watching the passing scenery.

They left behind the smoky chimneys of the myriad woollen mills and of the factories producing chemicals, furniture and industrial machinery. Streams of water pouring from the surrounding hillsides down rocky gills and cloughs had long been used to bring power to the factories and textile mills. On the outskirts of the city the wheels and slag heaps of collieries were to be seen; but farmlands, too, crept close to the city boundaries, and soon they were out in the open country. This was the rich farming land of the Vale of York, in a wide valley of rolling fields. But the hills were not far away. To the west were the dales, and over there, somewhere, was Grassington, Davey's birthplace. And to the east lay the north York moors. The tower of Ripon cathedral came into view on the horizon, and when they had passed that market town they began to travel through the wild countryside of the dales.

They passed waterfalls cascading down the narrow gills between limestone rocks. The lower slopes of the valleys were patterned with a criss-cross of drystone walls, between which hardy sheep were grazing. The villages and hamlets they passed were composed largely of little greystone cottages, with here and there a larger mansion set in its own grounds. In the distance, now and again, they caught a glimpse of the ruins of a castle or of an ancient monastery; then as they travelled further north the landscape became more stark and bare, the hillsides revealing scars where once there had been lead mines.

Jimmy had fallen asleep, lulled by the motion of the train, and Joanie had been persuaded to sit down instead of kneeling on the seat. She was busy now filling in a picture in a colouring book with wax crayons. Lily was amazed at their good behaviour and hoped it would continue for the whole of their visit.

'Are you feeling all right, Edith?' she asked. She had grown quite accustomed to using the older woman's Christian name now. Her companion had gone very quiet, after remarking about the diversity of the passing scenery and, as usual, she looked pale and washed out.

'Yes…yes, thank you,' replied Edith. 'Just a little tired. But it's the result of the operation. They've told me I can expect that.'

It was the first time she had referred to her operation. All Lily knew was that she had spent a while in hospital, but she had not divulged any details. Now it seemed as though she might want to talk about it. Lily waited, not wishing to pressurise her. Edith was a very self-contained woman as a rule. Lily had discovered she was a very nice person, too; not a bit stuck-up, although it was clear that she and her husband, Alf – whom Lily had met only once – had far more in the way of wordly goods than did Lily and her family.

Alf Dennison was a bank manager at a branch near the city centre and travelled there and back each day in his small Morris car. This, so Edith had told her, had been a recent acquisition, purchased only a couple of months before war had broken out. It had made it much easier for him to visit his wife whilst she had been in the Leeds hospital. Now, however, conscious of the war effort and the rationing of petrol – which had started almost as soon as the commencement of the war – he was sharing the driving with his deputy manager, the two of them taking it in turns to use their vehicles. And if their petrol ration ran out they would have to use the bus or tram, like thousands of others.

After a few moments Edith started to speak, in a hushed voice. 'I had an operation, you see, only a couple of weeks after our Audrey went up to Middlebeck. That's why we decided to send her, really. We thought it might be better if she was well away from it all. The trouble is we have no relations that she could have stayed with. Alf and I are only children, both of us, and our parents are long gone.'

'Yes...I see,' said Lily. 'Was it a serious operation? You don't have to tell me if you don't want to, but...'

'But I would like to,' interrupted Edith. She looked around anxiously at the other occupants of the carriage, but no one seemed to be taking any notice. The two RAF lads had gone, their places having been taken by two young soldiers who, Lily guessed, might be heading for Catterick camp in the far north of Yorkshire. They were talking and laughing together and the rest of the passengers were either reading or dozing.

Edith tentatively touched her left breast, then moved her hand away quickly. 'It was...here,' she whispered. 'A lump. I had part of my...er...breast removed. But the doctors say that they think I'm going to be all right. They think they've...they've got it all away.' Her voice was scarcely audible. 'I've been having treatment,' she went on, 'once a week at the hospital. Alf takes me there; he gets time off work. Radiation treatment, I think they call it. But it makes me rather tired...' She smiled weakly. 'I wanted you to know, Lily. Then you'll understand why I'm such a weary companion at times.'

'I don't think you are weary at all,' replied Lily. 'I think you are very brave, making this journey. And thank you for telling me about it.'

Edith nodded. 'It helps sometimes to talk to somebody. Alf is very good, very patient with me, but it's a woman's problem, isn't it? I think women understand these things far better than men do.'

'Yes, I'm sure they do,' said Lily. 'What about your husband though, Edith? Didn't he want to come with you today, to see Audrey? He's not working, is he? Not on a Saturday?'

'No...but he thought it was best if just I went. And then when I said I would get in touch with you, he thought that was a splendid idea. He's an old softie in some ways, is Alf, and if he was to see Audrey I think he might want to bring her back with us. And if Audrey saw both of us, together, it might upset her. Some of the children have gone back already, you know.'

'Yes, so I've heard,' said Lily. 'Not very many though. And they'll have gone back to school. There was no question of it closing because there were more stayed behind than left.'

'There'll be some changes though,' Edith told her. 'I've heard that the headmaster, Mr Ormerod, has joined the RAF.'

'Well, fancy that! I didn't know.'

'And you remember Audrey and Maisie's teacher, that Miss Patterdale? I think she used to make quite a fuss of our Audrey, but Audrey wasn't all that keen on her.'

'No, Maisie didn't like her much either,' said Lily. 'Anyway, what about her?'

'I've heard that she's gone and joined the ATS.'

'Well I never!'

'I can just imagine her in the army, the way she treated those children. At any rate, they've got an elderly man there now, in charge of the school, sixty-five if he's a day from the look of him. I don't know about a replacement for Mr Ormerod, but I believe a lot of married women are going back to teaching now.'

Lily smiled. 'You're a mine of information, Edith. Our two'll be pleased to hear the news from home, won't they?'

'You haven't thought about taking your Maisie back home, have you?' asked Edith. 'I've wondered, I must admit, with everything being so quiet. I mean, they're calling it the 'bore war', aren't they? Nothing much is happening, no bombs dropping, not anywhere. Not that we want them to, but...'

'Oh no, I don't think so,' replied Lily hurriedly. 'It's not that I don't want my little lass back, but things are not too good at home between me and my husband. He's Maisie's step-father, y'see, not her real dad and...well...she wasn't very happy. I wanted her to have a change, and more of a chance in life...'

'Oh yes...I understand,' said Edith, looking at her sympathetically. 'Only I've heard some folks say that it'll all be over by Christmas. But my Alf doesn't think so.'

'They said that about the last war, didn't they?' remarked Lily. 'And look what happened there. More than four years of it.'

'Oh, deary me!' Edith shook her head. 'Let's

hope and pray that the same things doesn't happen again. Four years! It doesn't bear thinking of.'

Jimmy began to stir on his mother's lap and the next minute his blue eyes were open wide. 'Mummy, I want to wee,' he said.

'So do I,' said Joanie, not wanting to be left out now that her little brother was awake. 'Come on, Mummy. I'm dying to go.'

Chapter Fourteen

I t was easy for Patience, also, to recognise the visitors. Who else could it be but Mrs Dennison and Mrs Bragg, plus the two children and a pushchair, the only people to alight at Middlebeck station? She welcomed them warmly, assisting with the pushchair and helping the little girl – that must be Joanie, she decided – to take a big jump from the step to the platform.

Both women shook her outstretched hand.

'How do you do?' said Mrs Dennison, very politely and with just a touch of reserve, very much like Audrey, in fact. 'I'm very pleased to meet you, Mrs Fairchild.'

'Hello there,' said Mrs Bragg, with the same warmth and friendliness that Patience had grown accustomed to in the woman's daughter. 'I've heard such a lot about you from my Maisie. It's grand to meet you at last.'

The two women were, by and large, as she had expected them to be; Mrs Dennison, though, a little older, maybe, that she had anticipated; and as for Mrs Bragg...well, Patience admitted to herself that this lady looked quite a bit smarter. She was a pretty woman with dark hair, like Maisie's, on top of which was perched a jaunty little red hat with a feather in the side. Her smile was Maisie's too, but her face was a trifle strained, with more lines around her eyes and mouth than a young woman of her age ought to have. From Maisie's chatter Patience had learned that Lily Bragg was not yet thirty. However, she appeared cheerful, much more so than she usually might be, Patience guessed; happy, no doubt to be enjoying a rare day away from her problems at home. And dressed up for the occasion, too, in the red hat and coat which made her look bright and eye-catching.

Mrs Dennison, at her side, appeared much more matronly and sombre, although it was obvious that her clothes were expensive, if unbecoming. Patience knew she had been ill, though not aware exactly of what had been the problem; but the woman had an unhealthy pallor which she did not like the look of at all.

As for the two children, Joanie and Jimmy, they were fair-haired, solid looking infants who resembled neither their mother nor their big sister. Patience supposed they must take after their father, the infamous Sid. There was no sign, as yet, however, of the bad behaviour that Maisie had complained about, but maybe time would tell. Jimmy was put into his pushchair where he sat silently and uncomplainingly, whilst Joanie trotted along at the side, one hand on the pram handle and the other holding on to her mother's

'Where're we going?' she asked, as they made their way out of the station.

'To see Maisie,' said her mother. 'I told you... You remember Maisie, don't you?'

The little girl shook her head, looking puzzled.

'Dunno,' she said. 'Don't think so... How far is it, where we're going?'

It was Patience who answered. 'Not very far, dear,' she answered. 'About ten minutes walk. It's about half a mile from the station to the church,' she told the two women. 'Can you manage that, Joanie? Just a little walk, then you'll be able to see your big sister again. Maisie's been looking forward to seeing you both, I can tell you.' She beamed at the child, but Joanie just regarded her stolidly, uncomprehendingly, it seemed. But three months was a long time to a child, Patience supposed, and the little girl might well have forgotten her sister.

'I'm tired,' said Joanie, pouting a little.

'No, you're not; you can't be,' said her mother. 'You had a good rest on the train. Now for goodness' sake, don't you start whining...' She fumbled in her bag. ''Ere y'are. There's a jelly baby, an' one for you an' all, Jimmy. Now behave yerselves, the pair of yer; think on!'

That seemed to do the trick, that first jelly baby, followed by two more. Patience hoped the sweets would not spoil their dinner, but she decided it was none of her business. She could well understand that a harrassed mother might have to give way to bribery now and again.

'We don't have a car,' she explained. 'My husband's parish is fairly compact, apart from a few outlying farms, and he manages his visits on a bicycle. And in these days of petrol rationing there is not much advantage in owning a car anyway. I wondered about bringing Maisie and Audrey along with me to meet you, but then I decided it might be better for me to have a word with you first. Now, Mrs Dennison, there is something we must talk about...'

'Yes,' replied that lady. 'Whatever has been going on? I've been really worried, Mrs Fairchild. My Audrey...she's not been a nuisance, has she, to that lady, that Miss Thomson? She is usually such a good girl.'

'So she is,' replied Patience. 'She's a credit to you, Mrs Dennison. And so is Maisie, Mrs Bragg. They are grand girls, both of them, and my husband and I feel privileged to be looking after them. No...it would not be fair to say that she has been a nuisance to Miss Thomson, but there was – what shall I say? – a little misunderstanding. It was all to do with the maid really, a young woman called Daisy.'

'Yes, Audrey mentioned Daisy in her letters,' said Mrs Dennison. 'She said she was nice and that she was looking after her.'

'Quite so,' said Patience. She went on to explain, as prosaically as she could, about the incident with the door and about Audrey's reluctant involvement in it. She did not say how fiercely Miss Thomson had reacted, how she had shaken and shouted at Audrey, even striking her across the face. It was sufficient of a shock to Mrs Dennison to hear of Audrey's part in the escapade.

'Oh dear, that's dreadful!' she exclaimed. 'It doesn't sound like my Audrey at all, behaving like that. How naughty and irresponsible... But I suppose it was that maid, was it, that led her on? It sounds as though the child is much better away from a flighty sort of girl like that. A bit of a trollop, is she, this Daisy?'

'No, not at all,' said Patience. She felt annoyed that such a word should be used about Daisy, but she did not let her indignation show. After all, Mrs Dennison was not to know. 'Daisy is a good-hearted girl, and – usually – quite a sensible one. But she is a young woman who is in love and, because of that, I think we can forgive her. Her young man has already joined the army, and now Daisy has applied to join the ATS. She is just waiting for her call-up papers. Miss Thomson dismissed her at first, but then she regretted it and asked her to stay on. And Daisy has agreed to do so – as I said, she's a very good-natured girl – but only till she joins the ATS.'

'So this…Miss Thomson, she will have to find another maid?' said Mrs Dennison.

'It seems so,' replied Patience. 'But that's easier said than done, I should imagine, with young women going into the forces and munitions work. And the Women's Land Army, of course; that has been started up again.'

'I should think it serves her right if she's left without a maid,' commented Lily Bragg. 'Anyroad, it's an ill wind, as they say, isn't it? It means that our two girls have ended up together. I'm sure they're glad about that, aren't they?'

'Yes…I do thank you, of course, Mrs Fairchild, for taking Audrey as well as Maisie,' said Mrs Dennison. 'I'm sorry…I should have said thank you straight away, but I was so concerned to hear about what had happened. Oh, I just can't wait to see her…'

Patience smiled. 'Well, you don't need to wait any longer. Here we are.' She pushed open the iron gate and led the way up the path.

But before she had a chance to get out her key, the door opened and there were Maisie and Audrey, with Luke in the hallway just behind them.

'Mum...' cried both little girls, simultaneously, and then both mothers and daughters ran to greet one another with a big hug and kiss.

'You look nice, Mum,' said Maisie, looking at her mother appraisingly as they stood in the hallway. 'Have you got a new coat and hat?'

'Yes, sort of new,' said Lily. 'I have to try and look me best, y'know... Eeh, Maisie love, it's grand to see you again. I've missed yer such a lot. And so have the little 'uns.'

Maisie was delighted at the warmth of her mother's greeting; there were tears of joy in Lily's eyes, something her daughter had very rarely seen. But the 'little 'uns' seemed singularly unmoved. Maisie doubted very much that they had missed her, or that they were pleased to see her again. Lily nudged the little sister and brother.

'Here's our Maisie, see. Aren't you going to say hello to her?'

Joanie was staring fixedly at her big sister. She pointed her finger. 'That's Nellie,' she said. 'I don't know no Maisie.'

Lily laughed. 'Oh yes, of course! That's what she's always called you. I was forgetting.' She stooped down to Joanie. 'She's got a new name now. She's called Maisie.'

'Yes, I'm Maisie now,' said the big sister, quite

indignantly. 'Hello Joanie, hello Jimmy. You've grown, haven't yer?' And they looked, to Maisie's eyes, unusually clean and tidy too. It seemed as though there had been some changes in her absence, unless it was just a special effort on her mother's part for today's visit.

'Why're you called Maisie then?' asked Joanie.

''Cause that's what I wanted to be called. 'Cause I hated being Nellie...'

'Why? Why did yer?'

''Cause I did, that's all!'

Patience stepped in, aware that Maisie was becoming a little distressed. 'Now, come along into the sitting room, all of you. There's a nice fire in there, and I'll go and make us all a cup of tea while you have a chat to Luke.' He had already introduced himself to the two women and assisted them in taking off their coats.

'It's why, why, why? all the time with our Joanie now,' said Lily. 'Tek no notice of her, Maisie love. She'll soon get used to you again, and yer new name. And Jimmy an' all.'

The little boy seemed to have totally forgotten her. He stared at her with a bewildered expression on his face. Then he smiled, still a little unsurely. ''Ello...Maisie,' he said.

Maisie felt a surge of affection for both the children, which surprised her, and she realised she was, indeed, glad to see them again, especially away from their home environment. Maybe that was what made the difference.

When Patience returned with the tea they all chatted together; light-hearted inconsequential talk about the school in Armley and the changes there, and about how the two girls were enjoying their new school and the various activities connected with school and church. Then Patience asked Maisie and Audrey if they could assist her for a few moments in the kitchen as she had a big meal to prepare that day, for eight people instead of the usual four. Maisie guessed that Luke might want to talk to their mothers without the two of them 'earwigging'. The little 'uns would take no notice. They were already playing a game with toy cars on the hearthrug...and how remarkably placid they were, she marvelled.

'My wife and I are delighted to have your two girls with us,' Luke told the women. 'There was a little incident recently – Patience will have told you about that – but, as it happened, it all worked together for good; and I'm sure Audrey will be happy with us, as I like to think Maisie has been.'

Both women nodded and murmured their agreement. 'I'd better not mention it to Audrey, then?' questioned Edith Dennison. 'About how she came to leave this Miss Thomson?'

'No, it's best forgotten,' replied Luke. 'And I want you both to know that your girls are safe here with us – God willing, of course – for as long as is necessary. You will be aware, though, I am sure, that several of our visitors have already gone back, to Leeds and to Hull.'

'But...do you think that is wise?' asked Edith. 'Alf – my husband – and I had wondered whether to have Audrey back home, just for Christmas, perhaps; but it might unsettle her, and us as well, of course. I don't think we would be able to bring ourselves to part with her again.'

Luke smiled and nodded understandingly. 'Yes, it's a thorny problem, I agree. It's my belief that this is just the calm before the storm. The parents who have taken their children back home, they may live to regret it.'

'I want Maisie to stay,' said Lily decidedly. 'Now as I've seen how happy she is, and how lovely it is round here I know I was right to let her go. I wanted her to have a chance, y'see, Reverend... Is that what we should call you? I wasn't sure.'

'Just call me Luke,' he said, grinning. 'That's what your two girls call me, at least Maisie does and I'm sure Audrey will soon do the same. I don't feel that it's disrespectful, and I want them to know that I'm a friend to both of them.'

'OK then...Luke.' Lily grinned back at him. 'And I'm Lily, and Mrs Dennison is Edith. We've only got to know one another properly today, haven't we, Edith? But we seem to get on fine together. Anyway, like I was saying, I'm glad Maisie's had the chance to come here. I don't mind telling yer that I've had problems at home, an' I didn't want Maisie to be part of them no longer... It seems like an excuse though, doesn't it? I mean, if the war hadn't happened, she'd still be with me in Armley, wouldn't she?'

'I don't think we can dwell too much on the ifs and buts,' said Luke. 'We have to look at the situation as it is. We have been only too pleased to help Maisie. She has told us a little... Ah, here is my wife.' He looked across and smiled as Patience came back into the room. 'I was just saying, my dear, that Maisie has told us a little about her problems at home.' But Patience and Luke had already agreed not to tell Maisie's mother about how distraught the child had been on that first night.

'Yes; we gather she did not get on too well with her step-father and his son,' said Patience. 'She hasn't said very much, but we are able to read between the lines, as it were, and we know that she has been worried about you as well, and your…situation with your husband. But we can assure you, Mrs Bragg, that this is confidential and it will go no further.'

'It doesn't matter very much any more,' said Lily. 'I'm Lily, by the way…I don't like being called Mrs Bragg. I think folks back home – some of 'em anyroad – know as Sid and me aren't happy. I've mentioned it to Edith here.'

'Yes, we are aware that both of you ladies have had problems,' said Patience. 'I've left your girls setting the table, by the way, so we can have a little private chat. They're such good girls and they're feeling very important being left in charge of the dining room… Yes, we know you have been quite poorly…er, Edith? I may call you Edith, may I? And we know a little about Lily's situation.'

'And we want you to know,' Luke continued, 'that if there is anything further we can do to help, then that is what we are here for. Anytime you want to come, either of you, then just feel free to do so. You can stay a night or two if you wish, your home circumstances permitting, of course.'

'Aye, that's the problem though,' said Lily. 'When Maisie first come up here I was all for coming with her. We'd had a bit of a set-to, y' see, the night before, and Sid told me to clear off and take the kids with me. Then he changed his mind and said I had to stay and look after him and his son. I'm between the devil and the deep and that's a fact. I daresn't leave; he'd only come after me and make me go back.'

Patience's heart went out to her. 'It isn't right that you should suffer abuse,' she said carefully, not wanting to admit to how much she already knew of the woman's problems. 'And you have the children to consider...'

'At least he doesn't hit me no more,' said Lily with a wry smile. 'He ignores me most o' t' time.'

That poor young woman, thought Patience. What a dreadful existence some folks had to endure. This war was showing up all kinds of misery and futility in people's lives. 'Well, you are having a day away from your problems today, aren't you?' she said. 'Your husband...he didn't mind you coming?'

'He wasn't interested,' said Lily. 'I told him, but I might just as well be talking to a brick wall.'

'Lily...' said Edith, a little unsurely. 'I didn't realise that things were quite so bad. If you ever want somebody to talk to...well, you know where I am and you mustn't hesitate to come and see me. I hope you will come anyway, not just because of your...problems. I feel I've made a new friend,' she added shyly.

'Well, isn't that nice?' said Patience. She guessed

that Edith Dennison did not find it easy to break down her innate reserve. 'It's lovely to make new friends.'

'Thank you, Edith,' said Lily, looking very touched at the other woman's overture of friendship. 'I'd like that. I suppose I thought you might be...well, a bit posh for the likes of me. I do cleaning jobs, y'see, at some of the houses near to Edith's,' she explained to Luke and Patience. 'And some of the women are a bit snooty, like. But Edith's not like that at all.'

'My wife and I are finding that this war is a great leveller,' said Luke, 'and I am sure it will be even more so before it's ended. The evacuation scheme is a case in point. We have had very few problems here, and it has helped us all to undestand one another a little better. And I am sure it is so in the armed forces as well, although...' He shook his head sorrowfully, 'We wish, of course, that it wasn't this wretched war that has caused us all to become more friendly.'

He and his wife exchanged a look of warmth and perfect accord, and then Patience stood up. 'If you would all like to come into the dining room, I will serve out the meal,' she said. 'Luke, could you seat everybody, please, dear? And what a good job you have made with the table, girls. Well done!'

The table had been extended to its full length and extra chairs brought from the kitchen. Jimmy no longer used his high chair at home, so he was able to manage with two plump cushions on his chair, as was Joanie. The meal was a delicious meat and potato pie topped with a suet crust, followed by apple crumble – there was still a plentiful supply harvested from the rectory garden – and creamy custard. Maisie had wondered how the two terrors would behave. She could not help thinking of them in that way, remembering how they had used to slop their food around, sometimes indulging in a game of throwing spoonfuls at one another. But they both conducted themselves very well, eating the potatoes and meat and the cut-up crust with a spoon, which was permissible, and with only a few dribbles on their bibs and little splodges on the tablecloth. Maisie, left in charge, had decided against Patience's carefully laundered white cloth, choosing instead a serviceable red checked one.

Patience knew that the two mothers and their children would want to spend some time alone together, and so, in the early afternoon the six of them set off for a walk in the surrounding countryside. Maisie and Audrey were pleased and proud to lead the way through the churchyard and along the lane that led to the farm and then to the squire's estate.

The early morning mist had cleared, but the day was still cold with a weak sun shining fitfully between the grey clouds. The trees were almost completely bare, with only a few decaying leaves hanging on the branches and piles of crinkly brown ones lying in piles beneath the hedgerows. But there was no denying the beauty of the scenery even in its sombre-hued autumn mood, nor the atmosphere of peace and tranquillity that prevailed.

'Our friend lives there, at that farm,' said Maisie, pointing to the farmyard where the hens were clucking and flapping around. 'Doesn't she, Audrey?'

'Yes; she's called Doris,' replied Audrey. 'Look, Jimmy and Joanie; look at the chickens. And there's the rooster, see; the one with the big red comb on his head.'

Joanie and Jimmy, from his pushchair, stared through the five-barred gate and the mothers exchanged amused glances.

'Quite the little country girls now, aren't they?' remarked Edith.

Lily nodded. 'Yes; I was just thinking the same. And don't they look well? They've both got roses in their cheeks, and I do believe Maisie has grown two inches.'

'And so has Audrey,' said Edith. 'And she's much more self-assured than she used to be. They've been lucky though. I don't suppose all the children have got such a nice home as ours have.'

Maisie decided that as Doris was nowhere to be seen they had better move on. 'We'll show you where the squire lives,' she said. 'It's a right big house with loads of rooms, but they've got evacuees, same as other people; mothers and babies...well, kids like Jimmy and Joanie, some of 'em. You could've stayed there, Mum, if you'd come with us.'

'Ah well; it wasn't to be, was it,' said Lily with a little sigh. 'Squire, eh? That sounds posh.'

'He's not posh really,' said Maisie. 'He's dead nice and friendly.'

'Yes, an' he's got a son called Bruce,' added Audrey. 'His dog frightened me the first day, but I've got used to it now.'

'Yes, you've got a lot more confidence now, dear,' said her mother. 'You've become quite grown-up, all of a sudden,' she added, a little sadly.

'We were just saying how well you both look,' said Lily. 'Yer hair's real nice, Maisie, now as it's grown again. And you've got some new clothes an' all, haven't you? I haven't seen that coat before, nor that jumper and skirt.' She looked rather crestfallen, and Maisie understood how she must be feeling. New clothes, back in Armley, had been very few and far between.

'Oh, they're not really new,' she explained. 'Aunty Patience got 'em from a collection they had in the church hall when we first arrived; second-hand things that kids had grown out of. Lots of us got new things. Audrey didn't, though, 'cause she'd got lots of nice clothes already.'

'Yes, she was a lucky girl,' said Edith dismissively, 'but never mind about all that. I'm so pleased that the two of you are such good friends. And that's what your mum and I are going to be, I hope, Maisie... I have been wondering though, dear...' She turned to Audrey. 'Do you really think you ought to call the Reverend Fairchild, Luke? I know he says he likes you to, but it seems...well, too familiar to me, too...irreverent. Of course I know I'm a bit old-fashioned.'

'I haven't called him anything yet,' said Audrey.

'But I do,' said Maisie. 'Y' see, Uncle Luke is hard to say, isn't it? You just try saying it...Uncle Luke, Unclook, Unclook...'

'Unclook, Unclook...' joined in Audrey, followed by a delighted Joanie who had been listening with great interest. The three of them fell about laughing, staggering all over the lane.

Lily and Edith laughed too. 'Eeh, it does me good to see 'em so happy,' said Lily. 'Oh look, d'you think that's the squire's place they were telling us about?' She pointed towards the large stone-built mansion just ahead, at the end of a long driveway. 'Oh, I say; fancy you knowing somebody as lives in a place like that, Maisie,' she shouted to her daughter.

'Well, we do, don't we Audrey?' said Maisie. 'We'll go along that path and we'll show you the garden at the back. But there'll be no flowers there now, I don't suppose.'

'Are you sure we can go up there, dear?' asked Edith. 'Won't we be trespassing?'

'No, 'course we won't... Oh look, there's Mrs Booth and Billy and Brenda.' Maisie started to wave. 'Yoo-hoo...hello, Mrs Booth...'

They all met in the middle of the path and stopped to say hello. Lily and Edith looked curiously at the young woman. 'I know you, don't I?' said Lily. 'I've seen you shopping in Armley, haven't I?'

'And so have I,' said Edith, 'but I only know you by sight. We're very pleased to meet you properly, Mrs Booth.' She held out her hand. 'I'm...er...Edith and this is Lily. We're visiting our girls for the day.'

'So I see; that's nice,' said the young woman, shaking their hands. 'I know Maisie and Audrey, don't I, girls? We were all in the same carriage on the way here. I'm Sally, by the way. Never mind all that Mrs Booth nonsense.'

'Out, out...' said Jimmy, struggling to get out of his pushchair, having seen two more children roughly his age and size. Lily released him and the four infants ran off together, seeming to make friends quite easily. The two bigger girls went too, to keep an eye on them.

'They'll be OK,' said Sally. 'No cars come along here; it's just for people on foot, like. We were just having a bit of a breather, the kids and me, before I go back to help Mrs Tremaine with the evening meal. There's not many of us left though, now. Only me and my two, and another woman, Dolly, and her two. An' she says she's going back to Leeds before Christmas, an' all. There's nowt happening, y' see.'

'Well, I suppose we must be thankful for that,' said Edith. 'It can't last for ever, though, can it, this...uneasy sort of peace?'

'That's what my hubby says,' replied Sally. 'He's in the army, so he knows what he's on about. He doesn't tell me too much, mind; their letters are censored, y' know. Aye, they have a big blue pencil line through all t' bits that might be giving away secrets, or else they cut 'em out wi' scissors. Anyroad, he said to me, "You stay where you are, love, where I know you'll be safe."'

'So you're not thinking of going back to Armley?' asked Lily.

'Not on yer life! No...I love it round here. I'm thinking of staying on, even after the war finishes, whenever that is. And Joe – that's my hubby – he thinks it might be a good idea an' all. The air's lovely and fresh up here, and talk about quiet! I couldn't get used to it at first after living in a big city, but I know it's a much nicer place to bring the kiddies up. Our house in Armley is only a little two up and two down, rented of course. So I think we'll stay on, if things work out.'

Lily felt quite envious as she listened to her. It seemed as though Sally Booth had got it made. 'But...what do you do all the time?' she asked. 'I mean...isn't it like one long holiday? I know you've got two children to look after, but...'

'Oh, I'm second-in-command to Mrs Tremaine now,' Sally replied, with some pride. 'I help with the cooking and cleaning and...well, everything really. Anyway, I was never able to sit on me behind all day and expect folks to wait on me. Mind you, that's what some of 'em did, the lazy devils! You wouldn't believe it! Mrs Tremaine was glad to see the back of 'em, I can tell yer.' She paused, fractionally, for breath.

'Actually...it's not definite at the moment, but there's some talk of making the squire's place into a hostel for the Land Army women. Just a small one, like, but there'll be room for at least ten or twelve of 'em and the rest'll be found digs in Middlebeck. And Mrs Tremaine is going to put me in charge of the girls, she says. So I'll have a proper job, and a proper wage an' all, I hope.'

'That sounds great,' said Lily. 'You've fallen on yer feet.'

'Aye, I'm not complaining,' said Sally, grinning. 'I'm glad I've met you both... Come on Billy... Brenda...' she called. The children were playing a game of tig, organised by Maisie and Audrey, some twenty yards away down the lane. 'Come on now, an' we'll carry on with our walk. It'll be getting dark soon.'

Although it was only late afternoon the day was drawing to a close, the sky darkening rapidly with the disappearance of the sun. As the little party continued with their walk, Maisie pointed out that the squire's terraced garden where, in the late summer, there had been a profusion of colourful flowers, had been now completely dug over.

'I expect they'll soon be growing vegetables there, not flowers,' Edith remarked. 'That's what they'll be wanting us all to do, I suppose, to dig over our back gardens. Alf's real proud of his flower beds, but I reckon they'll have to go eventually.'

Lily did not comment; all she had was a small paved yard with a communal lavatory at the end. She had certainly had a glimpse that day of how some other folk lived. To Edith, though, it would not have seemed so much of a contrast, she pondered. She knew she had no choice but to return to her – so-called – home with Sid and to 'grin and bear it'. It was some solace to her, however, that Maisie had got away and was so contented in her new life. And she now had a new friend in Edith. The future, on the whole was beginning to look a little less bleak.

When they returned to the rectory the black-out curtains were already drawn, and the village green and the road leading down to the town was in almost complete darkness. All too soon it was time for them to take that road down to the station. They all went, Patience, Maisie and Audrey, as well as their visitors, Luke leading the way, with his torch illuminating a pathway through the blackness.

The train, fortunately, was only some ten minutes late in arriving. It was cold standing around on the platform and Patience knew that the longer the girls stood there the more sad they were likely to feel. Partings were dreadful at the best of times, but Maisie and Audrey had insisted on coming to say goodbye to their mothers.

Lily and Edith, sensibly, did not prolong the farewell, although there were tears in both their eyes. The girls, dewy-eyed, too, waved and waved until the train vanished out of sight.

'Never mind,' said Patience. 'We have all had a lovely happy day, and I'm sure it won't be long before you see your mums again.' Edith, however, had confided in her, woman to woman, about her operation, insisting, though, that she should not tell Audrey. And in spite of her assurances that she was quite well again, Patience could tell that that was not strictly true. The next few months, she guessed, could be crucial.

'Off we go home,' she said, trying to sound light-hearted. 'And how about a nice cup of cocoa? And then we can listen to 'Happidrome' on the wireless. How does that sound?'

'Great...' said the girls, both of them manfully trying to hide their tears.

Chapter Fifteen

It was Doris Nixon who invited Maisie and Audrey and the fourth member of their little crowd, Ivy Clegg, to join the Brownies. They met in the church hall each Tuesday evening at seven o'clock, with their leader, Brown Owl, alias Mrs Jessie Campion, one of the stalwart members of the Women's Institute and the WVS.

The three new members had joined in September, soon after their arrival in Middlebeck, and by November they were proudly wearing their new uniforms; a brown tunic with a leather belt, a brown beret, and a yellow tie on which was pinned a little golden brooch, depicting a brownie. Doris's tunic already sported several badges on the sleeve, awarded for such things as knitting, recognition of wild flowers, tying knots, and homecraft, which meant making a simple meal of a cup of tea and toast. Doris was a sixer, too, which meant she was the leader of a group of six girls. Maisie was put into her six, whilst the other two were in a different one.

The sixes had the names of fairy folk. Doris's six girls were pixies, and there were also gnomes, sprites, fairies and elves. No goblins, it was noted, because those little folk had a reputation for being naughty and badly-behaved.

'Here we come, the friendly pixies,

Helping others when in fixes...'
Doris's six would chant, skipping around the giant papier-mâché toadstool that stood in the centre of the room.

There were suitable little ditties, too, for the other folk; the helpful gnomes (helping mother in our homes); the sprightly sprites, jolly elves and happy fairies. They learned to say the Brownie promise, which was a shorter version of the more adult Guide promise.

'I promise on my honour to do my best, to do my duty to God and the King, and to help other people every day, especially those at home.'

They played team games, took part in quizzes, learned to tie simple knots such as the reef knot, and to understand the basic steps in First Aid. The meeting finished soon after eight o' clock with a cup of orange juice and a biscuit, after a jolly good time had been enjoyed by all.

Maisie enjoyed it very much, but, if she were honest, she found some of it a bit babyish...well, soppy really, all that stuff about friendly pixies and jolly elves. But she would never have dreamed of admitting it, especially as the Brownies were continually being ridiculed by the members of the little clique led by Gertie Flint. The rivalry had continued – for no good reason except that once it had started in tended to go on – between Maisie's little crowd, and Gertie and her henchmen, Norma, Paula and Esme. This four tormented the other four, but only when Miss Mellodey or the teacher on playground duty was nowhere in sight. The forming of 'gangs' or any sort of bullying was frowned upon, but that didn't stop it from going on away from adult eyes.

'Soppy old sprites...potty old pixies...' they would jeer. 'Do yer best, do yer best... Go and tie yerselves up with yer reef knots...'

'Take no notice of them,' said Doris, with a haughty shake of her flaxen tresses. 'They're just being childish.' She told her friends that Gertrude Flint and Norma Wilkins had used to belong to the Brownies, but Brown Owl had stopped them from attending any more. There was no room, she had said, for girls who were badly behaved and could not take it seriously.

As well as tormenting them in the playground and at hometimes, Gertie and her gang sometimes hung around on Tuesday evenings, hiding behind the bushes, then jumping out when the Brownies dispersed, dancing round them and calling silly names. But only to those girls who were finding their own way home. Doris's mum or dad came to meet her to see her home along the dark country lane to the farm, and Ivy's Aunty Mabel, the elderly lady she lived with, was usually there to escort her back to her home further down the High Street. Maisie and Audrey were only a stone's throw away from the rectory, but when Audrey had lived with Miss Thomson she had had to suffer the jeers and insults whilst crossing the village green.

Ivy Clegg, from Hull, was the most timid girl of the little group, and the other three, knowing this, tried to protect her and her little brother, Timothy. One evening in early December Aunty Mabel was unable to meet Ivy from Brownies. Her husband was out, playing in an important darts match and Mabel had to stay and look after Timothy. Ivy was equipped with a large torch and she insisted that she would be able to get home all right on her own. What she did not tell her aunt was that she was terrified in case Gertie and her gang should be there that evening. They were not always there, though, and she crossed her fingers tightly when she came out of the hall, praying that tonight they would give it a miss.

She breathed a sigh of relief when she had waved goodbye to her three friends and they had still not appeared. But she had hardly gone twenty yards down the High Street, shining her torch bravely in front of her, when they all jumped out, seemingly from nowhere, and started to prance around her.

'Oh look, here's one of the potty little pixies... Is that what you are Ivy, a potty pixie?'

'No, p'raps she's a fluttery fairy,' said Esme Clough, fluttering her arms like wings and doing a silly little dance.

'Or a gruesome goblin. Grrr...' growled Gertie. 'Oh no; they don't 'ave goblins, do they? They're naughty, are goblins, like what we are. They don't know 'ow to behave 'emselves!'

'Actually...I'm an elf,' retorted Ivy, feeling very scared, but determined to stick up for herself. 'And I don't see anything funny about it neither.'

It was quite the wrong thing to say. The other four hooted with laughter and huddled together in a little group, allowing Ivy, momentarily, to get away. But they were soon after her, having thought up some more ribaldry. They pursued her down the High Street, linking arms a couple of yards behind her and yelling, 'Here I come, a silly old elf, crying 'cause I've wet meself... Silly old elf...soppy old elf...'

Ivy started to run, but the faster she ran the more they pursued her. Then, when she turned the corner into the street where she lived, close to the market hall, she fell. The torch dropped from her hand, the glass shattering on the pavement, and she felt both her knees landing hard on the stony ground. She put out her hands to save herself, so she was not badly hurt, just winded and very frightened. But when she got up, her knees smarting like mad and one of them bleeding, her tormentors had vanished. She staggered the rest of the way home, luckily only a few yards further down the side street, crying out loud now and grasping the broken torch.

'I fell...' she sobbed to her Aunty Mabel. 'I was running and I fell, an' I'm sorry about the torch...'

Mabel Roystone was a sympathetic woman who had had children of her own many years ago, who were now living far away from Yorkshire with their own families. She had grown very fond of Ivy and little Tim and had tended to spoil them. She blamed herself for not meeting Ivy from Brownies. She bandaged her bleeding knee and made her a cup of cocoa, and Ivy soon stopped crying.

But she did not tell Aunty Mabel about the girls who had chased her. Just as, the next day, although she told Maisie and Audrey and Doris all about it, she did not tell Miss Mellodey. Nor did her friends say she should do so. You had to fight your own battles, with your friends helping you sometimes, but telling tales was something that you just did not do.

In mid-December the first snow of the winter fell, transforming the little town of Middlebeck into a white and wondrous world. It happened overnight, and how different everything seemed when the folk at the rectory drew back the curtains and the blackout blinds the following morning. They looked out on to a changed landscape. A white blanket covered the village green, the early morning sun making it glisten like diamonds. The roofs and chimney pots were topped with white, like the icing on a cake, and the bare branches of the trees, motionless in the still windless air, were touched with a delicate tracery of silvery white.

Audrey and Maisie – though more particularly, Maisie – couldn't wait to get out and enjoy it. They had experienced snow, of course, many times, but in the city streets it very quickly turned to brown slush, trodden underfoot by hundreds of tramping feet. Here on the green it was likely to remain for days and days unless a thaw set in. Clad in their winter coats, woolly hats and wellington boots they joined the other children in the playground. They indulged in playful snowball fights and quickly built lopsided snowmen in the time left to them before the whistle was blown.

Miss Mellodey was quite tolerant that day about little pools of water dripping from coats and wellingtons – most children, fortunately, had brought indoor shoes to change into – and the several pairs of sodden mittens drying on the fireguard. But she did warn them not to be too boisterous when they went out at playtime or their coats would be soaking wet and would not be dry before they went home. On the whole the pupils took heed of the warning. But Miss Mellodey and the other teachers could not prevent what might happen on the way home.

Audrey, if she were honest, was not all that keen on the snow, except to look at it – it really was very beautiful – and to walk in. She liked to see the footprints that her feet made in the untrodden snow, like an explorer in undiscovered territory. But when Gertie and her crowd started throwing snowballs when they came out of school at the end of the afternoon, she kept close to Maisie, trying to hide her dislike and her nervousness. Bravely she made a snowball of her own and threw it, rather tentatively, in the direction of Norma Wilkins, the least aggressive member of the Gertie gang. But Maisie and Audrey soon made their way towards the rectory and the other four turned away.

'Come on,' said Maisie, tucking her arm through her friends. 'I know you don't like it much, do yer? I can tell. But you did right not to let 'em know, Gertie and them. Oh heck! I hope Ivy'll be all right, but there's nothing much we can do about it. Oh look; they're going after her and Tim...'

'She'll be OK,' said Audrey. 'She's not on her own. Look, Jean and Peggy are with her. Anyway, they've left her alone, haven't they, since she fell that time on the way home from Brownies?'

Gertrude Flint and her cronies had been a little scared lest there should be repercussions about their tormenting of Ivy Clegg. They feared she might tell on them, to her new aunt or to Miss Mellodey, and so they had lain low for a while. It was clear by now, though, that Ivy had not said anything; but the fact that she was not a telltale did not deter them from having another go at her. And this snow was a wonderful opportunity. They guessed, being the scared little creature that she was, that she would not like it.

When Maisie and Audrey had gone the four of them raced after Ivy and her little brother, armed with balls of tightly packed snow. They pelted the brother and sister on their backs, and Timothy, turning round suddenly, caught one on his chin and started to cry. Jean and Peggy, classmates of Ivy, but not close friends, threw a few snowballs in retaliation; then, realising they were not really part of this skirmish, shrugged and made their own way home. Ivy seized Tim's hand and they ran, blundering and stumbling through the carpet of snow with their assailants in hot pursuit, shrieking with laughter and bombarding them unmercifully. But when Ivy and Tim turned the corner into their own street they ceased their attack. The fussy old woman that Ivy and Tim lived with might be at the door waiting for them.

So she was; and Tim's tears were soon wiped away and they were both comforted with a hot sweet cup of tea. 'I'll meet you out of school tomorrow,' said Aunty Mabel, hearing about the snowball fight. 'Poor little Tim! What dreadful girls they must be.'

'No; please don't,' said Ivy, more bravely than she was feeling. 'It'll only make them worse, and they don't mean any harm. It's only snow...and most kids like it, don't they?'

'I never did,' said Mabel smiling. 'I was like you, Ivy. But...all right, dear, if you're sure then I won't come.'

The next day was Friday and the snow still lay on the ground.

'Are you going to the picture show tomorrer?' asked Doris of her three friends when they all came out of school. 'Two o' clock at the Palace. It'll be dead good. They're showing a Charlie Chaplin film an' a Donald Duck cartoon, an' I don't know what else. Try and come, won't yer?'

'We're going,' said Maisie. 'Aren't we, Audrey? Aunty Patience says we can go.'

'I'll ask Aunty Mabel,' said Ivy. 'I'll have to bring Tim with me, though.'

'That's OK. You'll like it, won't yer, Tim?' said Maisie. 'See you outside then just before it starts. Oh look, Ivy...Gertie and them are going the other way. You'll be OK tonight.'

Gertie, Paula, Esme and Norma, linking arms, were walking off in the opposite direction. For whatever reason, they had decided to leave the Clegg children alone for the moment, and so Ivy and Tim walked home without fear.

Although Middlebeck was only a small market town it did have a cinema. The Palace, although anything less like a palace would be hard to imagine, was in a side street off the High Street, just beyond where the shops ended. The property had, in days gone by, been a chandler's shop, then it had been bought in the early thirties by an enterprising family and converted into a small, privately owned cinema. They showed reruns of films that had had their first showing at the Odeons and Empires of the larger towns and cities, and occasionally a Saturday matinee show was put on for the benefit of the children.

The four friends, and little Timothy, met outside the Palace at ten minutes to two, paid their sixpences to the lady in the cash desk and made their way inside. The cinema had quite comfortable seats – tip-up red plush ones, though a little worn and shabby – at the back for the patrons who could afford to pay a few pence extra. At the front there were rows of forms and that was where the children sat when there was a special film show for them. The seats were more than half filled already with boys and girls, shouting and screaming and bobbing up and down waving to their friends. Maisie and her little crowd found an empty bench half way back and sat down. A surreptitious glance around showed her that Gertie Flint and her bosom pals were seated on the other side of the aisle, a couple of rows further back. Hastily, she turned to the front again hoping that they had not seen her. She did not want any trouble that afternoon, not whilst they had little Tim with them.

The noise lessened somewhat when the lights were dimmed and the silken orange curtain, a little threadbare in places, was drawn back to reveal the screen. There was a sequence of adverts shown first, for local shops and businesses, through which the children continued to chatter. Then, when the title of the first film appeared there was a concerted cheer from the audience and they settled down to watch the antics of Donald Duck.

This was followed by a short cowboy film. The cowboys pursued the Indians, galloping like wildfire on horses, sometimes riding in stagecoaches, or running along the roofs of railway carriages, and all the while there was the sound of incessant gunfire. Maisie glanced at Tim, two seats away from her. He was sitting on the very edge of his seat, staring goggle-eyed at the screen from behind his wire-framed spectacles, two fingers of his right hand pointing forwards in semblance of a gun. 'Pow! Pow!' he was muttering under his breath; timid little Timothy who wouldn't hurt a fly and who constantly looked to his big sister and her friends to protect him. The 'baddies' were shot dead and the 'goodies' remained alive; but Maisie knew that it bore no resemblance to real life, nor was it anything like the war they were supposed to be involved in with the infamous Hitler.

A nature film followed, about wild animals in the grasslands of Africa, during which the audience grew a mite restless, stamping their feet and beginning to chatter. They were waiting for the main feature, the Charlie Chaplin film, and when the title appeared there was a massive roar of approval. The ridiculous little man with his bowler hat and walking stick, his toothbrush moustache and his waddling way of walking, had them all in fits of laughter. There was no real story to speak of, only a series of absurd slapstick encounters which made them shriek and shout until they almost raised the roof.

It had all been 'dead good...terrific...smashing...' they told one another as they jostled and shoved their way out of the cinema and into the street, into the coldness of the mid-aftenoon. It was still only half-past three, but already the light was beginning to fade.

'Hurry along now, get yerselves home before it goes dark...and let's have no snowball fights,' said the cinema commissionaire, a rather short, self-important man with a silly little moustache; like Charlie Chaplin's, and like Hitler's, too, thought Maisie. He was dressed in a maroon jacket with brass buttons and a peaked cap, and he strutted up and down the pavement fronting the cinema as proudly as though it were the Odeon in Leeds City Square. But the children did seem to be taking notice of him and, on the whole, were dispersing without too much fuss.

Maisie and Audrey, linking arms, were just turning to make their way towards the High Street when a snowball hit Maisie in the middle of her back. 'Hey, give over!' she shouted, starting to turn round. 'You heard what that man said. We've not to... Oh, it's you...'

Sure enough, it was Gertie Flint, cackling gleefully, her arm upraised to throw another snowball, and behind her Esme, Paula and Norma. The next missile hit Audrey on the shoulder, followed my two more aimed at Doris and Ivy. All the girls were armed and they had obviously been ready and waiting to attack as soon as their rivals appeared.

Never mind what that pompous little man had

said, Maisie was not going to let Gertie and her gang have it all their own way. 'Come on, Audrey,' she said. 'Don't be soft. Stick up for yerself; why don't yer? If we don't do owt they'll just laugh at us, an' they'll only follow us. Come on girls, let 'em have it!'

Timothy began to whimper and he cowered close to his sister, his bravery in the confines of the cinema clearly forgotten now in the face of a real attack.

'Aw, diddums! Doesn't he like the snow then?' jeered Esma. 'Poor little boy! Here y'are; catch, Tim.' She hurled a snowball which hit him on the side of his face, nearly knocking his glasses off.

'Hey! Leave him alone!' shouted Ivy. 'He's only little. It's not fair. You're just a big bully, Esme Clough, fighting a little boy.'

'We're not fighting; we're only playing,' said Paula. 'What's up? Don't yer like a bit o' fun? Come on, you lot. Let's chase 'em…'

But suddenly the man with the peaked cap appeared on the scene. He had gone into the cinema, believing that most of the children had gone, but the sounds of ribaldry had brought him out again. 'Get off with you!' he yelled. 'Get off home. I've told you before… How dare you behave like that in front of my cinema…'

Shouting and laughing – at least some of them were laughing – they slithered and slushed their way across the street through the now partially melted snow. Timothy, frightened and cold, with driblets of snow running down his neck, managed to get away in front of the others whilst the girls re-armed themselves. He ran blindly, across the street and into a builder's yard directly opposite the cinema. He did not see the notice, KEEP OUT, but he did see a pile of bricks which he could hide behind until the others had gone past. He knew Ivy would come and look for him if she hadn't noticed where he had gone; and if she didn't, then he could easily find his own way home; it wasn't far.

But his sister had noticed and she followed him. 'Tim, Tim…come back. You're not to go in there…' And close behind her came the others, her own three friends and their assailants.

'Look, there he is!' yelled Gertie. 'Behind them bricks…' What might have started off as a game had now turned into something far more menacing. 'Let's get 'im…'

Tim ran out, racing across the yard. There was a patch of ice on the ground, in the shadow of a wall where the sun had not reached, and it was there that he lost his footing. He collided with a second pile of bricks and fell to the ground. The top layer of bricks tottered and then fell, one of them landing with a glancing blow on the side of the little boy's head. His glasses fell off and shattered, and he lay motionless, blood trickling from a wound on his temple. He looked deathly pale and his eyes were closed.

All the girls stood there, staring at his still form in horror.

'He's dead, he's dead!' shouted Ivy. 'Oh…oh, what are we going to do?' She burst into tears, then knelt on the ground, pulling at his arm. 'Tim! Tim, come on… Wake up!' But he did not stir. 'Oh, he's dead; I know he is!'

'We never meant it,' said Norma, in a tiny voice. 'But he can't be dead... He can't be!'

'We were only mucking about,' said Esme. 'We didn't meant to ki...to hurt him.'

'Oh, shut up, you lot!' snapped Maisie. 'We've got to do summat, quick. Look...oh look, Ivy! He's not dead; he's moving a bit...' Sure enough, Tim's arm was moving a fraction, but his eyes were still closed. Maisie quickly took charge of the situation. 'Doris,' she ordered. 'Go and tell that feller; you know, the one that shouted at us. He'll help us. He'll have to if you tell him what's happened. We might have to get an ambulance...'

'Yeah, OK,' said Doris. 'He's all right really. He's called Mr Lucas and me dad knows him.' She ran off and the others stood there waiting, watching Tim and talking in hushed voices.

'It weren't our fault,' said Gertie. 'We didn't make him come 'ere...'

'Oh yes it was,' retorted Ivy. 'It's all your fault!'

'Yes...it is,' said Norma, nodding sadly. 'It's our fault. We chased him...and we're dead sorry, Ivy. Aren't we, Gertie?'

Gertie shrugged. 'He'll be OK. He's got to be...'

It seemed ages, although it could only have been a few minutes, before Doris returned, running, with the cinema man, Mr Lucas, close behind her. He wasn't cross and bossy now. As Doris had said, he was all right really, and he had known her since she was a tiny girl.

'Oh dear, oh dear!' he said, shaking his head. 'Let's have a look at this little chap then. What's he called? Tim, did you say?' He knelt at the side of the boy, gently touching his face. 'Tim…Tim, lad; can you hear me?' The girls, all staring at the prostrate figure, and at the little man, as though he were a miracle worker, saw Tim's eyelids begin to flutter, and then he opened his eyes, blinking rapidly.

'He's waking up!' shouted Ivy. 'Look…Tim, Tim…'

Mr Lucas turned round briefly, casting an admonitory glance at the girls whom he guessed to be the culprits; he had heard a garbled version of the tale from Doris. 'Yes, he seems to be waking up. And aren't you lucky that he is? I did warn you about these silly snowball fights. Sometimes they get out of hand, like this one did.' Those were the only words of rebuke he uttered. He turned back to Tim.

'Come on now, laddy. You've had a bit of a tumble, but you're going to be OK. Steady now; let's see if you can sit up. Gently now.' He put his arm around the child, propping him against his shoulder.

'Me head hurts,' said Tim, shakily, 'and me arm an' all…' Indeed, his arm, the one on which he had fallen, was lying at a strange angle.

'Shouldn't we get an ambulance?' said Maisie. 'See; he's bleeding.'

'I think it's only a surface wound,' replied Mr Lucas. 'His arm though…I don't like the look of that. But I think it would be best to get him home first. Where does he live?' He looked enquiringly at the girls.

'I'll show you,' said Ivy. 'It's only just down the street and round the next corner. I'm his sister.

We're evacuees, y'see, and…and I'm supposed to look after him.' Her eyes filled with tears again.

'I'm sure you did your best,' said the man, kindly. 'But accidents do happen. Come along, young feller-me-lad, let's be having you.' Even though Mr Lucas was small in stature he was strong, and he lifted Tim from the ground, carefully and gently, supporting his weight with both his arms. 'Now, young lady, you can show me the way home… And the rest of you, you'd better run along an' all. And let this be a lesson to you.'

The four girls who had been responsible in the first place for the snowball fight exchanged sheepish looks and skulked away. It was only Norma who was muttering, 'We're real sorry; honest we are…'

Maisie, Audrey and Doris looked at one another. 'Poor Tim,' said Audrey. 'D'you think he'll be all right?'

'I hope so.' Doris shuffled her feet. 'All of us might get into trouble, 'specially if he's badly hurt.'

'But it wasn't our fault,' said Audrey. 'It was that other lot.'

'But we joined in, didn't we?' said Maisie. 'And it was me that said we should. I'm going to tell Aunty Patience all about it. I'll feel better if I tell somebody.'

Audrey nodded. 'Yes, she'll understand, won't she?'

'Me dad'll be mad with me if he finds out,' said Doris. 'He gets real cross sometimes, does me dad.'

'Does he often see that Mr Lucas?'

'No, I don't think so…'

'Well, don't say anything then, an' he might never know… Come on, let's get going,' said Maisie. They walked dejectedly up the High Street, saying goodbye to Doris at the village green.

Patience listened and understood how upset they were. 'No one is to blame, not really,' she said. 'No one wanted Tim to get hurt, and accidents do happen. But let's hope it puts an end to all this silly rivalry.' It was surprising how Patience knew what was going on without being told. 'I must admit that I've been watching Gertie Flint for quite some time. She's becoming a very wild sort of girl… Anyway, I'm sure Luke will pop down after tea to see Mr and Mrs Roystone and find out how Tim is going on.'

It was obvious to his guardians when they looked at him that Tim had broken his arm. Mr Lucas rang from the nearest phone box for an ambulance and the little boy was taken to the hospital on the outskirts of Middlebeck. What with the broken arm and the cut and bump on his head – he was still complaining of feeling dizzy – he was kept in overnight. The overnight stay was extended to two days, just to be on the safe side, although it was believed that he had suffered no serious injuries.

But his mother arrived, post-haste, on the Monday, and insisted on taking both Timothy and Ivy back home to Hull. She had intended having them at home for Christmas anyway, but now she announced, in high dudgeon, that they were going immediately.

'And they will not be coming back!' she declared to the confused and unhappy couple who had looked after them. 'I trusted my children to your care, and look what has happened. I know you say that you can't watch them every minute of the day and I know you are sorry, but it's clear that they have been allowed to run wild. I'm taking them home with me, back to Hull where they will be safe. This 'ere war is showing no signs of getting going at any rate.'

'Never mind, Mabel,' said her husband when Mrs Clegg and the children had gone. 'We did our best…'

But they had had to say goodbye to two children of whom they had grown very fond and their lives felt empty at their departure. And Maisie, Audrey and Doris had lost a very good friend.

'There's only us three now,' said Maisie. 'Ivy says she'll write to us. I wonder if she will… You're all right, Doris, 'cause you live here, but I hope me and Audrey don't have to go back to Leeds.'

Audrey hoped so too. She missed her mum and dad, but she did so enjoy living in Middlebeck, now she was with Aunty Patience and Luke and Maisie. Her mum was coming to see her again though, before Christmas, with Maisie's mum. She had promised that she would…

Chapter Sixteen

Lily was finding life a little more tolerable. She had learned to close her mind to Sid's insults and his bad temper, although it had to be admitted that he was still leaving her pretty well alone. They seldom spoke to one another, neither did he bother to speak very much any more to Joanie and Jimmy. Lily was sure, in her own mind, that he was seeing someone else; he might even be consoling himself with 'ladies of the night', several of whom hung around the mean streets of Armley. The thought of it made her shudder; on the other hand she was thankful that her body was now her own.

She was contented, also, that Maisie was so happy in north Yorkshire; although Lily had missed her even more after she and Edith had visited Middlebeck, and she had seen how her daughter had matured and was growing into a most attractive and spirited girl.

Please God, don't let us be apart for too long...she often prayed, fearing that the prolonged absence might mean, in the end, that she would lose her beloved daughter. But she knew there was no way, at the moment, that they could be together. Nothing but a miracle would bring their separation to an end.

Her friendship with Edith Dennison, which had

started so surprisingly, and then, since their return home, had flourished, was a comfort to Lily. And she realised that it was as pleasing to Edith as it was to her, Lily. The older woman did not appear to have many friends, only neighbours with whom she was on civil, rather than intimate, terms, and neither she nor her husband, Alf, had any close relations.

Lily and Edith saw one another a couple of times a week for a cup of tea and a chat. It was usually Lily who visited Edith's home, often calling on the way back from one of her cleaning jobs. Of course, she always had the children with her, but Edith, far from finding them to be a nuisance, enjoyed seeing them, and they had soon started to call her Aunty Edie.

The two women had decided, at Patience Fairchild's and their own two daughters' persuasion – although they had not needed much persuading – to pay another visit to Middlebeck before Christmas. Thursday, the twenty-first of December, seemed like a good choice of date. Christmas fell on a Monday that year and the trains were likely to be crowded beyond belief at the weekend. To Lily's surprise, Alf Dennison had decided to accompany them.

'I must see my little lass before Christmas,' he told Lily. 'Three months it is since I set eyes on her...' His eyes, blue like his daughter's, had started to brim with tears which he hastily tried to blink away. 'Look at me,' he joked. 'What an old softie I am, to be sure, but Edith here tells me how much she's grown, and grown up an' all. And I do miss her; I do that!'

'She'll be pleased to see you,' said Lily. 'Have you told her you're going as well as Edith?'

'Aye…' He nodded. 'Well, I've said I might. No doubt I'll get upset – that's what I'm afraid of – and want to bring her back home with us. But we've decided it's best to leave her there. The Germans won't wait much longer before they do summat drastic, I feel sure of that. Besides, my wife is still having this treatment, and it takes it out of her something shocking. In some ways it would be a comfort to her to have Audrey here with us; but Edith gets so tired, and our little girl seems happy where she is.'

Edith, indeed, looked dreadful at times. Her skin still had a yellowish pallor that Lily did not like the look of at all, but Edith usually insisted that she was all right, if a little tired. It was obvious, however, when Lily called to see her on the day before their proposed visit, that she was far from well. Her treatment at the hospital the previous day had made her feel even worse than ever, and, on top of that, she had developed a cold and was coughing and sneezing alarmingly.

She was not in bed, but sitting by the fire, wrapped in a tartan blanket. Edith was one of that breed of woman who believed that you died in bed, and seldom could she be persuaded to spend even a day there. Her operation and its aftermath, of course, had been an exception to this principle of hers.

'Oh, Lily love, don't come too near me,' she croaked. 'And keep those little bairns away from me. I don't want to sneeze all over them. I'm trying to get myself better for tomorrow.'

'Don't be silly, love,' said her husband, but very kindly. 'We can't go, and that's that.'

'But I might feel better in the morning, and our Audrey'll be so upset.'

Lily shook her head. 'You're not fit to go, Edith love,' she said. 'Even I can see that. You'd make yerself worse if you tried to go.' Edith's eyes were red-rimmed and moist, not just with the cold, but with tears of disappointment. 'Never mind; there'll be another time, perhaps soon after Christmas. What about that?'

'That's what I've been telling her,' said Alf.

'And I suppose I know you're right,' sniffed Edith. 'I was looking forward to seeing her so much, but I know when I'm beaten. You'll take our presents with you, won't you, Lily?'

'Of course I will,' replied Lily. 'What are you going to do? Shall you write and tell Audrey? If I get a letter in the post for you straight away, she should get it in the morning.'

'I don't know.' Alf shook his head. 'It's bound to upset her. But a telegram would be even worse. Telegrams always mean bad news, don't they? I think we'll have to leave it to you, Lily, to explain to her that her mum's real poorly...'

'But we've tried to keep it from her, haven't we, Alf, how bad I've been?' said Edith. 'I don't want our Audrey to think I'm dying.' Lily felt herself turn cold.

'She'll not think that, lass,' said Alf. 'It's just a bad cold you've got. Lily'll tell her. You'll be as right as rain in a day or two. It's just bad luck that it should happen just before Christmas.'

'Don't worry; I'll explain to Audrey,' said Lily. 'I know she's sure to be disappointed, but you've got some parcels for her, have you…?'

That poor little girl, thought Lily, as she walked home, with Jimmy's pushchair laden with parcels of all shapes and sizes. So many that they would put her own little gifts for Maisie in the shade, she pondered. But she guessed that Maisie would be more pleased to see her family than any amount of presents. And so, she guessed would Audrey have been…

'Our mums are coming tomorrer,' said Maisie to Audrey on the Wednesday, the day before the expected visit. 'I'm dead excited, aren't you? And we've got all those things that we made at school to give to them.'

'And my dad's coming too,' said Audrey. 'I haven't seen him since September, since that day when we first came here. That's more than three whole months.'

'Oh yes; yer dad…I forgot about him,' said Maisie. She looked a mite pensive, and Audrey guessed she might thinking that she hadn't got a dad, not a proper one, to make the journey with her mother. In reality Maisie was remembering Sid and feeling relieved that he would not be coming.

'You'll see your little brother and sister as well,' said Audrey. 'And you've got some presents for them, an' all, haven't you?'

Miss Mellodey's classroom had been a hive of activity in the weeks leading up to Christmas, as the children made calendars and cards and little gifts, for parents or for adoptive aunts and uncles. There was a shortage of paper and cardboard, or there would be before very long, and these commodities had to be used very sparingly.

Rectangles of card were cut from old cereal packets and covered with wallpaper – from surplus pattern books – to form the basis of the calendars, which were then decorated with pictures cut from last year's Christmas cards. A tiny calendar showing the days, weeks and months was then glued at the bottom – these were bought by the teacher at a few pence a dozen from Woolie's – and two holes and a string threaded through the top. The result was a work of art as good as anything that could be bought in a shop and which would grace a proud mother's kitchen wall from the beginning to the end of the year.

Each child had been allowed a precious sheet of cartridge paper to make a card, on which was their own choice of Christmas symbol – a robin, a plum pudding, a tree or shining stars – cut out of gummed paper, using templates that Miss Mellodey had made. Audrey had chosen a pudding, remembering how her mother had used to make a deliciously rich and fruity one each year, and Maisie a design of stars, a large one, which was the star for Jesus's birth, and several smaller ones. She loved the stars which seemed to shine extra brightly here in Middlebeck. She liked to look at them through her bedroom window, making sure there was no light visible from inside, of course.

And the two girls, along with all the other girls in

the class, had made a little needle-case out of 'Binca' canvas, embroidered with colourful cross-stitch. This had been a real labour of love for Maisie who was not much of a seamstress – Audrey had fared rather better – but Miss Mellodey had unpicked the stitches that had gone a bit wonky and helped her to put them to rights. And she knew her mother would be delighted with the finished result. The boys had made raffia mats, with rather less dexterity. All in all, it had been a happy time at school, singing carols and playing games in the classroom with the desks pushed back against the walls; and then, on the last afternoon, they had all gone into the church for a special Carol Service led by the rector of St Bartholomew's. That was Audrey and Maisie's very own Luke, and they felt very proud indeed.

Now they had broken up from school and could hardly wait for the excitement to begin; the decorating of their Christmas tree, a real one that Luke had brought home from Mr Tremaine's estate; the hiding away of secret presents; the Christmas dinner that Aunty Patience was planning; but, before all that, the visit of their parents from Leeds.

Maisie and Audrey skipped and ran all the way down the High Street on Thursday morning, with Patience hurrying along behind them. They were far too excited to try to 'walk properly' – as Miss Thomson would have exhorted Audrey to do, although Aunty Patience never bothered. The shops had made a valiant effort in this first Christmas of the war to put on a show of festivity and celebration. Chickens and ducks and strings of sausages hung in the butcher's window, and at the front, with a selection of the butcher's own homemade pork pies, there was a pig's head, staring out with glassy malevolent eyes and with an apple stuck in his mouth; and a hand-printed notice in red and green letters which read 'A Merry Christmas to all our customers'.

Cotton wool balls representing snow, and paper streamers adorned the windows of the baker's, the newsagent's and the Maypole Grocery Store. There did not appear to be any shortage of food as yet. There were fancy tins of biscuits and boxes of chocolates; Christmas cakes and puddings and mince pies – for those housewives too lazy or disinclined to make their own! – as well as such staple requirements as bread, butter, tea and sugar. Food had still not been rationed, although there were rumours that it soon would be. 'They'll let us get through Christmas, an' then we'll not know what's hit us, you mark my words,' said many a Job's comforter.

They arrived a few minutes early at the station and they knew they might have even longer to wait before the train arrived. Delays were frequent and had come to be expected. 'Don't you know there's a war on?' was the excuse for this, as it was for all sorts of other things.

Maisie and Audrey kept running to the end of the platform, peering into the distance for any sign of the approaching train. At then at last, 'Here it is! It's coming…' they both shouted.

They stood next to Patience as the huge engine

puffed and snorted its way into the station, clouds of acrid grey smoke billowing from its funnel as it slowed down, then halted with a squeal of brakes. Eagerly they scanned the windows of the carriages as the train passed by them and then stopped, but all they could make out was that it was crowded. There was a lot of the familiar khaki and airforce blue to be seen; soldiers and airmen seemed to be always on the move.

'There she is! There's my mum!' yelled Maisie, seeing the red-coated figure emerging from a carriage door some twenty yards away. 'Mum, Mum...we're over here...' she shouted. A soldier was helping her with Jimmy's pushchair, and then he lifted the little boy down from the big step and put him in the pram. Maisie's mum was smiling at him and saying thank you, and how pretty she looked when she smiled, thought Maisie. And there was Joanie as well, jumping up and down with excitement.

'But where is my mum?' said Audrey, looking puzzled. 'And my dad. He said he was coming as well. But they're not here.'

'I expect they're in a different part of the train,' said Patience although she, too, was looking rather anxious. 'Maybe they couldn't get seats together.'

Audrey shook her head. It was obvious that all the passengers that were going to alight had already done so. 'They've not come...' she said, her eyes filling up with tears.

Lily hurried over to them and gave Maisie a hug and a kiss. 'Hello, love,' she said. But she didn't make too much fuss of her daughter, before she turned quickly to Audrey. 'Audrey dear…' she said, kissing her cheek as well, 'I'm afraid you might be a little bit upset. You see…'

'My mum and dad, they've not come, have they? Why? Is Mummy poorly again?' Audrey's little face looked anguished as she stared pleadingly at Lily, with her tears overflowing and running down her cheeks.

The two women exchanged anxious glances, then Lily hurried on to say, 'Well, yes, she is a bit poorly, dear. She's got a very bad cold. She was coughing and sneezing all over the place when I saw her yesterday.'

'Oh dear! What a shame!' said Patience. 'I'm sure she's disappointed as well, isn't she?'

'She certainly is,' said Lily. 'But she knew she would only make herself worse if she came, as well as giving her nasty germs to everybody else. But she's sent you some Christmas presents, all sorts of exciting parcels, Audrey. And she says to tell you that she'll come and see you as soon as she can. And yer dad an' all.'

'Why didn't me dad come then?' Audrey whimpered. 'He could have come, couldn't he? I haven't seen him for ages. He's not poorly as well, is he?'

'No…but he has to stay and look after your mum,' said Patience. 'That's how it is, isn't it, Lily?'

'Yes…' agreed Lily. 'Aw, lovey, I'm real sorry.' She put an arm round Audrey and gave her a hug. 'Come on, cheer up now. I'm dying to hear what you and Maisie have been doing at the Brownies an' at that school of yours. And how's your nice Miss

Mellodey going on?'

Audrey had recovered somewhat by the time the little company had made their way back to the rectory. She was no longer crying, but she spoke very little during the meal that Patience had prepared; tasty shepherd's pie followed by jam roly-poly pudding and custard. Maisie, watching her friend concernedly, felt very sorry for her; she guessed that her thoughts were far away, with her mum and dad in Leeds. But her lack of conversation was not noticed overmuch because it was Joanie and Jimmy who were doing a great deal of the talking. They remembered Patience and Luke from their last visit – especially Patience's delicious dinner, it seemed, from the gusto with which they were attacking the food on their plates – and were vying with one another in telling their hosts about their journey.

'There were lots of baa-lambs in t' fields…'

'Don't say baa-lambs, Jimmy; it's babyish,' Joanie corrected him. 'Anyroad, they're not lambs; they're sheep.'

'All right; sheep…great big woolly 'uns…'

'An' there was a reight lot o' snow on th' 'ills. We haven't got none at home now,' said Joanie.

'No, it's all gone now,' said Lily. 'Like it has here. I thought it'd be snowing up here.'

'Oh, there's still plenty to come,' said Luke. 'The sky looks very heavy. I wouldn't be surprised if there's some more on the way.'

'Yes, we often have a white Christmas up here,' smiled Patience.

'An' we made a snowman,' chimed in Joanie. 'In

t' back yard. Didn't we, Jimmy?'

'Aye, wi' an 'at on 'is 'ead...'

'It were an old one of me dad's,' said Joanie.

'A very old hat,' said Lily, smiling meaningfully at Maisie. 'Else I would never have dared. It was one he'd chucked out ages ago.'

Audrey cheered up when it was time, after the meal, for the exchanging of Christmas gifts. There were several parcels for Audrey. Maisie counted four – or was it five? – all done up in bright wrapping paper as her mother drew them out of the big black hold-all.

'I'll save them till Christmas Day, shall I, Aunty Patience?' said Audrey.

'Yes, I think that's the best idea,' replied Patience. 'And yours as well, Maisie. We'll put them all underneath the tree. Oh, isn't it exciting?'

Lily had brought out two parcels for Maisie, and those, too, were gaily wrapped. 'It's not much, Maisie,' she said, shrugging apologetically, 'but it's all as I can afford. You know how it is, don't you, love?'

'Of course I do, Mum,' said Maisie. 'Presents don't matter. It's you that I wanted to see... Oh, I'm sorry, Audrey,' she added, as her friend, at her side, gave a little sniffle. 'I'm real sorry yer mum hasn't come, but you'll see her soon, won't yer? And don't forget we've got all them things that we made at school. Me mum'll take them back for you, and the presents you bought for yer mum and dad, won't you, Mum?'

'Of course I will,' said Lily. 'That'll cheer your mother up no end, Audrey.'

Lily exclaimed with delight at the calendar, card and needle-case. 'Oh, aren't they lovely? And the same for Edith an' all? Isn't that nice? She'll be ever so pleased.'

'An' this is a little present for you, Mum, that I've bought with me spending money,' said Maisie. 'Only I don't want you to open it till Christmas Day, same as I won't open mine. And these are for our Joanie and Jimmy,' she whispered, handing the little parcels over secretly so that her brother and sister would not see. They were playing a game of tig at the other end of the room, with Luke keeping an eye on them.

'Well, isn't that kind of you,' said Lily.

'Put 'em in their stockings, or tell 'em that Father Christmas has brought them,' said Maisie.

'No, I shall tell them that their big sister has bought 'em,' said Lily, her eyes suddenly feeling moist. 'It was a lovely thing to do.'

'I miss them, Mum,' said Maisie. 'I never thought I would, not really, 'cause they used to be dreadful little imps; but I do miss them...and you an' all.'

'I know, love, I know,' said Lily, swallowing a big lump in her throat. 'But it's best for you to stay here, honest it is. Things are just the same at home...you know what I mean. You haven't to worry about me though, 'cause I'm OK. I can look after meself, and the little 'uns are behaving 'emselves now.'

'Mrs Bragg...' said Audrey shyly. 'Would you take these back, please, and give them to my mum and dad?' There were two carefully wrapped presents as well as the things made at school. 'And tell them I'm sorry they couldn't come, and I hope my mum is soon better...'

Patience could see that everyone was starting to get emotional. It was only to be expected, but she wanted the day to be as happy as possible. 'How about a walk before tea?' she said. 'The sun's trying to get out, and it'll blow the cobwebs away.'

'And help us to walk off that lovely dinner,' said Lily. 'It was a real treat, Patience.'

Patience smiled. 'Thank you... And I'll come with you if you don't mind.' She wanted to have a private little chat with Lily. She could tell that the woman was putting on a brave face, but she knew, intuitively, that there was something troubling her deeply.

———

Lily was, indeed, worrying – although she was trying hard not to let it show – about what sort of a reception she would get when she arrived back in Armley. She had told Sid at breakfast time that she was going to visit Maisie that day; she would be setting off soon after he and Percy had gone to work in order to make an early start and have as long a day as possible in Middlebeck. She had mentioned it to him earlier in the week, but he had appeared to take no notice. But this time, when she told him, it was clear that he had remembered.

'Aye, so you told me, t'other day,' he said. 'D'you think I care what the hell you do? Bugger off and take them two little brats with yer.'

'Of course I'll take them with me,' she replied. 'What else would I do? Jimmy and Joanie are looking forward to seeing Maisie again, aren't you?' She turned to the children who nodded, staring fixedly at her and then at their father with their pale blue eyes. They did not react overmuch as they were used to their dad shouting.

'Oh, it's Maisie now, is it?' he jeered. 'Ne'er mind yer bloody fancy names. Her's Nellie to me, not that I want owt to do with her neither. I was damned glad to see the back of 'er, 'er and her flamin' lies, so don't you dare thing of bringing 'er back.'

'Don't worry,' Lily answered coldly. 'She won't be coming back, you can be sure of that.'

'And you don't need to come back neither, nor your two brats.'

'They're your children as well, Sid...'

'Aye, so you say. Aye, well, happen they are...' He cast a glance, that was half apologetic, at the two children before continuing his tirade. 'But me and t' lad here can manage very well wi'out the lot of yer, can't we, Percy?'

His son grinned maliciously. 'Aye; 'course we can.'

'So you can stay up in t' wilds of t' North Riding, if you've a mind, and bloody good riddance to yer. Come on, Percy lad. T' whistle'll be blowing, and we've been late once already this week, thanks to 'er an' 'er feckless ways.'

They grabbed their coats and dashed out of the back door. Lily was angry at his parting shot, knowing it was not true, but it was only what she had become used to over the years. She had always made a breakfast for him and his son before they left for the mill, even when she felt very disinclined to do so; and Sid knew that only too well. She guessed, too, that he didn't mean what he said about her not coming back. It was very tempting to take him at his word, but she knew there would be the very devil to pay if she did so. No; in spite of what he said, Sid would expect her to return and to continue to look after him and his children.

———

That was what she said to Patience later that afternoon. They were walking together, with the children all running ahead of them, along the country lanes at the back of the churchyard. Patience had enquired, tactfully and very concernedly, about how things were going at her home in Leeds. And Lily was glad to confide in her, but only to a certain extent. Patience was, after all, the wife of the rector, and Lily believed her to be quite an innocent and unworldly sort of woman. She might be shocked to the core about some of the things that Lily could tell her. So Lily thought, but it was not true. Patience was pretty unshockable, and as she listened to the unhappy tale she could read between the lines. Besides, she already knew, from Maisie's earlier outburst, about the dreadful state of affairs in that household.

'But there's nowt...I mean, nothing I can do,' said Lily. 'He's my husband, isn't he, and those two are his kids. He has his rights, I suppose, and wives can't just go buzzing off and leaving their husbands...can they?'

'It depends on the circumstances, I expect,' said Patience carefully.

'Anyroad, I know he doesn't mean it,' Lily continued. 'He's told me to clear off, but he's said that before then changed his mind. No; I'll have to go back and face the music, as they say.'

'You mustn't hesitate to let us know, Lily, if things get too bad,' said Patience. 'Luke and I are concerned and we want to help you if we can.' Patience knew, though, that it was not really right to interfere in other people's marriages.

'I'll be OK, don't worry,' said Lily, relieved to have unburdened herself of some of her anxieties. 'I'm worried about Edith, though, an' all. Don't say anything to Audrey – well, of course I know you wouldn't – but she's far from well, and it's not just the cold that she's got. She's a funny colour, yellow like; I don't like the look of her at all. She's not picking up after that op she had.'

'Poor Edith…' Patience shook her head. 'Yes, I know exactly what you mean; it was a serious operation. But we must hope for the best; hope…and pray. And you can be sure we will do that. Audrey is contented with us, bless her, and we must be thankful for that. She and Maisie are a great comfort to one another.'

'And how's that Miss Thomson going on?' asked Lily. 'Her maid was going to join the ATS, wasn't she? Did she get another one, a maid, I mean?'

Patience laughed, glad to change the subject to a less worrying one. 'No, she didn't; not a maid. But an extraordinary thing happened. Quite providential, so Luke and I thought. Miss Thomson now has a couple of land army girls staying with her.'

'Well, I never!' said Lily. 'And what does she think about that?'

'She wasn't any too pleased at first, I can tell you.

But she kept complaining about not having a maid, and so Muriel Hollins – she's one of the bigwigs round here, in charge of the WVS and the WI – she suggested that the first two land girls should go there. They're supposed to help with the chores, you see, wherever they are billeted, and as far as I know it's working out quite well.'

'Doesn't she boss them around, like she did with that Daisy?'

'She can't insist that they are in by nine-thirty. They have to be allowed a certain amount of freedom when they're not working. I think Miss Thomson has learned her lesson; well, we hope so. They seem to be nice friendly lasses; Priscilla and Jennifer, they are called.'

'So they work on one of the farms round here, do they?'

'Yes, right here, as it happens,' said Patience. 'Here on Mr Tremaine's estate. They're working for him and for Walter Nixon – that's Doris's father, the girl that Maisie and Audrey are friendly with. Walter is in charge of their initial training, I believe. He has two young sons as well, Joe and Ted, who work on the farm. But the other two young men who worked for the squire have both gone now; Andy, that's Daisy's boyfriend, the one she went to meet and caused all that trouble, and his mate, Tom. Yes, they've both joined the army, and so have a lot more of the young men from our parish. That's why the land girls are coming; there'll be quite a lot of them here soon to work on the outlying farms.'

'There was some talk of them coming to the squire's place, wasn't there?' said Lily. 'What's it called, Tremaine House? We met that young woman the last time we came and she was telling us she was going to be in charge of them.'

'Yes, that's right,' replied Patience. 'You mean Sally Booth. Plans are going ahead now and the land girls should be arriving soon after Christmas... Oh look, there's Bruce. You haven't met him, have you? He's Archie Tremaine's son. He's a grand lad, is Bruce; he's away at boarding school most of the time, just home for the hoidays.'

Bruce, a few yards further along the lane, was talking to Maisie and Audrey, with Prince, the dog, lolloping around them. Patience was pleased to see that Audrey no longer seemed to be scared of the dog, although she was standing very still and eyeing him warily. Tentatively she stretched out a hand and patted his head, and he reciprocated by licking her hand. She turned to Patience and beamed. 'I think he likes me,' she said.

'An' he likes me an' all,' said Joanie, fearlessly stroking the dog's back. Jimmy, by this time, was tired and he climbed back into his pushchair.

Bruce shook hands with Lily and said 'How do you do?' very politely, and that he hoped she was enjoying her day. Lily decided at once that she liked him. There was an air of assurance about him, without being stuck-up or over-confident.

'We've not seen Mrs Booth lately, or Billy and Brenda,' said Maisie, remembering that the last time her mum had visited they had met the little family in the lane. 'Are they all right? Or p'raps they've gone home for Christmas, have they?'

'Yes...sort of,' said Bruce. 'Haven't you heard

about it, Mrs Fairchild?' He turned to Patience. 'No, perhaps you haven't, because it only happened yesterday.'

'What has happened, Bruce? No, I haven't heard.'

'Well, they've gone for good,' said Bruce, 'or so it seems. Sally – Mrs Booth, I mean – had a telegram yesterday to say that her mother had been taken ill and that she was to go home at once. So she went back to Leeds – my father ran her to the station and she got the first train she could – but when she got there her mother had died. She phoned last night to tell my mother and father. It seems that her own father is an invalid. He was badly injured in the last war and he has never fully recovered. His wife looked after him, and she had hardly ever had a day's illnesss in her life. And then, well, it was a sudden heart attack and there was nothing they could do for her.'

'Oh, how dreadful!' said Patience. 'Poor Sally; what a shock for her. So…she is staying to look after her father, is she?'

'Yes, apparently she is the only daughter. I think she intends to stay and make her home with her father, for the time being, at any rate. It's very sad; and my mother says she was looking forward so much to staying here and being in charge of the land girls that are coming. It will be a lot for my mother to manage on her own.'

That young man has an old head on young shoulders, thought Lily, and what concern he was showing for his mother.

'Don't worry,' said Patience. 'You're a good lad,

Bruce, and I know you're concerned about her. But I'm sure your mother will find someone to help her, if Sally can't come back...'

A thought had struck Patience. What a splendid idea it would be, if only... But she did not see how she could possibly suggest it, so she did not even look at Lily. Besides, the young woman knew that she had to go back to Leeds.

But the selfsame thought had occurred to Lily, only to be dismissed as a hopeless dream.

Chapter Seventeen

✣

It was after ten o' clock when Lily and the children arrived back at Leeds City Station. The square and the surrounding streets were almost pitch black, with little light that night from the moon and stars, but she had her torch to help her to find her way to the bus stop. Jimmy was asleep, his head lolling sideways in his pushchair, but Joanie was trotting along stoically at her mother's side, indefatigable, it seemed, on this exciting day.

It was eerie to travel on a bus at night. There was only a tiny blue light to illuminate the interior and the headlamps were partially covered with masks. An unnecessary restriction, in fact it was a load of 'red tape', was the view of many people. Almost four months into the war there was still no sign of enemy planes or bombs falling from the skies. It was strange, too, to be given your ticket by a young woman conductress, doing the job of a man who had gone to serve in the war.

'We're nearly home now,' said Lily to the children as they alighted from the bus. The conductress helped with the pram, as she had when they boarded, and Lily popped a still very drowsy Jimmy inside. 'Not much further, just along this street and round the corner...'

She was beginning to feel sick with dread at the

thought of going into the house. Supposing Sid had meant what he said and he threw her out again? No; he couldn't do that, not with the two kiddies. It was turned half-past ten. He would, no doubt, have returned from the pub; they had closed earlier since the start of the war. But with a bit of luck he might have gone to bed.

There was no way of telling from the outside of the house whether or not he was still downstairs, because the blackout curtains did not allow even a chink of light to escape. She took out her key and opened the door, humping the pram, with Jimmy still in it, over the step. Her heart sank when she saw there was a light on in the living room. Quickly she closed the front door and took a deep breath, steadying herself to face her husband in whatsoever mood she might find him. She lifted Jimmy from the pushchair and then, holding him by the hand and with Joanie hanging on to her coat, she entered the room.

She blinked with amazement, then gave a gasp of shock and disbelief. A strange woman was sitting in one of the easy chairs, the one that Lily usually sat in when she had time to spare. A young woman, with brassy blonde hair in sausage curls all over her head, cherry red lips and pink cheeks like a painted doll, and wearing a bright blue jumper that clung tightly to the generous curves of her bosom. Lily was in little doubt as to who this person was, but she would not have imagined that even Sid would have had the nerve to invite her to his home. Nevertheless, the question came automatically to her lips.

'And who are you?' she asked. The woman met her questioning stare with a look that was unafraid, although she then looked across at Sid, seated in the other chair, for him to answer.

He was grinning with malicious delight. 'This young lady is Moira. She's a friend of mine; a very good friend, an' she's come to spend Christmas with me, 'aven't yer, luv? An' she can stay a good while longer an' all, for ever, if she's a mind. An' you don't need to bother yerself about where she's sleepin', 'cause she's sharin' my bed, aren't yer, Moira, me darlin'?' Lily, for the moment, was too flabbergasted to speak. She just gaped at Sid as he went on speaking.

'Oh, I'm forgetting me manners, aren't I? This 'ere is me wife, Lily.' He gave a sneering laugh. 'An' these two are me nippers. Say hello, you two, to the nice lady.'

Joanie and Jimmy just stared uncomprehendingly, and Lily, still at a loss for words, noticed for the first time that Percy was at the back of the room, an evil grin on his podgy face as he watched her discomfiture. Moira had not spoken so far, but now she managed a few words.

'Hello...' she faltered. 'Sid invited me... But he told me that you were...'

'Aye, I told her that you'd buggered off to see yer darlin' daughter and you wouldn't be comin' back. I told you this morning to sling yer hook, didn't I?'

'But...I didn't think you meant it, Sid. You've said that before, but you always changed yer mind.'

'Well, I meant it this time, didn't I? I've got meself fixed up very nicely with Moira here. You and me's finished. We 'ave been for ages, so I don't know what the hell you think you're doing here.'

'But...this is my home, and...and it's where the children live...'

'Not any more it ain't. Bugger off and take 'em with yer. Get off back to yer precious Nellie...'

'Sid, stop it!' It was Moira who intervened. She was looking a little worried at the turn of events. 'You can't just turn 'er out in t' middle o' t' night. Let her stay... There's been a mistake...'

At these words Lily at last saw red. She realised she was not dismayed or scared any longer by what had happened; she was just blazing mad, more furious than she had ever been in her life.

'You're damned right there's been some mistake,' she yelled at Sid, and ignoring the woman. 'How dare you move yer fancy piece into my home. This is my home,' she repeated, emphasising the last two words. 'It was mine and my family's long before it was yours. And this...lady...has the cheek to say "Let her stay". Let me stay, indeed, in my own home! Well, I can tell you that I won't be staying, not a minute longer than I have to... Come on, you two. It's long past your bedtime...' She hurried the children out of the room and up the stairs.

'What's wrong, Mummy?' asked Joanie.

'Who's that lady?' asked Jimmy.

'Don't worry yerselves about all that now,' said Lily. Quickly she put them into their pyjamas and bundled them into bed. 'Night night, sleep tight...' She kissed them both, knowing they were both too tired to be worried by the trauma surrounding them.

She still had her coat on, and when she had settled the children she hurried off to the house next door, the home of Fred and Kate Smedley. Luckily, they had still not gone to bed. Kate answered the door somewhat timorously at Lily's frenzied knocking.

'Good gracious, Lily; whatever's up? There's nowt wrong with your Maisie, is there?'

'No, thank God,' replied Lily. 'No, it's 'im, Sid. Youll never guess what he's done. He's only gone and moved his fancy piece in. Some painted hussy called Moira…'

She saw Kate and Fred exchanging uneasy glances. 'You knew, didn't you? Why didn't you tell me?'

'Sit yerself down, luv,' said Fred, and Lily collapsed gratefully on to an easy chair. 'Aye, I knew he had another woman, like. I told Kate about it. But I didn't know as how he'd moved her in. What a bloody nerve! Moira Higginbottom, she's called. She's a barmaid at the Rose and Crown.'

'I'm real sorry,' said Kate. 'Aye, I knew, but there didn't seem to be much point in telling yer. But what a cheek he's got! Of all the things!'

'She was there when I got back from seeing our Maisie, sitting there as bold as brass,' said Lily. 'To be fair, I think he'd told her that I'd left and I wouldn't be coming back…but he must have known that weren't true.'

'But the thing is, what are you going to do now?' asked Kate. 'You can stay here tonight if you like, can't she, Fred? And what about the kiddies?'

'They're fast asleep in their own beds,' said Lily, smiling a little. 'And that's where I shall sleep tonight, if I manage to sleep at all, in the bed in their room. Sid and me haven't shared a bed for ages, but I think you know that. But I'm only staying there tonight. I'll not stay where I'm not wanted, not for one minute longer than I have to. First thing in t' morning the kids and me'll be off back to Middlebeck.'

'D'you think you'll be able to find somewhere to stay up there?' asked Kate.

'I know I will,' said Lily. 'In fact...do you know...all this that has happened, it seems like an answer to a prayer.' She had only just thought of it like that, but now it seemed as though it was meant to be. It was the miracle she had been waiting for. A rather strange one maybe, but it meant that, at last, she would be able to escape from her disastrous marriage.

When she returned to the house next door – she could no longer think of it as home – the place was in darkness, Sid and his 'floosie' and Percy having retired for the night. She hoped it might be the last she would see of them for a very long time or, indeed, for ever, if everything worked out according to plan; a plan that she was desperately trying to formulate in her mind.

She reached up to the top of the wardrobe and pulled down the large suitcase which had not been used for ages, and then, by the dim light from her torch, she began to pack hers and the children's clothes inside it, as many as it would hold. She intended to set off in the early morning, before anyone else arose, if possible. She would make her way to the station and catch the earliest train she could, back to Middlebeck. But how would she manage, she wondered, with a huge suitcase, a pushchair and two young children? Don't be so spineless, Lily! she admonished herself; there would surely be somone to help her, both on the bus and on the train. One good thing about these wartime days was the way that complete strangers were trying to help one another. And quickly upon that thought came another; ought she to let Patience know she was arriving, and what time? If she didn't, then there would be no one to meet them when they arrived in Middlebeck. And what about Edith and Alf and the little presents that Audrey had sent for them? Audrey was relying on her and this was a trust she could not break, whatever the circumstances. She tossed and turned in her bed for ages, her mind in a turmoil; then at last, in the early hours, sleep overcame her.

She had set her alarm clock for six o' clock, and with the coming of the dawn her thoughts had assembled themselves into a more coherent pattern. Before waking the children she made a pile of sandwiches to eat on the journey. Fortunately there was a loaf that was not too stale and a remnant of cheese in the larder. She did not feel the slightest guilt in using the whole of it, then she spread the remainder of the bread she had sliced with margarine and strawberry jam. There would be no time to stop and eat breakfast; besides she did not want to set eyes on Sid and the others. Her idea was to get moving before anyone else was stirring; Sid and Percy were sluggards anyway, especially when it came to getting up in the morning.

She quickly washed and dressed herself, then she roused the children, giving them both a quick wash – a lick and a promise – at the kitchen sink before dressing them and making sure they had used the lavatory at the end of the yard. Thank goodness Jimmy was no longer in nappies, she thought; that was one less problem she had to face.

'Where're we goin', Mummy?' asked Joanie, as Lily bundled them both into their coats. 'Are we running away? Dad was mad at us, wasn't he?'

'Not with you, love; only with me...'

'Who was that lady? What's she doing in our 'ouse?'

'She's just a friend of Daddy's...'

'It's dark,' said Jimmy. 'Why are we going out in t' dark?'

'Are we running away?' asked Joanie again.

'Not really,' said Lily. 'Hush now...Try to be real quiet.' She put her finger to her lips. 'We're going on a train again – that's exciting, isn't it? – and then we're going to stay with Maisie and that kind man and lady for a little while, perhaps longer...I hope so anyway. But first we've got to go and see Audrey's mum and dad.'

Stealthily she opened the front door and lifted the pushchair out on to the pavement, balancing the big suitcase on the seat. 'You'll have to walk, Jimmy,' she whispered. 'Anyroad, you're a big boy now, aren't you? And Joanie, you watch that the case doesn't topple over...'

With scarcely a sound – it was amazing how quiet the children were being – she pulled the front door shut, then they hurried away through the dark streets. Lily was terrified lest she should hear a voice behind her, shouting for her to go back. But...no; she was certain that Sid, this time, had meant what he said. It was doubtful, too, that he would be awake yet, although that woman, Moira, might well be. Lily had heard a faint stirring as she passed the bedroom door, and a cough which was certainly not Sid's catarrhal wheeze. And Moira, she was sure, would say nothing at all if she had heard the hasty departure.

She knew it was early to be calling on anyone, but she guessed that Alf Dennison might be up and about and would not mind their premature visit.

'Lily... Whatever are you doing out at this time?' he exclaimed on opening the door. Then his eyes alighted on the suitcase. 'Oh...I see. There's something wrong, isn't there? Come on in, and tell us all about it.'

Even though it was only just turned seven o'clock, Alf was dressed, and Edith, on hearing voices, soon appeared in her red woollen dressing gown. Her nose looked red raw from her cold, but Lily noticed that her eyes were brighter than they had been two days ago. Alf put a match to the fire, which was already laid, and then they sat down and listened intently, but with alarm growing on their faces, as Lily told them what had happened.

'Well, we're real glad you had the sense to come here first,' said Alf. 'And you're not going anywhere until you've had something to eat. I was just going to make us some tea and toast, so now I'll make enough for five of us.' He beamed at the children. 'I bet you're hungry, aren't you?'

Jimmy nodded. 'And I'm cold an' all,' said Joanie.

'The fire'll soon get going,' said Alf. 'Go and sit on the rug and get warm… And while we're eating our breakfast we'll decide what's the best thing to do. Just leave it to me…'

'You're very kind,' said Lily, her eyes pricking with tears. 'I'm sorry to be such a nuisance.'

'Nuisance? You're not a nuisance,' retorted Edith. 'Is she Alf? Of course you're not. And we'll do everything we can to help you. That's what friends are for. You leave it to Alf; he'll know what to do.' She lowered her voice so that the children would not hear. 'You're doing the right thing, Lily, getting away from that brute of a husband of yours.'

Lily was relieved to let somone else take charge for a while. Alf was used to coping with problems at work and he took this dilemma in his stride.

'We'll send a telegram,' he said, 'as soon as the post office opens, to tell the Reverend gentleman and his wife what time you will be arriving in Middlebeck. Edith has told me what kind people they are; they'll take care of you and the kiddies, Lily.' He scratched his head thoughtfully. 'Oh aye; we'll have to find out the times of the trains first, won't we? And then I'll run you to the station in my car.'

'That sounds grand,' said Lily. 'You're so kind… But what about the petrol ration? You're not supposed to use cars, are you, only when you have to?'

'And what's this if it's not an emergency?' said Alf. 'Shut up, woman!' He grinned at Lily. 'That's what I say to Edith, isn't it, love? when she tries to argue with me. An' I'll not listen to any arguments now. You can't manage on yer own, not with a pram and two kiddies and all that luggage. Now then, just you relax while I see to everything. You don't need to be getting a train at crack o' dawn. Your husband won't come here looking for you, will he?'

'No...' said Lily. 'He won't know I've come here, and I don't think he'll bother to look for me at all. But I'll feel safer when we've got right away from Leeds.'

Lily relaxed and enjoyed the toast spread with butter and Edith's home made blackberry jam, and so did Joanie and Jimmy. She drank two cups of the good strong tea and felt the spirit flow back into her. 'I really called to bring you these,' she said. 'Some bits and pieces that your Audrey made at school, and here's some presents she bought for the pair of you.'

'Aw, bless her!' said Edith. 'That's lovely... Was she very disappointed that we didn't go to see her?'

'She was a bit upset, of course,' said Lily, tactfully. 'But I told her as how you'd go just as soon as you could, once Christmas is over... You're feeling better now, are you, Edith?'

'So so...' replied Edith. 'My cold's on the mend, I'm glad to say. I'm not coughing and sneezing as much. It's just this blessed tiredness that comes over me. Alf tells me to stay in bed, but I can't. I've not been used to it. You die in bed, that's what I tell him.' She laughed shakily. Lily had heard her say that before.

'You look better than you did the other day,' Lily told her. That was true, but it was clear that she was still far from well. 'I shall miss you, Edith,' she went on. 'You've been a real good friend to me, an' I can't thank you enough, you and Alf, for what you're doing for us now.'

Edith's eyes misted with tears. 'Just keep an eye on our Audrey, will you, while you're in Middlebeck? Tell her that we love her and we'll be seeing her real soon…'

Thanks to Alf, the plans for Lily's departure went ahead like clockwork. As he had said, there was no immediate rush to catch a train, and so they boarded one in the late morning. Alf insisted on being there to help with the luggage and to find seats for Lily and the children. He was his own boss at work, he assured her, and they would have to manage without him for an hour or two. The train was even more crowded than the one the previous day had been, but they managed to squeeze into a corner of a compartment filled with servicemen who willingly budged up to make room.

Alf kissed her cheek. 'Chin up, Lily,' he said. 'Let us know how you get on. Edith'll miss you. You're a good friend.'

'And so are you, Alf,' she replied, very touched by his concern for her. 'One o' t' best friends I've ever had...' She watched him waving as the train moved off, then he turned and walked away, a dapper little man in a dark overcoat and bowler hat, carrying a rolled umbrella.

They ate their sandwiches and Lily looked out at the now familiar scenery. It was incredible to think she was making the same journey again, only twenty-four hours after the first one. The children dozed on and off, growing restless as they neared their destination. The telegram which Alf had sent, to the Reverend and Mrs Fairchild, had read, CRISIS AT HOME. ARRIVING BACK IN MIDDLEBECK THREE O' CLOCK THURSDAY DECEMBER 21ST. LILY. That was allowing time in case the train should be delayed. She did not doubt that someone would meet her, most probably Patience again. But she was beginning to worry that she was being a nuisance. Supposing it wasn't convenient... Oh dear, she did so hope that she had made the right decision...

Patience was not on the platform when she alighted, but Luke, the rector, was there, and with him there was a man she had not seen before; a grey-haired man in a tweed jacket with a cheerful ruddy face. Luke stepped forward to greet her.

'Lily... Hello again. We're so pleased you've decided to come.'

Lily nodded. 'Yes...there's been a problem...'

'Yes, I understand,' replied Luke. 'There will be plenty of time to tell us about it later. We're just glad that you're here.' He turned to the other man. 'This is Archie Tremaine,' he laughed. 'Sometimes known as the squire.'

Archie held out his hand. 'How do you do…Mrs Bragg, I believe? But I hope I may call you Lily?' She nodded, feeling her hand enclosed in a firm grasp. She had guessed who this man might be, but she was too overwhelmed to speak.

'Come along, all of you,' he said. 'You two are Joanie and Jimmy, aren't you? I've heard all about you. Now then, I've got my shooting brake outside. And…do you know what? You're all coming to live at my house!'

Chapter Eighteen

✦

Mrs Tremaine was there at the front of the house when Lily, helped by Archie, stepped down from the shooting brake. She greeted her enthusiastically.

'Mrs Bragg...I'm so very pleased to meet you,' she said, shaking her warmly by the hand.

'Pleased to meet you an' all, Mrs Tremaine,' said Lily, still feeling very confused; so much so that the 'an' all' had slipped out without her realising it. She did try to hard to speak properly when she was with Patience Fairchild, and she knew she should when in the company of the squire's wife. But the lady did not seem to have noticed anything amiss.

'Call me Rebecca, please,' she said. 'My husband calls me Becky, and so do some of the others, but I really prefer Rebecca. And you are Lily, I believe?'

Lily nodded. 'Yes...I'm Lily. Rebecca's a lovely name,' she added, a little shyly, looking in some awe at the smartly dressed woman in the tweed skirt and pale blue twinset, with a string of pearls at her throat. She was tall and elegant with dark hair greying a little at the temples, and what Lily thought of as noble looking features; a longish nose and wide mouth and clear grey eyes. To Lily's way of thinking she was 'posh', and so was her voice, much posher than that of her husband, the squire.

'And here are Lily's two little 'uns,' said Archie Tremaine. 'Joanie and Jimmy. That's right, isn't it, you two? And we already know your big sister, Maisie, don't we, Becky?'

'Indeed we do,' said Mrs Tremaine. 'Come on in, all of you. I'm sure you're ready for a cup of tea after your journey, and I baked some scones this morning...'

Lily and the children followed her through the palatial hall into a large room which opened off to the side. She had thought that the sitting room at the rectory was posh, but this could beat it into a cocked hat, whatever that saying meant. It was truly elegant, like the lady of the house, decorated and furnished in varying shades of green. The floor-length velvet curtains, in what Lily thought of as a grassy green colour, matched exactly the green background of the carpet, which was patterned with black and yellow leaves. She had never seen such a luxurious suite, or one so large; two massive chairs and a sofa that could seat at least four, in dark green with chair back covers and cushions of cream linen with a crocheted edging.

'Do take your coat off, Lily,' said Rebecca, 'and make yourself at home. Because this is going to be your home, as I'm sure my husband and Luke will have explained to you. That is, if you are agreeable to staying with us, you and your two lovely little children.' She smiled fondly at Joanie and Jimmy, who, like their mother, were still very bewildered.

'Of course we want to stay,' said Lily. 'It's...it's...well, I can hardly believe it.'

'And we are very glad you are here,' said Rebecca. 'It seems...providential; I suppose that's the word; almost like an answer to a prayer, although I must admit I hadn't got round to saying a prayer about it.' She laughed. 'You deciding to come and live up here, I mean, in Middlebeck, after Sally had let us down. No...I really shouldn't say that. It was not her fault at all, poor Sally... But, it's an ill wind, as they say... Now, I won't be long, Lily, then we'll have a good chat over a cup of tea.'

Archie Tremaine, also, had disappeared for the moment, and Lily, mesmerised by her surroundings and by all that had happened, and so quickly, too, leaned back in the comfortable chair and closed her eyes. As Rebecca Tremaine had said, it was like an answer to a prayer. But Lily's prayer, on finding a strange woman in her house, had just been an impassioned plea, 'Oh, God please help me...' without any real belief that He would come to her assistance.

The thought had occurred to her when they had met Bruce and his dog in the lane – when was that? Only yesterday? That hardly seemed possible – that she, Lily, would be only too pleased to take over from Sally Booth, the young woman who had had to go back home so unexpectedly; if she was suitable, of course, and if it could be arranged. She had had a feeling that the same idea had occurred to Patience as well, but neither of them had voiced their thoughts, knowing that Lily was obliged to go back to Leeds that same night. And now, by some miracle, here she was. It had actually happened. She was to live here in Tremaine House, she and the children, and assist Rebecca in looking after the land girls who would be arriving in a few day's time.

It was Archie and Luke, between them, who had explained the plan to her on the drive up from the station. Would she be willing? Archie had asked. Would she be willing! Lily had felt like throwing her arms around him and kissing him, and Luke as well. She guessed, correctly, that it had been Patience's idea on receiving the telegram that morning, and Luke had gone round to Tremaine House to see what Archie and Rebecca thought about it. There had been no hesitation on their part, especially when Luke had explained a little about Lily's unhappy background. They were only too pleased to help her, and it would be solving a problem for themselves as well. And they already knew Maisie, the delightful little girl who had been living at the rectory since September.

Archie had stopped the shooting brake at the rectory gates and Luke had got out. 'We haven't told Maisie, yet, that you are here,' he explained. 'She doesn't even know about the telegram. We thought it was best for you to get settled with Archie and Becky, and then you can explain to Maisie yourself about what has happened. It's best coming from you, I think... Cheerio, Archie. Bye for now, Lily. See you soon; we're so glad you're here.'

Lily felt her eyes growing moist at the thought of the welcome she had received. But this surely must be a dream from which she would soon awaken, finding herself back in her nightmarish existence in

Armley... No; she was here and it was real. Joanie was pulling at her arm.

'Mummy, Mummy...I want to wee...'

'An' I do an' all,' echoed Jimmy.

'Of course you do,' said Lily. 'How silly of me not to think about it. You must be bursting by now. Come on; let's go and find out where the lavvy is.'

Archie, entering the room at that moment, summed up the situation and showed her to a little room to the side of the staircase. It was a wide staircase with carved oaken bannisters, which branched before reaching the upper landing. The little room was where coats and umbrellas and boots were kept, and as well as a toilet there was a little wash-basin with a nice smelling cake of soap and fluffy white towel. Lily guessed there would be a bathroom upstairs as well; maybe even more than one.

'Eeh...I don't know,' she murmured, more to herself than to the children. 'It's just like livin' in Buckingham Palace.'

'Where, Mum?' said Joanie, pulling up her knickers and and then helping Jimmy to adjust his pants; she was getting to be a very helpful little girl.

'Where the King and Queen live,' said Lily.

'Do they live here an' all then, the King and Queen?' asked Joanie.

Lily burst out laughing. 'No, of course they don't. I was only saying...well, it's posh enough for them...'

'When are we goin' to see Maisie?' asked Jimmy. 'You said we was goin' to see 'er...'

'Soon,' said Lily. 'When we've had our cup of tea...'

Rebecca explained, over tea, that Lily's job would be to assist in all manner of things. There was a cleaning lady, Mrs Kitson – the mother of Daisy, Miss Thomson's former maid – who came two mornings a week to help with what she called the 'rough'. Rebecca was used to doing her own cooking and baking because she enjoyed it. Even when they had had the influx of evacuees, now all departed, she had done most of it, helped sometimes by Sally Booth.

'I'm not much of a cook,' Lily told her, thinking it was best to be honest. 'Well, I do me best I suppose, but I've never really had the chance to do much fancy cooking, like.'

'These girls won't be wanting fancy dishes, I'm sure,' laughed Rebecca. 'It's all the same if they do, because they won't be getting them. Good old-fashioned Yorkshire fare, that's what they'll get.'

'I'm a good cleaner though,' said Lily. 'I love dusting and polishing and making things nice and shiny. An' I like ironing an' all...as well. Some folks don't like it, but I do.' It had been a joy to her to iron the shirts of the ladies' husbands for whom she had worked; pristine white shirts, crisp with newness, and casual coloured ones for weekends. Sid's and Percy's had been so grubby and stained with sweat that sometimes she could scarcely get them clean, never mind neatly ironed, and the collars and cuffs were all frayed; most times, though, they hadn't worn collars at all.

'I think one of our biggest jobs will be coping with the washing,' said Rebecca. 'I know how muddy Archie's clothes get, and there will be twelve of these girls, possibly more. We've had a big washing machine installed though, in the wash-house. We had it put in when we knew that the WLA were coming here. We've had a supply of single beds delivered as well. Iron bedsteads; army stock, I suppose. We've managed to get four of them in each of the three largest rooms. It'll be rather like school dormitories, but I expect the girls will be glad of the company. No doubt some of them will be homesick...

'And you can have the bedroom that Sally and her children used to have. It has a nice view over the hills and across to the ruined castle... Now, would you like to unpack your things, Lily, and then Archie will drive you round to see your daughter before we have our evening meal...'

Maisie's greeting was ecstatic. 'Mum, Mum...' she shouted, on seeing Lily and the two children on the doorstep. 'And you two an' all! What are you doing back here? Hello, Mr Tremaine,' she added, just noticing that Archie was with them as well. Then her smile faded a little. 'Is there summat wrong at home?' she asked. 'I mean...in Armley?' She thought of Middlebeck as her home now. 'Is it Sid, Mum? What's he done?' But her mother was still smiling, and so was Patience, so everything must be all right again now.

'There now! Isn't this a lovely surprise?' said Patience, as they all entered the house. 'Your mum and your little brother and sister have come to live here, in Middlebeck.'

'With the squire and Mrs Tremaine, though,' said Lily. 'Not here with you and Audrey. Yes...there was something wrong at home, love. Sid – well, I might as well tell you straight, Maisie love – he's got a woman living there with him, an' I'm not going to put up with that, am I? So...here I am!' The mother and daughter hugged one another. Lily had one eye on Audrey, though, who was standing there looking very forlorn. She turned and put an arm around her as well.

'I've seen yer mum and dad, Audrey,' she told her. 'I went to see them this morning, and yer mum's feeling a lot better. And she'll see you very soon, she says. When Christmas is over she'll come and see you, and yer dad as well. So cheer up, lovey. It won't be long...'

And this was the thought that Audrey clung to throughout that first Christmas of the war.

⸺

It was agreed that the rectory family and the family at Tremaine house should celebrate Christmas together. And so, after a short service at St Bartholomew's church, they all went back to the home of Mr and Mrs Tremaine. When the traditional meal was served at one o' clock there were ten of them seated around the long table in the dining room; Archie and Rebecca and their son, Bruce; Lily, Joanie and Jimmy, the Rev Luke and Patience Fairchild; and Maisie and Audrey. The three women working together in the spacious kitchen – far larger than even Patience, let alone Lily, had been used to – had prepared the roast turkey (reared on Walter Dixon's farm), the roast potatoes, home grown turnips and brussel sprouts, and Patience's homemade sage and onion stuffing. This was followed by Rebecca's special Christmas pudding and creamy white sauce, laced with a small glassful of brandy.

There was, as yet, no shortage of food. Especially in the country areas folks were not having to go without things that they had been used to. Stockpiling of commodities which soon might be in short supply was frowned upon. Nevertheless, there could scarcely be a housewife who did not have some dried fruit and ground almonds – for the marzipan on the cake – stored away in her kitchen cupboard to use that first Christmas of the war.

At the end of the meal Luke raised his glass of sweet brown sherry, and the rest of the company followed suit – even Maisie and Audrey had been allowed a thimbleful of the liquor – as he proposed a toast to the King and Queen, to the hope of peace, and to absent friends. They were thinking particularly of Audrey's mother and father, and of the servicemen from the little town who had not managed to get home to their families. Then they all gathered around the wireless set, encased in a large cabinet of mahogany, which stood in the sitting room, to listen to the broadcast by King George the Sixth. In his now familiar halting tones he declared, 'We cannot tell what the New Year will bring. If it brings peace how happy we shall be...'

The adults exchanged sceptical glances at these words. It seemed very unlikely.

After Christmas the snow returned with a vengeance. Not only north Yorkshire, but the whole of the country was covered by a thick white blanket. It was being said that it was the coldest January for half a century; even the River Thames in London had frozen over. There were stories of frozen pipes, snow-blocked roads and railways brought to a standstill. But how true it all was no one could be sure because the weather news on the wireless, as well as other news of importance, was censored for fear that enemy agents should be listening.

The expected food rationing came into force of January the eighth, but it was only bacon, ham, sugar and butter that were rationed. By that time Bruce Tremaine had returned to his boarding school, and Maisie and Audrey had gone back to a somewhat changed village school.

Anne Mellodey had spent Christmas with her parents in Leeds. To her great joy her fiancé, Bill, had been granted a forty-eight hour pass and they had been able to spend some precious hours together.

She returned to Middlebeck during the first week in January through a silvery white landscape. The hills were a wondrous sight with the early morning sun shining on them, but on either side of the railway track were shoulder-high piles of grubby grey snow. As yet there was no sign of a thaw. Anne was glad of her wellington boots, her warm coat and her woolly hat pulled down over her ears as she trudged up the High Street from the station. She had only a small case with her; even so she felt quite exhausted when she arrived at the greystone house next to the school.

Charity Foster greeted her warmly with a hug and a kiss on her cheek. 'Goodness gracious, child!' she exclaimed. 'You're as cold as a block of ice. Come on in and take those wet things off.' It had started to snow again, huge white flakes like goose feathers drifting down from a leaden sky. 'I must say you're looking well, though, Anne. You've had a lovely Christmas, I expect? And how is that nice young man of yours...?'

Anne told her headmistress all the news from home as they sat by the blazing fire drinking tea laced with a drop of whisky, 'to keep out the cold!' Charity explained. Bill had returned, late on Boxing Day, to his station in East Anglia where he had almost finished his training as a pilot. Thinking about him and wondering when she would see him again made her feel sad, but returning to the job which she enjoyed so much would help, to a certain extent, to take her thoughts away from her anxieties. And once they had exchanged chit-chat about the festive season there was a great deal to discuss about the forthcoming term at Middlebeck School. It had been agreed before the holiday that Anne should be the one to continue teaching there; and so Dorothy Cousins, the other teacher from Armley, had now returned home to Leeds.

'I have been giving some thought to the rearrangement of the classes,' Charity told Anne, 'More than half of our visitors have now gone back, as you know, dear, to Leeds or to Hull. They might live to regret it, or their parents might…' She shook her head a little sorrowfully. 'But I suppose one can't blame them; they want their children home again. But things won't stay like this for ever, with regard to the war, I mean.'

'Yes, that's what Bill says,' agreed Anne. 'He doesn't tell me very much. They're not supposed to give away secrets; besides, he knows it would only worry me. But this state of limbo that we're in can't continue.'

'Quite so… Anyway, Anne, instead of the six rather large classes we have had, we will be down to five rather smaller ones; three here on the school premises and two across at the church. We will be able to dispense with the one at the Village Institute; it was rather too far away in any case.

'But I'm afraid you will be having a mixed-age group, my dear; your own Standard Three and some of the Standard Four children as well. We are quite used to this in the village schools, but I know in the city schools that it is quite different. But you will adjust, Anne; you are a most competent teacher.'

'Thank you,' smiled Anne. 'I'll do my best. I shouldn't say this…but some of the troublemakers have gone back. Esme Clough – I knew her of old, back in Armley – and Paula Jeffreys from Hull. They caused no end of problems when they got together with Gertie and Norma. They're still here, of course – they live here – but they seem rather more subdued since that accident with little Timothy Clegg. They thought he was dead, you know, when he fell in the builder's yard; Maisie told me.'

'Yes, and speaking of Maisie...' Charity told Anne the news about Maisie's mother coming to live at Tremaine House to assist with the land army girls. 'They arrived a couple of days ago,' she said. 'But goodness knows how much farming they will be able to do in this sort of weather...'

———

'D'you think it's because of all this snow that my mum and dad haven't been to see me?' asked Audrey, towards the end of January.

'I'm sure it is, dear,' said Patience, for the umpteenth time. 'That's what she said in her letter, didn't she? You know that your mum was rather poorly last year when she had that operation...' Audrey had now been told about that, but not of the severity of it, '...and she needs to take care not to overdo things. This cold weather is not good for her. But it's beginning to thaw now. They'll be here before long, don't you worry...'

But after the snow there came the fog; dense fogs which were known in cities such as London, Manchester and Leeds as pea-soupers. You could hardly see your hand in front of your face as the greyish yellow blanket descended, obliterating buildings, traffic, street signs and the edges of the kerbs. You took your life in your hands in attempting to cross the road...

———

It was during the first week in February that the telegram arrived at the rectory. It was mid-morning and both the children were at school. Patience took the yellow envelope from the boy at the door with a feeling of dread. Whoever could be sending them a telegram? She feared it could only be bad news and her thoughts flew immediately to Audrey's mother in Leeds. Her continued absence was upsetting the little girl and Patience had wondered if she had take a turn for the worse.

Quickly she ripped open the envelope and read the stark messsage inside. Her cry brought Luke rushing from the study. 'Patience, my dear; whatever is it?'

'Just read this...' She thrust the paper at him. 'I thought it must be Edith, but it's...'

Luke read the printed words on the form. ALF KILLED IN ROAD ACCIDENT. LETTER FOLLOWING. PLEASE TELL AUDREY. EDITH. 'Oh no! How dreadful! How unbelievably dreadful,' he uttered. He turned to the telegraph boy who was standing there awaiting instructions. 'No, there's no reply; not yet. Thank you.'

'Sorry if it's bad news, sir,' said the lad. 'They usually are.'

Luke nodded. 'Yes, as you say. But it's not your fault, is it?'

He closed the front door and put his arms around his wife. 'Yes, it's terrible news. Poor little Audrey. Would you like me to break it to her?'

Tears were streaming down Patience's face. 'I'm not sure yet what to do, how to tell her. Poor Audrey...and poor Edith. She relied on her husband so much.

'Let's wait a little while,' said Luke. 'It says there's a letter following. It will arrive tomorrow, more than likely, then we can decide how best to break it to her.'

'That poor child,' breathed Patience. 'Maybe I will feel a little more composed by tomorrow…'

It was hard to put on a cheerful face when the girls returned at lunchtime, full of their news about the morning at school. They had both got full marks in the weekly spelling test, and that afternoon would be one of their favourite lessons, drawing and painting. Miss Mellodey wanted them to design a poster about some aspect of the war; the army, navy or airforce; the Women's Land Army; or perhaps about being careful with food, which was now on ration. It was a topical subject because you could hardly walk a few yards along the High Street without seeing a poster for something of other, on walls, billboards and the side of buildings. The latest one, depicting women gossiping on a bus, proclaimed that 'Careless Talk Costs Lives'.

The expected letter from Edith Dennison arrived the next morning. Patience kept it hidden from Audrey's eyes and she and Luke read it together when the girls had gone to school. It was surprising how Edith had managed to write so neatly and concisely. They knew she must be heartbroken and shattered beyond belief at the death of her husband, but it seemed as though she was managing to keep some control of herself.

He had been knocked down by a tram in the centre of the city, whilst crossing the road in dense fog. No one would ever understand fully what had happened. The tram could not have been travelling fast, and Alf was normally so careful, but he had received severe blows to his head and had been dead on arrival at the hospital. Edith explained that her neighbours were being very good to her and the local vicar was seeing to the funeral arrangements. She enclosed his telephone number as a point of contact. It was her final paragraph which devastated Patience and Luke, although they came to realise that it was inevitable.

'I would like Audrey to come back home to Leeds,' Edith wrote, 'not just for the funeral but to come back and live here. I have no more close relations, only a cousin or two elsewhere, and Audrey means so much to me, as she did to Alf. The funeral is on Tuesday. I can't come to fetch her, poor little lamb. I am not at all well as I expect you will understand. But if she is put in charge of the guard on the train I will meet her in Leeds, or someone else will. Thank you both for all you have done for her...'

'I'll take her back myself,' said Luke at once. 'I dare say Edith knows I will, but she wouldn't like to suggest it.'

'That poor woman,' sighed Patience. 'You can tell by the tone of her letter that she is far from well. And this tragedy coming on top of everything else; it's almost too much to bear. You will stay for the funeral, will you, Luke? And make sure that Edith has someone to keep an eye on her. I don't think she has any close friends there, and now, of course, Lily is living up here. I'm not surprised she wants Audrey back... But we are going to miss her, aren't we, Luke?'

'Most certainly,' Luke agreed. 'And so is Maisie. But what we have to think about now is breaking the news to her...'

When they had eaten their lunch it was Patience,

feeling calmer than she had on the previous day, who took Audrey into the sitting room. 'I have something very serious I want to say to Audrey,' she explained to Maisie. 'Her father has had a bad accident... So could you help Luke to wash up, dear, just for today?'

'I have had a letter from your mother,' she began, sitting on the settee with Audrey and putting an arm around her.

'Have you?' Audrey's eyes lit up. 'Is she coming to see me?'

'No...but you will be seeing her very soon,' explained Patience carefully. 'She wants you to go home because your daddy...well, he has had an accident, dear, and she needs you to be with her.'

Audrey's expression changed. Her eyes were grave as she looked at Patience. 'D'you mean...a bad accident?'

'Yes, I'm afraid so, Audrey. A very bad one. He was knocked down by a tram in the fog and...'

'And...he's been killed, hasn't he? He's...dead?'

The fact that Patience did not reply, but only held her more closely, was answer enough for Audrey.

'Oh...oh no! Not Daddy...' Sobs shook her body as she clung wildly to Patience. 'not my daddy...'

Patience let her cry, knowing it was necessary for her to do so. There was no sense in telling a little girl that she must try to be brave. How could she be brave when faced with dreadful tidings like that? Eventually her sobs diminished a little. 'And...and did you say I've got to go back and live with my mum? I won't be living here any more?' She lifted a tear-stained and perplexed face up to Patience.

'Well, that's the idea at the moment,' replied Patience. 'You mum will want you with her, or else she'd be all on her own, wouldn't she?'

'Yes…I suppose so,' said Audrey. 'But…I like it here. I miss my mum and…and my dad, but I like living here. Will I never be able to come back? Won't I ever see you again, and Luke?'

'You mustn't worry about all that at the moment,' said Patience. 'Of course we will see one another again. We are all friends now, aren't we? Luke will take you back to Leeds on Monday on the train, and stay with you for a day or two before he comes back.' She did not mention the funeral. There would be time enough later for Luke to explain to her about that sad event.

'Now…you don't need to go back to school this afternoon. I'll pop across and see Miss Mellodey and she'll understand. Perhaps you could help me to make some cakes for tea? How about that…?'

Audrey, understandably, was withdrawn and largely uncommunicative over the next few days. Luke phoned the vicar in Armley to tell him of the train times and he would pass the message on to Edith. Audrey was tearful again when it was time for her to pack her bags for the return home.

'What shall I take?' she asked. 'Everything? Or shall I leave some of my stuff here?'

'Oh…just take what you need for the moment, dear,' said Patience. 'We'll send the rest on to you by carrier.'

Both little girls shed tears on the Monday morning when it was time to say goodbye. It had been decided that there were to be no tearful farewells at the station. Archie was to drive Luke and Audrey down to catch an early train, and Maisie was to attend school as usual.

'Goodbyes are always sad,' Patience told them. 'But your mum will be looking forward so much to seeing you again, Audrey. Just think about that; you'll be such a comfort to her...'

But that was little consolation to Maisie as she watched the shooting-brake drive away. 'D'you think I'll ever see Audrey again?' she asked.

'Of course you will,' said Patience. 'Your home is in Armley, isn't it, as well as Audrey's?' She realised at once that that had been an unwise thing to say.

'No, Aunty Patience,' said Maisie solemnly. 'I live here now, don't I? This is my home, 'specially now my mum's living up here. I don't s'pose we'll ever go back there.'

'Well...perhaps not,' said Patience. 'None of us know, dear, what the future holds. But you'll see your friend again. I feel sure you will.'

***

'So there's only you and me left now, isn't there?' said Doris to Maisie in the playground, the following day. 'Ivy's gone and now Audrey an' all. I know you and Audrey were best friends, like...but d'you think you and me can be special friends now?'

'Yeah...I s'pose so,' replied Maisie. She was missing Audrey very much. She had felt so sorry for her, her dad being killed like that. She remembered now she had felt a bit peeved when Audrey had first come to live at the rectory, until Aunty Patience had explained that it wouldn't make any difference.

And it hadn't. They had all been so happy together. It was odd that she was living with Luke and Patience whilst her mother was somewhere else; but it was more convenient that way, they had explained to her.

'What's up?' said Doris. 'You don't sound very keen. Don't you want to be me best friend?'

'Yes…I don't mind,' said Maisie. 'But I was just thinking about Audrey. Real sad, isn't it? Hey up…look who's coming. Let's try not to fall out with 'em, eh?'

Gertie Flint and Norma Wilkins were approaching, but looking much less belligerent than usual.'

'We're dead sorry about Audrey,' said Gertie.

'Are you really?' said Doris, just a mite aggressively.

'Yeah…honest we are,' said Norma. 'It's real sad her dad bein' killed, an' her havin' to go back to Leeds an' all. She's gone for good, has she?'

Maisie nodded. 'I s'pose so.'

'We was wondering,' said Gertie. 'There's only you two now, and us two. Would you like to be friends with us?'

'Why should we?' said Doris, tossing her flaxen plaits.

''Cause we'd like you to be, honest we would,' said Norma. 'I know we've been dead mean sometimes. And we were horrid, teasing poor little Tim like that. We felt awful when he got hurt.'

'Shut up, Norma,' said Gertie. 'Yer don't need to go on like that. Leave 'em alone if they don't want to be friends. We don't care.'

'I thought we did,' said Norma.

'Yeah...all right,' said Maisie, decidedly. 'We'll be yer friends if yer want us to be, me and Doris. Won't we, Doris?'

'Oh...all right then,' said Doris, but still a shade grudgingly.

'We was just jealous, Maisie,' said Norma. ''Cause you're real clever, aren't you? Always top of the class, and so was Audrey. We thought you were a couple of swank pots, y'see. But you're not. You're dead nice really.'

Maisie shrugged. 'I can't help being clever,' she said, with an air of modesty.

'I'm not clever,' giggled Doris. 'You don't need to be jealous of me. Me dad sometimes says I'm as thick as two short planks.'

'No, you're not!' retorted Maisie. 'That's not very nice of him.'

'I don't care,' laughed Doris. 'He's only teasing.'

'But you're real pretty, Doris,' said Norma. 'I wish I had nice fair hair like that...'

'Oh...thank you,' said Doris. She gave a self-satisfied smile and tossed her plaits again. 'Yes, it's OK...you can be friends with us if you want, can't they, Maisie?'

Chapter Nineteen

The cold and miserable winter was followed by a warm and balmy spring, at least as far as the weather was concerned. Many people of the nation had begun to grow complacent as the months went by. Especially as the Prime Minister, Neville Chamberlain, remarked at the beginning of April, 'After seven months of war I feel ten times as confident of victory as I did at the beginning...Hitler has missed the bus.'

'What do you think about that?' Patience asked her husband. 'He should know what he's talking about; after all, he is the Prime Minister.'

Luke shook his head. 'I haven't forgotten Munich,' he replied, 'and neither have a lot more folk. I have as much confidence in Chamberlain now as I had when he came back waving his scrap of paper. Peace in our time... Yes, it was a comforting thought and I'm sure he wanted to believe it. But I doubt if he will be leading our nation for very much longer, my dear. We need a man of action.'

Four days later the Germans occupied Denmark, and then Norway, who had remained neutral. The British forces who went to their aid suffered heavy losses. Then, in May, the German army burst into Holland, Belgium and France.

'That's the end of our phoney war, the 'bore war' or whatever they called it,' said Luke. 'And the end of Chamberlain too, I fear... No, that's not true. There would be more to reason to fear if he were to stay.'

'Poor man,' said Patience. 'He did his best and he meant well.'

'I'm sure he did,' said Luke, 'but I am realising now that to be well-meaning is not always the best thing. It wasn't in this case.'

'So who do you think they will get to follow him?'

'There's only one man who can command the support of the House of Commons, and that is Winston Churchill. He's not always been popular, but most folks are coming round to his way of thinking now...'

Churchill's message was grim. 'I have nothing to offer but blood, toil, tears and sweat. What is our aim? Victory at all costs...however long and hard the road may be.'

The complacency of the British people, along with the apathy and the apprehension, was transformed to a new spirit of hope and determination. The glorious spring was followed by an equally golden summer. But every day, as that summer drew on, although it brought blue skies, brought increasingly bad news...

Andy Cartwright, Daisy's young man, was serving in France as one of the British Expeditionary Force. There was great concern for him in Middlebeck, and for thousands of others, when the British Army was forced to retreat.

'Say a prayer for my lad, won't you, Reverend?' Andy's mother asked Luke. She had been a spasmodic church-goer, but had attended more regularly since her son had gone overseas. In fact Luke had noticed that his congregation as a whole had increased since the beginning of the year, people realising that it might not be a bad idea to turn to the Almighty for help.

'Indeed I will, Mrs Cartwright,' Luke told her, 'and for all the others.' The news had just broken through of the armada of ships and boats, both great and small, involved in the rescue operation from the beaches of Dunkirk.

A tired and dishevelled, though not dispirited, Andy arrived home in Middlebeck two days later, and the following weekend his girlfriend, Daisy, was granted a pass from her ATS camp in Herefordshire and she travelled north to see him.

They called at the rectory the following day. 'We want to get married real soon,' they told Luke. 'In a few weeks' time if we can. We should be able to get leave and have a few days together.'

Luke did not even try to dissuade them or to advise them to wait a while. They were young and in love and they wanted to 'belong to one another' they told him. This was not the only speedy marriage that he had arranged. Time was of the essence and, although it was never spoken out loud, it was uncertain how much time might be left for young couples to spend together.

And so arrangements were made that very weekend for the wedding to take place on the second Saturday in July. Daisy, to the great delight of both girls, asked Maisie and Doris if they would be her bridesmaids.

'Why us and not your sisters?' asked Maisie.

'Oh, there's too many of 'em,' said Daisy, 'an' they'd only fall out about it, so I'll have you two instead. It'll not be a big posh do, but I want to have a white frock. Me mam said why don't I get married in me uniform, same as Andy will, but I've allus wanted to be a proper bride. An' you two can wear whatever colour you like; pink or blue or green, a pale green, like…'

'Not green,' said Patience. 'Green is supposed to be unlucky, isn't it?' She wasn't really superstitious, but she knew that bridesmaids very seldom wore green.

'Happen pink then,' said Daisy. 'Little girls always look nice in pink, but it's up to you. I don't mind. I mustn't say little girls though, must I? Look at the pair of yer! How you've shot up since I was last here.'

It was agreed that Patience and Doris's mother, Ada, would purchase material from the stall in the market hall and make the bridesmaids' dresses themselves from a paper pattern. And Daisy would buy a ready-made dress from a shop she knew of in Hereford, which was not too expensive.

She called again at the rectory on Sunday afternoon. 'I'm real sorry little Audrey's gone back,' she said to Patience, 'or else I'd've had her as a bridesmaid an' all. Well, actually, I'd've had her and not Doris, but I wanted two, y'see. And then I found out that Maisie and Doris had got friendly, like, and Andy has known little Doris since she were a baby.

Me and Audrey, though, we were real good friends when I was working for old Amelia…Miss Thomson, I mean,' she added with a grin at Patience. 'I'm goin' to pop over and see her now, then I'm goin' to tea with Andy and his mam and dad. I'm not taking Andy to see 'er Ladyship. She was never all that keen on him, but I might invite her to the wedding. What d' you think, Mrs Fairchild?'

'That would be a very nice idea,' replied Patience. 'It's a kind thought, Daisy. I think you will find that Miss Thomson has mellowed a little. She has two land girls billeted with her now, as no doubt you have heard, and they have a rota to help her with the housework and some of the cooking, although I have heard she is doing quite a lot of the cooking herself. And I believe your mother goes in a few mornings a week, doesn't she, Daisy?'

'Aye, that's right; so she does. She does the washing and scrubbing floors an' all that sort o' thing. She says Miss T. asks about me, so that's nice of her, isn't it? That's why I'm going to see her.'

'I like Priscilla and Jennifer,' said Maisie. 'They're the two land girls. Well, it's Priscilla that I know best. She's in the church choir…an' I am as well now,' she added proudly.

'Are you, by gum?' said Daisy. 'I didn't know you could sing.'

'Yes, she has a lovely voice,' said Patience. 'We could hear her singing all over the house, so Luke asked her if she would like to join the choir. She's one of the youngest choristers, of course.'

'I sing when I'm happy,' said Maisie, 'and I've been real happy since I came to live here, 'specially now me mum's up here an' our little Joanie and Jimmy. She's helping Mrs Tremaine with the land girls, y'know – me mum, I mean. An' our Joanie'll be starting school in September. An' I'll be in the top class then, Standard Four. I hope we still have Miss Mellodey. I 'spect we will, 'cause we've got some of the top class kids in with us now.'

Daisy laughed. 'You're still a little chatterbox, aren't you? And what about yer friend, Audrey? Does she write to you? How's her mam going on?'

'Well...' Maisie hesitated. 'Audrey writes now and again, not all that much though. I don't think her mum's very well.'

'Luke has kept in touch with her vicar,' said Patience. 'He met him when he took Audrey back home. I'm afraid Mrs Dennison is far from well. She wanted Audrey with her, which was understandable, and I'm sure the little girl is a comfort to her, but...' She glanced warily at Maisie who was listening intently. '...but, as I said, she's not well. We just have to say our prayers, Daisy, and hope for the best.'

'Yes...I see,' said Daisy. 'Poor little Audrey, poor kid... Anyroad, I'd best be off across the green to see Miss T. If I don't see yer before, I'll see yer when I come back for me wedding. Only six weeks! I can't believe it.'

Daisy was surprised at the greeting she received from Miss Thomson.

'Well now...Daisy, how lovely to see you...' Her former employer actually kissed her on the cheek, but very primly, then quickly drew away from her, looking rather flustered and embarrassed.

'I've come to tell yer that me and Andy's getting married,' said Daisy, following Miss Thomson into the room she called the lounge. Well, that was a turn-up for the book, being invited into the lounge! 'An' we'd like you to come to the wedding. It won't be a big posh do, but we're 'aving a bit of a get-together afterwards in t' church hall. I'll send yer a proper invite, like, but it's the second Saturday in July.'

'How very kind of you, my dear.' Miss Thomson turned quite pink and her lips curved in more of a smile than Daisy had ever seen on her normally forbidding face. 'I can't remember the last time I was invited to a wedding... And will you be staying in the army – the ATS, isn't it? – after you are married? I must say that you look very smart in your uniform, Daisy.'

'Ta very much,' said Daisy. She was proud of her khaki jacket and short skirt and her neat little forage cap which sat pertly on top of her dark curly hair, although she wasn't wearing the cap now, of course, in the house. 'Aye, I reckon I'll be staying on in the ATS. I'm down near Hereford, an' Andy...well, I'm not right sure where Andy'll be. He's just back from that Dunkirk place, y'know. We'll just have to meet when we can, him and me. Like folks keep telling us, that's what happens in wartime.'

'Yes, quite so,' said Miss Thomson. 'We have all had to make changes. I have two of those land girls staying here. Very nice young ladies they are, though; well-mannered and really very little trouble at all.' Daisy suppressed a grin. Miss Thomson sounded surprised that they were 'nice young ladies'. Or maybe she had mellowed, as Patience had said, and had seen the best in them.

'Perhaps you would like to meet them, Daisy? They are both here this afternoon, washing their hair, I believe. I will just pop upstairs and see if they would like to have a little chat with you, and then perhaps we could all have a cup of tea together.'

By heck! she has changed, thought Daisy, looking around the room which she had hardly ever sat in before, only cleaned and polished the old-fashioned furniture. It still smelled somewhat musty with lack of use; fires were very rarely lit in there. But there were now a few women's magazines on the sofa which surely did not belong to Amelia. Were the girls actually allowed into this hallowed place?

Miss Thomson was back in a few moments. 'Go up, Daisy,' she said. 'They are in the back room on the first floor, across from the bathroom. They will be pleased to see you.'

First floor, indeed! thought Daisy, and in one of the posh bedrooms an' all. Not banished to the attic floor as she and Audrey had been.

Two girls, one dark and one fair, although their hair was still damp and set in Dinky rollers, were sitting one on each bed. 'Hi there,' said the fair one. 'I'm Priscilla, and this is Jennifer. And you must be Daisy. We've heard a lot about you, haven't we, Jen?'

'Oh heck, have yer?' said Daisy. 'I don't like the sound o' that.'

'No, nothing bad,' said Jennifer, the dark-haired

girl. 'Miss Thomson's always singing your praises, isn't she, Prissy?'

'She certainly is,' replied Priscilla. 'Come and sit down and make yourself at home... You're in the ATS then? We heard how you'd joined up. Miss T. was very impressed about that. So how are you liking it?'

The three girls exchanged stories about the ATS and the Women's Land Army. They all admitted that they were homesick at times, but had learned to make the best of it. And there were compensations. Daisy enjoyed the company and friendship of a group of girls, something she had not been used to, working as a maid, whereas Priscilla and Jennifer, both town girls – Priscilla from Leicester and Jennifer from Manchester – were enjoying a very different sort of life in the countryside. But while Daisy was soon to marry the young man who was the love of her life, the two land girls were fancy free.

'There's an army camp not far away though,' said Priscilla, laughing. 'Up near Richmond.'

'Yeah, I know,' said Daisy. 'You mean Catterick camp. Have you got friendly wi' some of the soldiers then?'

Priscilla pursed her lips. 'No one special. They get transported down here now and again when there's a dance on at the Village Hall. And we go up to the camp if there's something going on in the NAAFI. Not just me and Jennifer; I mean a crowd of us land girls. There are a lot more billeted at the squire's house, you know.'

'And how do you get up there?' asked Daisy,

knowing that the bus service was practically non-existent.

'Well, we ride bikes, most of us, provided by the WLA. Or one of the sergeants might give us a lift in an army truck. There are ways and means,' laughed Priscilla.

She appeared to be the livelier of the two girls, the one who was doing most of the talking. Priscilla was small with delicate features, not the sort of girl you would imagine working on a farm, Daisy thought, whereas Jennifer was robust and pink-cheeked, seemingly much more of a farm girl. She was quieter, though, just smiling in agreement most of the time.

'So you're on one of the farms round here, are you?' asked Daisy.

'Yes, Mr Nixon's,' said Priscilla. 'We call him Walter, though; everybody does. He was responsible for our training, him and the squire. We were clueless when we arrived, weren't we, Jen?'

'Absolutely,' smiled Jennifer.

'Walter trains quite a lot of the girls,' Priscilla went on. 'He's a very good teacher, but he can get a bit short-tempered if you don't catch on at once.'

'Don't I know it!' said Daisy. 'My Andy used to work for him; well, for him and the squire. It's all Mr Tremaine's land, y'know.'

'The other girls are working further away though,' said Jennifer, 'the ones that are living at the big house. They get taken to their farms by lorry every morning, or sometimes they go on their bikes. Priscilla and I are lucky, working so near, aren't we, Prissy?'

'Yes.' Priscilla nodded. 'I sometimes wish we were with the others, though, at Tremaine House. But Miss Thomson's not such a bad old stick when you get to know her.'

'Huh! You don't know what she was like when I was here!' exclaimed Daisy. 'I must say she's changed, though. What time d'you have to be in, like, when you go off gallivanting?'

'Oh, half-past ten or so,' said Priscilla. 'We're never really late, though, because dances and all that sort of thing finish real early.'

'It were half-past nine for me!' said Daisy. 'There was no end of a row when I stopped out late once. She actually sacked me.'

'Yes,' laughed Priscilla. 'We've heard all about that, and about little Audrey getting into trouble.'

'Who told yer?' asked Daisy in surprise. 'It weren't Miss Thomson, were it?'

'No, of course not. It was young Maisie,' answered Priscilla. 'We had a good laugh about it, her and me. She's a grand little lass, isn't she?'

'Aye, so she is.' Daisy nodded. 'Her and Doris – you'll know Doris, of course; she's Walter's daughter – they're going to be bridesmaids for me and Andy.'

'We'll come and see you get married, won't we, Jennifer?' said Priscilla. 'We get time off on a Saturday afternoon.'

'You can do more than that,' said Daisy. 'Why don't yer come to the do afterwards in t' church hall? The more the merrier, and I know you both now, don't I?'

'Well, that's real nice of you,' said Jennifer.

'Thanks; we'd love to come,' said Priscilla.

There was a polite knock at the door. 'Girls…I've made a pot of tea,' said Miss Thomson, putting her head round the door. 'Do come and share it with me.'

'Well!' said Daisy, as the woman departed. 'I'll go to the foot of our stairs! Just wait till I tell Andy. A cup of tea with 'er Ladyship! He'll never believe me…'

When the wedding of Daisy and Andy took place, as arranged, in mid-July, there were not two, but three bridesmaids in attendance.

Patience and Luke had been increasingly worried by the news from Armley, passed on to them by Edith's vicar, the Reverend Keith Armstrong. Then came the news, in the middle of June, that Edith had been taken into hospital again; there had been a recurrence of her former problem. Audrey was being looked after by a neighbour. The woman was not a close friend of Edith, but she was willing to do what she could to help out for the time being. But Audrey, understandably, was not happy. She was worried about her mother and, according to the vicar, she kept asking when she could see Aunty Patience and Luke again.

The two of them were in a quandary. 'Do you think we should have her back here again?' said Patience. 'That poor child! I hate to think of her being so unhappy. Ring Keith Armstrong, my dear, and tell him you will go and fetch her, provided he thinks it is a good idea, of course.'

But the vicar in Armley did not think so. There

was a short silence when Luke made the suggestion, then he said, 'We are trying to remain positive, Luke, and we keep saying our prayers, of course, for Edith…but I have to tell you that the prognosis is not good. It would not be wise to take Audrey away at the moment. She is a sensible little girl, and I think she knows her mother is very poorly. It's quite possible that she realises Edith will not get better. My wife and I have had her round at our home, and she has a nice teacher at school who is caring for her there. And Edith's neighbours…well, they are doing their best.'

'How very sad,' said Luke. 'Patience and I only want to do what is best for her. Please, please Keith, do keep us informed…'

'Of course I will… By the way, Audrey misses her little friend; Maisie, isn't it? She said to give her love to Maisie, and to you two as well. She knows I keep in touch with you. So…just keep on praying, Luke. It's all we can do.'

Ten days later Edith Dennison passed away quietly in her sleep. It had not been possible to do very much for her other than to alleviate the pain, as her illness had progressed too far for a further operation. Audrey was said to be heartbroken and quite inconsolable. The Reverend Armstrong and his wife had taken her to stay at their home until the funeral, to be held in a few days' time, was over.

'And after that, we just don't know,' the vicar told Luke. 'The poor child is an orphan now. There is no way that my wife and I can care for her indefinitely, and I'm afraid that Edith's neighbours have made it quite clear that they are not willing to do so. Anyway, why should they? They are a middle-aged couple, and Audrey has not been too happy there.'

'Then she must come to us,' said Luke without hesitation. 'There is no question of it, Keith. I will come down for the funeral and take her back with me. I believe she was happy with us in Middlebeck, and we will do our best to make sure that she is again.'

There was an audible sigh of relief from Keith Armstrong. 'Well, I must say that is a weight off my mind, Luke. I was hoping you would say that, and I am not surprised either. You are a good man; one of the best men I know... It was only a short time arrangement before, though, wasn't it? She was an evacuee... Now it will be much more of a commitment. How do you feel about that?'

'It makes no difference,' said Luke. 'There can be no question of the child going into an orphanage and that is what would happen. Don't worry, Keith; I will look into the legalities of it all, and Audrey will come and live with us, permanently, I hope...'

He knew without asking her, that Patience would be in full agreement. She wept a little for Edith, and for Audrey, then she said quietly. 'Are you thinking what I am thinking, Luke? That we could adopt Audrey – legally, I mean, officially – and she would be like our own child.'

'Yes, that is what I thought,' agreed Luke, '...eventually. We must give her a little while to settle down with us first. It's not quite what we intended, my darling...' The thought was there in both their minds that they had intended, after ten years of marriage, to have had at least two or three children of their own. '...but maybe this is the answer for us.'

Luke brought Audrey back to Middlebeck when the funeral was over. He knew that it had been an ordeal for her, especially the part at the graveside; but she had seemed glad to have him there with her and he had kept her small hand in his all the time. The few mourners had gathered at the vicarage afterwards for sandwiches and tea provided by Mrs Armstrong. Then Luke and Audrey had set off in the mid-afternoon on the journey back to north Yorkshire. Luke had stayed overnight with Keith and his wife, but he knew it was imperative to get Audrey away from the place that held so many sad memories as quickly as possible.

Patience had warned Maisie not to say too much to her friend about her mother's death. 'She will know how sorry you are,' she said, 'without you telling her. And you mustn't tell her to cheer up if she cries. She needs to cry about her mum; but if you are there, just to be her friend, then that will help her a lot.'

Audrey was subdued when she entered the rectory again, and on seeing Patience her eyes filled up with tears.

'Hello dear,' said Patience. 'How lovely to see you again.' She gave her a hug and a kiss.

Maisie, too, gave her a bear hug. 'I've missed you,' she said. She looked at her and felt very sorry for her. How dreadful! Her dad and then her mum, both dead! 'I know you're a bit sad,' she said, 'but there's lots of things been happening here. Wait till I tell you...'

After a few days Audrey had shaken off some of her sadness and was ready to listen to her friend and to talk about the happenings in the little town. She was especially interested to hear about Daisy's wedding, and that Maisie and Doris were to be bridesmaids.

'Oh, how lovely!' she said. 'I would love to be a bridesmaid. I've never been one, you know.'

'Neither have I,' replied Maisie. 'Daisy would've had you, y'know. She told us, didn't she, Aunty Patience. But you weren't here, you see...'

Patience looked at Audrey's crestfallen face and came to a decision. 'There is no reason at all why Audrey should not be a bridesmaid as well,' she said. 'I know Daisy won't mind. I'll get in touch with Mrs Kitson, Daisy's mother, and when she writes to her she can tell her she will have three bridesmaids instead of two. How about that?'

Audrey's face lit up with delight, and Maisie looked pleased, too. But then Maisie frowned a little. 'But you've got the material, haven't you, Aunty Patience, and you've started making the dress.'

'No matter,' said Patience. 'I can easily get some more. There was still a lot of that material left on the market stall. And we've still got two weeks to go before the big day...'

Maisie and Doris had decided on pale blue, not pink, for their dresses. It was what Patience called turquoise blue. It was a colour that suited them both, and now it suited Audrey as well.

The wedding plans had to be arranged in the bride's absence, as Daisy, and Andy as well, were to arrive home only the day before the wedding. Patience had made a fruit cake and iced it. Mrs Kitson, who admitted she was not much good at baking, had given her some dried fruit from her store cupboard, as had a few members of the WI; and Patience had a few ounces of ground almonds left for the marzipan. It was not a large cake, but Daisy was fortunate to be having one at all.

The rationing of food was now starting to take effect. Dried fruit and butter and eggs were beginning to be regarded as luxuries, and future brides might not be able to have a wedding cake at all, or a very austere one. But the women of the WI had pulled out all the stops for Daisy and Andy, and they prepared a spread in the church hall which was, as Daisy's mother declared, 'a feast fit for a king'.

Daisy was a bonny bride in her white silken taffeta dress. Patience wished she might have been with her, though, to advise her about the style. She was not sure that the puffed sleeves and the full skirt were quite suited to Daisy's buxom figure, but it was the bride's own choice and she supposed that that was all that mattered. The short veil of stiffish net and the coronet of silken orange blossom were perched on top of her dark curly hair like the icing on a cake. In fact that was what Daisy resembled; a fancy three-tiered wedding cake. But she was a very radiant bride as she came down the aisle after the ceremony, on the arm of her new husband, grinning broadly at all her friends and relations. Andy looked smart and handsome in his soldier's uniform, proudly displaying his corporal's stripes which he had recently been awarded.

The three girls, Audrey, Doris and Maisie, smiled happily too, carrying their posies of mixed flowers. Like Daisy's larger bouquet, the roses, lilies, sweet peas and sweet williams had been culled from the rectory and other nearby gardens, and fashioned into bridal arrangements by one of the women of the Mothers' Union.

It was a cheerful crowd who gathered in the church hall to make short work of the 'banquet'. The salmon, corned beef and egg sandwiches soon vanished, as did the sausage rolls and meat pies; the trifle, sparingly covered with real cream; and the iced buns and jam tarts. And lastly, a small piece of the wedding cake, whilst Luke toasted the health and happiness of the bride and groom in sweet brown sherry.

Daisy and Andy departed, after Daisy had changed into her 'going-away' outfit – her best pink summer dress and matching cardigan; she could not afford to buy anything new after the expense of the wedding dress – to catch a train to Whitby, the nearest seaside resort on the east coast. They were to spend a precious three days there before returning to their respective army camps. To prepare for...who could tell what might happen in the unforseeable future?

'That was a really joyous occasion,' said Patience afterwards to Luke. 'Just what we all needed to cheer us up. Daisy and Andy looked so blissfully happy together, didn't they? I do hope that everything goes well for them, that they don't have to spend too much time apart. At least Andy will be stationed in England. She won't need to worry about him being sent overseas again, not at the moment...

For the war was now being fought in the air. What Winston Churchill was calling the Battle of Britain had started on the tenth of July with attacks on British ships in the channel and on the coastal ports. And the young pilots of Fighter Command – amongst whom was Bill Grundy, Anne Mellodey's fiancé – were engaged continually in dog fights in the skies above Kent and Sussex. Every day there was news of more and more casualties.

Chapter Twenty

'Aunty Patience, how long do you think it will be before the war is over?' asked Maisie. It was a warm evening at the beginning of September, 1940, on the day that the children had returned to school. And almost exactly a year since the evacuees had first come to Middlebeck, Patience remembered. She had gone upstairs to tuck the two girls into bed and to kiss them goodnight, as she did every night.

'I mean, there are so many people dying, aren't there?' Maisie went on. 'It's so sad. There was Audrey's dad and then her mum...although that was nothing to do with the war, was it, not really?'

'No,' answered Patience. 'But I suppose it was because of the blackout as well as the fog that Audrey's dad was knocked down.' There had been more deaths caused by the blackout in the first few months of the war than by enemy action. 'But her mum was very poorly... No, as you say; that had nothing to do with the war. You have been such a good friend to Audrey since she came back to us. I am very proud of you, Maisie.'

'But she's sad again now, isn't she?' said Maisie. 'We both are. We all cried this morning – well, a lot of the girls did – when Miss Foster told us about Miss Mellodey's young man. It's terrible, Aunty Patience. Why does it keep happening? Why do they want to go on killing one another? It doesn't make sense.'

'No, you're right, Maisie. It doesn't make sense at all,' agreed Patience. 'Nothing makes sense in wartime.' She found herself looking back to the Great War, which was now sometimes being called the last war, and the thousands upon thousands of young men who had died in the trenches, all to gain a few yards of territory either way. That had been pure carnage and utterly senseless. One would have thought that lessons would have been learned and remembered.

'You say how long is it going to continue? Well, nobody knows, do they? We just have to keep on saying our prayers and hope that God is...that God will answer them.' She had been going to say, 'hope that God is listening', but that was not a very wise thing to say to the child. One had to go on believing that He was listening, although Patience herself wondered about that at times. Or that He was on 'our side', as she had heard some people say. How could He be solely on our side, this all-powerful omnipotent God? He was the God of the Germans, too, wasn't He? And no doubt they were praying to Him, just as we were. It was all too dreadfully confusing.

'I know you are upset tonight, dear, about Miss Mellodey's fiancé,' she said to Maisie, gently stroking the girl's hair. 'Just think how sad she must be feeling, and Bill's parents too. Perhaps you could say a little prayer for her now, before you go to sleep. I know how much you and Audrey like Miss Mellodey.'

When the school had assembled for the first time after the summer holiday it was a solemn faced Miss Foster, the headmistress, who addressed them all. Miss Mellodey would be returning in a few days' time, she said, but at the moment she was at home in Leeds with her parents. She had recently received the sad news that her fiancé, Bill, had been shot down in his plane and killed. There were gasps of shock from the children and, as Maisie had said, several of the girls had shed tears.

'I know you are all very fond of Miss Mellodey,' said Miss Foster, 'especially those of you who have been in her class. She has been very popular with everyone since she came to join us here in Middlebeck. And she will know how sorry you are... That is why she doesn't want you to mention it to her when she comes back. She wants to carry on teaching you just the same as she did before. And you can help her best by being...well, by behaving normally. In the meantime Miss Mellodey's class will be divided up and taught by myself and Miss Bolton. It will only be for a day or two, and I am trusting you, boys and girls, to help us as much as you can...'

Patience could not, in truth, give any comforting words to Maisie when she asked how long the war would continue. The prospect, indeed, was grim. On the twenty-fifth of August German bombs had been dropped, for the first time, on London; by mistake, it was reported. But Bomber Command was then ordered to attack Berlin, a move which infuriated Hitler. And so the 'tit for tat' raids had begun, the large-scale bombing – the 'Blitz' – of

London and other major cities.

Anne Mellodey returned to take up the reins again at the beginning of the next week. Maisie thought she looked pale and her eyes were sad when she smiled at the children. She had a lovely smile, but now it was just her lips that smiled and not always her eyes. Maisie and Audrey had remembered that they were not to say anything to her, but Patience thought it would be nice to take her a bunch of flowers from the garden to brighten up her desk and, hopefully, to make her feel a little happier.

'Thank you, girls,' she said. 'I find that flowers are such a comfort, and these pale yellow roses are my favourite of all. It is very kind of you...and I know that you are thinking about me,' she added, smiling a little sadly.

But there was work to be done by the children of Standard Four, the ten and eleven year olds. Miss Mellodey reminded them that this school year was the one in which they would sit for the Scholarship examination. The following summer they would be leaving the school in Middlebeck, and in September – a year hence – they would be starting at the Senior School at the far end of the town (quite near to the railway station). And those who had gained a scholarship would attend the High School – there was one building for the boys and another separate one for the girls – situated lower down the valley, between Middlebeck and the village of Lowerbeck.

It was believed that Maisie and Audrey would be amongst that number, along with a few of the local children. And it seemed increasingly likely that the boys and girls who had at first been thought of as evacuees would still be there in a year's time when the move to the senior schools took place.

Doris entertained no hopes of passing the exam. She often, jokingly, told Maisie and Audrey that she was not a brain-box like the pair of them were. Besides, she had no wish to go to the High School. She would help her dad and her brothers on the farm, she declared, when she left school at fourteen. But that was a long time ahead.

Gertie and Norma, also, no longer showed any animosity towards the brainier members of the class. They knew that they, too, would be attending the Middlebeck Senior School. It was in no small degree due to Anne Mellodey that the children of Standard Four got along so well together. She showed no favouritism and regarded all her pupils – the bright ones and the not so clever, the obedient ones and those who were less so – with the same impartiality and genuine affection.

—

Maisie had picked up on the serious talk that was going on in the rectory between Luke and Patience, and sometimes Audrey was included as well. She knew it was something to do with Audrey having no relations now that both her parents had died, and they were talking about her becoming Luke and Patience's daughter. Although she couldn't be a real one, surely? To be a real daughter she would need to have come there as a baby, wouldn't she? Maisie was confused and, though she knew it was very wrong of her, a little bit jealous too.

'Aunty Patience, can I ask you something?' she said, one evening in October. The evenings were no longer light, but Maisie liked the drawn curtains keeping out the darkness, and the intimacy of the glow shed by her bedside lamp on to the silky blue eiderdown.

'Of course you can,' said Patience. 'I hope you know that you can ask me anything, Maisie. What is it?'

'Well, it's about Audrey... Is she going to be your daughter? I mean...will she be called Audrey Fairchild instead of Audrey Dennison? I feel a bit...well, a bit muddled up.'

Patience smiled fondly at her, then she put an arm around her. 'You mean...you're feeling a little bit upset? A wee bit...jealous, perhaps?'

Maisie nodded silently. There was a few seconds' pause, then she said, 'It's real horrid of me, isn't it? I know it is. But...if it had been me – I mean, if it had been my mum that had...gone – would you have wanted me to be your daughter, like you want Audrey?'

'But of course we would,' replied Patience. Maisie knew at once that there was no doubt that Aunty Patience meant what she said. 'You surely didn't need to ask that, Maisie? Listen...we have grown to love both of you very much. But you still have your mother. And you love her, don't you?'

'Yes...yes, I do,' answered Maisie.

'And now she is living up here, very near to us. You are really quite a lucky girl, Maisie.'

'Yes...yes, I know I am.'

'Whereas poor Audrey, she has been left an orphan, hasn't she?'

An orphan... The words sounded dreadful to Maisie's ears. Orphans featured in story books; there were quite a few in the Angela Brazil books, but those were usually rich, posh orphans. And there were poor ones too, like that little Oliver Twist who lived in that awful place and never had enough to eat. She hadn't read the book; Dickens's books were too difficult for her at the moment and the printing was hard to read, but she knew the story. She couldn't think of Audrey as being like that, and yet she was an orphan too.

Maisie looked at Patience intently, a new and surprising thought suddenly occurring to her. 'Aunty Patience, I've just been thinking...Audrey's really been dead lucky, hasn't she? I mean, if her mum hadn't sent her up here with the evacuees, she'd still have been in Leeds, wouldn't she? And she wouldn't have known you and Luke, and she'd have had nobody to look after her now, would she? And...and she'd have had to go to an orphanage...'

Patience laughed a little. 'Your reasoning is spot on, Maisie. Yes; I expect that is what might have happened. But we can't go through life saying 'if this' and 'if that'. We must be thankful that things have turned out the way they have for Audrey, and that Luke and I are only too pleased to adopt her. I suppose we might say that this is one good thing that has happened as a result of the war. It has been very confusing for her as well, you know. She still misses her mum and dad, but she is beginning to understand now what is going to happen. And I believe she is happy about it. So you must try to be happy as well, my dear.'

'Yes...yes, I am. Really I am,' said Maisie. 'Will she be called Audrey Fairchild?'

'I expect so,' replied Patience. 'That is what she will be called, legally.'

'And...and will she call you and Luke, Mum and Dad?'

'I very much doubt it,' smiled Patience. 'I guess we will always be Aunty Patience and Luke. But Audrey knows that her home is here with us, for as long as she wants it to be, and that is the important thing. Now...' Patience kissed her cheek. 'Off you go to sleep, and no more worrying!'

It might have been possible to imagine, in the northern dales, that there was no war going on at all. The skies above Middlebeck were clear and blue, or grey, as the autumn progressed, with never a sign of enemy aircraft. It was only the blackout and the rationing of food that made the inhabitants aware of the true situation; and, of course, the news reaching them every day of the bombing, not only of London, but of other large cities, Birmingham, Manchester, and Sheffield, and then the dreadful news in November of the devastation of Coventry. The major ports were suffering, too; Liverpool, Glasgow, Bristol, Portsmouth...and Hull. The thoughts of many of the folk of Middlebeck were with the evacuees who had come from Hull and had, all too soon, returned home again.

Patience opened the door one morning in early

December to find an elderly woman standing there. She was clearly distressed and it took Patience a few moments to remember who she was.

Then, 'It's Mrs Roystone, isn't it?' she said. The lady was a fairly frequent attender at St Bartholomew's church, but Patience and Luke had met her and her husband more particularly when little Timothy Clegg, their evacuee, had had the accident in the builder's yard. 'Do come in, my dear, and tell me what is the matter.'

The woman sat down or, rather, collapsed, into an easy chair. She gave a deep sigh, then blew her nose and wiped away her tears. 'It's dreadful news, I'm afraid, Mrs Fairchild. You remember Ivy and little Timothy, our evacuees? Well, I've just heard that Ivy has been killed in a bombing raid, and Timothy...'

'Oh no, not both of them! Timothy as well?' breathed Patience.

'Well, no; not Timothy, thank God,' replied Mrs Roystone. 'That is, if we can thank Him for owt at the moment, but that's another matter. No, it was Ivy, and her mam and dad as well. The three of 'em have been killed. A direct hit on their house, but by some miracle little Tim escaped. He's in hospital. He's got a broken leg, and he's in shock, of course, but...poor little lad, he's an orphan now, Mrs Fairchild. And God only knows what we can do about it.'

'Tell me,' said Patience, gently, 'how do you know all this? If I remember rightly those two children went back under rather a cloud. The mother was annoyed, wasn't she, about the accident, and insisted on taking them home with her?'

'Aye, you're quite right. But she came round, like, afterwards, did Mrs Clegg. She knew she'd been a bit hasty and that Bill and me weren't to blame. She kept in touch with us, and she must've left word that if owt were to happen, then we had to be told. It was a friend of hers that's wrote to us. Oh dear, Mrs Fairchild…I'm getting all upset again.' She sniffed and wiped her eyes, then opened her bag and took out a letter. 'Here; read it for yourself…'

Patience read the letter. It was a very sad one, from Mrs Clegg's friend. She was a woman called Enid Howarth who lived in the same area of Hull, but a few streets away, and her home had escaped the bombing. This time, she added. The raid in which most of the Clegg family had been killed had been a sudden one and many folk had been unable to get to their air raid shelters.

'So poor little Tim is now an orphan,' she wrote, 'and Sheila and Joe (Mr and Mrs Clegg) have no close relations, at least none that have come forward, to look after him. He is fretting, poor little chap. He's upset about his mam and dad and his sister, of course, and he keeps asking for his Aunty Mabel and Uncle Bill. That is why I am writing to you, Mrs Roystone, and also because Sheila said would I tell you if anything happened. She said to me many a time since this bombing started that she wished she had left the children where they were, safe with you up in north Yorkshire. But it seems as though it was not to be. I was wondering if you could see your way to having Timothy with you for a little holiday before it is decided what is to be done for him. There is some talk of him going into an orphanage. Me and my husband don't want that to happen, but we have quite a big family of our own. So have Sheila's other friends and we really don't know what to do for the best. I hope you will be able to help. It is all so very sad…'

Mabel Roystone looked anxiously at Patience whilst she read the letter. Then she said, 'It seems to me as though this woman, this Enid Howarth, is asking if we will do summat for him. Permanently, I mean, not just for a holiday, but I don't see as how we can. Bill and me, we're well into our sixties now. We had kiddies of our own – three of 'em – but they're all married now and have their own families. We can't start again, not at our age.'

'No…no, I quite understand. Of course you can't,' replied Patience. 'It's so terribly tragic. It is just the same thing that happened to Audrey, except that was not the result of a bombing raid. You know, I expect, that Audrey is living with us permanently now? We are adopting her.'

'Yes, I've heard about that. Poor little lass…but she seems very happy with you, Mrs Fairchild, and that other girl that's with you, that Maisie. Ivy was real fond of those two little lasses, and Doris from t' farm. Dearie me, I wish they'd never gone back.'

'I know,' said Patience gently. 'Believe me, I know how you feel. Luke is out at the moment, but I will tell him what has happened, and I'm sure he will agree to go down to Hull and bring Timothy up here for a holiday. He could stay with you and your husband, could he, for a little while?'

'Of course; we'd love to have him, but not for good, if you see what I mean. He was a dear little lad when you got to know him. But ever so timid and shy and – oh dear! – he used to get that upset if he thought he'd done owt wrong. He needs a loving home, Mrs Fairchild, not to be put in one o' them orphanages. I'm sure they do their best, but it can't be right for Timothy.'

'We will sort something out,' said Patience. 'Don't you worry. First of all we must make sure that it is in order for us to have Timothy up here for a holiday. My husband will see to everything... Now, Mrs Roystone, you and I are going to have a cup of coffee before you go back home.'

Patience waited until Maisie and Audrey had returned to afternoon school before telling her husband the tragic tale. She had not yet told the girls the sad news about Ivy. Luke smiled knowingly at her.

'I can guess what you are thinking,' he said. 'Little Timothy, as well as Audrey? Am I right?'

She nodded slowly and soberly. 'Yes...I think so, Luke. I feel it would be right. The child needs a home and someone to love him. We have plenty of room...and enough love to go round, haven't we?'

'Indeed we have, my dear. Yes...I, also, think it would be the right thing to do. But we would need to go into it more thoroughly, as we did with Audrey. There shouldn't be any problems. There must be scores of orphans – hundreds, possibly – and the powers that be will be only too pleased if suitable people wish to adopt them. First things first, though. We must try to find the words to tell Audrey and Maisie that Ivy has been killed…'

Both girls burst into tears at the news, but were then relieved to hear that Timothy, at least, was safe and relatively unhurt. Their motherly instincts came to the fore when they were told that he would be coming up to Middlebeck to have a holiday with Mr and Mrs Roystone, and then, possibly, he would stay at the rectory for a little while. That was as much as they needed to be told at the moment.

'He's a nice little boy,' said Maisie tearfully. 'Aw…what a shame! Poor little Timothy. He used to cling to Ivy; d'you remember?'

Audrey nodded. 'Mmm…We'll have to be big sisters to him, won't we, while he's up here?'

'Aunty Patience,' said Maisie. 'Will you go and tell Miss Mellodey and Miss Foster about Ivy? We don't want to tell them, do we Audrey? It's so sad.'

'Yes, I will,' replied Patience. Sad news is par for the course these days, she reflected. How she wished there could be good tidings, just for a change.

The children of Standard Four were distressed when their teacher told them that Ivy Clegg had been killed in a bombing raid. Several of the girls shed tears, as they had when they were told about Miss Mellodey's fiance.

At playtime Gertie Flint and Norma Wilkins came over to talk to Maisie, Audrey and Doris. Following their overture earlier in the year to make friends with their former rivals, there had been no dramatic upsurge of friendliness, but neither was there any cat-calling and spitefulness as there had been before.

'We feel awful,' said Norma, 'don't we Gertie?' Of the two of them it was Norma who had the finer feelings; she was the one who had always been slightly less aggressive.

'Yeah...s'pose we do,' said Gertie, but a trifle half-heartedly. 'Y'see...Norma thinks it's our fault, about Ivy.'

Maisie guessed at once what they meant. 'You mean because we had that snowball fight an' Tim got hurt, an' then their mum took them home again?'

'Yeah, that's right,' said Norma. 'If that hadn't happened, Timothy and Ivy might still've been here, and then Ivy wouldn't've been killed. An' I feel awful 'cause we were so horrid to poor little Tim.'

'But he's not been killed has he?' said Gertie. 'And we don't really know what would've happened. They might have gone back to Hull later, even if they hadn't gone at Christmas.'

'Aunty Patience says you can't keep saying 'if this' and 'if that',' said Maisie in a grown-up manner. 'We feel dreadful too, me and Audrey and Doris, 'cause we were in that snowball fight as well an' everything went wrong. We didn't mean for Tim to get hurt, none of us. But he's coming back here for a holiday when he comes out of hospital. So you'll be able to make it up to him, won't you?'

'Yes, we're going to be like big sisters to him, aren't we, Maisie?' said Audrey.

'Oh...all right,' said Gertie. 'We'll try and be nice

to him. Like Maisie says, we were all to blame, I suppose. But we're going to be friends now, aren't we?'

'Oh goody,' said Norma. 'I'm glad he's coming back. I liked little Tim really, but he was a bit of a softie.'

'Yeah…that's why we teased him,' said Gertie. 'But happen he'll have grown up a bit now. Do you lot want to have a go with our skipping rope before we go in?'

'No, thank you; I don't think so,' said Maisie seriously. 'We're feeling too upset, like, at the moment, to play games. Perhaps tomorrow…'

'There's a friend for little children,
　Above the bright blue sky…'
they sang in Sunday School the next time they met. Maisie's thoughts flew to Ivy, especially when they sang the verse about the 'home for little children'.

'No home on earth is like it,
　Nor can with it compare;
　For everyone is happy
　Nor could be happier there…'
Was Ivy really happy up there in heaven she wondered? Happier than she would have been in her own home? And…was there really a friend up there, above the bright blue sky, caring for all the children? Maisie tried so hard to believe it, but sometimes it was all so very, very difficult to understand.

Chapter Twenty-One

A rchie Tremaine raised his glass. 'So let's drink, shall we, to peace? Peace…in the near future, God willing. And to Victory for our brave soldiers, sailors and airmen…'

'Peace…' they echoed, and 'Victory…' as they all lifted their glasses and took a sip of the sherry, the wine which was always provided by Archie and Rebecca for the Christmas toast.

The company, this Christmas of 1940, differed slightly from that of the year before as the rectory folk were celebrating in their own home. Around the fully extended table in the dining room of Tremaine House twelve people were gathered; Archie, Rebecca and Bruce; Lily, Maisie, Joanie and Jimmy; and five land girls who had decided not to go home for Christmas as they lived too far away, but to take their leave at another time.

Everyone agreed that the meal was superb, just as sumptuous as it had been the year before. But Rebecca knew that there was less fruit in the pudding, less cream in the brandy sauce, and that the cake, to be cut at teatime, was covered this year with mock marzipan. They had still had turkey to eat, raised on Walter Nixon's farm; but the Ministry of Food was insisting that more and more land must be ploughed over for the growing of essential food crops. Folk living in the country areas were fortunate and they knew it, but in the towns and cities the shortages were felt more keenly.

Maisie and Bruce, sitting next to one another, exchanged smiles – a rather shy one, on Maisie's part – as they, too, raised their small glasses and took a sip of the sweet sherry. Maisie liked the taste, but her mother would let her have only a titchy amount. It made her feel all warm and glowing inside; but she knew that this feeling was not due entirely to the sherry. She was realising that she liked Bruce very much indeed. She was far too young, she knew, to think of him as a boyfriend; she was ten and would be eleven in May whereas Bruce was almost sixteen. But one of the reasons she liked him so much was because he treated her as though she was as grown up as he was and not just a silly kid. They met infrequently, though, with him being away at boarding school for the greater part of the year.

'I believe you have another little visitor at the rectory now?' he said. 'Timothy Clegg? I was really sorry to hear about Ivy. She was your friend, wasn't she? I remember seeing her with you and Audrey and Doris, but I don't think I ever saw her brother. Will he be staying long?'

'He's here for good; at least I think so,' replied Maisie. 'I think Aunty Patience and Luke are going to adopt him, like they did with Audrey. They haven't said very much, not to me and Audrey…but I can tell,' she added meaningfully. 'There's a lot of talk going on.'

'And you don't miss much, do you?' laughed Bruce.

'No, I don't,' agreed Maisie. She smiled. 'I try not to. I like to know what's happening. I think it's nice for Aunty Patience and Luke 'cause they've never had any children of their own. I remember when I first came here I asked if she had any boys or girls, and she got a bit upset and said no. Then afterwards she said she wished they had... P'raps she can't have any of her own, but now they'll have one of each, a girl and a boy.'

'And what about Timothy? Has he settled down? Poor little boy; it must have been dreadful, losing all his family like that.'

'Yes, he's OK,' said Maisie. 'He's been with the people he stayed with when he was an evacuee, and now he's come to us. Me and Audrey have been looking after him, like big sisters, y'see, instead of Ivy.'

'But you wanted to be with your own mum today, did you, and your brother and sister?'

'Yes, of course I did,' replied Maisie. 'Aunty Patience says Christmas is a family time. And they're my family really, aren't they? My mum and Joanie and Jimmy...'

At the rectory Patience and Luke, Audrey and Timothy, and Mabel and Bill Roystone had enjoyed a similar sort of meal. Patience had invited the elderly couple for the day to help Timothy to settle into his new surroundings.

He had been in Middlebeck for about two weeks. His broken leg was still in plaster, though only up to the knee as the break had been near the ankle. He had managed the train journey with the assistance of Luke and Mr Roystone who had gone to collect him, and then he had stopped at the Roystones' home for about ten days. He was hobbling along quite ably with the aid of crutches, and once he had recovered from the initial shock of losing his parents and his sister he had enjoyed being the centre of attention with his Aunty Mabel and Uncle Bill.

Now he had been told that his new home was to be at the rectory with Mr and Mrs Fairchild; he had gone to live there just a couple of days before Christmas.

'I am Aunty Patience to Audrey and Maisie,' Patience told him. 'Would you like to call me Aunty as well? And you can call Mr Fairchild, Uncle, or just Luke, if you would rather. He doesn't mind.'

The little boy nodded seriously, but although he started to call Patience 'Aunty', a little diffidently at first, he still did not call Luke by any name at all. He seemed rather in awe of the man, but Patience had every confidence that his shyness would disappear in time. She was pleased to see him smiling, and actually laughing occasionally, when he was with Audrey and Maisie.

Audrey had whispered to her on Christmas Eve, when she had gone to tuck her in and kiss her goodnight. 'Aunty Patience…Timothy is going to be my brother, really, isn't he? I mean…you're going to adopt him, aren't you, like you did with me? And then he'll be Timothy Fairchild, like I'm…I'm Audrey Fairchild now, aren't I?'

Patience felt her eyes grow moist; she was so

relieved that the girl had accepted her new name. It had been a gradual acceptance, without any pressure from herself or Luke. They had decided that she had to come to it in her own time.

'Yes...we are hoping to adopt Timothy,' she replied. 'But how did you know?' They had not told Audrey or Maisie what they had in mind.

'I just guessed,' said Audrey. 'And I think it's lovely. I always wanted a little brother.'

Patience kissed her fondly. 'Thank you, darling, for being so kind to Tim. You and Maisie have really looked after him since he arrived...'

Now all four bedrooms at the rectory were in use. It seemed strange to Luke and Patience because for the first ten years of their ministry three of the upstairs rooms had been unoccupied, although they had always had lots of visitors in the downstairs rooms. Now Tim was in the small room at the back of the house, next to the one where Audrey slept, with Maisie in the small front room, and Patience and Luke in the large front bedroom, the one they had always used.

'Are you happy, my darling?' Luke asked her as they lay close together in their double bed on Christmas night.

They had retired later than usual, as the three children had stayed up late, playing with their Christmas presents; the Snakes and Ladders, Ludo, and Chinese Chequers games; the jigsaws, yo-yos and puzzles; and Maisie and Audrey had had to be almost forced away from their latest Girls' Crystal annuals. Archie had brought Maisie back from Tremaine House after tea, then he had offered to take Mabel and Bill back to their own home. And when the children had gone to bed Patience and Luke had sat for a while on the settee, hand in hand, enjoying a glass of sherry, a special treat to celebrate a day that, in spite of recent bereavements and traumas, had been a quietly joyous occasion.

'Yes...very happy, Luke,' said Patience, snuggling closer to him. She threw her arm across his body and rested her head on his chest. 'Do you need to ask if I'm happy? It has been a lovely, lovely day.' She laughed out loud. 'And three children! Just what we always wanted. I know it isn't quite the same as we planned, and Maisie, of course, is only on loan to us. But...we are doing the right thing, aren't we, Luke?'

'Yes...we are. I am as sure about that as I have ever been about anything.' Luke reached out and threw off the eiderdown and blanket, a heavy weight on top of them. He propped himself up on one elbow, looking down at his wife. 'Except, of course, about loving you, my darling. That is something I have always been very, very sure of.' Tenderly he stroked her auburn hair, now greying a little at the temples, then he leaned down and kissed her passionately. 'I love you, Patience,' he whispered. 'I love you even more now than I did when I married you, and I didn't think that was possible.'

'I love you too, Luke,' she answered, 'more and more with every day that passes...'

After that there was no need for words as he

gathered her into his arms and made love to her, in a way that seemed to both of them more poignant and meaningful than it had ever been before.

Timothy's plaster was removed from his leg in due course and he was welcomed back at school by Miss Foster and his classmates, especially by Peter, his special pal, who had thought he would never see him again.

The children of Standard Four sat for their Scholarship examination during the month of February, then forgot all about it as the results would not be out until much later in the year. There were other things to occupy their minds and energies as well as school. Maisie, Audrey and Doris still attended Brownies, although at ten and eleven years of age this was starting to be regarded by them as somewhat childish. They were looking forward to joining the Guides, but that would not be until they went to the senior school.

The girls were busy, whilst the evenings were dark, making articles which would be sold in a few weeks' time at a Spring Fair and Bring and Buy Sale in the church hall. They worked away knitting kettle holders and dish cloths, sewing lavender bags, peg dolls and needle-cases, to aid 'our gallant soldiers, sailors and airmen'. The money raised would help to buy tanks and aeroplanes and ammunition, and adults and children alike were told that every little would help; everyone must try to 'do their bit'. And so they collected silver paper and milk bottle tops and waste paper, and bought sixpenny savings stamps at school on a Monday morning, then stuck them into a little book to help with the National Savings scheme. The news from other parts of the country was grim, with air raids still continuing, but it was good to think they were helping in some small way.

Life in Middlebeck, however, seemed to carry on quite uneventfully. Something that Maisie enjoyed, but which Audrey and Doris were not part of, was singing in the church choir. Maisie had always enjoyed singing, both at school and at Sunday school, and she always sang out loudly and confidently. When Luke had heard her carolling away happily at home he had suggested that she should join the church choir. Audrey had been back in Leeds by that time, but when she returned to Middlebeck she said, quite definitely, that she did not want to sing in the choir. She had only a tiny voice anyway, and she would not want everyone looking at her, she said, standing at the front of the church in the choir stalls. Doris, also, was not a member of the choir, although her father was the leading baritone singer. She laughingly said that her dad had told her she had a voice like a corncrake, whatever that was. Maisie thought that Mr Nixon was quite often rude to his daughter and said hurtful things, but Doris didn't seem to mind.

Maisie was the youngest of the girl choristers. The other three girls were twelve and thirteen years old and were at senior school, and there were four boy choristers too. The rest were men and women of varying ages, from seventeen to over seventy, she guessed. She quite liked being made a fuss of, as the youngest member, and she loved wearing the blue cloak over her ordinary clothes and the little squarish cap with a tassel at the back.

At the moment, during the season of Lent, they were practising songs to sing at the Easter services. Mr King, the elderly organist and choir master, called them anthems. There was one called 'This Joyous Eastertide', and another one called the 'Easter Hymn', which was from an opera. It was very difficult to sing, but Maisie loved the way the music started off quiet and then went louder and louder, with the voices of the choir echoing around the empty church. There was something mystical and magical about it when the church was in semi-darkness, lit only at the end they called the chancel. She often found herself humming the melody or singing the words,

'Rejoice for the Lord has arisen,
He has broken the gates of the prison...'
when she was at home.

She was beginning to understand the notes, the black ones and white ones and the ones with tails and how much you had to count for each one, like doing sums at school; and how they went up and down on the stave, going higher or lower; and what all the lovely Italian words meant; allegro, andante, diminuendo and crescendo, and her favourite one, rallentando.

She had a special friend in the choir and she was rather proud of this. It was Priscilla Meadows, the land girl who lived across the green in Miss Thomson's house. She had befriended Maisie as soon as she joined the choir and Maisie liked her very much. Priscilla was small and pretty with fair curly hair and she laughed and smiled a lot. Her friend, Jennifer, was not in the choir, but Priscilla had wanted to join because she had been in the church choir in Leicester, the town where she lived. She was one of the sopranos – the ones that sang the high trilly notes, the notes that the younger members of the choir sang, too – and you could tell by watching her singing that she enjoyed it.

Priscilla confided to Maisie, one evening in early March, that she had met a young man who was really nice. 'He's in the army,' she said, 'and he's stationed at Catterick, just up the road. Well, a few miles away, but it's not all that far. I met him at a dance last Saturday, and I'm seeing him tonight, after we've finished the practice.'

Her eyes were bright and sparkling and Maisie felt happy for her. 'What's he called?' she asked.

'Jeff…Jeff Beaumont; he's a lance-corporal. That means he has one stripe on his arm,' Priscilla explained, 'but I expect he'll be a corporal before long.'

'And…and you like him a lot, do you?' asked Maisie, all agog.

'Yes…I think so,' said Priscilla, smiling and blushing a little. 'I had a boyfriend at home, but we broke it off when he joined up and I came here. Yes, I think Jeff might be…rather special. Oh…we'd better shut up. Mr King is waiting for us.'

Maisie sat next to Priscilla at choir practices because the older members helped the younger ones to understand the music. But during the proper church services the young ones sat at the front with the grown-ups behind them. Mr King did not like them to talk too much, but there was always time for a little chat between songs.

'Hymn number 520, please, ladies and gentlemen, if you are ready,' he said now. 'Love divine, all loves excelling...' He nodded at Mrs Hollins, the pianist who played for practices, then they all started to sing again.

There were choir stalls on each side of the chancel, and in the one opposite was seated Walter Nixon, Doris's father. Maisie could see him now, looking intently at Priscilla, and then down at his music. But his eyes were upon her most of the time, or so Maisie thought. She had seen him looking at her before, and she had seen Mr Nixon and Priscilla talking and laughing together at the end of a practice. They knew one another quite well, though, because she had been working on his farm, and on the land that belonged to Mr Tremaine, ever since she came to Middlebeck.

Everyone seemed to like Priscilla, more especially the men, because she was so pretty and lively and friendly. She would talk to anyone, and she had a way of making you feel special. That was how she had made Maisie feel, and Maisie guessed that that was how she made the older men feel as well; there were no very young men in the choir, because they were all in the forces.

Maisie had overheard one of the choir ladies whisper to her friend that Priscilla Meadows was a flirt. 'You'd best keep yer eye on yer husband when that one's around, I'm warning yer,' she said. But Maisie did not think that that was true. Priscilla was just a nice agreeable young woman.

'I'm seeing Jeff again tonight,' she told Maisie the following week. 'He's getting a lift down from the camp, and I'm meeting him at the Green Man.' That was a public house halfway down the High Street. 'He's bringing a pal with him, and I'm going to introduce my friend Jennifer to him. Jen's a bit shy, you see, and... Hey up! Mr King's ready for us.'

'Have a good time,' said Maisie when the practice came to an end.

'Don't you worry; I will,' Priscilla laughed.

Then Maisie went to talk to Betty, one of the senior school girls who had offered to lend her a book all about the Guides. There were only Mr King and Mrs Hollins in the church when they left, sorting out the music and locking the piano.

'Tara, Betty,' shouted Maisie, then she set off along the path, through the church gate, and across the corner of the green to the rectory. There was a shorter way, a path through the bushes, which led to the back gate of the rectory, but it was dark and rather spooky in the blackout, so she always went the longer way round at night. Just when she reached the gate to her home she realised she had left her gloves behind. They were nice bright red ones that Patience had knitted for her and she didn't want to lose them. She supposed they would be safe there and Luke could get them for her in the morning, but she liked to wear them for school and she didn't want Patience to think she had been careless with them. She decided to go back.

She went round to the back door of the church, the entrance they used when they went for practices and meetings, but for proper church services they used the front door. But the door was shut and it was obvious that everyone had gone; Mr King and Mrs Hollins must have left almost immediately. Maisie turned to go back home, then she stopped dead in her tracks. She could hear voices coming from the other path, the one which led through the bushes. If it was Mr King and Mrs Hollins she could ask them to unlock the door so that she could get her gloves. She opened her mouth to shout, then she decided not to; they were both inclined to be a little short-tempered; no, it would not be a good idea. Then she froze, because the voices she could hear were not those of the organist and the pianist, but those of her friend, Priscilla and…Mr Nixon. At least, she knew it was Priscilla, and she was almost sure it was Walter Nixon.

'Leave me alone!' she heard Priscilla shout.

And then, 'Aw, go on; you know you don't mean it…' came the man's voice.

Maisie wondered if she dared to take a step in that direction and peep through the foliage, but then she heard Priscilla's voice again. 'Let me go, Walter! What d'you think you're doing?' So it really was Walter Nixon.

'I'm only doing what you've wanted these past months. Don't act all prim and proper wi' me. You know you want it as much as I do…'

'No, I don't… Let go of me!'

Maisie held her breath and tiptoed away. She had been in trouble for eavesdropping before, and she knew that Mr Nixon and Priscilla would not want her to hear them. She hoped Priscilla would tell him to get lost and that she was going to meet her boyfriend.

'I've forgotten my gloves,' she said to Patience when she arrived home. 'I went back, but the door was shut.'

'Never mind, dear,' said Patience. 'Luke will get them for you tomorrow.'

She decided not to say anything about what she had heard. And she was sure that Priscilla was well able to look after herself.

———

'You're very quiet, Maisie,' Patience said to her the following morning. 'Is there something troubling you?'

'No,' replied Maisie quickly. Possibly too quickly, because Patience then looked at her more closely. 'No...honestly, there's not.' She picked up her piece of toast and carefully took a bite. 'I think I'm just a bit tired, that's all. After I've been to choir practice my head's all full of tunes going round and round, and then I sometimes don't go to sleep for ages.' That much was true, but last night it had not been the tunes that had kept her awake, but her thoughts about Priscilla and Doris's dad. She wondered if she should have told Luke or Patience about what she had overheard, but that would have been 'nosy-parkering'. She just hoped that Priscilla had told Mr Nixon where to get off – the awful man! – and had gone to meet Jeff, her new boyfriend.

'I see,' said Patience. 'I know what you mean. I

don't always get to sleep straight away if there is something on my mind. You do look rather tired, dear, but you'll soon buck up when you get out into the sunshine. It's a lovely day; it really looks as though spring had come at last.'

Maisie was worried about seeing Doris that morning at school, knowing what she did about her father. Not that she would dream of saying anything to her friend – she would not even tell Audrey what she had overheard – but she would feel sort of awkward and embarrassed. It seemed as though Walter Nixon might be no better than her step-father, Sidney Bragg, although she didn't think that Mr Nixon knocked his wife about like Sid had done with her mother.

As it happened, the morning at school was just the same as any other. Maisie didn't avoid Doris, but neither did she go out of her way to talk to her. Doris seemed just the same as ever, happy and laughing, and they all rejoiced in the sunshine at playtime. It was warmer than it had been for months, and they soon discarded their coats, piling them up in a corner of the playground whilst they enjoyed their skipping and ball games.

Patience soon put her concern about Maisie to the back of her mind because she had something of much greater importance to think about. She had an appointment with the doctor that morning, one that she had not even told Luke about, and she hoped to have some very exciting news to report to him when she had seen Dr Forrester.

She had not had a monthly period since the middle of December, but she had thought nothing of it when the usual sign did not appear in January. Her monthlies were irregular; they always had been since she was a girl. This had made it more difficult when she and Luke, in the early years of their marriage, had desperately wanted to start a family. There had been several times when their hopes had been raised, only to be dashed again. She had had two early miscarriages as well, in the first few weeks of pregnancy. And since then they had come to the conclusion that it was their unfortunate fate to remain childless. They had decided to make the best of it, not to complain about their lot and make themselves miserable. And now they had adopted one child and the adoption of Timothy was almost complete.

What had happened seemed miraculous, too wonderful to be true, after all this time. She had not dared to tell even Luke, fearing that she might be mistaken. But in her own mind Patience was sure. She felt queasy in the morning, although she had not actually been sick, her breasts were tender and...she just knew in her heart that she had conceived a child of their own.

Her appointment was at ten o' clock at Dr Forrester's surgery, about ten minutes walk away, in a side street near to the market hall. He was a family practitioner who knew her and Luke very well, and he had attended to Timothy's broken leg and to minor ailments of Audrey and Maisie. He raised his eyebrows and gave a surprised smile when Patience told him the reason for her visit.

'Well, well, well…' he said. 'Let's take a look at you then, shall we, Mrs Fairchild, if you don't mind…'

She steeled herself for his examination, but he was very gentle and it was not as bad as she had expected. Anyway, what did it matter if the news was good? When she had gathered herself together the doctor beamed at her.

'Well, Mrs Fairchild, you are right. You are pregnant; about three months on, I would say. Your baby will be born towards the end of September, as near as I can tell. Congratulations to you, and to the Reverend! It's wonderful news.'

'It is indeed,' said Patience, unable to stop the tears of joy springing to her eyes. 'Thank you so much, Dr Forrester.'

He laughed. 'Don't thank me, my dear. You should be thanking that husband of yours.' His eyes twinkled. 'A Christmas conception?' he whispered.

'It seems like it,' said Patience, a little embarrassedly, thinking back to their night of love after the Christmas festivities.

Then the doctor became serious again. 'Of course you will need to be careful, Mrs Fairchild. A first baby at your age…I won't say that it is a risk. You are fit and healthy, but you are no longer twenty or even thirty.' Indeed, Patience would be forty later that year. 'But we will take very great care of you, and I will get you booked into Middlebeck hospital directly. Now, off you go and tell your husband the good news…'

Luke was in his study, working at his sermon for the following Sunday, when there was a knock at the back door. Patience was out – she had told him she had some shopping to do – so he hurried to answer the knock himself. He found his elderly verger standing there. Seth Jowett was nearer eighty thanseventy and had been the caretaker at St Bartholomew's church since long before Luke took over the living. He always wore a long black cassock as a sign of his office, a position of which he was very proud, having been a worshipper at the church since his Sunday school days. Now, his pale blue watery eyes were wide with fright and his hands were visibly shaking.

'Reverend, you'd best come wi' me straight away,' he said. 'There's summat in t' bushes betwixt here and t' church. I think it's a body, but I daresn't go any nearer to find out.'

'Very well, Seth, I'll come right now,' said Luke, but he was determined not to show any sign of panic. Seth was an old man; his eyesight was not good and it was possible that someone had thrown something away into the bushes. The path was frequently used as a short cut as it eventually led on to the lower end of the village green.

Seth led the way silently along the footpath near to the rectory's back gate. 'There… Look over yonder, Reverend,' he said, when they had gone some twenty yards through the bushes, which were just beginning to bud with the green of early spring. The old man pointed, but, as he had said, he did not venture any nearer; he rather seemed to cower away, averting his eyes.

The body, for it was obvious that it was, indeed, a body, was fully clothed and was lying a couple of yards away from the pathway, only partially concealed by the undergrowth. Luke gave a gasp of shock and horror as he recognised it was that of a girl; one of the land girls, because she was wearing a khaki greatcoat and those corduroy breeches they all wore. She had pretty fair hair which curled over her forehead and ears... And before he stepped forward to take a closer look, as he knew he must, Luke had guessed at her identity.

'Oh, dear God, no!' he breathed, as he looked down on the bruised and swollen face of Priscilla Meadows. Her coat was gaping open and he could see the red marks on her neck where someone must have handled her roughly – strangled her – and her blue eyes were wide open, staring sightlessly at him. Very gently he knelt down and closed them, although he knew he must not touch anything else.

'Rest in peace, my dear...' he whispered, but it was all too clear that poor Priscilla had come to a violent end.

He stood up, brushing the soil from his knees and turned to Seth. 'You were right, I'm afraid. It's Priscilla, one of our land girls, and a member of the church choir. She would have been here for a practice last night...' he added thoughtfully. 'Come along, Seth. You need a stiff drink after a shock like that, and I must phone the police right away.'

'Poor lassie,' said Seth. 'I'm still trembling like a leaf. Yer can't take it in, can yer, summat like this? Aye, I think I know the lass you mean; pretty little thing she were.'

Luke took the verger into the sitting room and gave him a glass of brandy and hot water. 'Here – drink this; it's good for shocks. And that's what you've had; a terrible shock.'

'D'you think...? Did somebody...kill her? Was she...murdered?' asked the old man.

'I'm afraid it looks very much like it,' said Luke. 'I'm going to phone the police now.'

'There's courting couples as use that there path,' said Seth. 'You can't blame 'em. And there's nowt we can do about it. Did she 'ave a young man, d'you know? The rotten bastard!' he added feelingly.

'I don't know,' replied Luke, 'but I suppose she must have had.'

The police arrived very promptly and cordoned off the area around the pathway. The inspector in charge of the case had come to ask Luke some questions and they were sitting together in the lounge when Patience arrived home.

'Hello, darling...' She burst into the room, then stopped dead at the sight of the policeman sitting there with her husband.

'Oh, Patience... This is Inspector Davies,' said Luke. 'Come and sit down, my dear. I'm afraid there is some very bad news.'

Patience felt her high spirits droop as she sat down next to her husband. Her good news would have to wait a while. Her mood of elation quickly evaporated even further on hearing the tragic tidings. Priscilla...dead! Most likely murdered... It was impossible to take it in. She shook her head unbelievingly.

'But…who? Who could possibly do such a dreadful thing?'

'That is what we intend to find out,' said the inspector. 'You knew the young woman, Mrs Fairchild? Your husband was saying that she was probably at the church last night, at the choir practice. You didn't see her yourself?'

'No…I have nothing to do with the choir, and my husband doesn't usually go to the practices, do you, Luke? One of our little girls is in the choir; Maisie, she came to us as an evacuee and she is still with us. She would probably have seen Priscilla…but I don't want her questioned, Inspector.'

'No, of course not; I understand. Did the young woman, Priscilla, have a boyfriend, do you know?'

'As a matter of fact, I believe she had,' said Patience. 'Our little girl, Maisie, whom I've just mentioned, was friendly with her. Priscilla used to chat to her and Maisie had beome quite fond of her. Oh dear…she is going to be so upset! And I remember Maisie mentioning, only a few days ago, that Priscilla had met a young man that she liked very much. He's in the army, stationed at Catterick; he's called Jeff, I believe… You know how little girls love to chatter, and Maisie was quite thrilled because Priscilla had confided in her.'

The inspector nodded. 'I see… Yes, that is very useful information.'

'But you won't have to question her, will you? Maisie, I mean?'

'No, I promise you, Mrs Fairchild, we will not want to ask your little girl any questions. It would be too upsetting, we realise that. My sergeant has

gone to break the news to Miss Thomson, the
landlady of the poor girl, and maybe the young
woman's friend, Jennifer Brewer, will be able to give
us some information. That will be all for now.'
Inspector Davies stood up. 'Thank you both for
your help... We will get him whoever he is,' he
added grimly.

Luke went to the door to see him out, then
returned to Patience who was sitting motionless,
stunned into shocked silence. He sat down and put
his arms around her. It was several moments before
she spoke.

'Maisie and Audrey; whatever are we going to
tell them? Maisie especially; she'd taken quite a
shine to Priscilla. Oh, Luke; it's so dreadful, so
wicked...'

'I'm afraid we will have to tell them the truth,' he
said. 'If we tell them a half-truth they will only find
out from someone else. Bad news travels fast; it will
be all over the village, you can be sure, by the end
of the day.'

'But there's never been anything like it in our
little town before. Middlebeck was always such a
peaceful little place. Hardly any crime to speak of,
certainly no...murders.'

'It's wartime, my dear. We don't know who was
responsible, of course, but there are lots of
newcomers round here who were not here a couple
of years ago.'

'You mean...the soldiers?'

'Maybe...but we mustn't speculate.'

'Maisie and Audrey will be back from school
soon,' said Patience, 'and Tim as well. I put a

casserole in the oven before I went out, so it should be almost ready.'

'Then I will go and see to it.' Luke got up and gave her shoulder a squeeze. 'You stay here and compose yourself.'

'No, I'll come as well. It's better for me to keep busy.'

Together they set the table in the dining room and Patience put the plates to keep warm. 'We'd better have our meal first before we tell them,' she said, 'or else nobody will want to eat anything at all.'

It was an uncomfortable lunchtime for Luke and Patience, although the children ate hungrily, as they always did, and chattered away to one another about their morning at school. Patience recalled how Maisie had seemed a trifle disturbed and quiet that morning, although she appeared all right again now. Had something happened at choir practice? she now wondered. Something which might have been connected with today's shocking discovery?

It was Luke who broke the news. 'We have something very sad to tell you,' he began. 'I am sorry, and I know you are going to be upset, but we would rather you heard about it from us.' Three pairs of eyes looked at him steadily as he went on. 'You all know Priscilla, the land girl who lived at Miss Thomson's.' They all nodded, Maisie the most interestedly. 'Well...I am afraid she has met with an accident. I am sorry...but the poor young woman is dead. She was found in the churchyard this morning.'

The three children looked stunned. Maisie, in

particular, turned pale, her mouth fell open and she stared at Luke in horror. 'You mean...you said she'd had an accident. Did she fall over or what? Or did somebody...? You don't mean she was...murdered, do you?'

Luke nodded briefly. 'It looks very much like it. I'm so sorry, Maisie. I know she was a rather special friend to you, wasn't she?'

'Nobody knows what happened, darling,' said Patience. 'She might have been going to meet her boyfriend. They will have to ask him some questions, and anybody else who might have seen her.'

'Jeff...' said Maisie quietly. 'She said he was called Jeff. But it couldn't have been...' She had turned as white as a sheet and her startled eyes were fixed on Luke in horror. 'Oh no,' she cried. 'Oh no, no! He can't have...' She laid her head on her arms on the table top and began to sob uncontrollably.

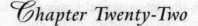

Chapter Twenty-Two

Maisie was far too distressed to go back to school that afternoon, and as it was Friday, Patience said she could stay at home.

'Just tell Miss Mellodey that Maisie is not feeling very well, and that I will explain to her later,' Patience told Audrey.

'All right,' said Audrey. She, too, was shocked at the news, but not so distraught as Maisie, and Timothy just looked puzzled as though he was unable to completely understand what had happened.

'And don't say anything – you mustn't say anything at all – about poor Priscilla; do you understand, Audrey, love? Not to anyone.'

Audrey nodded. 'I won't, Aunty Patience; honestly I won't. And you've not to say anything either, Tim,' she told the little boy.

'Because the news might not have got round yet,' Patience went on, 'and we don't want to start everybody talking before they need to, especially the children.'

'You're quite right, Patience,' agreed Luke. 'I know Audrey will be sensible, won't you dear? And you as well, Tim. But I must go across and see Miss Thomson. She will have heard by now and she is sure to be upset.'

'Very well, dear,' replied Patience. 'That is what you must do, of course. And Maisie and I will tackle this washing-up. Come along, Maisie.' She gave the girl a hug. 'It's better to keep busy, believe me. We've all had a dreadful shock, and it will take us a while to get over it. I am so sorry, dear; I know you were fond of Priscilla.'

Maisie burst into tears again. 'She was lovely...' she sobbed. 'I did like her. D'you think...? Will they find out...?'

'I'm sure they will,' said Patience. 'But don't start worrying your head about that. The police will find out who...who was responsible. Now, come along, Maisie. Come and help me in the kitchen and try to take your mind away from it all.'

But Patience knew that that was easier said than done. The child was clearly devastated by the news, and she seemed frightened, too. As for Patience's own wonderful news, that had had to be completely shelved for the moment. But she must find an opportunity to tell Luke when he returned from seeing Miss Thomson. She hoped it would alleviate, to some degree, the sadness and shock they were feeling. But the euphoria she had experienced earlier in the day had utterly vanished.

———

Jennifer Brewer, Priscilla's friend, was at home with Miss Thomson when Luke arrived. She was red-eyed with weeping, and it was obvious that Miss Thomson had shed tears as well, although she was trying to behave with her usual dignity and decorum.

'What a dreadful business, Rector,' she said, ushering him into the lounge. Jennifer was huddled into an armchair with a damp handkerchief held to her face. 'The police sergeant left us only a little while ago. He came to tell me the terrible news and, as it happened, Jennifer was here as well. Come along now, Jennifer; do try and pull yourself together. I know you've had a shock, but we knew something was wrong when Priscilla didn't come home last night... Do sit down please, Rector.'

'Take your time, Jennifer,' said Luke, sitting down opposite her. 'We are all distressed, of course, to hear about your friend.'

'She didn't come home,' the girl sniffed, 'like Miss Thomson said. We just had to go to bed, but I didn't sleep. And then when I went to work this morning Mr Nixon asked me where she was and I said I didn't know. He knew I was worried, though, so he told me to go home at the end of the morning to see if Miss Thomson had heard anything about Priscilla. And then the policeman came and he told us...' She started to cry again, quietly.

Luke nodded and waited until she had composed herself. 'The policeman asked me some questions,' she said after a moment or two, twisting her handkerchief round and round in her fingers. 'He wanted to know when I saw her last. And I told him it was last night. She went off to her choir practice, and we were supposed to be meeting later in the Green Man, but she never turned up.'

'Just you and Priscilla?' asked Luke gently.

'No... She's got, I mean, she had a new boyfriend. She only met him a couple of weeks ago, but she really liked him. He's called Jeff Beaumont and he's stationed up at Catterick. Well, he said he'd bring a friend along, like...' She blushed a little, 'and the four of us would have a drink at the Green Man.'

'And...did he? Bring a friend with him?'

'Oh yes...I went down the road to the pub, like we'd arranged, at half-past eight, 'cause I knew Priscilla would have finished her choir practice by then, but she wasn't there. Jeff was there – I've met him before, so I knew who he was – and his friend, Alec. He introduced us and we had a drink and chatted a bit. But I was worried about Priscilla and so was Jeff.'

'So...what happened?' asked Luke. 'Do you want to tell me?'

'Jeff went to look for her, but he came back after about twenty minutes and he said he couldn't find her. He'd been up as far as the church, he said, and walked round the green, but there was no sign of her. So when the pub was closing Jeff and Alec walked home with me, and then they were getting a lift back to the camp...and that's all I know.'

'Jeff didn't go up the little path and into the churchyard?'

'I don't know. He didn't say so. He only said he went as far as the church. You don't think...? No, it couldn't be Jeff. He really liked Priscilla... Oh dear; it's all so awful. I can't stop crying.'

'Have you had anything to eat?' asked Luke, knowing that the policeman had probably disturbed their lunchtime. 'You really should, you know.'

'No,' said Miss Thomson. 'I'm afraid we

haven't. With that policeman coming we haven't had time. Jennifer is not usually here at lunchtime and I usually have a little something on a tray. I will make some sandwiches and a cup of tea in a little while.'

'My sandwiches are still in my bag,' said Jennifer. 'I brought them back with me. We can have those, and I'll make a few more.' She got up, seeming a little more composed, and smiled sadly at the older woman. 'You stay and talk to the rector, Miss Thomson, and I'll go and see to things.'

'She's a good girl,' said Miss Thomson. 'Well, they both are...were. That poor poor girl! Such a nice well brought up young woman she was, you could see that. She came from Leicester and she'd been a shorthand typist. The policeman said that they would break the news to her parents and that I didn't need to do anything. And they will make arrangements for her body to be sent back if that is what her parents wish. It is all so dreadful, so impossible to believe. There has never been anything like this in Middlebeck. It used to be such a nice quiet little place.'

'No,' agreed Luke, 'there hasn't. That is just what my wife said. Now, Miss Thomson, I am going to leave you to have your lunch. Make sure you eat something, and Jennifer as well. And if there is anything at all you want, if you feel in need of a little comfort or support, then Patience and I are only across the green. God bless you...Amelia. You have the strength to cope with this; I know you have.'

'Maisie has gone up to her bedroom to read for a while,' said Patience when he returned to the rectory. 'At least, that is what she told me. She seems a little more composed now, but I think she wants to be on her own. Luke…there is something else that I want to tell you. No, darling…' She smiled understandingly at him, seeing his alarmed expression. 'It is not more bad news. In fact, it's just the opposite. I went to see the doctor this morning – that's where I had been when I came back to find Inspector Davies here – and, Luke…it is really the most amazing news…'

'What…?' He looked at her rapt expression and he could see, behind the sadness in her eyes, another very different look, one of wonder and joy. 'What is it, darling. You don't mean… You can't mean…'

'Yes, I do,' she nodded. 'We are going to have a baby at last. A child of our very own, darling.'

'Oh, my love, my dearest love…' He took her in his arms and hugged her so hard she could scarcely breathe. 'This is incredible. But what a day to find out about it. So much sadness, and then this utter joy. I really…I don't know what to say.' He released her from his arms and stood looking at her in amazement. 'It's a miracle, my darling; it really is.'

Patience smiled. 'Maybe… But it was an extra special Christmas, wasn't it? You remember…?'

'Of course I do.' In spite of the horror of recent events they found they were able to smile at one another. 'Is that when…?' She nodded. 'So the baby will be born…late September?'

'That is what Dr Forrester has estimated,' replied Patience. 'He is going to book me into Middlebeck hospital straight away. He says everything should be all right, but…'

'But you will have to take care; I realise that,' said Luke. 'And I shall make sure that you do. But you could certainly do without shocks, especially like the one we have had today.'

'Yes, that's true…' Patience nodded her head, the awfulness of Priscilla's death coming over her again. 'I don't think we will tell the children yet, about the baby, I mean. It might help to take their minds off other things, I know; but I would prefer it to be our secret, just yours and mine, Luke, for a little while.'

'Yes, I think that would be best,' agreed Luke. 'I can't get over it. We had resigned ourselves to having no children at all, and soon we will have three; four, if we count Maisie. That little girl will always have a special place in our hearts, won't she, even though she doesn't belong to us…You have no regrets, have you, darling, about Audrey and Tim, considering what has happened now?'

'Of course not. I feel – I know – it was the right thing to do. And maybe God has decided to send us a little extra blessing…' She smiled. 'Perhaps that is rather fanciful, but I do think that looking after the three of them has made me more…receptive, more ready for motherhood.'

'You will be a wonderful mother,' said Luke, kissing her gently. 'Now, you sit there and have a rest, and I will make us a cup of tea.'

'No, Luke,' she said firmly. 'My pregnancy is not going to be one long round of rests and cups of tea. I will carry on as normal and take a break when I need to. Don't worry; I will be sensible. I want this child more than anything else in the world, but at the moment it is better that I keep myself occupied. The children have had a terrible shock and we must help them to get through it as best we can. I'm going up to see Maisie now. I don't want her to be on her own for too long...'

But Maisie did not want to talk. She seemed more composed and was no longer weeping, but Patience was a little disturbed by her unusual quietude. Normally, if Maisie had something on her mind she preferred to talk about it rather than keeping it bottled up inside herself. However, she left her on her own, and when the other two came home from school Maisie came downstairs to join them.

'Nobody's said anything at school,' said Audrey. 'About Priscilla, I mean. I don't think anybody knows yet.'

'And you didn't even tell Doris?' asked Maisie.

'No, of course I didn't. Why should I?' said Audrey. 'Aunty Patience said we hadn't to tell anybody, so we didn't, did we, Tim?' The little boy shook his head solemnly.

'Is Doris OK?' persisted Maisie.

'Yes; why shouldn't she be?' replied her friend. 'She doesn't know yet. She'll be upset though, like we are, when she finds out.'

'I thought her dad might've said something to her, about Priscilla not turning up for work. She worked on Mr Nixon's farm, you know.'

'I know she did,' said Audrey, a little impatiently. 'But she hasn't said anything. I don't suppose her dad tells her much about what's going on on the farm. Why should he? I don't like him much, Doris's dad,' she added. 'He's not very friendly…'

'Now, come along, you two,' said Patience, determined to steer them away from morbid talk. 'You can help me to set the table. I think we'll have boiled eggs for tea, as a special treat. Mrs Nixon let me have six from her market stall, although new laid eggs are becoming quite scarce. And Tim, would you go and tidy your bedroom up a little, please, dear. You've left your clothes all over the place.'

'I'm going across to the schoolhouse to see Charity and Anne,' Luke told her quietly. 'They will have to be told, and I think it is better coming from me, rather than hearing it as village gossip. And it's just as well that it's the weekend as far as the school is concerned.'

In the early evening Luke went into his study to add the finishing touches to his sermon, and to adjust parts of it in view of recent events. It would be a tough one to preach to a traumatised congregation. Some five minutes later he heard a quiet knock at his door.

'Come in,' he said, although the other members of his household knew that he should not be disturbed whilst he was working on his sermon.

Maisie's head appeared round the door. 'I'm sorry,' she said, in a voice that was almost a whisper. 'I know you're working, but I've got to tell you something. It's very important. Please, Luke, can I come in and tell you?'

'Of course you can, Maisie,' he replied a little resignedly. He knew he must try to be patient, though, no matter how busy he was. This little girl must be feeling very confused and sad, more so than the other two children, as she had been closer to Priscilla. He guessed that that was what she wanted to talk about. 'Come along in and sit down, my dear.'

She perched on the edge of the leather chair and looked at Luke steadily across the desk. 'Luke...' she began slowly. Then she went on, talking more quickly, 'I know who did it. I know who it was that killed Priscilla...'

He frowned in puzzlement. 'Maisie...whatever are you saying, dear? How can you know? What do you mean?'

'I know you might not believe me, but I know, honest, I do. I heard 'em, the other night, Priscilla and...and Doris's dad.'

Luke felt himself turn cold. He knew that Maisie was not a fanciful child. She had had a great deal of trauma in her own life and was not one to make things up. He had always found her to be truthful. 'Maisie...I do believe you,' he replied. 'Just tell me exactly what you have heard, or seen. There might be a simple explanation.'

She shook her head. 'No, I'm sure it was him. It was last night, see. You remember when I came back from choir practice I told you and Aunty Patience I'd forgotten my gloves? Well, I went back for them, but the door was locked and everybody had gone. And it was then that I heard 'em; on that little path they were, that goes past our back gate. But they didn't see me. I kept ever so quiet, and then I crept away.'

'And what did you hear, Maisie?' Luke asked gently. 'And how did you know it was Priscilla and...Mr Nixon?'

'Well, I know Priscilla's voice, don't I, and I heard her say, "Leave me alone." And then the man said something like, "You know you don't mean it," and then she said, "Let me go, Walter; what d'you think you're doing?" So I knew it was him, Mr Nixon. Then he said something about knowing it was what she really wanted an' that she was acting all prim and proper. I can't remember exactly...an' I came away then. I've seen him looking at her, though, at choir practices. He sits opposite us an' he sort of stares at her as though he – I dunno – as though he thinks she's real pretty. Well, she is...was, I mean...'

The little girl would not know the meaning of the word lust, but Luke could imagine that was the way Walter Nixon had looked at the girl. 'And you are sure that Mr Nixon didn't see you?' he asked. He had no reason at all to doubt the child, and what she was saying was of great significance.

She nodded her head. 'Quite sure. They were further along the path, but I could hear what they were saying 'cause they were shouting. Well, Priscilla was when she said "Let go!" D'you think it was him that killed her?'

'I have no idea, Maisie. We mustn't jump to conclusions. The police are investigating the... matter.' He did not want to use the word murder, but that was what it was, and it looked very much as though Maisie, unwittingly, might have discovered the culprit. 'I really think we ought to leave it to them to find out.'

'You're not going to say anything, then, to the police?'

'No...I don't think so, Maisie. I don't think it would be right.' Luke was not a Catholic priest and did not listen to confessions. He was not sure that he agreed with the practice, but he was aware that there were many of that faith who would wish to talk to a priest, knowing that their confidences would go no further. He looked upon Maisie's disclosure now as confidential. He did not think she would have told anyone else, but he had to make sure.

'Listen, Maisie...' he went on. 'What you have told me, it must remain a confidence – a secret – between you and me. You mustn't tell anyone else at all, do you understand?'

'Not even Aunty Patience?' she asked.

'No...not even Patience. Your aunt has enough to think about at the moment. And I need to think very carefully about what I should do, and I must say a prayer and ask God to help me as well.'

Maisie was silent, then she said, 'If they catch...whoever it was that killed Priscilla...would he be hanged, d'you think? I know that's what happens,' she added, seeing the look of alarm on Luke's face. 'I'm not a little kid, an'...an' I have heard about it.'

Luke got up from his desk and came and put his arms round Maisie. 'My dear child, please...please, don't think about things like that. It does not always happen. Sometimes they go to prison... I have told you; we must leave the solving of this crime to the police.' He kissed her gently on the forehead. 'God bless you, and thank you for telling me. You have done the right thing. Now, off you go back to Aunty Patience. You can tell her that you wanted to talk to me because you were feeling sad. And that's the truth, isn't it? You'll feel a lot better now you've told me; really you will…'

And now it is my problem, he thought, as the little girl went out of the door. And what an enormous, horrific problem it was. The child's words about hanging had chilled him to the bone, and yet that was the ultimate punishment for murderers. It was the law of the land, indisputable and unchangeable. But how could he possibly contemplate this happening to one of his own flock, a member of the church choir?

Patience did not question Luke, but he told her that Maisie had been to have a talk with him because she was feeling confused and very sad. She nodded understandingly. All three children had seemed glad to retire to bed that night, rather earlier than usual.

By the next morning Luke had decided what he should do. He would go to Walter Nixon's farm and see if he could find the man on his own. He would talk to Walter, which would be a perfectly reasonable thing to do in view of what had happened, and see what came out of the conversation. He felt sure that the guidance he was seeking would become clear to him.

He caught sight of the farmer at the far end of a field. He was relieved that he had not needed to call at the farmhouse to enquire of Mrs Nixon about her husband's whereabouts; it was best to keep his visit confidential at the moment. It was Saturday, though, market day; so she might not be at home in any case.

Mid-March was the start of the lambing season, as Luke knew, having lived in the countryside for so long. As he approached he could see that one of the ewes had not long since given birth. A spindly-legged lamb was tottering around taking its first steps whilst the mother sheep watched it attentively. Walter, too, was looking broodingly at the little scene, his forehead creased in a frown and his mouth set in a grim unsmiling line. On seeing Luke approaching he raised his hand in greeting. His lips moved a fraction in a half-smile, but his blue eyes were wary. He looked worried, but Luke realised he could well be imagining that because of what he knew.

'Hi there, Luke,' called Walter. Those who knew the rector well, and others who did not regard him with overdue awe as a 'man of the cloth', called him by his Christian name. 'This 'un's just given birth. It's allus an awesome sight watchin' t' lamb get to its feet, no matter 'ow many times yer sees it. This little 'un 'll be reight enough now. I'll leave it with its ma.' He walked towards Luke. 'But I know you've not come to talk about lambs and suchlike.'

'Not really,' said Luke. 'I was so sorry to hear the dreadful news about Priscilla. I know she was one of your land girls.'

'Aye, so she was. It's a bad do, Luke, it is that. She were a nice lass…and so is Jennifer, the other 'un we've got. She's quieter though, but she's a good worker. She's real upset though, is Jennifer, about her friend.'

'She is sure to be,' replied Luke, watching Walter Nixon surreptitiously, but very much aware of every nuance in the man's voice and demeanour. It seemed as though Walter felt he must keep on talking as normally as possible. 'Have you had a visit from the police?' Luke asked. 'I suppose you must have had by now.'

'Oh aye; they came on Friday afternoon to tell us about finding…Priscilla. We were wondering what had happened to her when she didn't show up for work, like, and Jennifer had gone home to see if she'd turned up there. I can tell you, Luke, we had the shock of our lives, me and the wife.'

'Yes…I am sure it must have been a dreadful shock for you…'

'Anyroad, they asked me when I'd last seen her. They had to do that o' course; it's just routine. And I'd seen her the night before, as it happened…'

'Yes, at the choir practice…'

'Aye; we left at about the same time, Priscilla and me, and Tommy Allbright an' all; he were with us. We chatted on t' path for a while, and then we all went home… An' that was the last I saw of her, the poor lass.'

Luke nodded. 'I see… And did Priscilla say where she was going?'

'No, not as I can remember. She didn't say owt. But it seems now as though she might've been going to meet some feller she'd met, a soldier from Catterick. And…and they've taken him in for questioning, or so I believe.'

Luke regarded him steadily. 'You mean...the police have arrested him?'

'Well, I don't know as you'd say arrested, but they certainly want to talk to him.'

'And...how do you know all this?' asked Luke. 'Is it from the police?' If Walter thought the rector was quizzing him rather too intensely he did not show it.

'No, it was Jennifer. It seems that she's got friendly wi' one o' them soldiers an' all, an' he came to tell her last night that they'd taken his mate in for questioning. He was in a fair old state, she said – her friend, I mean – about his pal. And I don't suppose t'other chap's too happy about it neither.'

Luke continued to watch the farmer attentively. 'No, I don't suppose he is,' he replied, 'especially if the poor fellow is innocent.'

For the first time he saw a flicker of unease on Walter's face. It was, in fact, the first time during the conversation that the man had looked at him directly. Walter's eyes were wary. 'What d'yer mean?' he said. 'They must think it's suspicious, like, to take him in...' His voice petered out under the scrutiny of the rector's gaze. Luke could see the naked fear there now, in his pale blue eyes. If he had not been wholly sure, before, that Walter had committed this awful crime, the terror on his face now was all the proof that Luke needed. 'I mean to say...' Walter mumbled.

'Yes, exactly what do you mean to say, Walter?' asked Luke quietly. 'Do you mean to say that you would let an innocent man suffer, when you know all too well...'

'If the chap's innocent, then they'll prove it,' retorted Walter. His eyes narrowed as he stared back at Luke. 'What d'you mean...when I know? What am I supposed to know?'

They had walked as far as an empty barn and when Luke stepped inside the open door Walter followed him. Luke turned to face him. 'Walter, you were overheard,' he said, 'on the path behind the church, the night of the choir practice. You and Priscilla. She was shouting for you to let go of her, to leave her alone. The...person who was there heard quite enough of what was going on to be suspicious. And then when Priscilla's body was found...'

For a moment Walter looked defiant. 'And 'ow d'you know that what this...person says is true? It sounds like some busybody out to make trouble. Who was it anyroad? Because...it's a lie...'

'You don't need to know who it was,' said Luke. 'But I have no reason to doubt their word. Why? Are you denying that you were there on Thursday night with Priscilla, that you were...talking together?' Luke's steadfast gaze was too much for Walter. He shook his head confusedly.

'No, I suppose not. But they've got it all wrong. We were having a bit of a laugh, that's all. Me and Priscilla, we were friends, like...with her working on t' farm. I've got to know her...'

Suddenly Walter put his head into his hands. He was breathing loudly, in short gasps, then he began to sob. His words were forced out a few at a time on his rasping breath. 'I didn't mean it... I never meant to kill her... It were an accident. She was such a little thing...a little frail thing...'

Luke took hold of him by his upper arms. 'Walter, just tell me about it,' he said firmly, but quite sympathetically.

'I shook her...' said Walter, sounding bemused. 'That's all I did. I shook her to stop her from shouting. Me hands must've been round her throat. I didn't know...I didn't realise. She was making so much bloody row, so I kept on shaking her hard. An' then...she'd gone all limp in me hands, an' her head flopped over. I was frightened to death. I've never been so scared in all me life... So I just left her there. I tried to cover her up a bit... But we'd done nowt, honest we hadn't. I mean...it weren't rape or owt like that.'

Luke nodded. 'Yes...I see.' He would have liked to say that he understood, but he could not do so; neither did he know what he must do about this dreadful situation. Walter's head dropped forward, his chin on his chest. He started to mumble, as much to himself as to Luke.

'She was a tease, that girl. She led me on summat dreadful. Happen she didn't mean to. Happen she were t' same with all the men, wi' her smiles and her laughs. We had many a good laugh together me and her... An' if I wanted a bit more who could blame me, eh?' He looked up then at Luke. 'I'm a normal man, an' I've got me feelings and me needs an' all. Ada's not interested no more in that sort o' thing, an' I won't force meself on her. We've got our three kids, an' as far as Ada's concerned that's the end of it. She's a good wife, but I want a bit more than that. Priscilla were such a pretty little lass, so happy and friendly. I was sure she liked me...' He buried his head in his hands, still weeping quietly.

'But you mistook her friendliness for something that she didn't intend, Walter,' said Luke. 'I do know what you mean. It is possible that...she might have given the wrong impression.' He felt anger and revulsion at what Walter had done, but he felt compassion as well. He, Luke, was fortunate because he had a wife who was loving in every way; but he understood, too, the frailty of some men, and Walter Nixon was one of them.

'What are you going to do?' asked Walter gruffly. 'Are you going to tell the police that it was me?'

Luke was silent for a moment. Then, 'I can't do that,' he said. 'It would not be right for me to say anything. What you have told me, you have done so in confidence; and what the...other person told me must remain confidential too.'

'What about him...or her? Will they say owt?'

'I can give you my assurance that they will not,' replied Luke. 'But surely...it is up to you, isn't it? You cannot let someone else...suffer, when you know that he is innocent.'

'I can't let him hang, you mean,' said Walter. His hand went involuntarily to his neck and his eyes grew wide with terror. 'That's what'd happen, isn't it? He'd be hanged. That's what they do with murderers. No...' He shook his head. 'I know I can't let that happen. But I'm scared, Luke. I'm bloody terrified. I daren't give meself up.'

'You have told me it was an accident,' said Luke, 'and I, for one, believe you. I know you didn't mean to do it. And I would speak up for you; I would do anything I possibly could to help you. I know that, fundamentally, you are a good man. But it is for you to decide what you have to do. I am going to leave you now, Walter. No one has heard us talking and your secret is safe with me. Please tell Ada that I have been to commiserate with you about Priscilla. I don't feel that I want to talk to her just at the moment... God bless you, Walter.'

Briefly he touched the man's arm, then Luke walked away, leaving Walter rooted to the spot, staring after his retreating back.

Chapter Twenty-Three

'I 've just been over to the farm to have a chat with Walter Nixon,' Luke told Patience on his return to the rectory. 'I knew he was sure to be in a state of shock, with Priscilla having been one of his land girls.'

It was true that the farmer was in a state of shock, but what Luke was telling his wife was only half the truth. He felt conscience-stricken; he could not remember any other time when he had been less that completely honest with her. But the burden of his knowledge must remain his and his alone. It would not be right to trouble Patience with it, especially at the moment when she was in the early stages of carrying their child. That stupendous news had had to be put to the back of his mind, but he found it surfacing from time to time in his thoughts, bringing a momentary upsurge of joy in the midst of his consuming worry about Walter Nixon.

'Yes; I should imagine that Priscilla, and Jennifer as well, had become almost like members of the family,' said Patience. 'Ada Nixon told me that they were both very good workers. Oh Luke…it is such a tragedy, and such a wicked wicked deed! I suppose there is no news yet about…about who was responsible?'

Luke remained silent, for so long that Patience

looked at him curiously. 'What's the matter? Have they arrested somebody?' she asked.

'I believe…they have taken a young man in for questioning,' he replied carefully, 'so Walter told me. A soldier that Priscilla met recently, from the camp at Catterick. He is called Jeff Beaumont and that's all that I know about him. Jennifer told me – when I spoke to her yesterday at Miss Thomson's – that Priscilla was supposed to be meeting him in the Green Man, after choir practice, but she didn't turn up. Jennifer was there waiting for her with the two young men – Jeff and a friend – but there was no sign of Priscilla. So after a while they went back to their camp and Jennifer went home.'

'Then…why have they arrested this Jeff?' asked Patience. 'It sounds as though he didn't even see her that night.'

'That puzzled me too,' said Luke. He had, indeed, been turning the problem over and over in his mind. That young man was innocent, and there must, surely, be a way of proving it. But from what Jennifer had told him there were about twenty minutes unaccounted for when Jeff had been on his own, looking for Priscilla. He decided to tell Patience about this; she would think it strange if he did not tell her what he knew.

'Apparently Jeff was worried,' he continued, 'and, according to Jennifer, he went off on his own to see if he could find Priscilla. When he came back, twenty minutes or so later, he told Jennifer and his pal that he had walked up as far as the church, circled the green, and then had gone back down the High Street to the pub. But I suppose the police are jumping to the conclusion that there was time, during those twenty minutes, for him to have...committed the murder. They will try to prove that he went up the lane and met her there...' And it is up to me to prove that he didn't, thought Luke desperately. Please God, he prayed silently, let me – or the police – find a way of proving it.

'Of course, it is all what they call circumstantial evidence,' he sighed. 'There can't be any definite proof that he killed Priscilla. He's innocent...or so I firmly believe,' he added, aware that he might have said too much. 'We will just have to pray that there is no miscarriage of justice.'

'You seem very sure of his innocence,' said Patience, looking at him a little searchingly. 'You don't know this young soldier, do you?'

'No, I don't know him, but it's a feeling that I have, a very strong feeling.'

Patience continued to look at him steadily, then she frowned, shaking her head perplexedly. 'It was Thursday night, wasn't it?' she said, 'when this dreadful thing took place. I've lost track of time with all that's been happening, but there is something that is just coming back to me... Maisie came back from choir practice and she said she had left her gloves behind; do you remember, Luke?'

'Yes...I found them for her the next morning. Why? Did she say anything else to you?'

'No...but she seemed a bit worried about something. I asked her about it the next morning, but she said it was nothing. That wasn't what I want to tell you, though; it's something else... I went in to say goodnight to her, and to Audrey and

Tim, like I always do, and then I went into our bedroom, Luke, and I stood by the window looking out into the night. It wasn't quite as black as it is sometimes because the moon was shining, and it all looked so peaceful and quiet. I had really gone to pull the blackout blind and to draw the curtains, but I just stood there looking out at the green and the church and down the High Street.

'And I remember now that I saw that young soldier – it must have been Priscilla's friend, Jeff. He walked up from the High Street, and when he got to Miss Thomson's house he stopped and looked at it for a moment...'

'He didn't go and knock at the door?'

'No... If it was him, this Jeff – and I really think it must have been – perhaps Priscilla had told him that Miss Thomson wasn't very keen on them having followers. No...he went on walking, past the school, then across the front of the church, then he went past our house and back down the High Street. But, Luke, he didn't – he most definitely didn't – go into the lane. I was standing in the bay, and I can see from there quite a long way down the street. I remember hearing the plod plod of his army boots on the pavement, growing fainter as he walked away. He was the only person in sight. I couldn't say why I was watching him, but I was, and it's only just come back to me. I suppose my mind was mainly on the doctor's appointment I had the next day, and everything else just got pushed out.'

'Well, thank God you've remembered now,' cried Luke. 'This could be really important, darling.

Would you be willing to tell everything you have told me to the police? I really feel it might be a matter of life...or death.'

'Yes, of course I will...but won't they think it strange that I've only just remembered?'

'Probably not. It was only an insignificant little incident at the time, but it could save that poor fellow's life. Come along, my dear. There's no time like the present. You and I will pay a visit to the police station... Where are the children?'

'They've all gone down to the Saturday market. They have some spending money and I thought it was best to keep them busy. Luke...that night of the choir practice, do you think Maisie might have been worried because she had noticed something... strange?'

Luke pursed his lips. 'I shouldn't think so. She was probably just concerned about leaving her gloves. I wouldn't question her any further if I were you, dear. It is best for her to get back to normal, and in time she won't think about Priscilla quite as much. What time are you expecting them back for lunch?'

'I told them to be back at half-past twelve. It will be just soup and sandwiches, and I shall cook a meal at teatime.'

Luke glanced at his watch. 'It's only just turned eleven. We can go to the police station and be back before twelve thirty.'

Thank you, thank you, Lord...he was saying over and over in his mind. If Patience's evidence was enough to free the unfortunate young soldier, then that would be the greater part of his dilemma solved.

'Thank you very much, Mrs Fairchild, for coming in,' said the inspector after Patience had given him the details of what she had seen. 'And you too of course, Reverend. This information is just what we needed...'

He paused, putting his elbows on the table and leaning towards them in a confidential manner. 'Between you and me and the gatepost, we were just considering letting him go. There isn't enough evidence to convict him, but he was the obvious suspect. Recent boyfriend of the deceased, and by his own admission he had been up as far as the church and back that evening. He swore blind he was innocent; of course, that's what they all do, I know. But somehow I believed him – you get a nose for these things – and he seems a genuine trustworthy sort of lad. He went to pieces when he heard about the lass being murdered; that's nothing to go by either, but I do believe now that it was the first he knew of it.'

'We are glad to be able to help, Inspector Davies,' said Luke. 'Have you any more leads? Or perhaps I shouldn't ask.'

'It's early days yet, but we'll catch him, make no mistake about that. No...nothing definite, but I would be obliged, Reverend, if you could let me have the names and addresses of all the members of your choir. That was where the young lady had been on the evening in question, and it seems as though some of them might have been the last people to see her alive.'

Luke felt his heart give an extra loud thump. 'Of course, certainly I will. I take it you mean just the menfolk in the choir? There are ladies as well, and several children, but surely you won't want to question them?'

'No, not the children. I did mean the men, primarily, but we ought to question the ladies as well. They might have noticed something suspicious without even realising it was so at the time.'

'Quite so,' replied Luke, trying to remain calm and in control of himself. 'If you would like to call at the rectory I will let you have a list.'

'We have spoken to Walter Nixon, the farmer that the young woman worked for; and he is in the choir as well, of course. It seems, at the moment, that he might have been the last person to see her that evening; he and a man called Tommy Allbright. Mr Nixon mentioned that they had both been chatting with her after the choir practice, then they said good night and left Priscilla on her own.'

'Yes, I know them both very well,' said Luke. 'As a matter of fact, Tom Allbright is one of my church wardens.'

'We will be having a word with him,' said the inspector, 'to confirm Mr Nixon's story that they left Miss Meadows at the end of the lane. It is only routine, of course; we have no real reason to suspect either of them.'

Luke nodded. 'Yes, I see...' He felt quite sick with the worry of it all, but he knew he had to stand aside and let events take their course. Tempted as he was at that moment, he knew it would be very wrong to speak to Tom Allbright and ask him to substantiate Walter's story. It would be encouraging him to tell an outright lie. He turned to his wife. 'Come along, my dear. You have done your duty now and it's time we were getting home.'

Patience smiled, gathering together her bag and her gloves. 'Yes, and what a relief it is to have told you, Inspector Davies. I'm glad I've been able to help that young soldier.'

He stood up with them and accompanied them to the door. 'Thank you both once again. I will call round for that list quite soon, or I will send my sergeant.'

The Sunday morning service was just about the most difficult one that Luke had ever had to conduct. The congregation was subdued and the choir sang less heartily and convincingly that usual. Luke noticed that Walter was there in his accustomed place, but to be absent, of course, would only have drawn attention to himself. Luke wondered what Maisie, sitting opposite to Walter, was thinking. What was going through that astute little mind of hers? She had not said anything about the murder to Luke since her disclosure; neither had Luke told her that Walter Nixon had actually admitted to the crime. Maybe, eventually, he would tell her. He might, in fact, be forced to tell her if things went badly for Walter. At the moment, though, he knew it was best not to mention either Priscilla or Walter to her at all.

He had chosen the words of his sermon carefully. It was the season of Lent, a sombre time in the church's calendar, in any event. The hymn they had sung,

'Forty days and forty nights
    Thou wast fasting in the wild...'

seemed appropriate, telling of Jesus' temptations in the wilderness. He spoke about the temptations of man, as he had planned to do before the terrible events of Thursday night; the temptations of the world, the flesh and the devil. But Luke was not a rabble-rousing, tub-thumping type of preacher, so he spoke quietly, with sincerity and directness, as he always tried to do. He could see from his position in the pulpit that there were a few women in the congregation who were moved to tears, as handkerchiefs were taken stealthily from pockets and bags to mop at brimming eyes. Walter was not in his line of vision, but Luke had no intention of haranguing the congregation with an appeal to repent of their sins. He had decided that the decision to confess, or not, must be Walter's alone.

He prayed for the family and friends of Priscilla Meadows that they might, somehow, find comfort in the knowledge that others were thinking about them. He did not pray, as his Catholic brethren might have done, for the soul of Priscilla. It was his belief and the belief of his church that she was already in Paradise. But that was small comfort for those who loved her, he knew only too well.

After the final hymn he stood at the door to shake hands and bid farewell to all his flock. Walter, after changing out of his choir regalia, departed with a brief 'Good morning.' Luke had not expected anything different. There was nothing more that either of them could say.

When all the members of the congregation had departed Luke went into the vestry to take off the surplice and stole he always wore for services. One of his church wardens, Albert Carey, was just leaving, but the other one, Tom Allbright, was still there.

'May I have a word with you, Luke?' he asked. 'There's summat that I'm concerned about, summat that's puzzling me, and I don't rightly know what to do about it.'

'Certainly, Tom,' said Luke. 'You know that anything you tell me will not go any further.' He had already guessed that it might have something to do with the subject that was uppermost in all their minds.

'Well, it's about Walter Nixon,' said Tom, as Luke had thought he would. 'Him and me, we left at the same time the other night, after the choir practice, and we stood chatting for a while at the end of the path...and Priscilla was with us an' all. She was a lively lass, Priscilla; we all liked her, especially the men. Now I don't mean there was owt wrong about it, Luke. We just enjoyed her company, an' she had that way with her of making you feel good about yerself, as though you mattered, if you know what I mean.'

'Yes, I do, Tom,' replied Luke. 'I know just what you mean. Go on... What is it that you're concerned about?'

'Well, I couldn't help but notice, like, that Walter seemed quite fond of her. But I know it was because they worked together on the farm, an' he'd got to know her better than the rest of us did. Anyroad, like I said, we stood there chatting for a while, then I said cheerio to them an' I went off home, out of the front gate. And Walter was still there, chatting to Priscilla...' He paused, shaking his head bemusedly. 'And now...well, he's asked me if I'll say that he left her at the same time as me, that she was on her own; if the police start asking questions, like... And I don't know what to do, Luke, and that's a fact.'

'I see...' said Luke. 'And...have the police questioned you?'

'No, not yet. But they're sure to, aren't they? We all thought as how it must've been that soldier she was seeing, but now they've let him go. Of course, I know it couldn't've been Walter; the idea is just ridiculous. But I suppose he's panicking, like, in case they get round to thinking that he was the last one to speak to her and they try to pin it on him. You know what the police are like; they're determined to get a conviction.'

Luke hesitated. 'They try to get to the truth,' he said, 'and if someone is innocent then they should have nothing to fear. A man – or a woman, of course – is innocent until he is proved guilty; that is the law of our land.'

'Aye, that's as may be,' replied Tom. 'But you know as well as I do that it doesn't always work out like that. There must've been many miscarriages of justice in the past, fellows that have been hanged, even, when they've had nowt to do with it. Not that we're likely to find out; the police keep that sort of knowledge to themselves. But Walter's a mate, and for the sake of a white lie...'

'It's rather more than a white lie, Tom, if you are telling me you left him alone with Priscilla, and you tell the police something different. Tell me; what do you think happened?'

'I reckon he walked along the path with her, to make sure she was safe. It's dark down there between the trees; it was dark there even before we had the blackout. And then...well, I dunno. I suppose she must've met somebody, either somebody she knew or a stranger; we all knew she was a friendly lass. We thought it was her boyfriend, but it seeems he's in the clear. It's a problem, Luke, an' it gets worse the more I think about it.'

'What did you say to Walter?'

'I said I'd have to think about it; that it was a serious matter to lie to the police. But he looked so bloody scared – pardon me language, Luke, in church an' all, but it's enough to make a saint swear, all this lot – he looked so scared that I more or less said, "Aye, all right then."'

And none of us are saints, thought Luke; not Walter, not Tom, not Luke himself. 'If you are asking me if I think it is permissible that you should lie, then I'm afraid I can't give you that assurance, Tom,' he said regretfully. 'But you know that, don't you?'

Tom nodded. 'Aye, I reckon I do.'

'All I can say is...just do as you feel you must; it is a matter for your conscience. It has to be your decision and no one else's. But I think you have known that all along, haven't you? You just needed someone to confide in; am I right?'

'You're right, Luke, as you always are.'

'Not always, Tom. None of us are always right,

nor do we always know what is the right thing to do... I want Walter to be innocent of this crime just as much as you do. He certainly seems to have got himself into a dreadful predicament.' And that was no more or no less than the truth. It was an evasive answer, maybe, but it was true that he, Luke, did want Walter to be innocent. He was the only one, though, apart from Walter himself, who knew of the man's guilt. Even Maisie did not know for certain. The burden of his knowledge was not getting any easier to bear, but bear it he knew he must. Otherwise it would mean he had to betray a trust, and be partly responsible for sending not a wicked, but a vulnerable and morally weak, man to the gallows.

'I'm real sorry to have bothered you,' said Tom. 'I can tell by your face that you are deeply troubled, aren't you, Luke?'

'Yes...I am.' Luke nodded. 'There has never been anything like this before. I have had plenty of ups and downs in my ministry, but nothing has affected me the way that this has.' He smiled sadly. 'Come along, Tom; let's go home. We both have happy homes to go to, and that is a comfort.' They left the church together and walked along the path to the gate.

'I suppose I shouldn't say this,' said Luke, 'but I am relieved that I don't have to face the ordeal of Priscilla's funeral. That, I feel, would have been too much...'

'Oh, I see. It's going to be in her home town, is it? Leicester, wasn't that where she lived?'

'Yes, her parents live in Leicester. It's a terrible

tragedy for them to bear, but when the police release...the body, she will be going home to her family and friends... God rest her soul,' Luke added.

'Aye, God bless her,' said Tom. 'And whichever way you look at it, Luke, there's nowt we can do – or not do – that'll bring her back.'

———

'That's another lead that's taken us nowhere,' said Inspector Davies to his sergeant, midway through the following week. 'That Walter Nixon; it all pointed in his direction. But Mr Allbright swears blind he was with him, chatting to the lass, then they left her and went off together. He even said that he walked with Nixon as far as the back gate of the churchyard, because they were deep in conversation; talking about the anthems they were singing for Easter, he said, when I wanted to know what they were talking about that was so important. And then he saw Nixon go along the lane that leads to his farm. Mrs Nixon said her husband came in at more or less the same time as usual; happen a few minutes later, but that's because he was talking to Mr Allbright. And he's a church warden, is Tom Allbright, so I can't see him lying.'

'It doesn't always figure, though, sir,' said Sergeant Taylor. 'They're not bound to be speaking the truth, just because they're church folk. It's funny how many of 'em there seem to be involved with this case.'

'That's because she'd just been to choir practice

and they were the last people to see her.'

'Aye, an' it were the men, weren't it, who said what a nice lass she were; real friendly and suchlike. Walter Nixon's name came up a few times, but they all spoke well of him, said he was more like a father to her because she worked on his farm.'

'The women weren't too sure about her, though, were they?' remarked the inspector. 'I reckon they were a bit jealous; a pretty young lass – a newcomer an' all – getting all the attention. But none of them, neither, would say a wrong word about Nixon. And let's face it, Mike, we've nowt much to go on, except that he knew her better than the others did, and he seemed a bit shaken up, but then I suppose he would… There's no material evidence to link him to it. No finger prints, no blood; it's not as though she was stabbed; there would have been more to go on if she had been. And she hadn't been raped; there were no signs of sexual activity. She didn't seem to have put up much of a fight neither; no scrapings under her finger nails…'

'And no footprints neither; the ground was dry. If this was one o' them murder mysteries we were reading, there'd be a nice little clue at the scene; a cufflink or a shirt button.'

The inspector nodded. 'Aye, you're right. But this isn't Agatha Christie, and it seems that neither of us is Hercule Poirot. We'll have to release the poor girl's body now and let the family get on with what they have to do. And we'll have to go on searching and questioning folk even though the trail's gone cold.'

'I can't help thinking though, sir, like I said

before, how much the church is involved in this little lot. It was the verger that found her, wasn't it, and then the rector? All the folk concerned are church folk except for that boyfriend we had in, Jeff Beaumont. And who was it who gave her an alibi? None other than the rector's wife.'

'You're not accusing her of lying, are you, Mike?'

'No, of course not. She's a lovely lady, is Mrs Fairchild. You only have to look at her to know that she's sincere. No; I was only thinking that maybe the Lord looks after his own, or summat like that. I dunno; it's a rum sort of how d'you do...'

Chapter Twenty-Four

Life at the rectory gradually returned to normal, although Maisie continued to brood and to look sad from time to time. The murder of the land girl had been a nine days' wonder at the school; some of the children had known Priscilla, but a lot of them hadn't.

Then it was the Easter holidays and the school broke up for almost two weeks. Maisie was able to spend more time with her mother at Tremaine House, and with her little brother and sister whose company she now enjoyed much more than she had when they were in Armley. Those days seemed a long long time ago. Bruce, also, was home from boarding school, and that was an added pleasure to Maisie.

She had to share his company, though, with Audrey and Doris. He seemed to enjoy being with the three girls although they were a few years younger than he was. He had lots of friends at school, but those boys, like him, had all gone home for the holidays; and being away at boarding school he had not had the chance to become acquainted with many of the boys in Middlebeck.

He suggested to the girls, as they chatted together one day on the green in front of the rectory, that they should all go on an 'expedition', as he called it, to the ruined castle on the hill. Doris, being a local girl, had visited it before, but Maisie and Audrey, although they had often looked at its grey towers from the rectory windows, had never ventured so far.

'We'll take a packed lunch and have a picnic,' said Bruce, taking it upon himself to do the organising. 'If you all bring sandwiches, I'll ask Maisie's mum if she will let us have some of her special ginger cake and rock buns. They're scrumptious! She's getting to be a dab hand at baking, Maisie, is your mother, with looking after all our land girls.'

Maisie smiled at him. She was pleased that her mother was happy and enjoying her job so much. She had told Maisie that she was happier than she had ever been in her life; since Maisie's dad had died, that was, she had added. Lily certainly looked very fit and healthy, and younger, rather than older, since coming to live in Middlebeck. She looked just as young as some of the land girls she cared for.

'And I'll bring some lemonade and Tizer for us to drink,' said Bruce. 'I'll carry that in my haversack, 'cause it'll be a bit heavy for you girls. You don't mind drinking out of the bottle, do you? Unless you want to bring a cup... Yes, perhaps that would be a better idea.'

'Can Timothy come?' asked Audrey. Since she had been told that the little boy was to be an adoptive member of the Fairchild family, as she was, she had become very protective of him.

'Do you think he will be able to walk so far?' asked Bruce. 'It's about four miles.'

'Oh yes; I'm sure he will,' said Audrey. 'His leg doesn't bother him now, and I'll look after him. Anyway, he's getting bigger now. He's eight, and he's not such a baby as he used to be.'

'All right then,' agreed Bruce. 'It'll mean there's another boy to keep me company as well as all you girls. And Prince, of course. I can't leave Prince behind.'

'What about our Joanie and Jimmy then?' asked Maisie, feeling just the teeniest bit jealous. Audrey had well and truly laid claim to Tim as her own little brother just recently. 'Joanie's started school, you know, now, and Jimmy'll be going in September.'

'Oh, I don't really think they can come,' replied Bruce. 'Do you, honestly, Maisie? They would be too much of a responsibility,' he added, in a very grown-up manner. Bruce, of course, was sixteen, which seemed to her to be terribly grown-up. The only other boy of that age that she knew at all well was Ted Nixon, Doris's brother. He was sixteen too, but he seemed far more mature, even, than Bruce. Ted worked on the farm and had done so ever since he had left school more than two years ago. There was no chance of him coming with them, though, on their outing, as he would be working. Bruce and Ted, she thought to herself, were just about as different as they could be; like chalk and cheese, she had sometimes heard grown-ups say.

'Yes, p'raps you're right, Bruce,' she said now, 'I don't suppose me mum'd let the little 'uns come anyway...' And even if she did, then she, Maisie, would have to look after them. As Bruce said, it would be too much of a responsibility.

'What about you, Doris?' asked Bruce. 'Your mum will make sandwiches for you, will she?'

'I'll make me own,' said Doris. 'Me mum's busy, extra busy, you know, since Priscilla...' She stopped for a moment, biting her lip. None of the others made any comment; they tried not to talk about Priscilla now. 'We've got another land girl to help Jennifer,' Doris continued, 'but we'll have to get another one as well, p'raps two, because there's only me dad and our Ted now, since Joe joined the RAF.'

'Yes, my father told me that your brother had joined the airforce,' said Bruce. 'Where is he stationed?'

'Oh, somewhere near Lincoln,' replied Doris. 'He fancies himself as a pilot, does our Joe, but I don't think they'll ever let him fly aeroplanes. You have to be real brainy to do that, don't you, Bruce? I 'spect he'll just get a job mending the planes, seeing that the engines are working properly an' all that. That's what he was good at; he always looked after the tractors for me dad.'

'Yes; I expect he will be one of the ground crew,' said Bruce. 'But they are just as important as the fliers in their own way... I would like to join the RAF,' he went on, nodding confidently. 'I would really like to be a pilot...but of course I'm not old enough, am I? Not yet.' He gave a rueful grin. 'Now, is it all settled? We'll set off in the morning at ten o' clock. We'll all meet by Doris's farm gate. Is that OK?'

'Yes, great,' they all agreed. 'Cheerio then; see you tomorrow…' They went off their separate ways, Doris and Bruce heading for the path to the farm and Maisie and Audrey to the rectory gate.

Bruce, in the RAF? pondered Maisie. Her little heart had given quite a jolt at the thought of it, remembering Miss Mellodey's fiancé and countless others who had been killed. Thank goodness he was not old enough, and surely the war would be over, wouldn't it, before he was?

———

It was one of the first really warm days of spring when the three girls, two boys and Prince, the dog, set off on their excursion to the castle on the hill. Maisie realised she was almost happy again as she felt the rays of the sun warm on her face. It was not a day for sadness, although it still came over her sometimes when she thought about the dreadful thing that had happened to Priscilla.

Had Walter Nixon killed her? Or had they just had an argument, and then she had gone off and met somebody else? Maisie knew that they had talked to Priscilla's boyfriend, Jeff, and then they had let him go, because they must have decided he hadn't done it. And they – the police – didn't seem to have latched on to Mr Nixon at all, although Doris had told her that they had been to the farmhouse asking her mum and dad a lot of questions. She had felt really awkward talking to Doris just after it happened, with that awful secret burning away inside her. But it was gradually getting a little bit easier to bear as the days and weeks went by, and talk of the murder, which had been on everybody's lips at first, began to die down.

Maisie and Luke, and Patience as well – although she did not know what Maisie had overheard that night – never spoke about the matter at all. She had heard grown-ups say, when something awful happened, that life had to go on. It seemed so heartless, though, to think like that when somebody had died. And so many people had died just recently…Audrey's mum and dad, Timothy's parents and his sister, Miss Mellodey's boyfriend, and Priscilla… But Timothy and Audrey seemed happy again now, and Miss Mellodey was smiling more than she had at first. And Jennifer, Priscilla's land girl friend, was now walking out, as the grown-ups would say, with Jeff, who had been Priscilla's boyfriend. Yes…life was going on, and there was nothing to be gained on this lovely day by being miserable.

Their walk took them along the path past Nixon's farm, then through a little wood to a waterfall. Maisie had been as far as this before with Luke and Patience, and she had been enthralled then, as she was now, by the wonder and beauty of it all. It was not a gigantic waterfall – she had seen pictures of Niagara Falls in America, and she knew it was nothing like that – but a series of gentle cascades rippling over the rocks in frothy white waves, like soapy washing-up water. It was a part of the river that ran through the dale, and there were boulders along the bank where you could sit and watch the water and listen to the soothing gurgle and splash it made as it tumbled over the stones.

They sat for a while and Bruce handed round a bottle of lemonade for them all to have a drink. 'Don't go too near,' he warned the girls and especially Tim, who had ventured close to the water's edge. 'We don't want any wet feet; it's too cold for paddling anyway, at the moment. And we'll cross the river by the bridge, not the stepping stones. It's my job to look after you lot!'

They had all been warned by the adults, before they set off, about the dangers of the water. But Patience and Luke, and Doris's mum, knew they could trust Bruce to take care of the younger children. There was a path of stepping stones across a smooth flowing stretch of the river, where the more intrepid might cross. Prince was the only one to get his feet, and a good deal more of himself, wet. They all laughed as he stood on the bank shaking the silvery drops from his coat, barking and wagging his tail excitedly.

They crossed the river by a single-arched stone bridge, and then the path led upwards over moorland where shaggy sheep were grazing. The fields were divided by greystone walls, and in the distance they could see lonely farmsteads, much more inaccessible than the one where Doris lived, down in the valley.

Maisie thought to herself that it was rather like an outdoor history and geography lesson as she listened to Bruce telling them what he knew about the area. He certainly knew his stuff, and if he was showing off – just a tiny bit – then you could not blame him. He went to a posh school, and he had told Maisie that they had a different teacher for each subject, not just one for everything like they had at the school in Middlebeck (although she was sure his teachers couldn't be any better than Miss Foster and Miss Mellodey).

'The castle where we're going is called Middleburgh Castle,' said Bruce, speaking quite loudly so that they could all hear, if they wished to do so, 'because Middlebeck is the nearest town; it was only a small village, though, when the castle was built. And that was in the fourteenth century – more than six hundred years ago. It's a ruin now, but it was built to defend the dale against the Scots...'

The girls listened more or less attentively – Maisie hanging on his every word – but Tim had switched off his ears and was lagging behind a little.

'Audrey...' he called. 'Can we stop for a bit? Me leg's hurting.'

'Oh, I'm sorry,' said Bruce. 'Yes, we'll have a rest. We've not much further to go though now, Tim. And when we get to the top you'll be able to look back and see how far we've come... I was telling you about the castle, wasn't I? It was a very important one in the area, because it is said that Mary Queen of Scots was in prison here for several months. You've heard of her, have you?'

'Yes,' agreed Maisie, and the rest of them nodded dutifully. They were more interested in getting to the top and eating their sandwiches.

'I'm OK now,' said Tim, after a few minutes. 'Me leg just gets a bit tired sometimes, that's all, but it'll be easier going downhill, won't it, Bruce?'

'It surely will. Come on; let's have a sing-song;

it'll help us to walk a bit faster…. One man went to mow, went to mow a meadow…' Bruce started to sing and the others followed suit.

In about ten minutes they were at the top, a little breathless, but filled with a great sense of achievement. Bruce lifted Timothy on to a ruined wall. 'There,' he said. 'Now you're the King of the Castle.'

'I'm the King of the Castle,' chanted the little boy in glee, his tiredness and his aching leg forgotten. 'Gosh! Look, Audrey…I can see for miles and miles.'

They all wandered around the ruins, gazing down into the valley where they could make out the distant roofs of Middlebeck, the church tower and the village green.

'And there's our farmhouse,' said Doris, 'and look, Bruce, that's your house, a bit to the right.'

'I'm hungry though, now,' said Tim. 'Can we have our picnic?'

They sat on the prickly grass with their backs against a stone wall and opened their packets of sandwiches. It was amazing how much better everything tasted out of doors; the various sandwiches – salmon paste, corned beef and cheese and onion – which they shared amongst them, the sausage rolls that Patience had provided, Lily's buns and ginger cake, and crisp apples, all washed down with a drink of bright orange Tizer.

Doris had been quiet all morning, not joining in the conversations very much. When they had finished eating she suddenly said, 'I've got summat to tell you… Me mum's real upset this morning, an'

I'm feeling a bit sad an' all.'

They all looked at her, and Maisie felt a tremor of fear run through her. Whatever was it? Surely Doris's dad hadn't told them what he had done?

'It's me dad...' she said. There was a pause, during which Maisie held her breath. 'He's joining the army,' Doris continued. 'He told me mum last night, and she's right upset. He's been and enlisted, an' now he's just waiting for them to send for him.'

'Well...I think that's jolly brave of him,' said Bruce. 'You should be proud of him, Doris.'

'Yeah...I suppose I am, but he doesn't really need to go, y'see, that's what me mum's upset about. Farmers don't have to join up, 'cause they're doing important work. It's called a reserved occupation, or summat like that. And me brother's already joined the RAF so that makes it worse. That's why...we're feeling a bit upset, like...' Her voice petered out and she gave a loud sniff. 'Me dad's quite old an' all. He's turned forty, and me mum says he's being ridiculous. They had a row about it, but he won't take no notice of her. He says he wants to go and do his bit, like the rest of the men.'

'Never mind,' said Maisie, not knowing what else to say. 'P'raps the war won't go on very much longer. Then they'll all come home again.'

'If it lasts for two more years, though, I'll be able to join up,' said Bruce. 'That's what I want to do when I'm eighteen; train to be a pilot.'

'You sound as though you want the war to go on,' retorted Doris. 'I think that's dead mean of you, Bruce. You wouldn't say that if your father had joined the army, or your brother.'

'I don't have any brothers; you know that. I have two brothers-in-law though; one is in the army and the other's in the RAF... I'm sorry, Doris. Of course I don't mean that I want the war to continue. We all want peace...but there's nothing to stop me being a pilot even if there is no longer a war going on. There is civil aviation as well as the Royal Airforce.'

'Your dad won't have to go overseas, though, will he, Doris?' said Audrey. 'All the soldiers came back, didn't they, after that Dunkirk thing? And most of them are in camps in England now, aren't they?' She addressed her questions to Bruce who seemed to know more about the progress of the war than the rest of them did.

'You're partly right, Audrey,' he answered. 'But a lot of our soldiers have gone to the Far East, and we're fighting the Italians in the African Desert as well. As a matter of fact, one of my brothers-in-law is over there; they call them the Desert Rats.' He turned to Doris. 'But I should think your father will be posted somewhere in England, Doris. It's mainly the young and fit ones that are sent overseas.'

'Me dad's as fit as anybody,' argued Doris, 'an' if I know me dad he'll want to do his share of fighting, like the young ones. He's not a coward, an' I know he'll volunteer to go if he can.'

'You'll just have to wait and see then,' said Bruce. 'But he'll be in this country for several months I'm sure. He'll be able to come home on leave to see you. And tell your mother, Doris, that we all think he is a very brave man,' he added.

Maisie felt rather uncomfortable with them all talking about Doris's dad and saying how brave he was. He hadn't shown much courage when he had killed Priscilla; he hadn't owned up to what he had done. But then she didn't know the whole truth, and it might well be that he was innocent after all. At all events, she knew she would feel easier when Mr Nixon had gone and joined the army, and then she would no longer have to look at him, and worry and wonder.

They arrived back in Middlebeck in the mid-afternoon, tired, but only comfortably so, having enjoyed their day in the sunshine and the fresh springtime air. It had been a happy day, apart from Doris's momentary sadness when she had told them about her dad. But she had seemed to cheer up on the way back, heartened by hearing her friends say that he was a brave man. She had already known herself that he was brave. She had seen him catching rats in the barn and fearlessly breaking their necks, although she guessed that fighting armed men might require a different kind of bravery.

Doris also knew, which she had not confided to the others, that her father had been quite odd and jumpy, and more than usually irritable, too, since Priscilla had been murdered. It was only natural that he should be upset – they all were, and her mother had cried a lot – but Doris suspected that her dad had liked Priscilla rather more than he should have done. She had seen him looking at her, and certainly not in the way he looked at her mother or at her, Doris. She hadn't told her mother, of course, but there had been times when Mum had seemed unhappy, even before Priscilla had died. So maybe, she told herself, her father was joining the army to help him to get over losing Priscilla. And perhaps he would realise when he was away from her, that he really loved his wife. There was a proverb that Miss Mellodey had told them at school; absence makes the heart grow fonder.

Patience had prepared a special tea as she knew they would be hungry when they arrived home. They all tucked into the sausages cooked in batter – Aunty Patience called it toad-in-the-hole – with fluffy mashed potatoes and carrots, followed by rhubarb crumble and custard.

Tim's usually pale cheeks glowed with health and his blue eyes, behind the round lenses of his spectacles, shone with delight. He was no longer the odd little chap he had seemed when he first came to Middlebeck at the start of the war, or when he returned after the death of his family. His spindly legs and arms had filled out, he had grown a few inches, and Patience had brushed his pale golden hair so that it lay flat and he no longer resembled a frightened hedgehog. He had thoroughly enjoyed his day out and he chattered more than anyone whilst they ate their meal.

He had discovered that he had another friend that day. He had not known Bruce Tremaine very well before, but now his conversation was scattered with pearls of wisdom that had fallen from the lips of the older boy.

'Bruce says that castle we've been to is more than

six hundred years old...' and, 'Bruce says there are lots of castles up here, 'cause we're quite near to Scotland, and the Scots used to come down and invade the English... And now the Germans might come and invade us, mightn't they, Uncle Luke?'

'Well, we hope not, Tim,' replied Luke, a little anxiously. 'Bruce didn't tell you that, did he?'

'Oh no; he didn't say that. But I know we're still fighting the Germans, aren't we? Bruce says there's a war going on in the desert somewhere, and I thought the Germans might come and invade us. Like William the Conqueror did; we learned about him at school.'

'Well, it was a very long time ago,' said Luke, 'and that was the last time our island was invaded, Tim. We just have to go on hoping and praying that we will be safe. Try not to worry about it.' Poor little lad, thought Luke. It was only natural that he should be fearful of the enemy, having lost all his family in that dreadful air raid.

'I'm not worried,' said Tim, ''cause we're safe from bombs up here, aren't we Uncle Luke?' He was using the name confidently now, but he preferred the honorary 'uncle' title rather than just Luke. Audrey, also, sometimes addressed him as Uncle Luke now, but Maisie did so rather less often. It was as though she was aware that she was not quite one of the rectory family.

It was Maisie who spoke now, quietly, and not really looking at either Luke or Patience. 'Did you know that Doris's dad is joining the army?' she said.

There was a few seconds' silence, then Luke said,

'No...I didn't know that, Maisie. Doris told you, did she?'

Maisie nodded. 'Mmm... He's going soon; he's just waiting for them to send for him. I just thought you should know...' She stared down at her pudding plate, busily spooning up the last scrap of creamy custard and buttery crumbs.

'Walter's not been the same since...well, since Priscilla...' said Patience; then she stopped herself from saying any more. It had been a happy day for the children and she didn't want anything to spoil it. She and Luke had decided that they would tell them the news about the baby when they had finished their meal. 'Perhaps it will be good for him to be in the army,' she added. 'I expect he feels he wants to do his bit.'

'It's certainly a surprise,' said Luke thoughtfully, 'although – I don't know – perhaps it's the best thing for him...' He and Patience glanced at one another. He had not told his wife about Walter's terrible secret, although he sometimes wondered if she had guessed that he, Luke, knew a good deal more than he had disclosed. 'I think that's quite enough talk about the war, though, isn't it, my dear?' he said.

They exchanged a private little smile, then Patience said, 'We have something to tell you all. It's been a secret between Luke and me until now, but we would like you to share it with us...' Three pairs of eyes, two blue and one brown stared back at her. 'There is going to be another little person in our family before very long...Luke and I...we're going to have a baby!'

'A baby?' said Maisie. 'You mean…a proper tiny little baby?'

Patience smiled. 'Yes, that's what I mean.'

'Ohh…!' breathed Audrey. She looked too overcome to say anything else.

Tim looked puzzled. 'Aunty Patience…' he said, wrinkling his forehead in a frown. 'D'you mean you're going to 'dopt a baby, like you did with Audrey and me? Only we weren't babies, were we? Can we have a boy, please?'

Patience and Luke both laughed. 'It isn't as simple as all that, Tim,' said Luke. 'We can't choose, you see…'

'You mean… It's one of your own, isn't it?' said Maisie. 'You…and Uncle Luke, you're going to have a baby of your very own, aren't you, Aunty Patience?'

'That's right, dear,' said Patience. 'Isn't it exciting news?'

'Oh…how lovely,' exclaimed Audrey. Then she asked, rather shyly, 'When…when is it going to be born?'

'In September,' said Patience. 'I know it seems quite a while away yet, but we thought you ought to know.'

''Cause we'd notice, wouldn't we, Aunty Patience, when you got bigger?' said Maisie. 'I remember when me mum had our Joanie and Jimmy.' Patience nodded, feeling slightly embarrassed. It was all so new to her, and Maisie was such a knowing little girl.

'I still hope it'll be a boy,' said Tim. 'I'd like to have a little brother.'

'I don't mind,' said Audrey, 'whether it's a boy or a girl, and you mustn't mind either, Tim. You won't have to be disappointed if it's a girl, 'cause Aunty Patience and Uncle Luke'll be pleased whatever it is. Won't you?' she asked them.

'Yes; we both know we're very lucky,' said Luke. 'Well...blessed is the word really, not lucky, after all this time.'

'I've already got a little brother, and a little sister as well haven't I, Aunty Patience?' said Maisie, sounding just a trifle envious.

'Of course you have, dear,' said Patience. 'Your Joanie and Jimmy. And what a lovely little boy and girl they are, too. You and your mum must be very proud of them.'

Patience recalled the horror stories she had heard from Maisie about the 'little 'uns' before they had come to live in Middlebeck; and she thought how well Lily had coped with them since she had brought them to the countryside, away from the traumas of their home life in Armley.

'Aunty Patience...' said Maisie thoughtfully, 'when you have this new baby, you'll let me have a share of it, won't you, same as Audrey and Tim? I know it won't really be my little brother or sister, but...you know...' She shrugged and shook her head, looking very perplexed.

'Maisie, of course you can share our baby with us, dear, and with Audrey and Tim,' replied Patience. 'You are a member of our family while you are living here, just as much as anyone else. And you've got your other family as well at Tremaine House, haven't you? There are lots of people who love you.'

'Mmm...yes; I suppose I'm quite lucky really, aren't I?' said Maisie.

But Patience knew that the girl was feeling somewhat left out of things, and not for the first time either. She and Luke loved her just as much as they loved Audrey and Tim. How could they help but love her? She had endeared herself to them in all sorts of ways. And yet...there was a difference, and the child knew it. It must be confusing for her to be living apart from her mother and her siblings. She was still, virtually, an evacuee, whereas the other two children were now members of the Fairchild family. But space was limited at Tremaine House – more land girls had come only recently – and it had seemed the best thing to do for Maisie to remain at the rectory. It was just one of the many complications that had come with the advent of war. How much longer would it be, Patience wondered, before families were reunited and life returned to normal?

Chapter Twenty-Five

Lily had kept in touch by occasional letters with Kate Smedley, who had been her next door neighbour in Armley. Kate had been a good friend, one of the few that Lily had had in Leeds, and the only one, apart from Edith Dennison, who had known of the parlous state of Lily's marriage. But even Kate had not known the whole of it; Lily had not confessed to anyone about the abuse of Maisie by her step-brother.

Lily had been delighted to hear Kate's own happy news, that she and her husband, Fred, were expecting their first child at long last. It was due in September, the same month as Patience and Luke's baby was expected. Now that had been a surprise, to be sure! It had been Patience herself who had broken the news to Lily.

'If I don't tell you myself, then Maisie is sure to,' she said, smiling joyfully. 'All the children are excited at the thought of having a new baby in the house, and Luke and I, well, we can scarcely believe it.'

But how is this going to affect Maisie? Lily pondered to herself. There were three children already in that household, and how ironic it was that having adopted two children, the rector and his wife were now to have one of their own. It was often the way, though, that adoptive parents suddenly found themselves to be parents in their own right.

Lily knew though, in her heart of hearts, that Maisie's proper place was with her own mother, and she began to wish, more and more, that she could have all her three children together, like a proper family. There was no father, of course, but they were all better off without such a one as Sidney Bragg. She had been tempted to ask Rebecca Tremaine if it could possibly be arranged for Maisie to come and live at Tremaine house. She was still classed as an evacuee whilst she remained at the rectory; and that had been a wartime emergency which, by and large, had come to an end as the majority of the evacuees had returned home again.

But then several more land girls had been billeted on them. Even Bruce's bedroom was having to be used whilst he was away at boarding school; the lad would just have to squeeze into a corner somewhere when he came home for the holiday. So Lily had found she was busier than ever, and the problem of Maisie had had to be put to one side.

In July Lily received a letter from Kate which worried her. Apart from the usual chatty account of how they were looking forward to the birth of the baby, of the Betty Grable film they had seen at the local cinema, and the moan about the latest Government measure, clothing coupons, there were two other items of news. The first one that was Percy had joined the army. This gave Lily quite a jolt until she realised that by now the lad must be almost eighteen. Well, good for him, she thought, trying to feel magnanimous about it. She hoped it might do him a power of good; it might even be the making of him. She was able to have more charitable thoughts when she was away from him.

The second item of news was that Sid was on his own again. Completely on his own, because soon after his son's departure his lady friend, Moira, had walked out on him. Kate had heard the rows going on, she wrote, and then she had seen the woman leaving with a large suitcase. Sid was moping around like a 'bear with a sore behind', she reported, although she and Fred had tried to keep their distance from him.

Lily was staring at the letter in her hand when Rebecca came into the kitchen. 'What's the matter?' she asked. 'Have you had some bad news, Lily? Do forgive me – perhaps I'm being nosey – but you do look worried.'

Lily shook her head. 'I'm not sure,' she replied, 'whether it's bad news or not. It doesn't matter to me what happens to Sidney Bragg, unless...' She looked at Rebecca. 'It's my husband, y'see. His lady friend – you know, I told you about Moira, the woman he had living with him, well, she's upped and left him. I can't say I blame her; I'm surprised she's stayed as long as she has. Like I say, I couldn't care less what happens to him, unless...unless he comes looking for me. You don't think he will, do you, Rebecca?'

'No...I shouldn't think so,' said Rebecca, but rather unsurely. 'He told you in no uncertain terms to clear off, didn't he? And you've made a new life for yourself up here. He has no claim on you...'

'He has though, hasn't he?' said Lily. 'I'm still his wife. You don't know what he's like...' She could feel the panic rising in her throat and her voice was harsh with anxiety.

Rebecca put an arm round her. 'Now calm down, dear. He doesn't know where you are, does he? You have had no communication with him, have you? And who is your letter from, if you don't mind me asking?'

'It's from a good neighbour; she keeps in touch with me.'

'And she wouldn't give him your address, would she?'

'Would she hell as like! I mean, no, of course she wouldn't. But he could find out, couldn't he, if he really wanted to? There are ways and means. Oh, Rebecca; I'm scared, I really am.'

'Here, sit down and I'll make us a cup of tea,' said Rebecca. 'Let's just try and look at it sensibly.' Rebecca Tremaine was a very calming sort of person, and in a few moments Lily began to feel more composed.

'Now why should he come all this way looking for you? From the sound of it, he would be far more likely to get himself another...floozie, wouldn't he?' The word sounded strange on Rebecca's lips and Lily actually smiled.

'Yes, I suppose you're right. I've been so happy up here. I don't want anything to spoil it. I know the war's still going on, and maybe I haven't the right to be happy with so many people dying and being killed in other places. But I feel that

Middlebeck is my home now. I couldn't go back to Armley.'

'Then we will make sure that you don't,' said Rebecca.

The school broke up at the end of July for the long summer holiday. The scholarship results had not brought many surprises. Both Maisie and Audrey had passed the exam and would be starting in September at the High School near the next village of Lowerbeck. Doris had known all along that she would go to the Middlebeck Senior School along with the majority of her classmates. She was quite resigned to this; in fact she was looking forward to leaving school at fourteen and starting work on the farm with her brother, Ted, and her father, who would, she thought, be back from the war by then.

'We'll still be friends though, won't we?' she said to Audrey and Maisie. 'I'm still not right keen on Gertie and Norma, but I know I'll have to put up with them 'cause we'll be at the same school. You won't get all stuck-up and lah-di-dah, will yer, in yer posh uniforms?'

Maisie and Audrey assured her that they wouldn't. Doris, in fact, began to help her mother more and more with the household chores and on the market stall, whereas the other two girls and Timothy revelled in the long days of freedom. They helped Patience, of course, with little jobs around the house. She was getting very big now with the coming baby, and needed to rest in the afternoons; but Luke assured the girls that she was very well indeed. The doctor was pleased with her and there was nothing for them to worry about.

'Shall we go and have a look round the market?' said Maisie one afternoon in early August. 'I 'spect Doris'll be there helping her mum, and she likes us to go and see her. I tell you what. I'll go and see if our Joanie wants to come as well.' Maisie and her little sister were becoming quite pally and Joanie often wanted to tag along with the older girls.

'All right,' said Audrey, 'but Tim'll want to come as well. We can't leave him out.'

They walked to Tremaine House and collected Joanie who had been 'helping' her mother with the baking; but she was delighted to be asked, and Lily, too, seemed pleased to be able to get on with her job in peace. Jimmy declined the offer. He didn't want to go looking round 'some silly old market'. He was playing with his toy soldiers in a corner of the kitchen.

'Tara, then,' shouted Lily. 'Joanie, you keep hold of Maisie's hand, there's a good girl, and don't go running off…'

She put the scruffy bits that Joanie had been playing with to one side, and went on rolling pastry for the apple pies. She was feeling contented and far less worried now by thoughts of Sid. Several weeks had gone by and she had not heard any more from her former neighbour. It was peaceful in the kitchen and cool away from the heat of the sun. Lily found herself singing quietly as she worked, something she only did when she was feeling happy; that song she liked so much – it was always on the wireless these days – about the nightingale that sang in Berkeley Square.

Suddenly the light from the back door, which she had left open, was blocked by a dark shadow. She looked up, then dropped the rolling pin with a clatter when she saw who was standing in the doorway leering at her. It was the all too familiar, but dreaded, figure of her husband.

'Somebody sounds happy,' he said. 'Glad to see me, are yer, me little Lily flower?' He advanced towards her, his pale blue eyes gleaming with a malicious light. He looked larger and coarser than ever; his face and bulbous nose were mottled with purplish-red veins, his fair hair was long and greasy and his bristly chin and cheeks showed a two-day growth of stubbly beard.

'Get away from me!' yelled Lily. She picked up the rolling pin, but Sid wrenched it out of her hand.

'Don't be so bloody silly, woman. Yer don't need that. I only want to talk to yer...' He turned and looked at the child playing on the floor. 'And who's this 'ere? Well, if it isn't me little Jimmy! Hello, Jimmy lad; aren't yer going to come and say how do to yer dad?'

The child stared at him, a puzzled frown on his little face. Sid turned away, drawing closer to Lily. 'Ne'er mind; he'll soon get to know me again. And so will you, me darlin'. Now, you're going to be a good girl, aren't yer, and get yer bits and pieces together, 'cause yer comin' 'ome wi' me.'

'No!' cried Lily, 'Never...get away from me, Sidney Bragg. I want nowt to do with yer. You told me to go, and so I did. An' I'm stopping here...'

'Oh, you are, are yer? We'll soon see about that...' He moved round to the back of the table where she was standing and grabbed hold of her. She could smell the stale sweat on his clothes, and his beery breath. She turned away in revulsion as he tried to bring his slobbering mouth down on to hers. She landed out at him with her fists, beating him wherever she could on his head and chest.

'Oh, so yer want a bit o' rough stuff, do yer?' he smirked. 'Well, that just suits me fine.' He took hold of her arms and shook her violently, then he lifted his hand and slapped her hard across the face, one way and then the other. She staggered backwards, stumbling against a chair, then she fell to the stone floor, banging her head against the table leg as she fell. He stood looking down at her.

'Don't you try any funny business wi' me. You're me legal wife, an' yer comin' home wi' me. Now, get yerself up.' He kicked her savagely in the groin, and when she winced and made no move to get up he kicked her again in the stomach. She tried to protect as much of herself as she could with her arms, but she felt his boot strike her time and time again and she knew he had completely lost control of himself. She had suffered before when he was in a drunken rage. She felt his heavy boot make contact with her temple. Her head lolled sideways and that was the last blow she felt.

Sid hadn't noticed Jimmy scurrying round the side of the room, and before he was aware of it the child was out of the door and running for his life.

'Somebody help! Somebody help!' he yelled as he ran through the garden and into the nearest field. 'It's me mum. There's a big man an' he's fighting her...Bruce, Bruce, come an' help me mam...'

Bruce was at the far end of the field throwing sticks for Prince to retrieve. On seeing the little figure of Jimmy racing towards him, shouting wildly, and not quite comprehensibly, he ran to meet him, a long stick still in his hand and with Prince yapping excitedly at his heels. He caught hold of the little boy.

'Whoa, Jimmy. What is it? What did you say? Something about a man?'

'Bruce, you've got to come, now!' He pulled at the older boy's hand. 'It's me mam. She's lyin' on t' floor...' His breath was coming in short gasps as he tried to get the words out. 'An'...an' there's a big feller; he's kickin' 'er. I think he's goin' to kill 'er...'

'Get your breath back, Jimmy...and just stay where you are,' said Bruce. 'I'll go and see what's happening.' He set off running towards the house with Prince lolloping after him. 'Go and see if you can find my father,' he shouted back over his shoulder. 'He's in the top field...'

Bruce reached the garden just in time to see the man escaping through the back door. He gave chase, brandishing his stick, but it was Prince, barking madly, who outstripped him and caught up with the intruder. The dog snapped at his trouser leg and managed to get his teeth into it, but the man, armed with what appeared to be a rolling pin, landed out, hitting Prince on the side of his head and then on one of his front legs. The dog was momentarily stunned and taken aback; he was not used to treatment like that. And in those few seconds his assailant was off round the front of the house and down the lane.

'Prince, Prince...here, boy,' shouted Bruce. 'Let him go. I'll ring the police. They'll soon catch up with him.' The dog limped towards him and Bruce gave him a quick hug. 'Well done, boy; you nearly had him. Come on; let's go and see what has happened to Lily...'

He entered the kitchen to find his mother on the floor cradling Lily in her arms. Lily seemed to be unconscious and Bruce could see blood trickling from a wound on her temple.

'I was up on the top floor,' said Rebecca, turning a frightened face towards her son, 'and I heard some shouting. But by the time I got down here poor Lily was on the floor and the brute was escaping through the door. Then I heard you and Prince... Couldn't you catch him?'

'No; Prince nearly did, but he got injured for his trouble. Listen, Mum...I'm going to ring the police, and I'll ring for an ambulance as well. It looks as though Lily needs one. Who do you suppose he was? Somebody trying to rob us?'

'No...' Rebecca shook her head. 'I'd make a guess that it was Lily's husband. And by the look of her I'd say he's pretty well done for her this time.' She leaned closer to the recumbent, seemingly lifeless, figure of Lily. 'Lily, Lily...it's Rebecca. Can you hear me? Oh Lily...oh, please God, don't let anything happen to her. Bruce, hurry up and get some help...'

By the time he had made the first phone call, for an ambulance, Archie had arrived on the scene holding Jimmy by the hand. 'Oh...dear God!' he whispered. 'I got a garbled tale from Jimmy, but I couldn't make out just what was going on.'

'We think it was her husband,' said Rebecca. 'He's...well, you can see what he's done to her.'

'Is me mam dead?' asked Jimmy. His pale blue eyes were puzzled as he stared at Rebecca and at the prone figure of his mother.

'No...no, dear; of course she isn't,' said Rebecca. She was still kneeling with her arms around Lily, and just as she spoke she heard her give a faint moan. 'I think she's coming round... Hurry up and ring the police, Archie. Bruce was just about to do it.'

'But I phoned the ambulance first,' said Bruce. 'It shouldn't be too long now, Mother.' He glanced at Jimmy who was standing motionless, staring at the scene as if in a state of shock. 'Come along, Jimmy,' he said. 'Come and help me to look after poor old Prince. He's had a bang on the head and he's feeling a bit sorry for himself. Don't worry; my mother and father will look after your mum. She's going to be all right.'

Rebecca gave him a grateful smile as the two boys and the dog left the room. Lily was stirring a little, but had not yet opened her eyes. Rebecca guessed she might have other injuries as well as the wound to her head.

The ambulance arrived quite speedily, and whilst the men were carrying Lily, on a stretcher, into the van, the police arrived on the scene.

'Are you able to give a description of the assailant?' asked Sergeant Taylor. 'Although I should imagine he will be easy enough to spot, and he can't have got very far.'

'Quite tall, well built,' said Rebecca. 'Dirty fair hair and a sort of brownish jacket. Scruffy looking chap altogether...'

Bruce, called from the dining room, could not add much more. 'Grey trousers,' he said. 'They might have a tear in the leg where my dog snapped at him,' he added, grinning a little. 'And he was carrying a rolling pin, although he'll probably have thrown it away by now.'

'Thank you, young sir,' said the constable. 'Don't worry, Mr and Mrs Tremaine, we'll soon catch up with this 'un.'

'I should imagine he'll head for the railway station,' said Archie, 'unless he lies low for a while. We have good reason to believe he is Mrs Bragg's husband – estranged husband, of course – from Armley.'

'And from the sound of him, he is probably known to the police there,' said Sergeant Taylor. 'We'll get on to it straight away...'

Maisie arrived home with Joanie to hear the news that her mother had been injured and taken to hospital. There seemed to be no point in hiding from the girl the fact that it was, more than likely, Sidney Bragg who had attacked her.

Maisie turned pale. 'Sid...he's not up here, is he? And what about...Percy? You don't think he's here as well do you?' She knew, of course, that Percy had joined the army – her mother had told her, feeling that it was right for her to know – but the news she had just heard had awakened her old fears.

'No, he was on his own, Maisie love,' said Rebecca, 'and the police are on to him already. He will be brought to justice, don't you worry, for what he has done to your mother. Now...Archie is going to take you back home to your Aunty Patience and Luke, aren't you, Archie? Try not to upset yourself too much. Your mother will be fine, I'm sure...'

❧

Lily was kept in hospital for several days as her injuries were quite severe. As well as the blow to her head which had caused slight concussion, she had a broken arm and bruises all over her body from the assault of her husband's boot, and abdominal pain from a particularly vicious kick in her stomach.

It was obvious that she would need to recuperate for some time before resuming her duties at Tremaine House, but Rebecca and Archie promised they would care for her as though she were a member of their own family. Because that, in fact, was how they thought of her now.

The good news which Lily, and Maisie, too, were relieved to hear was that Sidney Bragg had been caught and arrested the very same night. He had managed to get as far as Middlebeck station and had boarded a train without being apprehended, but the police from Leeds were awaiting him at the other end.

It turned out to be the break they had been waiting for. He was wanted already for burglary. There had been a spate of burglaries of late, some using violence, in the Armley area; and after the latest one a so-called mate had grassed on him. Sid was not popular, even amongst the criminal fraternity. And a vicious attack he had made on a policeman as he escaped from the scene of a crime would be enough to put him inside for several years, even without the grievous bodily harm he had caused to his wife.

Lily demurred at the thought of giving evidence. She never wanted to set eyes on him again, not even in the dock standing trial for his crimes. But she was assured that she would not need to be called as a witness. There were plenty of others who would be pleased to see that he got his just desserts.

'How do you think he found out where you were, Mum?' asked Maisie, on one of her visits to see her mother, after she had returned from hospital.

'I don't know,' replied Lily. 'But I dare say it was easy enough once he'd made up his mind. He would be able to find out from the school which town we had gone to; anyway, I expect that is common knowledge by now. And a lot of the evacuees went back, you know. Some of 'em would know you were staying at the rectory and that I was here. And once he got to Middlebeck somebody'd tell him the way to Tremaine House.' She shuddered. 'Let's not think about him no more, Maisie. We've got rid of him, and let's hope it's for good an' all. What I've got to think about now is getting back to work. Rebecca's got a woman from the village to help with the land girls for the time being, but me job's still there when I want it... If I want it,' she added.

'You can't go back yet, Mum,' said Maisie. 'Your arm's in a sling an' you're still not well enough...

What did you mean, if you want it? D'you think you might not want to go back to being in charge of the land girls?'

Lily smiled. 'Happen it's time for a change,' she said. 'To be honest, love, I want you with me as well as the two little 'uns.' She reached out a hand and stroked Maisie's hair. 'I want us to be a proper family again. Well, we never have been really, because it was always spoiled in Armley by...him, and Percy. I was frightened, love, that you might get too fond of Patience and Luke with living there for so long...but I don't think that has happened, has it?'

'No, of course not,' replied Maisie. 'They've been real good to me, an' Aunty Patience says I'll always be special, like. But with them having Audrey and Tim now, and with the new baby coming...I'd really like to be with you, Mum, and our Joanie and Jimmy. D'you think I could come and live here, at Tremaine House?'

'No...I don't think so,' said Lily. 'I think we need a place of our own... Good heavens! Whatever am I saying?' She shook her head in bewilderment. 'I must be stark ravin' mad. We haven't got two ha'pennies to rub together, an' it's wartime an' all. What chance have I got of finding somewhere to live?'

'P'raps Luke might know of somewhere,' said Maisie. 'He gets to know all sorts of things. Shall I ask him?'

'No...' said Lily. 'Not just at the moment. Besides, I don't want Rebecca and Archie to think that I want to leave them; they've been ever so good to us. No; summat'll turn up, I feel sure of it, if it's meant to be.'

But Lily was happy, knowing that when the time came for her to make a move, her eldest child, Davey's child, would want to be with her.

Chapter Twenty-Six

A t the beginning of September, whilst Lily was still recuperating from her injuries, Maisie and Audrey started at the High School near the village of Lowerbeck. It was too far to walk from Middlebeck and very few of the parents had cars; even if they had, the rationing of petol had curtailed the use of them. A school bus served the town of Middlebeck and the outlying villages, doing a round trip to take the pupils, both boys and girls, to and from the High School. The sexes were taught separately, in different buildings, which was a big change after the co-education of the village school.

They boarded the single-decker bus each morning at eight fifteen, outside the gate of their old school, neatly dressed in their new school uniform. The outstanding feature was the school hat, of navy blue felt with a wide brim encircled with a pale blue ribbon. They both felt very proud of this headgear which singled them out as High School girls.

The scarcity of new clothes to buy, particularly since the introduction of clothing coupons earlier that year, had affected the enforcement of school uniforms. Regulations, therefore, had had to be relaxed a little. Schools could no longer insist on a particular type of coat or skirt, for instance, as they had used to do. But Lowerbeck High School still expected the pupils to conform as much as possible, particularly with regard to the colour of the uniform. As this was navy blue, a colour favoured by many schools, there were very few problems. Maisie and Audrey both already had navy blue garberdine raincoats and gymslips. The rest of the items on the list provided by the school could be obtained from the draper's shop in the High Street. At least, those items that were available could be bought; shopkeepers of all commodities were continually waiting for allocations of goods to be delivered.

'Sorry, dearie, they haven't come in yet,' said Mrs Jenner, the owner of the draper's shop, when Patience, together with the two girls, had gone in there just before the start of the autumn term. 'They keep on promising, but you know what it's like these days. An' I suppose ties and girdles are classed as luxury items. I'll give 'em a tinkle on t' phone and try to hurry 'em up a bit. There's other folks waiting as well as you.' The items they were awaiting were ties of navy and pale blue stripes, and woven girdles which were worn around the waist of gymslips, again in navy and pale blue.

'Never mind,' said Patience. 'Thank you for trying so hard, Mrs Jenner.' She turned to the girls. 'Your headmistress won't have to mind if you haven't got a proper tie for the first few days, and you can wear your old school girdles just for the time being. Mrs Jenner has been able to let us have everything else we needed, hasn't she?'

The white blouses, grey knee socks, navy blue

cardigans and navy blue knickers – with a small pocket at the side, to Maisie and Audrey's amusement – had all been purchased a few weeks ago. Mrs Jenner did a brisk trade at this time of the year when school uniforms were being renewed; and for the rest of the year she had a pretty steady turnover as well, of the various items she stocked.

Maisie had always been fascinated by the myriad variety of goods that could be bought in Jenner's Draper's shop. Underwear for both men and women was possibly the most popular item, although this was of a rather old-fashioned kind. Striped winceyette pyjamas, high-necked vests and long-legged underpants, and an odd garment called combs, which was a combination of both woollen vest and trouser. Ladies voluminous knickers in pink celanese with elastic in the legs, and corsets with bones and hooks and eyes, with suspenders dangling from them, which Maisie thought looked a very uncomfortable sort of garment. Then there were overalls, scarves, gloves, handkerchieves, stockings, mob caps and aprons such as maids wore, and all manner of baby clothes; towelling nappies, bibs, tiny nightgowns and vests, matinee jackets, and minute bootees and shoes. Some of these items Mrs Jenner had had in stock for ages, from the look of them in the window. Everything was in 'short supply'; that was the axiom of the day.

Patience had already bought a supply of napkins and some little vests and nightgowns, but she was making the rest of the garments for the baby herself. Mrs Jenner's shop was a haberdashery as well, selling knitting wools, a selection of materials for dresses (a rather limited selection), buttons, braids, lace, needles, thimbles, cotton, safety pins... Everything that was needed, in fact, for both knitting and sewing.

'I'll have another two hanks of that pale lemon wool, please Mrs Jenner,' Patience said now, 'while you've still got it in stock. I want to make another matinee coat. You can't have too many, or so folk keep telling me,' she added with a laugh. 'And lemon's a safe colour, isn't it, suitable for both a boy or a girl?'

'So it is, Mrs Fairchild,' said the shopkeeper. 'It won't be long now, eh? And you're keeping well, are you, dear?'

'Yes, thank you; I have surprised myself at how well I have been,' said Patience, 'considering my age.'

'Nonsense, you're nobbut a young lass,' laughed Mrs Jenner. 'You look years younger, if you don't mind me saying so, since this babby was on its way. You've got that bloom of youth about you...'

'Thank you,' said Patience. 'Yes; I must admit that I do feel better than I have for quite some time. But you are quite amazing as well, Mrs Jenner, still keeping this shop going.'

'At my age, you mean,' smiled the woman.

'No...I wasn't meaning that. But I know it is several years since Mr Jenner retired from the mill, isn't it?'

'Oh aye; getting on for five years now. He's seventy-one next birthday, and I'm the same.'

'Well, you certainly don't look it,' said Patience, and she meant it. The woman was grey-haired, to be sure, and a little plumper than she had used to be, but her face was scarcely lined at all. Her cheeks were smooth and rosy, her eyes were bright, and she was alert and lively with not a sign of the hesitance and stiffness that sometimes affected the elderly.

'No, I suppose not,' she replied, 'but Cyril keeps on at me to give up the shop, or at least to get somebody in to help me.'

'Yes; you run this shop single-handedly, don't you?'

'Aye; I always have done. It was an old aunt who left me this place in her will, God bless her, and it's been a real thriving little business. I must admit, though, that it's getting a bit harder for me to manage than it used to be. Cyril's got his eye on a little house at the other end o' town. It's near to t' railway station; not what you might call posh, just two up and two down, but we could afford to buy it. We've got a fair bit stashed away; we've always been careful, like, with our brass, and we've never had any bairns... More's the pity, of course. We'd've liked kiddies, but the good Lord never saw fit to send us any... You're a fortunate lass, Mrs Fairchild; but I dare say you know that, don't you?'

'I do indeed,' said Patience.

'Anyroad, like I was saying...Cyril and me, we've been talking things over, and if we could find somebody to run this place for us we could happen rent it to 'em, or even sell it, maybe, the shop and the living quarters. It's quite roomy upstairs where we live. Then we could move to that little house we fancy; an happen I could still keep an eye on t' shop.

I don't want to give it up entirely, y'see; it's been me whole life for so long… Hark at me, rambling on like this! I'm sorry, Mrs Fairchild; I tend to go on a bit, but you're such a good listener. You're the first person I've mentioned it to, as a matter of fact.'

'I've been glad to listen,' said Patience. 'I think you would be well advised to take things a little easier; and then you could spend more time with Cyril, couldn't you?'

'Aye, I'd like to do that, but he's gone and joined this 'ere Home Guard now. What with that, and digging for victory in the little plot we've got at the back he's pretty busy. If you hear of anybody that you think might be suitable to take over here, happen you could let me know? I don't want to put an advert in t' paper. You never know who you're getting, do you?'

'I'll listen out for you, Mrs Jenner,' said Patience. She looked anxiously at the two girls. She hadn't been bored listening to the woman's chatter, but she feared that Audrey and Maisie might have been. Maisie, however, appeared to be listening with great interest to the conversation.

When they had said goodbye to Mrs Jenner and were walking back up the High Street Maisie took hold of Patience's arm. 'Aunty Patience, you know what Mrs Jenner was saying about wanting somebody to help her in the shop? And that they might be able to go and live there? Well, I was wondering…what about me mum?'

'Do you mean…that if your mother was to help Mrs Jenner, then you could all go to live there; you and Joanie and Jimmy as well?'

'I'm not sure about that,' said Maisie. 'I was listening to what Mrs Jenner was saying. P'raps I shouldn't've been, but I was. You know what I'm like for earwigging, don't you, Aunty Patience?' she giggled. 'I didn't really understand all that about renting the shop and everything. I don't think me mum could afford it. But I thought it might be nice for her to work there. She's tired, y'know. She's been working real hard for Mrs Tremaine, an' then there was that awful attack on her...'

'Do you know, Maisie, I think that is quite a brilliant idea,' said Patience. 'What a clever girl you are! I must admit I hadn't thought about your mother when Mrs Jenner was talking, but now when I come to consider it, it might just be the answer. Of course it all depends on what your mum says about it, doesn't it? And she would need to talk it over with Mrs Jenner. Like you, I'm not sure about all the details.' She hesitated to say that she, too, doubted if Lily could afford the rent of a shop and living accommodation. But the idea was certainly worth considering.

Lily, when Patience told her later that day, also thought that the notion of looking after a nice little shop was very tempting. And if she could have her three children with her, then it would be better than ever. But she knew she must be realistic.

'I don't know owt – er, anything – about shop work,' she said to Patience. 'And I've scarcely got two ha'pennies to rub together, never mind enough to rent a property. I said the same to our Maisie not long ago. She'd full of bright ideas is that one,' she added fondly. 'Trust her to think of it. I know she wants what is best for me and the kiddies, bless her.'

'As far as the work in the shop is concerned,' said Patience, 'I can see no problem. You are a very intelligent woman, Lily, and you would soon pick it up. And as for anything else, I'm sure some arrangement could be made. I think – if you are agreeable – that we should go and see Mrs Jenner as soon as possible. She's a very amiable sort of woman; but I expect you know her, don't you, with going in the shop?'

'Yes, just to pass the time of day, like. She's always very pleasant and friendly. Actually, I'm not entirely skint, you know, Patience. I was exaggerating when I said I hadn't even got a couple of ha'pennies. I've managed to save up a bit while I've been working for the Tremaines. They're a generous couple. All the same, it's only a few pounds here and there; not a fortune.'

'The girls start at their new school on Monday, don't they?' said Patience. 'So how about us going to see Mrs Jenner on Monday morning?'

'Yes, that sounds OK to me,' said Lily. 'Then we won't have our Maisie sticking her two penn'orth in,' she laughed. 'And that reminds me, our Jimmy starts school an' all on Monday. Can you believe it? So I'll just make sure that he's all right with his new teacher, and Joanie as well; then we'll go and see what Mrs Jenner has to say. I'm really grateful to you, Patience, for thinking of it.'

'Thank your Maisie,' said Patience. 'It was her idea.'

Mrs Jenner took to Lily at once. She remembered her from the times she had been in the shop, on her own or with the children.

'You're like an answer to a prayer, dearie,' she said: 'A bonny young woman like you in t' shop. That's just what we need to liven the place up a bit, and the customers'll be pleased to see a different face behind the counter... And ne'er mind if you don't know much about running a shop. You'll soon pick it up. If I can do it, then anybody can. I'll show you how to do the ordering and bookkeeping and such like. There's nowt to it when you know how.'

It was agreed that Mrs Jenner – or Eliza, as she soon insisted that Lily should call her – would come into the shop for three or four mornings a week, possibly less as time went on. Patience and Lily both realised that the older lady was loth to let go of the reins and give up her work entirely. As she said, her husband was busy with his own concerns and the shop had been her life for so long. Only recently had she begun to tire a little and to realise that, 'I'm not as young as I used to be,' as she put it.

Most importantly, after consulting with her husband, Cyril and Eliza Jenner had decided that they would still continue to own the property – at one time they had considered selling it – and that Lily and her children could live there...rent free! What this meant, in effect, was that Lily was to be the manageress of the draper's shop, and she would be paid a weekly wage plus accommodation for herself and her family. The proceeds of the shop, of course, would belong to the Jenners, but Lily was more than happy to comply with this. She felt that all her dreams had come true at once.

There was ample room in the living quarters for the four of them. As well as the living room, bedroom, kitchen – and even a small bathroom – on the first floor above the shop, there was an attic floor, hardly ever used until now except for storage, with two rooms that could be made into bedrooms for Maisie, and for Joanie and Jimmy.

Furnishing the rooms was something of a problem, but Lily, with the help of Patience and Luke, and Rebecca and Archie Tremaine, was able to gather together the essential items; beds, chairs, table, wardrobe, dressing table and two easy chairs. Mr and Mrs Jenner were to leave a few pieces of furniture behind, and all the carpets and curtains. Some items were purchased, very reasonably, from a saleroom in Richmond, and other bits and pieces – kitchen utensils, crockery, cutlery and the like – were provided by various friends and neighbours. Lily, whilst working with the land girls, had become a very popular member of the community.

In mid-September, when her broken arm had healed, her bruises had died back, and she was feeling altogether much fitter and stronger, Lily started work at the shop, gradually learning more each day from Eliza Jenner. But the family would not be going to live there until the middle of October. Cyril Jenner and a couple of his Home Guard pals were decorating the attic rooms and making them habitable, and moving the stock which was stored up there to the store room on the ground floor. There was also the Jenners' new home, the little house at the far end of the town that they had purchased, to be put to rights.

It was a busy time for everyone and Maisie could scarcely contain her excitement. All the same, she was pleased that she was still living at the rectory when Patience and Luke's baby was born.

It was on the last day of September, in the early hours of the morning, that Patience awoke with labour pains. Archie Tremaine had insisted, whatever time it was, day or night, that he must be called and he would drive Patience to the hospital in his car.

Luke accompanied her into the ward, leaving her in the care of a nurse and doctor. They assured him, after examining her, that all would be well. He trusted them unreservedly; all the same, he felt that he had never prayed so hard as he did that morning for the safety and well-being of his beloved wife…and the child. Even now, at this late stage, it seemed almost impossible to believe that they were to have a child of their own.

He returned home to the other three children who were still fast asleep in their beds. They were loth to go to school that day, but he insisted that they must. He went back to the hospital, cycling that time instead of riding in a car, and there he waited in an ante-room, along with another expectant father.

It was mid-afternoon when the doctor came to call him. 'Mr Fairchild, you may come and see your wife now. You have a fine healthy son... Congratulations to you, Reverend!'

The baby, by no means a small one, but what one might call a 'bouncing baby boy', was cocooned in a blanket in his mother's arms. He was a miracle of perfection to Luke. His eyes were closed, shielded by eyelids of mottled pink with tiny purplish veins, but Luke could see from the pale red-gold fluff, as delicate as thistledown, on the crown of his head, that he would have his mother's auburn hair. He kissed her tenderly. 'Thank you, my darling,' he whispered. 'This is the most wonderful thing you have ever done for me.'

'Yes...and it's a boy!' She laughed quietly. 'I think – secretly – that I hoped it would be a boy. Or else Tim might have been so disappointed.'

'They will be thrilled, all of them,' said Luke. 'I'll bring them to see you...when the doctor says you are allowed to have visitors. You must rest now, my dear. I'm sure it must have been...a tiring experience.'

'That's the very least of it,' said Patience with a rueful grin. 'But it was worth it. Yes, I am tired, but I'm looking forward to seeing the children. And they will be pleased to see...John, won't they?' They had already decided on the name. John, meaning Jehovah had favoured us, and also the name of the favourite disciple.

'Yes...one of the most popular names of all time,' said Luke. 'But one of the best; I always think it sounds so strong and purposeful.'

'Luke...would you mind very much if we gave him a second name?' asked Patience.

'No...I don't think so. What is it?'

'You know how I love the novels of Trollope, the Barchester stories? And Septimus Harding is a favourite character of mine. A true servant of God, I always thought, just like you are, Luke... And our baby was born in September, so it seems fitting.'

'John...Septimus?' said Luke. He pursed his lips. 'A mite old-fashioned – and he might not thank us for it! – but, yes, it has a certain something about it... Yes, I think I like it. John Septimus he is then. John Septimus Fairchild, God bless him...'

Chapter Twenty-Seven

There was a ring and then what sounded like an urgent knock at the rectory door, one early evening during the second week of October. Patience had been home from hospital for only a few days, and they were all still getting used to the arrival of the youngest member of the family into their midst. It was amazing how much difference little John Septimus was making to the smooth running of the household. Patience, at that moment, was bathing the baby on the hearthrug downstairs, where it was warm, surrounded by a mountain of towels, baby clothes, nappies, talcum powder, baby lotion and feeding bottles, and watched by a trio of wide-eyed children.

'You go, please, darling,' she said to her husband, who, for once, was taking his ease in a comfortable chair. Neither of them had had much sleep for the past few nights with the baby still proving restless, although, ironically, he slept for most of the day. Luke had insisted on taking his turn with feeding the child. Patience had found that her supply of milk was limited and had had to be supplemented with the powdered variety.

Luke opened the door to find Archie Tremaine standing there looking very distraught. 'I have some bad news, I'm afraid, Luke,' he said, 'Very bad...'

'Come in then and tell me.' Luke ushered him inside, closing the door quickly as they had all learned to do with the blackout regulations. The ARP wardens were very quick off the mark with their constant cry of 'Put that light out!'

'Come into my study,' he said, 'Then we can talk in private... It's Archie, darling,' he called to his wife. 'He's come to tell me something.'

'It's Walter,' said Archie, as soon as they entered the study. 'Walter Nixon... He's been killed.'

'What?' cried Luke. 'But I thought... He's not gone overseas, has he? I thought he was still down south somewhere, Salisbury way...'

'So he is...was. It was just a training exercise; army manoeuvres, and it sounds as though he got in the way of a bullet. He was killed instantly.'

'Ohh...' Luke sank down into a chair, putting his head in his hands. 'I don't know what to say... It's such a shock...' He shook his head disbelievingly.

'Aye, it's that all right,' replied Archie, sitting down opposite him. 'Although I do believe there's a fair number that gets killed during training as well as them on the battlefield. Ada's in quite a state, as you can imagine. She got the telegram this afternoon, and she couldn't understand it at all. She even thought it might be a mistake, and then the Second Lieutenant phoned her, long distance; they were so concerned about it. It was a tragic accident, he told her, but no one was to blame. She came straight round to tell Becky and me, then she had to go back to tell little Doris. The girl's heartbroken – I've just called there again now – and young Ted an' all. And Joe's in the RAF, as you know. Poor Ada...'

'Yes, I'll go round and see her, of course,' said Luke.

'I should wait till tomorrow if I were you, Luke,' said Archie. 'Give her a chance to come round a bit. What makes it worse, to my way of thinking, is that I don't think they'd been getting on too well of late, Walter and his missus. Of course she was upset when he joined up, but there had been summat funny going on. It was all to do with our land girl, Priscilla; the one that was killed…'

Luke raised his eyebrows, looking at the other man questioningly, but not wanting to react too much. As far as he knew, he, Luke, was the only one who knew, or had guessed at the truth, apart from Maisie. 'Yes, that was a tragedy,' he said carefully.

'Aye, it was an' all,' Archie sighed, 'and I don't think Walter ever got over it. It's my belief that there was something going on between him and that lass, and I think Ada knew it as well.'

Luke nodded briefly, but non-committally. 'Walter had an eye for a pretty face,' he commented, 'but then so have a lot of men of his age, without there being anything wrong going on. And Priscilla did work for him, as well as for you, didn't she, Archie? He was responsible for her training, from what I remember, so I'm sure he must have been rather fond of her.'

'I suspect there was rather more to it than that, but there's no point in dwelling on it now. She's dead, and so is Walter… God rest his soul. I don't suppose we will ever know the truth about that poor girl's death. I still think that it was one of those lads from the army camp; not her boyfriend, but another of 'em, maybe. She'd got herself rather a reputation as a flirt.'

'And that's most likely what it was between her and Walter,' said Luke decidedly. 'Nothing more than a flirtation.' He had breathed an inward sigh of relief that Archie had not guessed at the truth. 'But at the moment, our chief concern must be for Ada. I will call and see her in the morning… What about the funeral, I wonder? I suppose they will be sending…him home.' He always tried not to refer to the dead person as 'the body'.

'I hadn't thought about it, to be honest,' said Archie. 'Yes, I suppose with Walter being in the choir and a member of the church council there could be quite a lot of folk at the funeral.'

'Mmm… We'll see what Ada thinks about it,' replied Luke. He was feeling that a big funeral with crowds of parishioners, and eulogies in praise of Walter might be too hypocritical for him, as the rector, to conduct. 'Thank you for coming to tell me, Archie,' he went on. 'I'm still finding it difficult to understand that Walter should have been killed so…meaninglessly.' Maybe it was no more than the man deserved, a tiny part of his mind was saying, but Luke could not believe in a God who would bring about retribution in such a way as that. 'A very tragic accident…' he said.

Archie stood up. 'I'd best get back. This has given Becky a shock an' all. We've known Walter for many years. He was a good friend as well as being my tenant farmer.'

'Yes…of course. So what will happen now?'

'About the farm, you mean? Ada will stay there,

of course. There would never be any question of her leaving, unless she wished to do so. She works just as hard as Walter did, in her own way, and Ted's still there and the land girls. Becky and I will take care of Ada.'

'I'm sure you will,' said Luke, seeing him to the door. 'Bless you, Archie. Rebecca's all right is she, apart from…this?'

'Yes; she has two women to help her to look after the land girls. They'll be taking over from Lily when she leaves us. She's already working in the shop, of course… Lily has proved to be a real godsend and we'll miss her; but we're so happy about the way things are turning out for her.'

'Yes, and for Maisie as well,' replied Luke. 'She's looking forward to being with her own family, although she's besotted with our little John at the moment. Aren't we all?'

'Aye, there's happiness as well as sadness, Luke. Isn't it always so, all through life? Goodnight, then… Don't put the light on; I can see my way out. God bless, Luke…'

'Yes, God bless, Archie,' replied the rector.

'What did Archie want?' asked Patience when he returned to the room. Baby John had been tucked up in his cot, but the other three children were still there.

'Oh, something to do with the farm,' replied Luke evasively. 'I'll tell you later, dear. It will keep.' A tacit nod of his head conveyed to her that he would tell her when the rest of the family had gone to bed.

Patience listened in stunned silence when he told

her the news about Walter's accidental death. 'Ohh…' she breathed. 'Poor Ada…and poor Doris; she was so fond of her dad. But as far as Walter's concerned, I can't help feeling it might be providential, not…accidental.'

'Whatever do you mean?' asked Luke, feeling himself start involuntarily at the shock of her words.

Patience looked at him steadily for a few seconds. Then, 'He killed that girl, didn't he?' she said quietly. 'Priscilla…it was Walter, wasn't it?'

He could not lie to her. Very slowly he nodded his head. 'Yes…he did. He confessed to me, but I would never have told you. I couldn't tell you, darling. Not even you, you understand? But…how did you know? Did Maisie tell you?'

'Maisie? No, of course not. Why?' She stared at him incredulously. 'How does Maisie…? She doesn't know about it, does she?'

'Yes, I am afraid she does. At least, she guessed at the truth…' He told her about what the girl had overheard on the night of the choir practice, her disclosure to Luke, and then about Walter's confession.

'Oh…the poor little girl,' sighed Patience. 'Keeping that dreadful thing to herself, and her being a friend of Doris as well.'

'She only guessed,' said Luke, 'and I never told her that Walter had actually confessed to me. I thought it was best if we tried to forget it, especially as he had gone and joined the army. But how did you know, if Maisie didn't tell you?'

'Don't ask me how I knew, Luke. I just knew.

Intuition, I suppose. I was watching Walter...and you. I know you very well, my darling, and I knew that something was troubling you.'

Luke nodded. 'But you surely don't think that his death was...providential? That is what you said.'

'No...maybe that is not quite what I meant. But perhaps it is for the best, for Walter. Fatalistic, you might say. It must have been a dreadful burden for him to bear.'

'He wasn't really a killer, my dear. It was not intentional... And I hope that Ada has never guessed at the truth. I will go and see her tomorrow...'

Ada's eyes were red-rimmed, and she was pale and looked very tired. She had clearly wept a lot and not slept a great deal. But she was manfully carrying on with her work; she was baking a batch of scones, she told Luke when he arrived. They sat down together at the kitchen table.

'I could sit around and weep for evermore,' she told him, 'but what's the use? Nothing'll bring him back. I've got to carry on as normal, as much as I can, an' I've tried to make sure that the kids do the same. Ted's out in the fields somewhere and Doris has gone to school. She wasn't for going, but Ted ran her there in the shooting-brake just for once. She's got lots of friends, has our Doris; she'll be all right. An' we've sent word to our Joe. I reckon he'll get compassionate leave for a day or two for the funeral.'

'Yes...the funeral,' said Luke. 'It will be here, will it Ada? I assumed it would be.'

She nodded. 'Aye, this is Walter's home, and St Bartholomew's was such a big part of his life. They're sending him back, after the post-mortem I suppose. I got this letter this morning, Luke. It's from a fellow called Stan. He was Walter's mate, he says, and he's wrote to me to say what a shock it was... Here, read it for yerself, and tell me what you think...'

She produced a crumpled letter from her apron pocket and handed it to him. 'It's a bit hard to take it all in...'

The letter was fairly brief, expressing condolences from a soldier called Stan Shuttleworth in the same platoon as Walter and obviously quite a close comrade.

'We were on manoeuvres,' he wrote, 'and I saw what happened. It was uncanny really, but I want you to know that Walter didn't suffer at all. He was killed instantly by a bullet fired at point blank range. It almost seemed as though he ran out deliberately in the line of fire, and the poor chap who fired the shot hadn't a hope in hell of missing him.' It went on to say how Walter would be missed and how he had often spoken about Ada and his sons and daughter.

Luke read it in silence, but was at a loss, momentarily, as to how to express his thoughts to Ada. It appeared to him as though Walter had wanted to be killed and had brought about his demise deliberately. It was, possibly, not the most tactful thing for this man, Stan, to have told his friend's widow, but it made sense to Luke at least.

'Very strange,' he commented, handing the letter

back to Ada. 'I don't suppose we will ever know exactly what happened. It was a tragic accident, that much is certain… I know it is no consolation to you, Ada, but these fatalities during training exercises are by no means uncommon. It all seems senseless, I know. If he had been killed in action then maybe it would have been easier to understand.'

'Aye, you're right,' said Ada. 'I know it was an accident; at least it was for the poor chap who was responsible. He must be feeling an awful sense of guilt, but he's no need to feel any self-reproach. You see…I believe that what this Stan says is just what happened.' She tapped her finger against the letter. 'Walter did it deliberately. He wanted to be killed.'

Luke watched her keenly. 'You really think…?' he began.

'Yes, I do. There's something that I know, y' see, summat that I've been trying to keep to meself these last few months. It's about Walter and that girl, Priscilla…'

Luke continued to watch her steadily. She seemed to have full control of herself and he guessed that she had done all her weeping for the moment. 'What is it that you know, Ada?' he asked gently. 'Would you like to tell me?' He feared the worst and he still had no idea how he should react or how much he should divulge to Walter's widow.

'They were carrying on together,' she said, 'the pair of them. I'd thought so for some time. I'd seen the way he looked at her, and then, when she was killed, he just went to pieces; he never got over it.'

Luke felt a deep sigh of relief escape him. What

Ada knew – or thought she knew – was not what he had feared. 'It was only natural that Walter should be distressed at her death,' he said carefully. 'Everyone was. It was such a dreadful thing to happen...'

'Aye, well, that's true, I suppose. But it was then that he started going on about joining up. And there was no need for it. He was in a reserved occupation; he didn't need to go. But he wouldn't listen, and I know that what he really wanted was to be sent overseas, to be in the thick of it all. We had some terrible rows, him and me. An' I told him, an' all, that I knew what was wrong. I said to him, "You were having an affair with that lass, weren't you? And now you can't get over it." Well, he went barmy, shouting and swearing at me. But he swore blind that he hadn't, that there had never been 'owt like that", he said. He was just fond of her – he admitted that – and he wished they'd catch the bastard that did it... But they never did, did they, Luke?'

'No...and the chances are that they never will now,' replied Luke. 'You made it up with Walter though, did you, before he went away?'

'To a certain extent, yes, but I never really believed him about Priscilla. Walter and me, we'd not been – what you might say – husband and wife in the fullest sense, not for some time.' She looked a little discomfited. 'You know what I mean, Luke, and I suppose I realised he was only human. But we were closer again by the time he went, and he was very tearful, saying goodbye to me and the kids. As though he knew it was for the last time. At least, that's what I'm thinking now...'

'Ada...' Luke leaned across the table and took hold of her hand. 'I think that what Walter told you was true. I don't believe he had an affair with Priscilla. He was fond of her, yes; but you must try to believe that that was all.' Walter had been adamant, when he had confessed to Luke, that the friendship had not progressed so far, despite his wanting it to do so, and what Maisie had overheard pointed to the fact that it had not been in Priscilla's mind at all. And so it made sense to Luke to reassure Ada on that point at least. 'He was upset at her death, but who wouldn't be, especially when he had worked so closely with her?'

Ada nodded. 'Thank you, Luke. Yes...you may be right; I hope so. It's just the thought that he might have killed himself – well, made sure someone else did – because of her. He was unbalanced though. I knew that when he went away. Not all the time, but it would come over him now and again, and then he didn't seem to know what he was doing.'

'It's the effect of the war,' replied Luke. 'It has affected us all in different ways, some more than others.'

'I'm trying hard to think of the good things about Walter now,' said Ada. 'We were real happy here on t' farm, especially at first, and then when the boys and our Doris came along we were thrilled to bits to have a family. And the lads love the land just like Walter did. I dare say Joe'll go back to farming when he comes out of the RAF. And Doris is showing no desire to do anything else.'

Luke smiled, feeling a sense of relief. The dark

truth must remain hidden, but it was good that Ada was remembering the happier times of their marriage and not just the quarrels and distrust.

'He could be a bad-tempered so and so,' she went on, 'and irritable with the kids as well as me. But he loved them, an' they loved him an' all. So did I...' She stared musingly into space for a moment, then her expression changed. 'I don't want a big funeral, though, Luke. I don't think I could bear it, and I'm sure our Doris and the lads won't want it either. Could we just have a quiet family affair; no fuss and to-do?'

'Yes, certainly,' replied Luke. 'Whatever you wish, Ada. But members of the congregation will want to pay their respects. Walter was well liked.'

'A brief church service then,' agreed Ada. 'But no baked meats and funeral feast or what have you.' She shook her head. 'I've never liked that sort of carry-on. I'll make a few sandwiches for the close family, but nothing else. Me and the kids, we just want to remember him quietly...'

And that was just what Luke, for reasons of his own, had hoped would be Ada's decision.

The church was half full of mourners. Walter had been well known in the town of Middlebeck and the nearby farm lands and, on the whole, liked and respected for his fairness and reliability. At Ada's request the choir had not been asked to sing, as sometimes happened at the funerals of members of the congregation. Luke was relieved, again, at this, and he conducted what he hoped was a dignified, but not too effusive service. He said that Walter would be remembered as a good and loving husband and father, a loyal member of St Bartholomew's church and choir, and as a respected member of the community.

After the burial in the churchyard only the immediate members of the family, with Luke and the Tremaines, returned to the farmhouse. Joe had been granted compassionate leave for a few days, and he and Ted and Doris were seen to support their mother throughout the service and the commital at the graveside. It was evident that they were a close and loving family, and Luke had few worries about their future or about how they would cope without the head of the family. He knew that was how Walter had thought of himself, but Ada was a strong woman – he had discovered more about her strength during the past week – and she would be able to take up the reins without any difficulty.

Doris, that day, was subdued and thoughtful, though not unduly tearful. It was strange not to see her laughing and chattering in her usual carefree way; but she would come through it, he was sure, and remember her father with nothing but affection. She was not alone in having lost a beloved parent. Audrey and Timothy, too, had suffered the loss of both their parents, and as the war dragged on relentlessly there would be many, many others in the same situation.

Maisie had looked grave on hearing the news of Walter Nixon's sudden death. It was Luke who had told her, before Audrey and Tim were informed, although Tim had scarcely known the man. He had anticipated Maisie's question; it was the first time she had mentioned the matter since her disclosure several months ago.

'Did he do it, Uncle Luke?' she asked in a whisper. She sometimes called him that now, as did Audrey and Tim. 'I mean...was it him that killed Priscilla?'

Luke nodded. 'I think we can assume that was what happened, Maisie. But no one else knows... Oh no; Patience knows; she stumbled on the truth of it all. But it must never, never be talked about. You understand, don't you, dear?' She nodded soberly. 'Yes, I know you do, Maisie; you are such a sensible girl. And you can resume your friendship with Doris without feeling awkward about it. I know it's been difficult for you, knowing what you did. But Doris will need her friends now. Perhaps you could call round and see her sometime soon, you and Audrey?'

'We haven't seen her much lately,' said Maisie. 'She's at a different school now and she's got some new friends.'

'But sometimes old friends are the best,' said Luke, 'and I expect Doris might think so too.'

'OK; we'll go and see her tomorrow,' said Maisie. 'She was real nice to me and Audrey when we first came here, when we were evacuees, and some of the others were horrid. I'll see if Audrey'll go with me after school tomorrow.'

'Wait till after the funeral, dear,' said Luke. 'Mrs Nixon will be busy and...it would probably not be a good time.' He guessed that the coffin containing Walter's body might soon be arriving.

'OK,' said Maisie again, quite cheerily. She sounded as though a weight had been lifted from her mind.

Soon afterwards, the trio of friends were seen mooching around Woolie's, their favourite store, or the market stalls. Doris, however, spent a good deal of her time, when she was not at school, helping her mother, either in the home or on the market stall; and Maisie, too, soon found that she was extremely busy.

She and her mother, and Joanie and Jimmy, moved into their new home above the draper's shop at the very end of October. As this coincided with the half-term holiday from school she was able to spend the few days helping her mother to arrange the furniture, to sort out their belongings into the various cupboards and drawers and – most importantly – to get to know one another again, the mother and three children, as a secure and happy little family.

'We're so lucky, Maisie, so very lucky,' said Lily on the first evening as the two of them sat companionably by the fireside. The 'little 'uns' were in bed and mother and daughter were enjoying a cup of cocoa and a Nice biscuit. 'And haven't people been kind to us?'

Lily had managed to buy the two easy chairs and a rather old-fashioned sideboard, and some essential bedroom furniture herself; but the red carpet and the matching damask curtains – both of which were only slightly worn – had been left by the Jenners. Their feet rested on a rag rug, donated by a customer at the shop, and the brown plush cushions and the plush tablecover by Rebecca. They even had a wireless set with a sunray design in the front, a glass fruit bowl – for the rare occasions when fruit could be bought – and a china biscuit barrel with a silver handle, all given by friends who wanted to wish them well in their new home.

'Nothing is going to spoil it for us now,' said Lily. 'I hope we will be able to stay here for ever, even after the war ends…touch wood.' She tapped the end of the chair's arm. 'Please God, I suppose I should say really,' she added. She laughed. 'I know your Uncle Luke might not go along with my superstitions.'

'You are my family now, Mum,' said Maisie. 'You and Joanie and Jimmy. I do love Aunty Patience and Uncle Luke, but I'm back home again now, aren't I?'

'Yes, where you belong, love. And Sid Bragg's in prison where he can't get at us, thank the Lord.' Lily smiled as she gazed into the embers of the fire. 'Aye, we've been lucky,' she said again.

Chapter Twenty-Eight

M aisie was thrilled to be able to help in the shop. She dashed home from school each day so that she could take over from her mother whilst Lily got the tea ready. She soon learned to operate the till, and giving the correct change to customers was no problem to her at all. Sometimes she helped on a Saturday morning as well. This was a day when Mrs Jenner came in the afternoon – the shop was extra busy then because it was market day – but on Saturday morning Lily caught up with her housework, leaving Maisie in charge of the shop, but always on hand if her daughter should need assistance or if there was an emergency.

It was about eleven o' clock on a Saturday morning in mid-November when Maisie heard the familiar tinkle of the door bell and looked up to see a young soldier entering the shop. This was quite an unusual occurrence; soldiers from the nearby camp were often seen wandering around the little town, but they did not often come into the draper's shop.

'Good morning; can I help you?' said Maisie politely, as her mother had taught her to do. Then she stopped and stared at the newcomer. She cowered back against the shelves behind the counter, feeling herself turn cold and her hands begin to tremble. Because as he came closer to her she recognized the young man; his stocky figure, now dressed in khaki, his ruddy face and pale blue eyes, and his spiky blond hair which she could see more clearly as he took off his forage cap. It was Percy... She opened her mouth, but no sound came out. She was so terrified she could not speak, let alone scream, which was what she wanted to do.

But he was smiling in what seemed to be quite a friendly manner. 'Hello...Maisie,' he said, but a little unsurely, unlike the bold and nasty person she remembered. 'That's what you call yerself now, isn't it? Much nicer than Nellie...' Suddenly, he looked down, in some embarrassment at his shuffling feet.

She continued to stare at him, rooted to the spot with terror. He looked back at her, then half-smiling...but not sneeringly, she thought, almost as though he really might want to be friendly. But she did not trust him; never, never could she trust this awful lad who had done all those bad things to her. 'I'm...I'm sorry, like,' he muttered, 'an...an, well, I meanter say...yer don't need to be scared of me no more. I've just come to say...hello.'

'Go away...' she cried feebly, then again, more loudly, 'Go away!' as she found to her relief that her voice had come back. 'I don't want you here! Mum, Mum...' she yelled at the top of her voice. 'Come quick! There's somebody here...'

It was a minute or two before Lily appeared through the door at the back of the shop, during which time Percy had made no move, but just stood regarding his step-sister with a resigned but sorrowful look. 'I suppose it's only what I can expect...' he murmured.

'What is it? Whatever's the matter?' cried Lily. She looked at the young soldier, then her mouth dropped open in shock and, at first, in fear. 'Percy Bragg...you! Get away from my daughter! Don't you dare try to come near her...' She dashed towards him as if to strike him. He backed away, holding his hands up in front of him, in a gesture of defeat.

'Lily...Lily, listen, it's all right. I don't want to hurt Maisie. Honest I don't. I've just been trying to tell 'er, but she's...she looks scared to death.'

'Is it any wonder,' retorted Lily, 'after what you did...? What are you doing here anyroad? And how did you know where we were?'

'I found out. I had to,' replied Percy, hanging his head as though ashamed. 'I could've come sooner – I've been up at Catterick camp y'see ever since I joined up – but I've been trying to get me head round things, sort meself out, y'know; an' I wasn't sure how you'd take me.' His voice was quiet, and his words tumbled over one another, so that Maisie and Lily found it difficult to catch all that he was saying. 'Well, I guessed as I wouldn't get a reight warm welcome. Maisie...I didn't mean to frighten yer, just now, I mean. I want to be friends with yer, and yer mum; well, as much as we can be. An' I'm sorry an' all for...well, you know what I mean, don't yer?' He looked down at his feet again.

Maisie continued to look at him in bewilderment. It was Lily who spoke first, but before doing so she went to the shop door and bolted it, turning the sign round so that it said 'Closed' instead of 'Open'.

'Are you trying to tell us that you've changed?' she asked. 'If so, then it takes some believing.'

'Aye, I know it does,' replied Percy, 'but...I have changed, at least I'm starting to. It was living with me dad, y'know, all that time. He weren't any good for me. He shook his head vehemently. He was a real bad lot, was Sid. I couldn't see it when I were a kid. I were his favourite, y'see; God knows why, but I were, with me being t' youngest, I suppose.' He was speaking more confidently now.

Lily was watching him closely. It really did seem as though the lad might have changed somewhat. He looked different for a start, smarter and cleaner, and he no longer had that shifty and villainous expression in his eyes. He was sure to be smarter, though, being in the army, and maybe it had done him good in other ways as well. But she still felt that she could not trust him completely. She nodded. 'I see...Yes, I know your dad used to make quite a lot of you. But you decided you'd had enough of him in the end, did you? Is that why you joined the army?'

'Aye, that was t' main reason, I suppose. But I wanted to do me bit an' all. You might find that hard to believe knowing me but it's true. An' I was beginning to see what a bad lot he really was. But you knew that, didn't yer, Lily? You guessed what he was like soon after yer married 'im. I was always expecting you to clear off and leave 'im.'

'How could I, Percy, with three children to look after?' Lily surprised herself that she was even able to use his name.

'Me mam did,' he replied. She frowned at him, puzzled at the remark.

'Your...mam?'

'Aye, she cleared off and left 'im when I was – let's see, about eight or nine, I think. I know he said he was a widower, like, but he weren't. There were two more of us, me sister and me brother, older'n me, an' me dad used to knock 'em about summat awful, and me mam an' all; but not me.' He was looking Lily in the face now, as he spoke, instead of staring down at the floor. 'Anyroad, like I say, she upped and left 'im and took the other two wi' 'er, but she left me with me dad... An' I suppose – well – I got more and more like 'im, didn't I?'

Lily, in spite of herself, was starting to feel that this put a different complexion on things. The poor lad, she was almost beginning to think, what sort of a chance did he have after all?

'I see...' she said again. 'And...did you see them again, your mother, and your sister and brother?'

'No, never a word from that day to this. I don't even know where they are. Me dad told me, years later, that they were divorced, and good riddance he said. He had a few women friends over t' years, but never a proper lady like you are, Lily. Then he met you, an' I thought he might change, but it didn't last long, did it? An' as for me, well, I was jealous, like, I suppose. He'd got two more little kids, an' he were fond enough of 'em at first, weren't he? Aye, Joanie and Jimmy... Where are they, by the way?'

'They're upstairs playing together,' said Lily curtly. She still could not tell whether this new and different Percy was trying to 'soft soap' her, or had he really changed?

'Can I see 'em?' he asked. His eyes had more of

an interested light in them than she had ever seen there.

'I don't know, Percy. I'm not sure. This is an awful lot to take in.'

'Aye, I can see that… It were when me dad started thieving that I knew I'd had enough of 'im. I know I were a bad sort o' lad; I did a lot of awful things, but I couldn't go along wi' that – thieving, I mean. Neither could Moira – you know, the woman he was living with. She was quite a good sort, was Moira; her and me got along quite well. I left before she did, though.' He paused, but Lily could not think of any comment to make; she was dumbfounded by the turn of events. She let him go on talking, which was what he seemed to want to do.

'Y'see, I'd got a girlfriend by then, a proper one, a real nice girl she is, an' I started to see as how I weren't doing meself any good, living wi' Sid. An' so I decided to volunteer for th' army.'

'So…you still have this girlfriend, do you?' asked Lily. 'A girl from Armley, is she?'

'Aye, that's reight. She worked at t' mill with me; well, she still works there. I'd always been a bit scared o' lasses. T'other lads I knew were always boasting, like, about the girls they took out…an' all that. But I never… That's why…' He cast an apologetic glance in Maisie's direction, but she was looking anywhere but at him. He hung his head. 'Anyroad, I'm trying to forget all that. I'm ashamed of it acksherly, an' I'm sorry. That's why I've come, to say sorry.'

'Well, that certainly takes some doing, to say you're sorry,' said Lily. She was feeling a certain –

not warmth, not quite that yet – but sympathy for him. 'It was brave of you to come, Percy. But how did you find us, exactly where we were, I mean? I suppose it would be common knowledge that we were in Middlebeck?'

'Aye, I knew that. But this girl as I'm friendly with, her name's Peggy Clough, an' her sister was up here when t' war started, but she went back.'

Maisie spoke for the first time, quite involuntarily. She hadn't intended speaking to him, but before she had realised it she said, 'Esme Clough... Is it her sister that you're going out with?'

'Aye, that's reight.' Percy turned to Maisie. 'She told me that you and yer mam and the kiddies were still up here. She knew that you were staying wi' that rector chap an' his wife. And then – would yer believe it? – when I joined up I was sent up here to Catterick. But it took me a while to pluck up courage to come and see yer. I asked around, like, an' then I found out you'd just moved into t' shop. So that were that.' He shrugged and gave a weak sort of grin.

'Esme and me weren't friends,' said Maisie, a little testily. 'She caused a lot of trouble when she was up here, her and some other girls.'

Percy nodded. 'Aye, she can be a bit of a terror, that 'un. Peggy's not much like her; she's gentler, much nicer really...'

'You must miss her then?' said Lily, warming to the lad a shade more.

'Aye, so I do...'

'And...if you go back on leave to Armley, where do you stay?'

'Oh, I've no fixed address now, not since me dad's been inside. I knew about what he did to you, Lily, an' I'm real sorry. Anyroad he's banged up for a few years now, and serve him bloody well right! Er...sorry; I'm trying not to swear an' all. Peggy doesn't like it... Like I was saying, I've got no proper address. I'll be able to stay at Peggy's place, though. Her mam's not a bad sort; I'll make out somehow. I'll probably be sent abroad soon, but we're not allowed to say owt about that. Top secret, y' know.' He tapped at his nose importantly.

Lily moved suddenly, making towards the door. 'We're keeping customers out,' she said 'and that'll never do, not on a Saturday morning. If we shut 'em out they might never come back.' She drew back the bolt and turned the notice to 'Open'. 'Now, Percy, you an' me'll go upstairs, then you can see your little sister and brother. Don't be surprised, though, if they don't know who you are. It's been a long time; well, two years is like a lifetime to a small child...'

'It's all right, Maisie.' She smiled at her daughter who was staring at her in amazement. 'I know what I'm doing. You stay here and look after the shop for me. That's what you like to do on a Saturday morning, isn't it?'

'Aye, it's all right, Maisie,' said Percy. 'Honest, it is. I'm real glad to see you and yer mum again. But I know you're not all that pleased to see me, an' I know how you feel. But there's a war on, i'n't there, an' we've got to try and make peace where we can.'

'OK,' said Maisie, briefly. She glanced at him, then quickly looked away again. 'I'll see to the shop, Mum...'

They closed each day from one o' clock until two, as was customary with most of the shops in the town. This gave Lily the chance to prepare a meal for the two children when they came home from school. Maisie's school was further away so she had her dinner there each day. But on Saturdays they all dined together.

Maisie was slightly miffed, but not altogether surprised, to find that Percy had been invited to stay and have dinner with them. The young man tucked into the meat and potato pie, which had been cooking slowly in the oven all morning, with great relish. She glanced at him surreptitiously from time to time from under her eyelids. His table manners seemed to have improved; she would say that for him. He no longer burped loudly nor wiped his sleeve across his mouth as he had used to do. No doubt he had been imitating his loutish father, and she thought she could understand that.

She had been listening to what he had told her mum, downstairs in the shop. She had known that he had no mother, but she had believed that she had died. It must have been awful for him, she pondered, that his mother had deserted him and that he had never seen her since. And to be left with such a dreadful person as Sidney Bragg... Maybe there was some excuse, after all, for the way he had behaved in the past. All the same, Maisie felt that it might be a long, long time before she could speak to Percy in a normal sort of way, if ever.

She did not say much during the meal. Most of the conversation that was taking place was between her mother and Percy. He was telling Lily that he was enjoying army life. He had made new friends and he thought that the scenery up in the northern dales was 'reight grand'.

Joanie and Jimmy stared at him and were unusually quiet. It was doubtful that they remembered him at all, although there was just the slightest glimmer of recognition in Joanie's eyes. Towards the end of the meal she said, 'I 'member now…. You lived with us in Armley, didn't yer, a long time ago?'

'Aye, that's reight; so I did,' laughed Percy. 'And happen the next time I come this young feller'll know me an' all, won't you, Jimmy lad?' Jimmy looked up from his rice pudding to give a brief nod.

Maisie glanced at her mother. So there was to be a next time, was there? Lily did not return her glance, but continued to look down at her pudding plate.

Later on, however, as they sat drinking a cup of tea – which was the way that all true Yorkshire folk finished a meal – Lily asked him if he would like to come and visit them again… Sometime, she added, not making her invitation too enthusiastic.

'Aye, I'll let you know when I can come again,' Percy replied, quite humbly. He clearly knew that he was fortunate to have received any sort of a welcome at all. He stood up and put on his greatcoat. 'Ta very much, Lily, for t' meal…an' everything. I'd best be off now and let you open up t' shop again. Tara then, you two.' He waggled his fingers at Joanie and Jimmy. 'Happen you'll talk to me a bit more next time… Tara then, Maisie…look after yerself.'

'Tara...' she muttered, still unable to do more than glance at him.

Her mother went downstairs with him to see him on his way. 'I know how you feel,' she said to Maisie when she returned. 'It was a big shock to me as well as to you. But at least the lad has tried to make amends.'

'I don't see why you asked him to come again though,' said Maisie. She knew she was being peevish and unforgiving, but it had been so nice lately; just her and her mum, and her little brother and sister.

'He won't come all that often, love,' said Lily. 'He just wanted to make his peace with us. There was no one who disliked Percy more than I did – there were times when I hated him – but I can see that he really has changed. We've got to try and give him the benefit of the doubt, Maisie love. Do you know what that means?'

'Yes, I think so...' replied Maisie.

'There's so much unhappiness in the world at the moment.' Lily shook her head sorrowfully. 'Young men are being killed fighting for their country, when they should really be looking forward to getting married and having a family; folk are being bombed out of their homes; and there's still no sign of this flippin' war coming to an end. So when we find that somebody wants to be friendly and say they're sorry, well, we've got to try and believe them, haven't we? At least Percy's trying to do what's right.'

'OK, Mum...I'll try to understand,' said Maisie. 'I remember Peggy Clough; she was a lot nicer than her sister. I can't imagine her wanting to go out with Percy; but p'raps if he's different now…Mum, can I go and see Audrey this afternoon? P'raps she could come for tea, if Aunty Patience says it's all right…'

As it happened, Lily and her little family saw Percy only once more before he was sent overseas. General Rommel, the Desert Fox, for almost a year, had been leading what seemed to be his invincible Afrika Corps in northern Africa. Percy, in December, became a member of the British Eighth Army, endeavouring to drive the Germans and Italians out of the Western Desert.

*

At the end of 1941 the news was grim. On December the seventh, Japan bombed the American Naval base at Pearl Harbour; more than two thousand Americans were killed and almost every major unit of the US Pacific Fleet was sunk or maimed. On December the tenth the Japanese sent shock waves through Britain with the sinking of two great warships, the *Prince of Wales* and the *Repulse*. And on Christmas Day Hong Kong surrendered to the Japanese.

It seemed that there was little cause for celebration when the Fairchild family and Lily's family met together for their Christmas dinner at the rectory.

'We must drink to the future, though,' said Luke, 'whatever it holds for us.' Winston Churchill, the Prime Minister, had gone to spend Christmas in Washington with President Roosevelt, to cement the new alliance with the USA. 'It might be somewhat late in coming…but we now have a powerful ally. And all we can do is hope and pray. This past year has brought its share of sadness, but so many blessings as well to our families…'

The Fairchild family – Luke and Patience, Audrey and Timothy, with baby John asleep in his pram; and the Jackson family, Lily having decided that this was the name they would use from now on – Lily and Maisie, Joanie and Jimmy, knew that they had much for which they must be thankful.

Luke raised his glass. 'To the future,' he said. 'To victory, and to peace, please God… And to our families; God bless us all.'

'To the future…God bless us,' they all replied.

a&b